Looking Through the Shadows
◇ Book 2 ◇

I0602347

After the Wreckage

Michelle Lee

BLUE FORGE PRESS
Port Orchard, Washington

Blue Forge Press is the print division of the volunteer-run, federal 501(c)3 nonprofit company, Blue Legacy, founded in 1989 and dedicated to bringing light to the shadows and voice to the silence. We strive to empower storytellers across all walks of life with our four divisions: Blue Forge Press, Blue Forge Films, Blue Forge Gaming, and Blue Forge Records. Find out more at: www.MyBlueLegacy.org

Blue Forge Press
7419 Ebbert Drive Southeast
Port Orchard, Washington 98367
blueforgepress@gmail.com
360-550-2071 ph.txt

*For every person out there who has suffered
the ravages of PTSD, this is for you.
You aren't alone.*

Looking Through the Shadows
◊ Book 2 ◊

After the Wreckage

Michelle Lee

Chapter One

Jake

Five o'clock in the morning. I'm on leave. Why the hell is my phone going off? I sat up, realizing I'd fallen asleep on the couch. Instead of in the room with Francesca, where I should be to make sure she's okay. Damien's funeral yesterday had thrown her for a loop. Not like it hadn't done the same for me, I shook at the thought.

Not even a week had gone by yet. And I was only beginning to understand what life would feel like without my best friend and brother by my side all the time. I fucking hated it. I was grappling with some serious depression issues because of it, too. Half the time, I wanted to die; the other half, I longed to beg Francesca to love me through it.

Every time I thought about her, I felt guilty. Damien had fallen in love with her instantly, which made her off-limits—fallen hard. While I admit to the attraction when I first saw her, the falling in love part didn't happen until I knew who she was. It was a forgone conclusion at that point. Regardless, I would have never stepped between them. I let go of her then, not of her, of the chance to be with her.

Damien knew how I felt; we had no secrets. We both knew Francesca had feelings for me, though she kept a pretty good lock on them. After I had broken down in front of her, she kissed me once, getting me through the episode. The chemistry between us was off the charts insane, and I confessed what had happened the same day to Damien.

All he'd done was laugh. There were no hard feelings. His love was absolute and unconditional for both of us. Yet it still felt like I was doing something wrong for wanting to drown in a kiss from Francesca right now. It felt wrong, but it also hurt because being with her was right. Damien had even tried to get me to promise to marry her and keep her safe.

The constant rollercoaster of emotions was dizzying and exhausting. Damien was everywhere and nowhere. I only wanted him here with us. Not his ashes that sat there on the counter staring at me like an accusatory victim. Not the DNA he'd contributed to the life growing inside Francesca. Him.

We've been by each other's sides for almost every day of the past nineteen years. We fought in a war on each other's sides, fourteen of those nineteen. There was significant history there, life-altering history. It felt like we'd never left that place, and at times it felt like eons ago. Then there were the days when we were still trapped there, reliving the shit that had left permanent damage inside and out.

The fissure Damien's murder had left was wide and deep in both Francesca and me. Now, she was all I had left, and I was all she had left. One of the many tragic stories around the world, sure. But it for damn certain looked bleak when you were right smack in the center of the travesty.

My phone went off again, and I felt tempted to throw it against the wall. I silenced it instead. I didn't want it to wake Francesca up. Giving in to the rage inside me would sure as shit wake her up *and* scare the life out of her. I didn't even know if I'd be able to come back from that; it was so powerful inside me. A living, breathing force that demanded retribution for destroying us. Again.

"Goddamn it, Demon," I grumbled, "tell me what to do!" I leaned forward and clasped my hands behind my neck, holding my head down. "How do I fucking get through this? You lead, I follow, remember? Only I can't now! I can't fucking follow you without killing what's left of Francesca."

I needed a meeting, and I needed one bad. In every direction I turned, a trigger was waiting to set me off on a path I wasn't strong enough to step off. I wanted to be strong for Francesca, I wanted to be what she needed, and all I could see happening was me pulling her down with me. She'd lost enough. Fuck, I'd lost enough.

I grabbed my phone and sent a text to my club.

I need a meeting. Organize what you can for today. Must be today.

The urge to throw my phone hit me hard again.

My phone vibrated in my hand, and I glanced down to see a message from Mike from the club. I looked at the missed calls to see who at the station had been contacting me and saw the Chief's name.

We've been waiting for the call from you. Kind of expected it. Noon. Clubhouse. I read Mike's text.

Knowing that, a little of the tension built up in me was released. That would take me away from Francesca for a bit. I could offer to bring her with me. *If she's going to run, she won't go with me.* That made me pause. I'd let her go, at least for a little bit. She needed space; I could understand that.

I was still worried about the murderer on the loose out there. Her safety and the baby's safety were top priorities now. Not because those had been some of Damien's last words, but because I loved them. Jesus. I was a mess. Pushing Francesca away because I felt guilt, pulling her back in because I needed her. She deserved better than this.

I picked up my phone and called the Chief. "Thought you wanted me on leave?" I said when he answered.

"You *are* on leave. I need you to come in for a conversation. Got a fucking shit storm happening, and only you can fill in some of these missing pieces. The sooner, the better, and I still need a statement from you. I'm busting my ass on this Foxwood, trying to keep it away from you."

I cringed, knowing it was true. The Chief was doing everything in his power and pulling no stops to close this for me.

"I'll be there in an hour. I need to go home, shower, change, and get some clothes together."

"I'm sorry, Jake. I wouldn't ask unless it was important," the Chief softened his tone. "Are you getting help?"

"Meeting today at noon," my voice cracked again, despite resolving to keep my tone even.

"See you in a bit, then," the Chief ended the call.

I grabbed a piece of paper from the office and scrawled out a note. "I had to run to the station and am going to get clothes. I'll be back this afternoon after a meeting. I love you."

I left it by the coffee pot, where I knew Francesca would see it. I hated being away from her right now, but I didn't have a lot of choices. More to the point, the options I did have sucked and wouldn't help either of us.

Francesca

I woke right before the scream ripped from my throat. My body became frozen in terror; the only thing I was able to move was my eyes. I blinked slowly, noticing that Jake wasn't in here with me right off the bat. The second thing I noticed was that I heard him talking. I couldn't make out what he was saying, there was still the echo of the nightmare playing in my head, but I listened to his voice.

He hadn't left me. I lay there for a minute, trying to get my body to move when he walked in silently. It had always amazed me how quietly Damien and Jake had moved. I never heard them, only saw or felt them. If I had still been asleep, I would never have known he had been in here. I saw him walk in this time. He began to put his shoes on, and I started to panic.

"Francesca, are you okay?" Jake was at my side in a second. Even in the dark, the strain was evident on his face; the heavy grief shadowed his green eyes.

My words wouldn't form, and I was gasping for air. Jake couldn't leave. I couldn't keep him safe if he left. The immediate thought followed that thought that even if I went with him, I couldn't keep him safe. I hadn't been able to keep Damien safe.

"Shh, it's okay. I'm right here. I need to run home to get more clothes, and then they need me at the station. I have a meeting with the club after that, and then I'll be back. You can come with me if you want," Jake offered.

Fear slammed into me so hard that I jolted and broke free from the paralysis that had gripped me moments before. My ribs protested the sudden movement of flinging myself at him, but I didn't care.

"Don't leave," I breathed into his neck.

"You can come with me, Francesca," he stroked my hair. "I need to go to the station, though."

"What if something happens to you?" My pitch rose with fear.

"Nothing will happen to me. I'll be back. Then we are going to start to talk. I'll turn off my phone, and it will be just us." Jake slowed his movements as if the thought hadn't occurred to him. It probably hadn't.

It was just us anyway. I had acquaintance friends,

but no one I was very close to the way I was with Jake and Damien. That list had only just gotten shortened to Jake now. He wouldn't leave unless necessary, and I needed not to let my fear override everything. Easier said than done.

I didn't know if I could leave or if I should leave. If Jake left, it gave me an opening to get out for a minute and try to find stable ground. See if I could stand on my own two feet instead of letting him carry me all the time. He was hurting more than I was.

"What are you thinking?" Jake kissed the side of my head.

"That being away from you terrifies me bone-deep because if I lose you too, I have nothing left. Nothing is holding me here," I blurted out in raw honesty.

"That's not true, Frankie," he said softly into my hair. "You have this baby, and you have so many people that admire and respect you. I'm not planning on doing something to make you lose me, I promise."

"Neither was Damien. I could have gone to that appointment alone, and he would have been safe. He'd still be with us now, and neither of us would be hurting like this." My tone went numb as I voiced the thought I'd been afraid of letting go. "Because of me, you are hurting in a way I can't fix."

"You don't need to fix me, babe." I felt him flinch. "None of this is your fault. It's not my fault. We both have issues with past trauma. We also have each other. We've both got a strong case of grief and survivors' guilt. Do you want to come with me?" he asked

13

me again, his tone slightly defensive.

I shook my head. Jake was a cop. I was going to have to come to grips with that. He'd always be in danger, and if I wanted him in my life, I had to accept that. It was a little harder now with Damien gone, but I wasn't willing to push him away. No matter how much guilt it caused me, I loved Jake.

I wound my fingers in his hair and leaned away from him, taking in every shadow, line, stubble, texture, and color of his face that I could. His full lips beckoned me, begging for a chance to see if that spark was still there or if my grief had killed it.

Before rational thought could change my mind, I kissed him. The reaction was instantaneous heat between us, a pull, unlike the one I'd had with Damien. If it was possible, this one was even stronger. I swept my tongue across his lower lip, and he let me in, each touch showing me how real it was.

I broke away when I realized we were both crying. Oh yeah, my feelings for Jake were intense, and so was the guilt for having them. I un-fisted my hand from his hair and rested my head on his chest, feeling the rapid thumping of his heart.

"I'm sorry, Jake."

"I'm not," he whispered, sniffing. "I love you."

I let go, and he laid me back down and kissed my head.

"I love you, too," I returned, not knowing if he could hear me or not.

"Rest. I'll be back," Jake held my hand to his face, then kissed my palm and walked away.

I turned the light on when I heard his truck pulling away and saw the article he'd left on the pillow that he should have been sleeping on next to me. The words that he had said helped him. I let the tears flow then. I had several choices to make, several extremely hard choices.

Chapter Two

Jake

I was driving borderline recklessly and forced myself to slow down. I had no clue how to navigate the emotions taking me apart. That kiss broke my fragmented heart. It was so real, so substantial, and nothing had ever come close to feeling that way. And I kept wondering if Francesca only did it to distract herself from the grief?

It could have been the fear because that had been potent and like a live wire. The moment I'd said I had to go to the station, it zapped hard and fast. It ripped my heart out seeing it. I didn't want Francesca to kiss me out of fear or as a way to escape grief. I couldn't replace Damien, and I didn't want to. It was a no-win situation.

My head wasn't in the right place for this. Facts were battling with emotions that became shaded with remorse. I have known Francesca for long enough to see that she loves me. There was a conflict that was happening within her. I couldn't tell if she was acting on that or on a need to connect and get back on her feet. I couldn't be a rebound.

Fuck. I was overthinking, overtired, and way too

emotional to be anything close to logical on this. I needed to stop and put my head somewhere else. Like on the road so I didn't crash and turn myself into a liar by not making it back to her. Noon couldn't get here fast enough.

I made it to my house in record time, showered and packed a duffle bag with clothes, and flew back out the door on complete autopilot mode.

"Head in the game, Jake," I reminded myself as I pulled back down my driveway and made my way to the station.

I parked in my usual spot and went straight for the Chief's office. "Captain Foxwood," his assistant Rebecca said, startled at my appearance in his office.

"He's expecting me," I replied curtly. I didn't want Rebecca's sympathy or her attention.

"Foxwood," the Chief called out, "get in here." The gruff voice didn't faze me. "Close the door," he said quieter when I walked in.

"I resign." I pulled it shut and yanked out my wallet and gun.

I'd failed to notice the rest of the brass in the room. Damn it. My head definitely wasn't in the game. It didn't change my decision, but I could have done it better than I just did, especially in front of the top brass.

"I don't accept that. Put it away, and we'll discuss that later." His eyes bore into mine. "We've got a situation developing, and I'm doing my best to keep a lid on it."

"I'm taking it that it involves me," I remarked dryly, snapping my gun back into its holster.

"It involves veterans, and more specifically, you, Damien Ocasta, Darius Baker, and Caleb Grayson," his voice was the only warning I got to speak very carefully. He knew this was a subject I was very tight-lipped on, even with him.

"We served together overseas in the Navy, sir." I used my peripheral vision to take in the rest of the brass. I couldn't even begin to think of their names right now.

"A very hard-to-come-by fact that the media seems to have gotten a hold of somehow." One of the uptight guys in the corner told me. Shit, that was the commissioner.

"Sir, me resigning will take whatever heat is on you guys off. I'll get it written up and handed in as soon as possible," I blinked slowly, trying to figure out what was going on. The lack of sleep wasn't helping.

"Your employment here isn't the issue," the commissioner snapped. "It's the very secret nature of what you were doing overseas, putting you in the spotlight. Something the chief is trying to put the kibosh on."

What the fuck was happening? "Everything we did was classified, sir. Only the highest levels of the government were involved. The only people left to talk about that are Darius Baker and me. I can assure you that it wasn't something either of us said. Nor would Damien have ever spoken of it."

"I notice you didn't mention Caleb Grayson in that," said a different guy in the corner. I didn't recognize this one, but he set my internal warning sensors off.

"Why would I? He died over there in the war zone

19

nine years ago. Kind of hard to talk about things if you aren't breathing," I retorted sarcastically. "Let's cut the shit, why don't we? Tell me what's going on. I've been holed up in a house grieving, except for my time spent at the funeral yesterday. I'm walking if you are about to smear dirt over any of those names."

The chief gave me a stern look. "I've told you repeatedly, gentlemen, Jake Foxwood isn't behind this. I don't even know what he did overseas, and I'm his chief. All I knew was he served with Damien Ocasta."

"Who's in that car?" The man that had gotten my trouble radar pinging pulled out his phone and turned on a video of Damien's murder.

"We'd be having a very different conversation in a different location right now if I knew the answer to that," I replied coldly. "No need to show me the video, that man you hear screaming is me. I'm well aware of what transpired that day."

"We believe the shooter is the culprit spreading information," the commissioner butted back in. "If the only two alive that know of you and your unit are you and Darius Baker, is it possible he has shared information?"

"Shouldn't you be asking Darius that? Anything is possible, sir. Is it likely? No. All of us became traumatized by what we saw and were a part of in that desert. Not only that, but we also all lost people. People close to us. Darius was a part of two very deadly attacks that have left us all permanently scarred. It's not dinner-time conversation. We didn't even speak with each other about it." I took in a slow breath, trying to calm my breathing down.

"Which leads me to my next concern," the nameless man went on. "Your mental health."

"My mental health isn't of your concern. Nor really of anyone here, after I hand in my resignation. I sought help for PTSD, and I continue to do so. I am not unstable nor a danger to anyone or myself. I am, however, suffering deep grief at the loss of the person closest to me. Take that as you want," I went rigid, remembering Dr. Waters's warning.

"Your witch hunt is over," the chief told him. "Whatever you think is happening isn't happening with this man. I have actual police business to discuss with Captain Foxwood. If you don't mind, you can see yourself out."

He stood up. "Someone's always watching, Jake."

"They can watch all they want. I have nothing to hide. If you want information on my missions, seek out the War Cabinet. Beyond that, you won't get shit from me," I snapped.

The commissioner gave me a level look but didn't comment as the man left the office, leaving the door open behind him out of pure pettiness. I got up and slammed it closed, and sat back down. "Want me to type out my statement?" I asked the men.

"Do you know who that was?" The commissioner moved to stand behind the desk next to the chief.

"Nope. Truthfully, sir, I don't give a shit either." I crossed my arms and met his steely glare with one of my own. He would get rudely awoken if he thought I would bow down to his authority.

"Darius Baker is building up a rap sheet, yet you just want to bat for him with National Security," the commissioner said as if I hadn't spoken.

"Darius Baker is an adult and can do whatever he wants with his life. Purely speaking of our time together in service, there isn't anything he would reveal; he kept watch over Damien while lying dead in the morgue, so our brother in arms wasn't alone. Is that the actions of a man who would spill classified missions? In front of Damien's fiancée and sister to Caleb Grayson, he broke down in tears. Whatever actions he is doing now are separate from what happened then," I spat angrily, losing my grip on the minimal control I had left.

"What happened with Caleb Grayson?" the commissioner asked me.

"He was killed overseas," my jaw ticked. The only tell my chief had that I was in dangerous territory was that tick.

"That's classified information, Dean," he broke in, rescuing me.

"Doesn't it seem odd that they would bring up a name that's been dead for several years?" The commissioner didn't know when to stop.

"Whatever it seems like, it's out of our hands. Our job is to find that shooter and bring him to justice. Disparaging the memory of a military man killed while in service to our country will not get us there," the chief ended the conversation.

The commissioner took his cue finally and left, closing the door behind him. "Sorry, sir." I slumped over.

"Son, are you truly resigning?" he cut right to the chase.

"I am. Francesca's fear when I told her I was coming here was volatile. I can't do that to her, and she's all I have left now. It may be a snap decision, but it's the right one; I'll give a thirty-day notice," I offered politely.

"Very well." He deflated a little. "Take me through the details of the murder. I will take your statement personally and ask you some hard questions you might not be inclined to answer."

"Let's do it then. I have a meeting I desperately need to attend at noon," I said, resigned.

Francesca

Pregnancy brain was real as I was finding out. It could be a mix of mind-numbing grief and pregnancy brain, but I was scattered everywhere. I finally gave up and decided if I forgot something, I could stop and buy it.

Except for the ashes, I grabbed a small blown glass container I had leftover from something and scooped out a bit from another mahogany box that I shouldn't have. The loss of Damien hit me again, and I lost focus for the hundredth time since Jake left.

I slid the container of ashes into my camera case, put both in the small bag I packed, grabbed my purse, laptop, and the article Jake had left on my pillow, and went to my car only to realize I didn't have my keys. It wasn't looking good if this was a sign of how my day would go.

After the Wreckage

Finally loaded, I headed out; destination: wheat boat. I was pretty sure I remembered how to get there. It soon became irrelevant as I blasted Damien's playlist through my speakers and drove through stretches of road I didn't remember driving through.

I thought through everything I knew of him from Caleb's letters and everything I had learned in our short time together. A time that was apparently long enough to get engaged and pregnant. I knew we still had a lot to learn about each other, but I figured we had time like anyone else.

I knew for a fact that Damien was a good man, and I knew I loved him. It had been enough for me to agree to marry him. Foolish, maybe, but it had felt right. The persistent voice in my head that told me Jake felt righter was becoming louder and harder to ignore. And not because Damien was gone and I was scared.

It was part of why I was going to the boat Damien had perched out in Eastern Washington. The other purpose was I wanted to leave a bit of him there in the place that had meant so much to him when he needed it.

There was a genuine chance the whole thing could backfire on me since I was trying to get out of the house that felt like Damien and get some air to breathe. I needed space to let these feelings go. The boat was all him. It was where he had asked me to marry him. There would be no escaping him there.

It still felt like where I needed to be. While our relationship didn't start there, it's where the promise of commitment started. Maybe it's where I needed to be to end it. I didn't know anymore. It was movement on my end, which I needed at the deepest level of it all. If I kept lying there in that bed I had shared with Damien, I would drown.

Caleb's death taught me that. I needed to keep moving; it was what worked for me. I had to pull over when I couldn't see through my tears. I was in the middle of nowhere too. Jake had told me at the end that Damien had seen Caleb. There were so many emotions tied up in that, but under them all was peace, knowing they were together.

Back under control, I resumed driving and found the exit I needed; I thought I had taken the right side road, but I still hadn't seen the boat, and I'd been driving a while. I backtracked and took a different one that had the same results. After the third attempt, I burst into tears and called Angela.

"I'm trying to find the boat, and I'm lost," I sobbed into the phone when she answered.

"Oh, Mamacita. Are you in the fields?" Angela's sympathetic tone made me cry harder.

"Yeah. I have no idea where, and I don't have Hector's number," I leaned my head on the steering wheel.

"Stay put, Mamacita; I'll send him to find you and give him your number. If you need anything, you call me, okay?" Angela made me promise.

My phone rang with a number I didn't know five minutes later. The area code was this area, so I assumed it was Hector and answered with another sob. "Honk your horn for me, amiga, or kick up some dust with your tires," he said gently. I did both. "I see it. I'm coming. Turn around and follow me out," Hector instructed.

I hung up and waited, and then after a few minutes, I saw him driving backward down the road. He waved at me, and I followed him out and then to the boat. When we arrived, I dissolved in more tears when he opened the door and held his arms out.

"It hurts, I know. Where is Jake?" Hector held me while I sobbed into his chest.

"I needed some time alone," I wiped my face on my sleeve. "Now, I miss Jake. I felt like I needed to be here. I'm sorry for crashing in on you. And making you come to find me."

"Francesca," Hector said, pulling my bag out of the car, "you have no water and food." I shrugged helplessly. He shook his head at me and called Angela. "She has no food or water," he said, then looked at me for a moment. "Did you bring your vitamins?"

I hadn't thought of any of that. I shook my head at him, breaking down in tears again. "I'm going to be a shitty mother."

"Thanks, Angela." He hung up and put his arm around me. "Come on, Francesca. Are you sure you want to stay on the boat?" Hector's eyes were sad, and it struck me how much the loss would affect him too. I hadn't even considered how Hector would feel.

"I think I need to," I said quietly and let him lead me up the stairs on the deck. Hector unlocked the cabin, another thing I hadn't thought about, and gestured for me to head down before him. It felt like the air was getting sucked out of my lungs; the memories were so strong.

Hector caught me as I sagged and led me to the stateroom. "Maybe rest a bit. Angela will leave water and food on the counter for you. If you need anything, you call either of us."

"Thank you, Hector. Sorry to be a burden," I mumbled apologetically.

"A friend is never a burden, amiga." He gave me another hug and left me with my overwhelming sadness.

I opened up each of the windows allowing the air to flow through, hoping it would take some of the pain inside me with it. Wishful thinking and grief didn't work that way. I dug through the bag Hector had set inside the door and pulled out the camera case, then the container of ashes, and my article.

I set the container on the counter on top of the article, a reminder of why I was here. I pulled out my phone and contacted my accountant. "Hey Greg, I need your help," I told him as he greeted me. "I need an adoption lawyer, a real estate agent, and an estate lawyer. Do you have recommendations, or can you find me those?"

"Francesca, you shouldn't make big decisions in a time of grief," Greg advised me kindly, almost undoing me again.

"Yes, I should. If you can't help me, just say so," I said impatiently.

"Of course, I will help you. Should I send the contact information to you or pass your number on?" Greg asked after a pause.

"Both? Please. Life is short, Greg. Way too short

for some of us. I'm trying to make the most of it, and I know I'm all over the place, but trust me," I begged him.

"The news said you were pregnant. Are you sure you want to give up your child?" The concern in his voice was touching.

"That's not what I'm doing. I'm ensuring my son has a father. I'm not doing anything Damien wouldn't want me to. I know that much." Damien had told him to marry me if Jake's words had been true. I held on to that tightly.

"Very well. My family is here if you need us, Francesca. I'm glad you called." The kindness was appreciated but killing me. At least the questioning of my sanity had me momentarily focused.

"Thanks, Greg. I'll be in touch," I promised and hung up. I didn't pull any sheets out of the closet; I didn't need Damien's smell all around me. I seriously hadn't thought this through. I had brought a sweatshirt of Damien's that I washed, so it only smelled like fresh laundry.

I pulled that out of the bag, put it on, and curled up in the middle of the bed to cry myself to sleep. My phone chiming woke me up a few hours later, and I glanced at it to see the security cameras from my house showing me a frantic Jake running through the hallways.

Shit. I hadn't even left Jake a note. *I'm at the boat;* I texted him. I hadn't meant to make him worry like that. Too late, I realized I probably hadn't even shut the garage door. No wonder he was like that.

A few minutes later, my phone rang with another unknown number. I almost didn't answer it, but then remembered my request to Greg. "Hello?"

"Francesca Grayson?" an elderly-sounding man asked.

"Yes," I replied.

"My name is Nelson Markham. I was given your information with the note that you needed a lawyer well versed in adoption?" His words were soft-spoken.

"I do." Laying under the boat felt right. "Let me lay out what I am looking for, and you tell me if you can make it so," I started, getting up off the bed.

Chapter Three

Jake

"Can you pick me up at the Pullman airport?" I asked as Hector answered.

"Absolutely. You knew Francesca was here?" Hector asked cautiously.

"Not until she texted me. I'm landing at five-forty. If you can't make it, I'll rent a car. I was hoping to avoid that if possible because I don't want her driving back alone," I explained as the taxi dropped me at the airport.

"Does she know you're coming? I don't want to upset her any more than she already is," Hector's voice was heavy with concern.

"I didn't tell her, but she probably suspects I am. Did she say she doesn't want me around?" Cold panic that she was already pulling away from me clutched my heart. "No, not at all. The last time I checked on Francesca was when Angela brought food and water since she had none with her, which wasn't too long ago. She was asleep but in rough shape. The odd thing was, she was asleep under the boat, not in it," Hector

31

said cautiously.

"Under?" I cursed. "Is she back inside?"

"She is," Hector confirmed. "Angela woke her up, made her eat something, and talked to her. We left her alone after that, probably twenty minutes ago. Francesca looks haunted. I'm going to go out on a limb and guess you aren't looking any better?"

"Probably not. Thanks for this, Hector. All of it. I have papers for you to sign too. Picked them up today," I warned him ahead of time. Hector was a proud man, and the property was an emotional topic for him. His returned silence was enough to tell me that hadn't changed any.

"I'll see you soon."

I raced to the check-in counter, barely in time for the boarding call, and got on the plane. Coming back and seeing the garage door open, the alarm not set, and Francesca's car gone had sent me through the roof. I expected her to be gone, but not that disarray. My heart hadn't stopped pounding since then.

The small consolation was her telling me where she was before I went complete meltdown. If she hadn't wanted me to come after her, she wouldn't have told me where she was. That was my reasoning anyway. Right or wrong, I was going to her.

The flight would be quick, yet it allowed me too much time to think, worry, and think more. Damien had been a practical man and not given to flights of fancy, spontaneity, or impulsive decisions. That he fell in love as fast as he did had shocked me initially, but I never doubted it was real. That's just who he was.

His heart ran deep, and he was trustworthy, an anchor for us all when we desperately needed one. He never disregarded our advice and only made snap decisions without asking our opinions if our lives were on the line. Each decision he made that way saved our skin. Damien had been one of those candles that burned very brightly on both ends. Caleb and I had been the ones that burned slower but longer.

I trusted no two other men to have my back more than Caleb and Damien. One of those burning ends of Damien's candle had gone out when Caleb died, but Damien had still kept us together. He kept us alive and anchored until we were in that hospital, and then he broke down.

Still practical and logical about it, Damien chose the way he thought Caleb wanted him to go, and that was to try and find his sister and stay the course until she was safe. We turned down the offer of medical discharge.

Everything I knew about Damien, his secrets, and his hidden emotions pointed to me going on and doing what was best and right, regardless of what anyone else thought. No matter what. It's no different than what I would expect of him if the roles reversed, but I'd often thought that Damien was closer to that recklessness, not caring if he died, closer to that line than I had ever been.

Shit, this was way too much time to think. I had a lot to talk to Francesca about. Hector too. I'd met with Boomer before I went back to Francesca's house and filled him in on what I'd been a part of that morning. He let me know where he was in tracking down who had done this, which wasn't a lot farther than the police were. I honestly didn't want to see Boomer arrested, not after he stepped up the way he did when Damien died. He was there for all three of us.

The world was heavy, and it felt like it was on my shoulders. Even more massive than the world was my grief and questions that I had no answers to. Guilt sat like a lead weight in my heart because all I wanted was to curl up with Francesca and just let it all go. Cry it out until we couldn't cry anymore.

"You look troubled," a female voice said next to me.

I jumped a little because the seat had been empty. Some blonde young thing sat there. I probably would have gone for it purely as a distraction fling to get it out of my system in my past. Not now. This girl didn't hold one tiny bit of my interest.

"I'm fine. Thank you for checking, though," I replied, my voice coming out unexpectedly steely.

"I'm going back to college. Are you staying in Pullman?" She ignored my signals and persisted.

"No. I'm meeting my pregnant wife," I said bluntly, asking silent forgiveness for the lie.

"Oh," she said, disappointment crossing her young face. "Well, have fun."

Relieved when she left, I felt a moment of regret for being so hard, but I was over that life. The moment Damien died, that part of me went with him. Aside from the fact that no one compared to Francesca in the slightest.

I closed my eyes and rolled towards the tiny

window, angling my body so people couldn't see my face. I knew I was good-looking, but I wasn't conceited about it. I just wanted the flight over with; I dozed for the rest of it and woke when we landed.

I made my way off the plane as fast as possible and scouted for Hector. I heard his truck before I saw it and beelined for it. Hector climbed out and grasped me in a bear hug I didn't know that I needed. Tears stung my eyes as I clung to the man.

"Thanks, Hector, I needed that," I rasped out as he let me go.

"So did I, amigo. So did I." Hector got back in, and we headed back to the farm. "Storm has moved in."

"Fitting," I mumbled. "Damien loved the storms out here. I know you don't want to hear this, Hector, but I have to tell you. You know I'm the executor of his estate, right?" I waited for his grunt before saying, "He deeded the farm to you. There was a letter that I put a copy of in the paperwork for you. It was a general letter of his wishes, but he spoke to you in it. He just wants the boat to stay there and to be maintained. The proceeds you paid to him, he put in a maintenance fund for the farm. He hasn't touched it; it's just grown and collected interest, and that he left to you." I pulled the folder out of my bag and set it between us.

"Why?" Hector's voice was hoarse.

"It's in the letter," I looked out the window. The sky ahead was dark and threatening. The fields next to the road showed the crops bent sideways with the wind that tore through violently. "Damien considered you one of his brothers."

"He has a child to leave it all to now," Hector continued to protest.

"Damien's son will be cared for, trust me on that. As a personal favor, if you decide to sell, can you give me the first option of buying?" It was incredibly selfish of me to ask, but the boat had been significant to Damien, and I wanted to make sure it stayed there.

"Of course," Hector agreed immediately. "I'll change my will accordingly to ensure that whoever inherits will keep it that way."

"Thank you, Hector." Relieved, I sat in silence and watched the clouds as we drove straight into the storm that had settled over the area. Rain and wind were slamming into the side of the truck, rocking us.

When we pulled up, I hesitated before getting out. Hector sensed the reason why. "Francesca's resilient, but she's struggling. I checked on her before I left to get you, and she was asleep again. There's food on the counter and water."

I nodded, sucked it up, pushed against the door held closed by the wind, and darted up the stairs and down to the cabin, soaked. I hadn't heard the music from outside, the wind and rain had been too loud, but now, it was all I heard.

Damien's playlists were blaring from the Bluetooth speakers he had up around the place. The only sign I saw that Francesca was even here was the article I had printed on the counter with what looked like a small jar of Damien's ashes holding it down. I didn't see her bags or anything else of hers.

The food was on the counter, along with vitamins

and water, as Hector had promised. There were windows open in the stateroom, I could tell, going by the sound of the wind whipping through I heard between songs. That's where she probably was. I set my bag down on one of the chairs and pulled off my wet shoes and coat.

The music was deafening, so I wasn't surprised she didn't hear me. I made my way back to the stateroom and stopped in the doorway; my heart cracked wide open. Francesca lay on the floor. Her back was right against the bed. The windows in front of her were wide open, the wind and rain streaming in, puddles forming on the planks. She was still. So completely still. I grabbed her camera from the bag inside the door and took a few photos of her before setting it back down, proof of one of the conversations I needed to have with her.

Francesca

The wind crashed through the open windows in a display of violence that I wished I could feel. The rain was streaming through, leaving puddles on the floor. I huddled my back against the bed, my feet inches from the spreading wetness, and all I could think of was Damien's blood. Had it spread across the ground like this? I was there for his death but not conscious.

I'd made several life-altering decisions today and drowned in grief in between those decisions, and in the middle of it all, battling my thoughts and guilt over my next steps. The storm was a welcome reprieve. It almost made me feel like Damien showed me how spectacular it could be just watching it play out, showing me how it soothed him.

It was cathartic how the music told me so much about Damien. It matched the storm and my emotions. I still felt numb, though, because I missed Jake. Jake wasn't gone, but I'd selfishly left him alone after begging him not to do it to me. I missed Damien too, but my heart knew he was gone; it was familiar with the hole left behind.

As if my longing for Jake had materialized him, I felt his arms slide around me and pull me up off the floor. "Babe, you're freezing."

"You're here," I breathed out a sigh, wrapping my arms around him.

"I'm always going to follow you, Frankie," Jake warned, kissing my head. He reached over to the iPod and shut the music off.

"We need to talk," I told him. He stiffened under my arms.

"After we clean up the water." Jake let go of me, grabbed a couple of towels, threw them on the puddles, and closed the windows. He left the ones on the other side open and felt the bed, checking if it was wet. He dried the floor up and then took the wet towels out to set in the sink in the other room and then returned.

Jake pulled a blanket out of the closet, led me to the bed, sat me down, tucked the blanket around me, and then stretched out next to me. "Is this the talk where you tell me you don't want to see me anymore because I remind you too much of what you lost?"

Dumbstruck, I could only look at him for a

moment. Blinking slowly, I unwrapped the blanket from around me and lay next to him, pulling it over us. "I'm not entirely sure why you would think that, but no. Not even remotely close."

Jake let out a strained sob, rolled to me, buried his face in my neck, and broke down in tears. I couldn't make out what he was saying, but his anguish triggered my own, and we just lay there and cried together. Mother nature outside of the boat cried out her agony over the situation.

When he calmed, "Jesus, Frankie, when I got there, saw you gone, the garage door open, I freaked out. When I got here and saw you lying so still on the floor, again, my brain just flipped. Then you said we had to talk, and it was like I was losing you too."

"I'm sorry," I murmured, stroking his back. "I went about this so wrong. I wasn't thinking clearly and was going on pure reaction. I needed to get away. I was so terrified something would happen to you that I bolted. I needed to think. I needed to bring Damien here too, and under it, I think I needed to come here to finish breaking, so I could start to rebuild as you said."

"I resigned today," Jake lifted his head to look me in the eye.

"You what?" My heart skipped a beat.

"I resigned, gave them a thirty-day notice. I saw how it affected you, and I don't want you to worry about me like that. It's just a job. I'll find something else to do." There wasn't a sign of regret on his achingly handsome face.

I was stunned and speechless. Everything I had

planned to say flew right out of my mind. Jake had quit his job so that I wouldn't worry about him. "Will you marry me?" I blurted out.

"Did you just propose to me?" His entire body froze, his eyes riveted on mine.

"I did, but there's so much more to it than that. I'm sorry." Great. I'd scared Jake off with my unintentional proposal. I started to shiver, having uncovered myself. "I'm screwing this all up."

"We are definitely coming back to that. Before you go farther and possibly say something you don't mean, like a proposal, I want to finish breaking us so we can both rebuild." He pulled me closer to him, wrapped an arm around me, my head laying in the hollow of his shoulder, and he recovered us.

"Jake, I meant the proposal; I just did it wrong," I protested. "I'm not going to stop whatever plan you have to finish breaking us because we need it. You have to let me finish first, though. Please?"

"What if what I have to say changes your mind?" I felt his breath catch at the question. I let the howling wind be the only sound in the room for a minute as I pondered the question.

I think the only thing that would change my mind is if he told me he couldn't ever love me the way I loved him. Or that he already had a wife. "Unless you tell me you are already married, my mind won't change with whatever you have to tell me."

"You can't possibly know that," he chastised gently.

"I do know that, Jake. Can I explain?" I slid my

arm across his chest to hold on to him, feeling a bandage under his shirt. "Wait, are you injured?"

"No, babe, my injuries are all on the inside," he chuckled lightly. "We'll get to that later. Go ahead and explain."

"Leaving that article was a stroke of genius on your part," I started. "It reminded me of how much I struggled after Caleb's death. How lost I was. Neither of us is a stranger to death, and two of them have bonded us in ways neither could have seen coming. But what I learned from it is that life keeps going, even though it feels like it's stopped. To get through it, I need to keep moving too."

"I'm listening," he reminded me. Jake's arm tightened a little around me, and I moved my arm back to his chest and gently stroked my fingers over it. The feel of his heartbeat was more reassuring than he could understand.

"A doctor once talked to me about a loss she suffered and how she started to look at things differently. Being here helped me see that different level, even though it felt like my heart was being ripped out of my chest while still beating. I'm not overly religious, nor am I overly scientific. I'm somewhere in the middle of those two, but her talk returned to me while I was lying under the boat trying to find Damien," my voice cracked slightly.

"This is going to hurt, isn't it?" Jake's voice had a lower tone than usual that let me know his emotions were close to the surface.

"Maybe," I admitted softly, angling my head to

look at him.

He shifted and brushed his lips lightly across mine, that spark jumping to life between us. "I'm ready," his hold didn't loosen or tighten, but his eyes were intent on mine.

"What if there are different dimensions where Damien is alive right now, and we are getting married? The possibility exists; the universe is far too vast and mysterious for it not to. What if there are multiple dimensions? Each with a different path that could have been taken and playing out. This situation is what was supposed to happen in this one. I *hate* thinking that because losing Damien wasn't something I ever wanted. I can't dismiss the possibility, though. Just as this doctor once told me that she was still with her husband in some other dimension, and they were planning a family, but in this one, she had a different purpose that he wasn't a part of," I fumbled my way through it.

"Okay, I'm with you. I don't like thinking about it either, but I'm still with you," Jake whispered.

"My heart knows he's gone. It's accepted the loss, but I'm stuck in it because everyone I have ever loved is gone, except you. Before you jump to conclusions, that's not why I asked you to marry me. If I could have figured out how to have two husbands legally, I would have told Damien I wanted to marry you both. Maybe in one of these other dimensions, that's happening. It's a thought I like because, from the start, I wanted both of you."

I paused to let that sink into him. I continued stroking my hand over his chest, paying attention to the cadence of his breathing. I felt the rhythm of his heart, watching for changes, but it held steady.

"Jake, Damien was intense in a way that you weren't. You've been steady and supportive even though I knew you wanted me. Through my entirely too short time with him, my feelings for you only grew stronger. To me, that was the most telling thing of all. It is also one of the hardest for me to admit because of how it hurts. My path was always you. This reality, dimension, or whatever, would happen no matter what. I was always going to lose him." The tears came back, and I started to shake.

"I don't want to believe that," Jake's emotions came out. "Damien loved you in a way no one else ever came close to."

"I know," I cried. "Except you. That's why it hurts. But it also helps to think in another dimension, Damien's still alive, and we are still together seeing where this goes. I think that's why I'm pregnant. My destiny was to lose him, and maybe God took pity on me and gave me this small part of him to keep. I don't know. Maybe Caleb knew Damien would die, and he fixed it, so I met you both, fell in love, and made it so this baby exists. I can rationalize it a thousand different ways, but it keeps coming back to he's gone, and I'm not. You're not. I knew Damien well enough to know he'd hate to see us hurting like this when he knows how we both feel about each other."

"You're right about that." A tremble washed over Jake.

"I never had that spark when I kissed Damien.

There was heat, fire, and passion, but not that spark I get with you. That tells me something too. I'm not comparing you two because that's unfair to both of you. I loved him, and I love you. Differently, but no less intensely. I was more scared of telling you about this baby than telling Damien. That was telling too. All of it was telling me I wanted to be with you. Some small part of me made me feel like thinking that made that whole situation happen, which I know is ridiculous. I know," I repeated.

"Frankie," Jake started to say something, but I interrupted him.

"Let me finish," I tapped my fingers on his chest, and Jake closed his mouth. "Caleb told me once on a visit back home after one of his nightmares that he wished I could meet someone like you. What Caleb wasn't saying was that he wished I could meet you. Caleb wouldn't say that because you were still enlisted, still serving, and the thought of something happening to you hurt him so much that Caleb wouldn't ever allow me to consider dating someone in the military. Not that I would have given him a choice, but he never brought either of you home. After he died, I didn't only lose him. I lost both of you too."

"We lost you, too," Jake reminded me.

"I know. Life is so damn short, Jake. I know we both carry a lot of baggage, and I know that it won't be easy to get over all this, just as I know we shouldn't wait for that to happen before starting us. I'm not trying to pressure you because a simple no will suffice. I'm in love with you, and I want a life with you. If you can't see it happening, I want you in my life in whatever capacity you are comfortable with; however, I want this baby adopted by you. I've started the paperwork. I talked to a lawyer about it today. The baby will have Damien listed as his father on the birth certificate, but I want you to be his dad. It will, of course, be easier if we are married, but he can still make it happen if we aren't. I'm also looking for a new house because mine feels haunted now. I want to turn my house into a non-profit place for people living with PTSD who need a safe place to transition."

I stopped talking and looked back at Jake's face. It was unreadable. His grip on me hadn't changed, but now his heart was racing, despite the controlled breathing. Some rational part of me told me I should be scared by his silence, but I wasn't. I knew Jake would never hurt me intentionally. It was one of those deep instincts that I knew I could rely upon without fail.

"I fell in love with you the first letter Caleb read aloud to us," Jake finally said. "The way your voice came through, the humor, the worry, the love, and biting sarcasm had us in hysterics. Then I saw the pictures you'd sent, and I fell a little more because I saw you through the pictures you took. Caleb knew. I wasn't shy about telling him I would find you and run away with you. He constantly punched me over it. It never was the *idea* of you I was in love with either; it was *you*. It was the voice of the person who wrote those letters. The intelligence and strength, the cavalier way you went through men that drove Caleb insane, the wit that kept us all going when we all wanted to give up. If I'd had an inkling that the mini tornado that walked into the bar that night was Caleb's sister, I would have run Damien flat over to get

45

to you."

"Does that mean we get to tell our child that Mommy proposed to Daddy?" I asked, somewhat hopefully.

Chapter Four

Jake

"We'll get to that," I told her gently. "First, I need to tear us up into little pieces. After I left you today, it hit me hard, the fear on your face. *Everything* hit me all at once. I knew I would resign before I even walked into the station."

"You don't have to quit for me, Jake," Frankie said softly.

"I do. Not just for you, but for me. I'm over being a soldier; a cop is just another soldier. I want to do something meaningful. I'm getting off track here," I tried to get a grip on my thoughts. I was still stuck on her telling me she was *in* love with me. I'd known it, but hearing it was even better. "I also decided that I would do just what I tried to get Damien to do, and that was to tell you the truth."

"The truth?" she asked, confused.

"Yeah. All the stuff we aren't supposed to talk about, the reasons for the nightmares, the way your brother died. I told Damien to have no secrets with you. I'm taking my advice, but it's not only to give you the closure you need; it's also to give me the closure I need. We *both* need to heal. I went to a meeting after my time at the station today because I was severely on edge. Then I went to see the lawyer about Damien's estate, and then I went to get a tattoo. That's what you are feeling," I spilled.

I watched Francesca's face as she processed it all. "You're going to tell me about Caleb's death?"

"I will. I will answer any questions you have. If this is going to be real, I don't want those questions or the past hanging between us. I want you to understand why I'm triggered. I don't want you to have to guess. I will spare you the details you don't want, the gore, the parts that won't help you get closure, but if you want them, I will give them. I will give you everything you ask for; I want the same from you. By that, I mean total truth. It doesn't mean I will pick your life apart with questions. For instance, this morning, I knew you were going to run. I saw the look on your face. Your brother got the same look on his when shit got to be too much. I followed him too," I moved my hand to set it on top of hers on my chest.

"Yes, I should have told you," she agreed readily. "I can agree with total honesty. I want more kids. I want to have babies with you."

"One at a time, babe." I almost choked on my tongue. "Are you ready to hear about Caleb?"

"No," Francesca admitted in a sigh. "That doesn't mean I don't want you to tell me, though. So, go ahead."

"It may trigger me," I warned her.

"I know. I've got you," Francesca shifted her body closer until she was pressed entirely against me, my train of thought completely gone for a minute. I was getting everything I ever wanted, but it had cost me two best friends and part of my soul. I wasn't sure I was enough for her.

"It was supposed to be a routine surveillance assignment combined with a supply run. Of course, our routine surveillance was still considered a dark operation, but the supply run was our cover. We had some extra troops we were delivering to the base catching a flight out. And some who were meeting back up with their squad. We had Army, Navy, and Marines with us. Boomer and our communications guy were in the front vehicle of the convoy. Damien, Caleb, and I were in the second vehicle with an Army guy and a Marine. Caleb and I were on the outside. I was on the gun and Caleb on the door. We don't usually ride like that, but our intel had told us the route was clear. We were going to break off from the convoy before it reached base and do a trek up into the hills to do some recon on some caves that had gotten spotted."

"How many vehicles were in the convoy?" she asked quietly. Her expression told me she was picturing it in her head.

"This one, we had seven vehicles. Our three in the lead, two supply trucks in the middle, and another two vehicles in the back," I answered Francesca. "We were about at the halfway point when Caleb's attention got pulled to the right of us. There were dunes and some rocky hills in that direction, and to the left was rocky

49

mountain-type terrain. At first, he thought it was an animal looking for a hiding spot, and he didn't halt us. We had gone another fifty feet when the vehicle in front of us slowed down enough that Caleb started paying close attention to our right area. We'd heard Boomer through our coms that he was studying the road for buried IED. While Caleb was watching the right, I spotted something odd to the left. It looked like sunlight glinting off metal, but I didn't spot it again. Some of the rocks in that area have naturally occurring crystals that form in that intense heat, and it tripped me up a few times. My instincts told me to watch, so I kept my eyes that way and relayed the info to Damien."

I glanced back down at Frankie's face to see her eyes squeezed tightly shut. I paused and kissed her forehead until she looked back up at me.

"I'm okay," she said, but her eyes held a haunted quality that I knew all too well.

"I'm going to sidetrack for a moment. Caleb had become the type of person he thought your mom wanted him to be. He was offered a leadership position and turned it down more than once. He was a part of us, and that's where he would stay. He had several loyal soldiers that would have followed him anywhere, Damien and I included. Your brother was one of the best people I have ever had the pleasure of knowing. Yes, that place and what we had to do and see traumatized him, scarred him, and left its mark. It only made him try harder to do things he thought would make you and your mom proud of him. That's what drove Caleb, and that's what we all did. We all tried to find at least one thing every day in that place to do that would make Frankie and her mom proud of us. He succeeded in it, too, every day. Whether we were on assignment or not." I kissed her forehead again, noticing the glint of tears.

"I was proud of him no matter what," she whispered. "He never believed me. He thought I was just saying it to make him feel good, but I meant it. I was trying to do things to make him proud of me."

"God, Frankie, he was incredibly proud of you. Every one of us in that squad was. I'm going to veer back to that day now, okay?" I waited until she nodded and brushed the tears off her cheeks, careful of the cracked side.

"Caleb had called out a halt, having spotted what had drawn his attention again. He'd gotten off the vehicle and walked out from the road a little way when Damien followed and called him back. My attention became divided between the mountains and them. Boomer had gotten out, and the comms guy and our medic were watching the same place I was, which validated that what I had seen wasn't my imagination. I rotated my gun to point to the area I had seen something when Damien called me down. I instructed the Army guy to take my spot and watch that area. The medic and I met the rest of our team when Caleb broke out into a run. Your brother was fast. Probably the fastest out of all of us, and Damien and Boomer couldn't stop him. I wasn't close enough, but I had finally spotted what he had seen. A pregnant woman who appeared to be in distress."

"Yeah, that would do it," Francesca breathed

out. "Damsel in distress was Caleb's thing."

"Very much so." I laughed at the truth of that. "Damien was hot on his heels with the rest of us right behind him. Damien was shouting through the comms, 'it's a trap.' His instincts were deadly accurate on these things, and he'd never been wrong. But the visual presented to us was also a strong incentive. She looked pregnant, beat up, and had blood running down her legs. It wasn't farfetched given the shit we'd all seen happen to women over there. Caleb had gotten to her, laid her down on the ground, and tried to help her. Damien was the closest to him, with me directly next to him and the medic next to me. I saw Caleb move the woman's clothes, and he was starting to back up when the bomb went off. She wasn't pregnant. It was a bomb. I saw enough to know that the blood running down her legs wasn't from a baby. She'd cut herself and had the bomb strapped around her belly; Caleb didn't stand a chance. It blew him apart and tore into Damien's side, almost killing him. It took out a huge chunk of my leg," I lifted my pant leg to show her the extensive scarring.

"The scars on Damien's side," Francesca's eyes widened. "Those are from then?"

"Those scars were," I nodded sadly. "The gunfire from where I had spotted movement started while we were stunned by the bomb, killing the comms guy and severely wounding the medic. Boomer got shot a couple of times as well, but somehow Damien managed to get him out of the line of fire before passing out. We were getting ambushed. Screaming everywhere, smoke, chaos, body parts, death. Damien woke up and tried to find something of your brother to bring back; he was fanatic about it. He was bleeding out, trying to keep us together and fighting back. He saved six lives from that attack; how, I'll never know. That bomb blew the vest right off him. Because we weren't supposed to be there, we weren't officially; we got silenced about it. Damien won two medals from that day, and no one will ever know."

"Caleb died thinking he was helping a woman who was losing her baby," Francesca said, tears pouring down her cheeks. "*I'll* know how Damien got those medals. Our baby will too."

"Boomer took the discharge offered to him as one of the bullets shattered part of his collarbone, and the other nicked a lung. Losing Caleb broke the squad in a bad way. Boomer thinks that the guy who killed Damien is related to one of the casualties from that day. Somehow our being stopped and ambushed was the fault of Damien for not keeping Caleb inside the truck. The ambush would have happened anyway and possibly killed more of us than it already did. It takes a pretty heartless bastard to walk away from a hysterical pregnant woman with blood running down her legs. Damien was the only one that suspected that it was a trap."

I couldn't stop the words once I'd started. The sounds, smells, and sights from that day assaulted all my senses, but Francesca's tear-stained face kept me grounded in the present. It didn't keep me from the guilt, but I wasn't lost in it as I was last time.

"I'll never forgive myself for not having followed

Caleb the moment he stepped off the vehicle. We always had each other's backs. Always. Damien blamed himself, as he did any time we lost someone. But not one person blamed Caleb," I said reverently.

"That's ridiculous. If anyone were to blame, it would have been Caleb. He broke away from the group. He was my brother, and I loved him dearly, but even I can see that," she said through her tears.

"What would we blame him for, being human? Empathetic? Being a good person? As I said, it would have happened anyway. It would have happened between whoever was in the hills and the woman, and probably more lives would have gotten lost. The sad reality of the situation is that Caleb kept the bomb away from the convoy, saving many lives and paying for it. I saved one person, and it wasn't enough. Damien saved six other people and paid for it with his sanity. So many things went wrong that day," I sobbed openly now.

The guys at the meeting had been right to encourage me to do this because while it hurt like hell to reopen all those wounds, it also freed me from carrying them in silence all these years. I'd tried desperately for a long time to get Damien to talk to me about it, but he was stalwart in his decision to remain silent on the matter.

Francesca had pulled away from me and sat up, using her shirt to wipe her face clean. She pushed a few of the lights in the room to turn them on and moved to pull up my pant leg and examine my scars. It evoked another wave of emotion in me when her gentle fingers traced the ugly flesh.

"What happened?" she looked up at me, her hands around my leg, the only person outside of the doctors treating me that I had let touch me there.

"Shrapnel from the bomb. It was the same that took the vest off Damien. I'm not sure if he didn't have it fastened all the way or not, but he was hit in the shoulder by something, and I think it tore or burned the seams apart, and the vest was hanging off him. The shrapnel from the bomb tore through his side and into his lung. It broke a few ribs and punctured his spleen and appendix. The concussion knocked me backward, and a piece tore half the muscle from my leg; shredded it. It was a lot of surgery and therapy to rebuild the muscle. Despite that, we still went back."

"Damien wouldn't tell me about those scars. He told me about the rest, but not those. I can't say the knowledge will help me rest easier, but it answers questions I've had. Thank you for telling me and letting me in," she said softly, still holding my leg. "You were lucky. This wound could have killed you."

The words caught in my throat, but the look on her face said she knew what I was going to say, that I wished it sometimes had. Francesca bent over, kissed my leg, and lowered the pant leg, moving back to my side. She used her shirt to dry my face and then covered us both and lay down.

"Does this change anything for you?" I hesitated before asking.

"In what way?" she shifted and looked up at me with a slight frown.

"About me?" I braved the fear building in me

and asked.

"No. There's no reason it would. It raises other questions that I need to think about—about Damien and my brother, and when I'm ready, I'll ask. It helps me understand the circumstances of that day. The people who came to notify us about his death were vague, only telling us he was killed in enemy action by an explosive device. They didn't tell us where, when—anything at all. Just that there was no body to recover, actually, they worded it in a way that led us to believe his body wasn't in a place where they could safely retrieve it. It breaks my heart that Caleb died in the way he did, trying to do the right thing, but it also proved to me he was who I thought he was exactly. It's even worse knowing you were all stuck in a place where things like that were common. It does not change how I feel about you or for you."

"I wanted Damien to tell you. It would have helped him. You are the only person I have ever told about that day outside the chain of command we answered to. I feel like I burdened you while freeing myself," I confessed.

"You didn't burden me. It's never a burden, Jake. I had many vets telling me worse things than that. This time was just more personal to me," she assured me. "If it helps you, tell me everything you want to. Every time you feel triggered, tell me. Get rid of the poison."

"You are my light in the dark, Frankie." Pure love washed through me.

"I love it when you call me that," she smiled at me softly.

56

"I think you are both Frankie and Francesca. To me, calling you Frankie feels more intimate. If it doesn't bother you that I call you that, I will," I melted at her smile.

"Okay," she smiled again. "Now, Jake Foxwood, are you going to rebuild with me, together? Will you marry me and be this baby's dad? Help me raise him so he knows who Damien was? Help infuse all that goodness in you into him? Can you love me the way I love you? Was that a better proposal?"

"I'm not a rebound?" Jesus, this woman slayed me. I almost didn't ask, but I had to, and her emphatically shaking head soothed my fears. "Yes, to everything. I don't know how you love me, but the way I love you is pretty all-encompassing. I don't think it will be easy because the grief is deep, and the guilt is there. But I swear to God, Frankie, I will do my best to give you everything you ever ask for and the things you don't. You are everything I have been looking for since I was in that hell. I don't care how sappy I sound, but you are offering yourself on a platter, and I'm selfish enough to take it."

"It's a little sappy, but I don't mind. You could never be a rebound, Jake. We are in this together then. We'll screw up together; we'll succeed together. We can go to Pullman tomorrow and get married at City Hall. We need our own place. You don't have to sell your house; we'll get a new one or an old new one. Just somewhere fresh. No ghosts. My mom and Damien are everywhere in my house, and I had to get away."

"I understand." I did. I agreed with her too. I sat up and pulled off my shirt, my first time shirtless in front

57

of Francesca. I didn't have as many tattoos as Damien did, nor was I as built as he was. Her eyes were glued to me, nonetheless stroking the fire inside me. I peeled the plastic off the tattoo and turned to show her what I had done.

Her breath caught as she took in the work I had done. It was a large tattoo, a set of dog tags that spanned my side at an angle spreading to my back. The chain wound up to lay across the back of my shoulders. On the tags were the words Never Forgotten, the names of my lost team members, and the date I lost them. I'd had Damien's name added.

"It's beautiful, Jake." Her fingers traced over her brother's name and down to the side of Damien's.

"I think we've found the wreckage, babe. Just one more thing I want to bring up. Why the hell were you afraid to tell me about this baby?" I forced the question that had been bothering me.

"Because it felt like a door was closing that I didn't want to be closed. Not because I was afraid of your reaction. I was honestly certain you would have been beyond thrilled," Francesca said in a small voice.

When she put it that way, I understood. "Okay, I get it. I don't want you ever to be scared to tell me anything. I'm not going to lie; it hurt to hear that, even if I now get what you meant. Total honesty, right?"

"Right," she pulled me back down and cuddled up with me, careful of the fresh tattoo. "No more making me sleep alone, either."

I could live with that condition.

Chapter Five

Francesca

I woke up a mess. Jake was right; this was going to be very hard to navigate. I felt closer to Jake than ever and closer to him than I had felt with Damien, which caused immediate guilt, and I tried to tamp it down. After our talk last night, I had started to see there was a lot more to Damien hidden than I had thought. That wasn't bad, but it solidified my creeping feelings that Jake had been the right choice. Again, that didn't ease the guilt as much as it did make it worse.

I heard thumping footsteps coming down from the above deck, and my new fiancée popped his head into the stateroom.

"Having second thoughts?" Jake asked me.

"No. Guilt, yes, but no second thoughts. It struck me how little I knew about Damien and how willing I was to jump into a life with him without knowing things," I rubbed the heel of my hands into my eyes.

"You knew the type of man he was and that you loved him. It was enough to make that commitment. You didn't have that wrong," Jake came and sat next to me.

"You knew Damien loved you. Hell, I knew he loved you that first night."

"The love on both our parts was real," I nodded. I snatched Jake's hand before he could retreat. "It's real with us too. I don't know how to say this without sounding like an ass, so I'll say it anyway and hope you understand what I mean. The love I had for Damien was strong. It felt right, and I was safe; the sex was fantastic, our personalities meshed, and the boxes were all marked. I didn't question it. I question now that my feelings for you came up more often than not, and they cast doubt over what I had with him. I was not too fond of that because I knew it was real. That is a very shitty way to say that my feelings for you are stronger than for Damien, but I believe that's what it boils down to. If they weren't, it wouldn't have come up. It makes me feel guilty because I would commit to a man who deserved more from me than divided feelings."

"Damien knew you had feelings for me. You wear them on your face. What sticks out for me is when you said your heart knows he's gone. Mine does too, and while PTSD made us both live in the past, we can't do that. We are moving forward and rebuilding from the wreckage. Damien knew how we felt, and he did what he's always done. He charged forward and claimed his victory. Maybe the relationship would have fizzled and burnt out; maybe you both are so stubborn that you would have made it work. We won't ever know because the choice got taken from us. We can only forge our path now if you still want to," Jake brought my hand up and kissed my palm.

"I do. I haven't changed my mind, Jake. I'm just verbalizing the mess in my head to help you understand. I also don't want you to feel like you are getting a divided me. Wow, it's a lot easier dumping someone than letting them in," I mumbled. Jake let out a sharp laugh and kissed my uninjured cheek.

"As long as we aren't having the breakup talk, I'm good with the mess in your head. We already knew this would be hard; we'll get through it. Get dressed, babe. We need to go ask Hector to be a witness for us, probably his sister too, if you want me for your unemployed trophy husband," Jake's small smile burrowed into my heart. "At least I'm delivering on his asking me to promise to marry you."

"Well, I didn't lie that first day I met you. You *are* pretty; you'd make a nice trophy." I stood up and gingerly pulled off my shirt and stripped my pants. Jake didn't break eye contact with me once. That wouldn't do. "You know, as your wife, I'll want you to look at my body. Touching it will become a necessity for making more babies."

"If I do, we will not make it out of this room," he said huskily. Equal parts guilt and lust tore through me.

"Oh. I thought you didn't find me attractive," I whispered.

"I thought you were beautiful when I didn't even know what you looked like," Jake stepped into my space and pulled me flush against him. "Now that I do, my opinion has changed to thinking you are the most gorgeous woman I've ever encountered."

I moved to pull him down into a kiss, but he

stepped away and shook his head. "Why not?" I pouted.

"I'm saving myself for my wedding night," he grinned and left the room, me standing there in my underwear, stunned silent.

"I need a shower," I called after him as I pulled my dirty clothes back on and grabbed a set of clean ones. I picked up my phone and followed him into the central part of the cabin, where he thrust a vitamin and bottle of water into my hand.

"I also took the liberty of making your follow-up six-week appointment with Dr. Waters," Jake said as I swallowed the vitamin.

"Glad one of us is thinking," I mumbled. I'd forgotten all about that. I downed the water and grabbed my purse, not knowing where my keys were.

"I've got the keys, babe," Jake guided me to the steps. "I've got a set of clean clothes in the car already for myself."

"Are you going to shower with me?" I asked automatically.

Jake groaned, "You're going to kill me. I'll proudly walk around all day with a hard-on if I have to. I don't give in as easily as Damien does."

"Wait, if I remember right, you were the playboy of the group," I protested, thinking fast.

"*Was*. No more. I'm an engaged man now. Did you know I got punched in the dick because of you?" he asked me as I climbed the stairs.

I laughed, "By Caleb?"

"No, by an army girl that I was casually seeing. The story goes: Caleb had read us one of your letters, and

I said I was in love with you. I had no idea she was anywhere near me until I saw Damien's face. I turned around, and she nailed me. I dropped like a sack of rocks. I have never seen Damien laugh so hard before. Your brother smirked and told me he was glad he didn't have to do it," Jake chuckled.

"Poor baby. If Hector does that, I'll kiss it and make it better," I promised, looking over my shoulder to see him falter and almost miss a step.

Jake shook his head slowly, "I swear I can hear both Caleb and Damien laughing their asses off."

I stopped on the top stair and waited until he was in front of me a couple of steps lower, putting us at the same height. "I'm sorry. It's a habit. I'm not trying to make you suffer. I'm just one of those women that have a revved-up sex drive. I did the same thing to Damien."

"Don't apologize for that, Frankie. It's karma biting me in the ass." He leaned forward and brushed his lips barely across mine, the touch so light, I wasn't sure it had happened, except that spark that lit between us told me it had.

"Do you feel that? When we kiss?" I whispered in awe.

"I feel something every time I touch you," he whispered back. "I've never taken this many cold showers as I have these past three months."

Humbled, I moved to let him come up, and then I followed him down to the car. "How'd you get here?" I didn't see his truck or bike.

"Flew. Hector came and picked me up. I didn't want you driving back alone," he said, opening the door for me.

I held his hand on the way to Hector's and stayed put while he came around the car to help me out. "I'm not doing this because I'm scared to be alone, you know that, right?" I asked Jake.

"I do," he replied quietly. "I know what fear looks like on you." He ran his hands down the side of my face. "I know what pain and grief look like, anger, humor, passion too. Most importantly, I know what love looks like; I wouldn't let you do this if I thought it was a fear reaction."

Mollified, I followed him into Hector's house, who was just sitting down to eat. "Oh, good. I made enough for both of you," he said, seeing us.

I rerouted myself from heading straight to the shower to sitting down at the table while Jake brought us both plates of food, my stomach rumbling loudly. "Thanks, Hector. I have a favor to ask you," I said while Jake sat next to me and poured me some juice.

"Did you take your vitamin?" Hector asked.

"I watched her take it," Jake answered.

"Okay, then I'll talk," Hector smiled easily. "What can I do for you, Francesca?"

"Will you and Angela be witnesses for Jake and me today at City Hall? I asked him to marry me last night," I said after swallowing a bite of scrambled eggs.

"Are you sure that's what you want, amiga?" I saw the alarmed look he gave Jake.

"Yes, Hector. I know what I'm doing. My feelings for Jake are just as real as they were for Damien. They always have been. I'd also like to ask you to be a godfather to our son," I added, hoping that Jake was okay with that. I should have asked him. "Sorry, Jake, I should have asked you about that first. I don't think I'll be an easy wife."

"Jake's up for the challenge, amiga," Hector laughed openly. "I'd be honored on both accounts."

"It's all good. Hector's a choice I would have made myself. We'll head to Pullman after we shower and see if we can get an appointment time. I'll pull some strings if I have to and let you know. I want to head to the store first and get a decent set of clothes. I didn't know that I would be getting married today when I packed," Jake smiled.

"Crap. We need to get rings too," I thumped my head. "Here, I thought I had it all mapped out, and I'm forgetting many things."

"Teamwork, babe. We'll get it taken care of; the worst-case scenario is we wait until tomorrow or fly to Vegas." Jake shrugged and kept eating.

I pushed my plate away, the list of things we needed to do growing disproportionately large in my mind. I went to stand when Hector glared at me until I sat back down, withering under his intense stare.

"That look means finish eating because he's worried about you." Jake pushed my plate back.

"After you eat, I'll call Angela and see if she has time to be the second witness for you," Hector lost the glare and smiled once again as I continued to eat.

"Thank you," I told him, again humbled. "Leave the mess. I'll clean it up while Jake showers, and then we'll be out of your hair."

"Deal." I saw a look pass between the two men, but I ignored it. They could hash it out between themselves while I showered.

Jake

Once we heard the shower turn on, Hector turned to me, "Are you sure, Jake?"

"I am. I wouldn't have agreed if Francesca wasn't in her right mind. We talked a lot. It boils down to Damien's gone, and nothing will change that. He wouldn't want us to ignore what's between us, and she pointed that out. The feelings are genuine, Hector. She's also started adoption paperwork for me to legally be the baby's dad, with Damien's name on the birth certificate as the father. She's started a real estate agent looking for a new house. This momentum is how she gets through the grief; she keeps going," I tried to explain.

"I only want to make sure this isn't a grief reaction. Will this baby know who his father is?" Hector pulled no punches.

"I'll make damn sure he does," I replied with a bit of heat to my words. "Francesca wants that too. Damien tried to get me to promise to marry her. Did I tell you that?"

"No," Hector looked startled. "Why?"

"I think Damien knew something was going to happen to him. He wanted to make sure she was loved and safe. He knew how I felt about her; he always did."

Satisfied, Hector stood and pulled out his phone,

calling his sister. "Hey, Francesca asked if you and I had time to be witnesses to her and Jake getting married at City Hall today?" he cut right to the chase.

A string of loud Spanish burst through the phone as Hector grinned at me, answering back in English, so I knew what was going on. When he hung up, he nodded, "Angela had the same concerns I did, but apparently, she already knew about Francesca's feelings for you."

I thought about it briefly. "Francesca will probably ask your sister to be godmother then."

"Angela would love that," Hector's eyes watered a little. "Do this right, Jake. Book a room in a hotel for tonight, at least. Don't consummate your marriage in a place that was uniquely Damien's. Give her a clean start."

"I was going to. Hopefully, we can get in at City Hall without me having to make a ton of phone calls to government people to make it happen," I mused.

"I know one of the judges. I'll give him a call after you guys leave and see if he can make it happen. I'll text you a time if he can," Hector offered generously. "Don't forget to bring her camera."

"Will I be a good dad and husband?" I asked him directly.

"Without a doubt in my mind," Hector's immediate answer calmed my nervousness. "You simply have to be a good man first, and you are that."

"I've loved Francesca for so long that this feels surreal to me. Like I'm going to wake up and find out I've been dreaming this whole time. Part of me wishes that were true because it would mean Damien is still alive," I said quietly. "God, I wish he was still alive. Every woman

I've ever been with has been competing against Francesca all these years."

"The universe works in mysterious ways, Jake. Treasure her and every moment with her," Hector patted my arm. "She's a rare jewel."

I stood and cleared the table, rinsing all the plates but leaving them as Frankie had said. I didn't want to start our wedding day by irritating her. Hector saw and laughed at me, winking. He glanced at his watch and then stepped outside and made a phone call.

Finding myself alone, I took the opportunity to talk with Damien. "Man, I hope you can hear me and that you don't hate me. I'm beyond angry that you left us both, and the guilt is crushing me. But I love Francesca. Words I have never said about any woman other than my grandma. I promise you, Damien, this baby will know who you are. I'm going to love them both and take care of them."

"I hope you are with Caleb," I leaned back against the counter and closed my eyes against the sudden sting of tears. "I also hope that Caleb doesn't hate me either. I never lied about loving her back then. Please don't hate me, Damien. Please don't hate me. I'm doing what I think is right, and I feel selfish because my heart wants it so bad, even while I feel like the worst friend in history since you haven't even been gone two weeks. Fuck, Damien, so much so I quit my job. I can't put Francesca through that, wondering if I'll come home or not." A sudden sound had my eyes flashing open to see Hector standing in front of me.

"He knows, Jake. You two were so close that I

know you wouldn't be here doing this if it felt wrong to you. Damien loved Francesca with all he had in him, but I will say this; he loved you more. I believe you have his blessing, and there is no one he would have trusted more than you to take care of what mattered most to him. To love her as he loved her."

I heard the soft pad of Francesca's footsteps and tried to straighten up, but instead, I let her see the emotion. Her step slowed as she came into sight and then picked up until she had wrapped her arms around me in understanding. It was a rare and raw moment that Hector witnessed, but his face told me he was glad that he had.

"We'll get through this," she promised me. Her muffled voice came from my chest as she pressed kisses over my heart.

"I might not ever let you out of my sight," I warned her, my voice thick with tears I refused to shed. I didn't even want to let her out of my arms.

"Should I shower with you then?" she tipped her head up to smile at me.

"If I had met you during my man whore years, it would have been a battle to see which of us could outdo the other. I'm happy to concede you the winner before I cave in, and we are no longer welcome in Hector's house," I kissed her head.

"I'm headed out to get some work done. Francesca, Angela and I will be there. Judge Roberts, my friend, will meet us at City Hall in Pullman and do the ceremony for you at four. It gives you time to get the license and do everything else you need to do," Hector smiled at me. "You would have been able to get an appointment, he said, but he wants to do it himself."

I smiled my thanks at Hector and kissed Francesca's head again before releasing her to shower. When I left, she was hugging the life out of Hector.

Chapter Six

Francesca

We went to get the marriage license first because the jewelry store that Jake wanted to go to wasn't open yet. Once finished, I fielded a call from Greg and promised him a copy of the license to set the beneficiary things up on his end. He'd already spoken to the adoption attorney he'd found for me.

Then I got a call from the real estate agent, and I gave my search parameters. To my surprise, she'd already found a place she thought was hot and wasn't even listed yet. She sent me the link, and Jake and I took a few minutes to look at the information.

"That's a bit expensive, isn't it?" Jake asked cautiously.

"No. Greg is my accountant, but he's also my investor. He's a genius with the market, and he's more than quadrupled the money in the trust, which was already a significant amount. We will outright buy the house skipping the mortgage process, and the title will be buried under the trust's name but will have both our names attached to it. It would just take some digging for people to uncover that information," I replied, watching his face.

"You know I can contribute, right? I'm not penniless, and everything Damien had he left to me. We can dump all of it together into the trust he already manages. I'm not opposed to that," he tucked some hair behind my ear.

"I want you to do what you feel comfortable with, Jake." I wasn't sure if what I was doing emasculated him or not.

"I don't have an accountant, but there is a lawyer Damien and I both used when we inherited. If this Greg is someone you trust, I don't have a problem following your lead. I just want to be clear that I'm in it too. I don't expect you to support me. I'm not marrying you for your money and am more than happy to pool mine in with yours."

"I didn't think you were. Here," I held out my hand for Jake's phone and punched in Greg's number. "Call and talk to Greg and see what he advises. I trust him implicitly with my money and investments, and he has yet to steer me wrong. Before you call, though, what do you think of this place?"

Jake took back his phone and set it down on the dashboard, and we looked over it again. It had four bedrooms and four bathrooms. It sat on three wooded acres with a private drive, and the house looked out over the sound. I'd specified that because I thought he would like to keep the water view.

"Tell her to do what she has to do to keep it unlisted, but I want to see at least three other options as well," he conceded. "We can go look at them all on Monday. That gives her three days to wow us. I like this. I just want to see what it feels like in person."

"Okay. I don't want to sleep at my house," I said slowly, wincing as a pain reminded me I still had a cracked rib.

"We can stay at mine. No other woman has been in my bed there. No other woman has been there, period. I guess I should probably sell the house," he thought aloud.

"Talk to Greg about it first. I'm not selling mine; he said the value would skyrocket, which would be a great inheritance for the baby. I'll rent it out or turn it into a safe house or meeting place for a non-profit. I haven't fully figured that out yet. That's a married couple talk, and we aren't married yet," I rambled on.

"Okay," he agreed readily. "Call the agent back, and I'll call Greg. To be clear, I'm buying your ring. Me."

"Deal," I smiled. I climbed out of the car to give him privacy and called the agent back. I relayed Jake's requests and then backed it up by telling her whatever house we picked would be a cash deal, no mortgage paperwork. I gave her Greg's number as a backup if she needed to verify funds. I went over what I liked about the house she sent me. She promised to have four homes for us to view on Monday.

We parked outside the jewelry store, and I wandered over to look in the windows. I heard the car door open and saw Jake get out, still talking on his phone, his eyes glued to me. It took me a minute to realize that I had walked out of his line of sight, and he was just making sure he could still see me. A warm feeling filled my chest.

I liked that Jake didn't crowd me, but it also thrilled me to know that I was precious enough for him to keep in sight. Damien had been the same way, but he would have been within touching distance. I hadn't minded that, but I preferred being allowed to have some slack in the leash.

A few rings caught my eye. One's for Jake, that is. I saw a clerk come and flip the sign to open and unlock the door. I motioned to Jake that I was going in, and he nodded at me. I walked in and was given a cool look by the woman who had opened the door. I was in jeans and a t-shirt and didn't look like I could afford anything, but it was also rude to assume, and her attitude irritated me.

I gravitated over to the titanium rings, wanting something that wasn't quite ordinary, which our situation emulated. I noted a few that I wanted to see with my fingers and moved to look at the tungsten ones as well, thinking about Jake and what made him so special. It didn't pass my notice that I found several that Damien would have loved. I wished that we hadn't waited to get married.

The woman still hadn't acknowledged me verbally, so I continued to ignore her and peruse the selection of rings that the cases had to offer me. I wandered to look at some of the women's bands and found several that caught my eye. I moved over to the earrings, my eyes landing on a beautiful pair of peridot or emerald earrings that almost precisely matched Jake's eyes.

"May I see those, please?" I pointed to the earrings, looking over at the woman who eyed me like I was about to rob the store blind.

She stalked over and pulled the earrings out. They were emeralds. The emeralds were a color I hadn't seen before, and they were exquisite. I heard the door open and turned, putting them back on the counter where I saw her snatch them and stow them away. I also didn't miss the way her jaw dropped when she looked at Jake.

"Sorry that took so long. Greg's a genius, you're right," Jake said, his eyes only for me. "Are we going to keep our selections secret from each other?"

"I think we should," I said quietly, noticing he hadn't once looked at the woman behind the counter. "Makes it a little fun."

"Are you going to get down on one knee and ask me properly?" Jake grinned at me, the earlier sadness in him gone for the moment.

"If we were at the police station in front of all your co-workers, you bet your ass I would. In front of the lady who seems to think I'm going to steal her inventory, it's not quite as impressive," I shrugged. "If it will make you give me that smile, I'll do it in a heartbeat."

"Which smile is that?" His eyes watched me closely.

"I can't tell you. You'd use it against me all the time, and I'd have to cuff you to the bed." The gasp from behind me made it all worth it. The twinkle in his eyes matched those earrings perfectly.

"Where's the manager?" Jake finally looked at

75

the woman, the smile leaving his face. Instead, I saw the SEAL side of him take its place. Almost as terrifying as that side of Damien's that I had seen creep up on occasion.

"H-he's in back. Can I help you?" the clerk asked meekly, still openly admiring him, making me want to slap her.

"You will be helping me. Get the manager out here to help my fiancée, and please stop ogling me. It's rude," he snapped.

I bit my lip to keep from laughing as she scurried away, her face beet red. "Definitely love you. Why is she helping *you*, though?"

"Because I'm going to make sure she knows what customer service should be about; I saw how she ignored you when you came in here. I don't miss much, babe," Jake kissed my head again. "By the way, we also have a room at the fanciest hotel Pullman has to offer tonight. Only the best for my bride."

"As long as it's not a Motel 6, I'm good." I giggled. I couldn't help it.

"There is one, but this won't be that," Jake laughed. "Do you want a real honeymoon, Frankie?" His question was quiet, for my ears only. "I'd love to take you somewhere."

"Ireland," I answered immediately.

Jake's face softened, "Your brother loved it there. I'll make it happen."

A stodgy-looking man came out of the back with the snooty woman following him. "Good morning, sir. Can I help you?"

"Yes, I'd like you to help my beautiful fiancée pick out a ring for me. Your assistant will help me as I feel she needs to learn what customer service should be, not what was presented to my fiancée when she came into the store," Jake said matter-of-factly.

The manager frowned back at the woman and then turned back to us. "I apologize on behalf of my daughter. I'm happy to help and allow you to work with her on that."

"Thank you. Also, I'll need these rings ready today. I'll pay extra," Jake added.

"Your fiancée is already wearing one of my rings," the manager said. "I'm happy to help a repeat customer, but you didn't buy that ring."

"Damien Ocasta bought this ring for me," I felt my face fall. "He got killed over a week ago. Our circumstances are a little strange, sir, but I assure you that we both know what we are doing, and it's what Damien would want."

"Oh, my dear, I'm so sorry," the manager's face changed. "Come with me," he gestured down to the cases I had been looking at earlier.

"Francesca," Jake turned me to look at him, "you don't owe explanations. Trust your heart."

"I wouldn't be here if I didn't, Jake. I like that he remembered who bought the ring, and I love that when you walked in, your eyes were only on me." I stretched up and kissed his chin. "He's not judging us. She might be, but he isn't."

"I'll take care of that. Go find me a ring, woman," Jake patted my ass.

I walked back to the manager and held out my hand, "Francesca."

He shook it, "Sam, a pleasure to meet you, Francesca. I'm truly sorry to hear about Mr. Ocasta. He was a true gentleman."

"He was. So is Jake. They served together with my brother overseas during the war on terror. Both are remarkable men, and I'm lucky to have been loved by all of them. Oh crap, I don't know his ring size," I mumbled.

"Hold on, Francesca," Sam pulled out a sizer, measured mine, then ran over to get Jake's, informing his daughter on my size, then came rushing back. "Easy enough. Was there something you were specifically thinking about?"

"The titanium or tungsten rings," I told him.

"Titanium, I think," Sam said, glancing back at Jake. "Tungsten is a harder metal but can shatter. Titanium can take a beating and hold up."

My eyes flew up to Sam's. He understood. I moved over to that case and pointed at two that stood out to me, and Sam pulled them out and angled his body to block the view. My eyes kept gravitating to the one. I pointed to it, and Sam nodded.

"This here," he pointed to the middle of the band, "is what we call hammered. The achieved effect is from just that. This channel here could support some small stones, and if I have a few hours, I can make that happen. This channel, the outside, is gold. You picked a unique ring in that aspect."

"We have an appointment at City Hall at four. So we have until maybe three o'clock for you to do what you need?" I guessed.

"May I ask you a personal question, Francesca?" Sam lowered his voice.

I wasn't sure where he was going with this, but he seemed to understand what I was looking for in a ring for Jake, so I nodded.

"You mentioned he served with Mr. Ocasta and your brother. I'm guessing, and this is only a guess, that your brother has passed away as well?" Sam tried to ask delicately.

"He did. He died overseas, and both Damien and Jake were with him. Part of what makes this so special to me is that they were closer than brothers. My brother spoke of them often, and in my heart, I believe my brother would have picked Jake for me. Not that Damien was wrong, but he got taken from us violently. Jake is all I have left in this world, and I love him. I love him every bit as much as I love Damien. Jake is the captain of a S.W. A.T. team back home; he's a gentleman and one of the best men I have ever met."

Jake must have felt my eyes on him because he turned and gave me a smile that cemented in the words I'd said in a way I couldn't have even if I tried. I smiled back at him before turning back to Sam.

"I miss Damien with every breath I take, but Jake does too. It hurts so bad that I'm not sure how I remember to breathe. Together he and I will get through this and build a life that both Damien and Caleb would be proud of, and it will honor them. I know how strange it must sound to hear that I love them both so much, but it's true. Love isn't a word I hand out loosely or freely either." I looked up at Sam to see tears in his eyes.

"I believe you, Francesca. My suggestion would be to have a birthstone from each of you added to this small channel. I can put them in there loosely or anchor them in. It would be a way to honor the relationship between all of you," Sam said gently.

"You might think me a complete ass, but I don't know Damien's or Jake's birthstones," I mumbled.

"I can find out Mr. Ocasta's easily enough, and I can have my daughter request his birthday on the information form he will be filling out. It's the same form I had Damien fill out, including his birthday," Sam smiled at me. "Adding the stones will also make this ring one of a kind."

"I trust you, Sam. You picked the same ring I did for the same reasons," I smiled tremulously. "Do it exactly as you see fit. Can you help me pick out a watch to give him as a wedding gift? Something that's befitting a seasoned Navy SEAL, a cop, and under it a tender man who loves as hard as he fights."

"Of course," Sam pulled out a pad of paper. "What's your birth month? And your brothers?"

"October is mine. June was Caleb's," I responded. "Can you add March? Maybe to the bottom?"

"Of course." His eyes searched mine carefully. "I'll finish it up in a way that will allow me to add future stones as well."

"Sam, I'll gladly drive across the state to be your customer." My happiness surged.

Jake

"Now show me what she was looking at when I walked in here, and you rudely snatched it away," I demanded.

"She was quite enamored with them." Mary, the saleswoman, meekly headed to the case next to us and pulled out a pair of green earrings.

"Wrap them; I'll take them now. Ring me up and have that ring ready no later than three. Tack on any additional fee that needs adding to make it happen," I kept my tone hard. I'd ridden her ass the entire time about how she had treated Francesca.

Mary handed me some forms to fill out, and I didn't question them. I filled them out and slapped my card on the counter. She rang up the sales, had me sign the receipt, and then went in the back to wrap the earrings, coming back out with the small box tied with a pretty bow.

"Will we be called, or do we just show up?" I asked, wanting to drum into her head the importance of this.

"We will call," Mary assured me.

I slipped the box into my pocket and looked back to see Sam smiling widely at Francesca. She had won him over in a matter of seconds. Her easy and gentle nature was hard to resist. Even when she was angry, it was hard to resist. I watched as he came around the counter and hugged her, my heartstrings tugging like crazy that she would be my wife before the night was through. Damn it; I felt torn between elation and utter sorrow.

Francesca slung her purse over her shoulder and

walked with Sam back over to me. "You are a lucky man," Sam smiled quickly at me.

"I know it," I agreed. "I'll do something that earns Francesca's love every day."

"I believe you, son. These will be ready on time; I promise you that." Sam led us both out of the store.

"Ready to go shopping?" I looked down into the eyes that were already looking up at mine.

"No. I hate shopping, but yeah, I don't want to marry you in jeans. Is naked a possibility? That has merit," she quipped.

"It does, but I'd rather not have others seeing my wife naked," I hugged her lightly, wondering how her rib felt. I knew better than to ask after having hugged her. "At least not on our wedding day."

"How many people have seen you naked?" Francesca leaned against her car and smiled innocently.

I laughed hard. "Way too many to count. I was in the military, remember? Walking around naked wasn't a concern for us when we had to wash up in the field. Or after training or waking up. Honestly, we had no modesty," I said bluntly. "I will not ask you the same question, so don't even think of telling me. I heard your letters; I know you aren't a virgin."

"Not all of them saw me naked," she argued. I groaned.

"Frankie," I took one small step closer to her, "unless you want me to find each of these guys and give them a beat down, don't tell me more."

"Caleb beat you to most of them," Francesca laughed.

"Most? I don't doubt that there were many you didn't mention. I'm on to you. I was the same way," I stepped back and pulled her forward so I could open her car door. I waited until she sat before saying, "Your brother was probably worse than you."

Her jaw dropped open as she pulled her legs in, and I shut the door before she could say anything else. I rounded the car, smirking, and got in. "He was not!"

"Oh, babe, I was Caleb's wingman. Yes, he was. He was smooth too. He flashed his dimples and half of wherever we were, came running. I hardly had to do any work. When we wanted to go home, all either Damien or I would have to do is talk about you and wanting to meet you," I grinned, remembering the many times we cock blocked him that way. "Drove him insane. It became a game for us."

"Effective," she laughed delightedly. "No wonder Caleb punched you so much."

"He was the king of bathroom sex," I laughed, remembering our escapades.

She threw her head back and let out a loud groan, "Way too much information."

I took the victory and drove us to the bridal store the rude Mary had told me about during our shopping spree. I'd also sent a text to Hector asking him to make reservations at the best restaurant in town afterward. He replied that he'd done it and told me that Angela would bring a bouquet for Francesca.

Things were moving along, and despite the moments of intense heart-stopping grief that gripped me at odd times, I was happy because she was. Francesca had the exact moments I did, they showed on her face, but when our eyes met, she always smiled. It was good enough for me.

I'd also asked Greg if he could recommend a travel agent, and he'd asked me if I would allow him to make our reservations for Ireland. Greg said he had some strings he could pull, and he had Francesca's information on file already. I would send him a copy of my passport when I got home. I told him to make the flight out the day after Francesca's doctor's appointment. That gave us time to move and settle before we took off again.

"A bridal store?" she asked when we pulled up.

"It was the easiest choice for somewhere local," I told her. "They have other dresses besides wedding dresses. Get whatever you feel you want."

"Are you going to see it?" Francesca gave me a look.

"Do you want me to?" I countered.

"Yes," she sounded nervous. "I'm not good with the whole girly thing."

She made me want to slay dragons for her. "Be you. That's all I want."

We walked in and immediately got surrounded by salespeople. Francesca followed one woman over to a rack, and I followed another to where tuxes were. "Do you have suits and not tuxes?"

"A smaller selection, yes," she showed me, and I dug through until I found a pair of charcoal-colored pants I thought would fit and then a softer gray button-up shirt. I picked out a green tie to match the earrings, and I went to the dressing room to try them on.

The pants were a little too long for my taste, but the girl assured me she could shorten them in the time it took Francesca to settle on what she wanted. She took the measurements and suggested bringing in the waist a bit; I agreed because I didn't know much about this stuff.

I sat outside the dressing room while Francesca was trying on dresses, watching as dress after dress was flung up over the door, the other saleswoman running back and forth with different styles. It was almost laughable. After about forty minutes, I heard a small sigh.

"Jake? Are you out there?" she called out.

"Right here, Francesca," I answered softly.

"I think I found the one," was her timid response.

"You can show me if you want," I told her.

"I want," she opened the door slowly, revealing a sight that almost sent me straight to the floor. "Yep, this one," she told the saleswoman, who breathed a sigh of relief.

The dress had thin shoulder straps and was long. The gown had a side slit that went up above Francesca's knee, hugging curves so that every man in the vicinity would lust after my bride-to-be. White satiny material flowed with her movements sensuously, making my pants uncomfortably tight.

"I need shoes," she said. "I'm not good at walking in heels."

"I'll carry you," I grumbled, trying to adjust myself discreetly.

The saleswoman laughed and ran off to bring back several shoes. Thankfully she picked those out quicker than the dress and was soon changing. The saleswoman ran out with a stack of things and to steam the dress for her quickly.

"That is a dangerous dress, Frankie," I softly whispered when she came out. "Damn near gave me a heart attack."

"I saw," she smiled softly. "That's how I knew it was the right one. I think Damien would have liked it too."

Chapter Seven

Francesca

"You need a coat, babe," Jake told me again. "Nights get chilly, and we are going out to dinner afterward. There's an outlet store here. Let's run in, grab a coat, and check into the hotel. It gives us enough time to relax for an hour before getting dressed and leaving to grab the rings."

"Fine," I relented, knowing it was true. I needed makeup too.

I went straight to the makeup aisle, grabbed what I needed, and then beat feet to the coats. I quickly agreed to a knee-length gray one Jake held out because I didn't care what it looked like as long as I didn't freeze.

"Anything else before we go?" he asked.

"Oh! A brush!" I ran back to the cosmetics and grabbed a brush and a package of hairpins. Jake met me at the checkout lane with a couple of toothbrushes and a grin.

We checked into our room and lugged all the purchases up, declining help. We got the clothes hung up so they didn't wrinkle, and Jake flopped back on the bed.

"Are you going to go shower?" he asked.

"Yes, but how did you know that?" I stopped in my tracks.

"The way you were staring at the tub gave it away," he chuckled. "It will take you longer, so let me clean up first."

"Okay," I agreed, setting down the makeup and hidden lingerie bag the saleswoman had been friendly enough to recommend. "Damn, razor. I'll be right back; I need to run down to the front desk and get a razor."

Jake kissed my forehead, handed me a room key, and shed clothes behind him as he made his way to the bathroom. It was distracting until I heard him laugh and knew he'd done it on purpose. Our sex life was going to be fun; I could already tell. Sex was a grief coping mechanism for me, and I wondered if I would be able to go through with it. There was a fractured rib, but Damien also hovered in the front of my mind constantly. I fought back the wave of pain that accompanied the thought with a sense of betrayal.

I grabbed three razors from the front desk, her smile telling me she knew what I was up to, and made my way back to the room. It took a strong man to agree to the plans I had laid out for Jake last night, especially on the tail of his best friend's murder, who was also my fiancée.

Not one other man I knew, other than Damien, would have so quickly agreed to marry me, move after quitting his job so that I didn't worry, and decide to adopt a baby that wasn't his. I also knew Jake wouldn't have agreed to it if he hadn't already loved me.

My past didn't concern him the way it had Damien. It hadn't seriously concerned Damien, but it had bothered him a little. Jake's history didn't bother me. He was playful and open with me; he had been from the start, which endeared me to him. I didn't have any reservations about this at all. Something I can't say about my engagement with Damien; the uncertainties had all come after I had accepted his proposal, though. All of them had been about Jake.

A stab of guilt shot through me at the thought right as Jake came out of the bathroom wrapped in nothing but a small towel around his waist. I bit my lip, suddenly glad the saleswoman had talked me into the lingerie.

"This is foreplay to the foreplay," Jake brushed his lips across my cheek as he moved to the foot of the bed and picked up my dress. He sauntered by to hang it on the back of the door to the bathroom.

I took it a step farther, just for payback. I stripped all my clothes off, leaving them in a small pile, and strutted past Jake buck naked, swinging my hips. "Challenge accepted," I looked back over my shoulder to see his heated stare.

"You win," he called out as I closed the door and tried to stifle my laughter.

I shaved, showered, got out, and dried off. I checked the time and started to blow dry my hair. Then I pinned it up in a way that hid the stitches on my head, probably the only genuinely girly thing I knew how to do. I grabbed my scented lotion out of my purse and moisturized my body. While my skin was soaking that in, I pulled the tags off the lingerie and got that on.

Makeup was always trickier for me, but I did a passable job with barely any time left to spare and slid the dress over my body carefully. I studied myself critically in the mirror, hardly recognizing the person staring back at me. He liked me without the makeup, so he'd probably like this too.

I cleaned up quickly, grabbed my purse, pulled the watch out, and opened the door. The sight of Jake standing there looking undeniably gorgeous almost sent me face-first into the ground. His suit molded his body in a way that had my mouth watering, the green of his tie a perfect match for his eyes.

"Holy shit, Frankie," Jake breathed out, breaking my trance. "You are perfect."

"So are you," I squeaked out. I fought back the tears as I thought I should have seen Damien this way.

Jake's breathing was a little ragged as he handed me my shoes. I slipped the heels on, my shorter height not quite as pronounced now. "I got you a wedding gift," his breathy voice washed over my ear, making me want to rip my clothes off. Sex and grief went hand in hand for me, and that it would be with him was even better.

Focus, I told myself. "I got you one too." I pulled the gift box from the top of my purse.

Jake moved to kneel before me, his eyes soft on mine. "You got me a gift? *You* are my gift."

"If you make me cry and ruin this makeup, you are in trouble," I smiled. My eyes filled, but I kept the tears from falling. I handed Jake the box, and he gave me one as well. I pulled the bow off and carefully opened the paper and the box to reveal the green earrings I'd been looking at earlier.

"Those are the ones you were looking at, right?" he asked me softly.

"They are. I wanted these earrings because they match your eyes." My hands shook as I tried to get them out of the box.

"That's why you liked them?" Jake's voice dropped an octave, getting husky.

"Yeah," I said, managing to get one of the earrings out. I quickly swapped and then got them on, standing to look in the mirror.

"I don't deserve you, Francesca Grayson," Jake came up behind me.

We looked good together. Damn good. "Francesca Foxwood, soon," I corrected him. "Open yours."

He cleared his throat, his heart in his eyes as his gaze raked over me, but he finally stepped back and looked at the package in his hand, pulled the paper off, and saw the brand name on the box. "You got me a TAG Heuer?" his stunned voice asked as he opened the box.

I smiled at the look of astonishment on his face. It was a beautiful piece, rugged and elegant at the same time. The perfect blend of badass tough, and sexy as hell. "Do you like it?" I asked, worried because Jake just stared down at it.

"You're kidding, right?" his quiet voice sounded, and his eyes met mine. "I fucking love it." He set the box down and took off the one he was wearing. "It's already set."

"Yeah, I had Sam do it at the store," I smiled at his expression of wonder.

He put the watch on and then swept me off my feet. "I'm not kissing you again until we are married, but I want to." He set me down gently and put the coat on me. "Let's go get our rings and do this. I want to see what that dress looks like on the floor."

"Yeah, I'm not going to lie. I want to see that too," I laughed. It was hard feeling elated while also feeling like I was dying. I grabbed my purse, Jake grabbed my camera, and we headed out. We turned heads.

"People can't keep their eyes off you," Jake murmured in my ears. "I might have to fight our way out of here."

"Um, look in the mirror, handsome. These people aren't just looking at me," I pointed out.

"Those people looking at me wish they *were* me," his lips tickled my ear.

We made it back to the jewelry store in record time. Sam came outside to greet us and exclaim how fantastic we looked. He handed Jake and me a box each once we entered the store. He expectantly watched as we tucked them away. His eyes flicked from my ears to Jake's wrist, and a gentle smile graced his face.

"Is there a necklace that matches these earrings?" Jake asked out of the blue.

"There is," Sam told him and led us over to the counter. He held the chain out to Jake, who fastened it around my neck and handed his card over. Sam quickly rang it up and sent us on our way with warm wishes.

"Jake, you didn't need to do that," I said, staring down at the beautiful stone that rested over my heart.

"It was purely selfish, so you think of my eyes when you look at it," he smiled at me.

Jake

We walked into City Hall, and with the way people looked at us, I felt like royalty. Hector and Angela waited outside the judge's chambers, letting out surprised little yelps as they spotted us. I felt a jolt of happiness and grief that this wasn't Damien's wedding.

"Amiga, you are stunning." Hector kissed Francesca's cheeks lightly while Angela helped her out of her coat and handed her a beautiful little bouquet. "You clean up well, Jake."

"Look at my motivation, Hector," I laughed. "You'd clean up well too."

"All too true," Hector agreed. "Are you ready?" His even tone let me know that he'd spotted the moment of sadness and understood.

"Never been readier." Francesca took my arm as Hector opened the door and led us in.

"Welcome, you two." A tall, thin, slightly older man belted out. His voice wasn't what I expected it to be. It was deep and booming, where I had expected it to match his frame, thin and reedy. "Hector filled me in a little on the unique circumstances of this sudden marriage, so I'll skip the lecture. I will, however, say to you both that I offer my deepest condolences for the loss you both suffer."

"Thank you, sir," I replied automatically. Jesus, my brain spun out of control because this should have Damien standing here. The thought wouldn't let go, and it hurt deeply. It didn't change anything because I wanted this, but it felt right that he brought up Damien.

Judge Roberts nodded respectfully at me. "A heartfelt thank you to you, soldier, for your service. Now, I want to stress marriages of convenience are never worth it. That said, I don't believe that is why you are here. I'm just obligated to point that out." He made a chuffing sound. "Losing someone so important to you isn't convenient, and Hector wouldn't have called in a favor unless he agreed with your reasons."

Francesca moved closer to me, something the judge didn't fail to notice. "It hardly seemed worth it to plan a traditional wedding when the only two people that matter to me are here with us. This way just felt easier, and since we are here, it felt right," she said softly but firmly.

Judge Roberts nodded at her, and his face lit up with a big smile. "Practical thinking, young lady. Do you two want to say your own vows?" he looked between us, getting straight to the point.

"I'd like to, yes." I cleared my throat nervously.

"Proceed," Judge Roberts instructed me.

"Frankie, everything about you is a light that shines brightly on my life. From when you were nothing but words on paper to when you walked into our lives in a moment of pure hell. You've never stopped surprising me since that day. I promise to love you and our family with everything I have, strive to make your life easier and happier, and work by your side to make all of our dreams come true. I will find ways to make you proud. I promise to work hard every day to earn your love, protect you and our children, and take care of you. There is not one thing on earth that I want more than I want to spend the rest of my life loving you."

The judge nodded his approval at my words, then looked at Francesca. She took a deep breath and looked deep into my eyes.

"Jake, I once told Damien the words I love you were overused and that you didn't truly understand their meaning until the one you loved was gone, and you can no longer say it." She paused before continuing, grappling with her emotions. "I still think it's mostly true, but there are exceptions. I've been lucky enough to find two men to show me the word's meaning again. You show me in every little thing you do. I've seen how hard you fight, and I've seen that the way you love me is harder than you fight. I promise you that I will do my best to keep seeing the little things you do that add up to so much more than I could ever expect. I promise to love you just as hard as you love me. I'll fight anything that stands in our way, and I will always pull you out and bring you back to me, no matter what. The road may be hard, but we are stronger together."

There was nothing in the room but her. Francesca had found a way to honor Damien when she declared her love for me. She reached up and wiped the tears from my cheeks; her face radiated love and confidence with the shadow of grief lingering underneath.

"Let's exchange the rings," Judge Roberts said surprisingly gently. He appeared as moved to emotion as Francesca and I were.

Hector handed me the box, and I pulled her ring out while Angela gave her the other. "Do you, Jake Tanner Foxwood take Francesca Olivia Grayson to be your lawfully wedded wife?"

"I do," I responded immediately, a stupid grin splitting my face.

"Do you, Francesca Olivia Grayson take Jake Tanner Foxwood to be your lawfully wedded husband?" the judge asked her.

"I do," she smiled back at me. She took my hand and slid a ring onto my finger, and I think my heart stopped.

I looked down at my hand, realizing I still held Francesca's ring. Sheepishly, I took hers and gently slid the band I'd picked for her onto her finger. My heart slammed against my ribs. She looked down at her hand in wonder. Her eyes snapped back up to the judge when he pronounced us man and wife.

"Kiss her, son," Judge Roberts smiled kindly.

I stepped close and pulled Francesca gently up against me. This woman could bring me to my knees so quickly. I slid my arm around her waist, anchored her to me, mindful of her rib, dropped my face a breath's width from hers, then lowered to capture her mouth in the hottest kiss I've ever had. I imagined this is what heaven tasted like, these lips of hers. Electricity zapped between us like a solar flare, and she melted into me.

When she moaned, I pulled away because my control was slipping, and we were putting on a show. We stared at each other, dazed until the judge broke into our thoughts and had us all sign the license.

"Go file it now, you still have fifteen minutes, and I bribed a clerk to wait for you." Judge Roberts winked at me. No need to tell me twice. "You'll get your certificate today, too, and any copies you need."

Chapter Eight

Francesca

I stood there, waiting at the counter for the clerk to do her thing, and stared at the most perfect ring I had ever seen. The band underneath was flat and thin and widened up to a flat brushed top that flared out and took up the space between my lower knuckle and hand in an almost oval shape. Diamonds lined the edges, and in the center on the top and the bottom rim was a gemstone, two different colors.

"This is my birthstone, topaz," Jake said softly, pointing to the beautiful blue stone at the top. "This one is Damien's—garnet. I see we had the same idea. Do you like it?"

"It's perfect," I stretched up to kiss him. "Do you like yours?"

"Perfect," he echoed me. "Explain what drew you to this."

"I saw it and thought of you," I glanced at his face. "It's titanium, except the edges Sam said are white gold. The center is titanium, one of the strongest metals out there, and he said it's hammered to get that look.

You've been hammered pretty hard but are still precious and gorgeous. No question about your strength," I winked at him. "The stones were Sam's idea. A way to incorporate Caleb and Damien into our lives and our marriage. Sadly, I didn't know either your or Damien's birthdays, so I had to use Sam to figure out which stones. The other two on the top are mine and Caleb's, and the one on the bottom is March. This little guy I'm carrying. Sam said he'd be able to add other stones later."

"Caleb is June. What's the stone?" he asked me.

"Alexandrite. For mine, it looks like Sam went with tourmaline instead of opal," I slipped my hand in his.

"You are October; I knew that from Caleb. Coming up pretty soon. Mine's after yours; I'm November. Damien was January." Jake filled in the blanks with a wistful look at Damien's name on his lips. I desperately wanted his mind off Damien because we needed to feel something other than the painful ache of loss.

"November what?" I asked right as the clerk came back with our copies and certificate. Jake took them and the envelope she offered, hooked my arm through his, and walked us out to where Hector and Angela sat waiting.

"Thirteenth," he told me. "I'm a Scorpio, and if you are wondering, we are extremely compatible. I looked it up one year to torture Caleb with and secretly hoped that I'd get a chance to find out if it was true or not, and here I am, married to you."

I laughed out loud. "Did Caleb punch you?"

"For about a week. It was well worth it to keep

listing why our signs worked so well together. It also helped get Caleb through a couple of rough spots where he woke up with nightmares. I'd pull him back with the reasons we worked," Jake explained.

"Here's the address where the reservations for dinner are," Hector said as we stopped in front of him. "Angela and I will meet you there."

Angela handed me my camera. "I got a few perfect ones."

"Thank you," I let go of Jake's arm and hugged her. "Will you be the baby's godmother?" I whispered in her ear.

Her breath caught. "I'd be honored." We parted ways with Hector and Angela as we headed to our cars.

"Why'd you choose this ring?" I asked Jake.

"I'd have bought the biggest diamond they had if I thought that's what you wanted, but you don't strike me as flashy. I wanted something that spoke to me of simple beauty, and when the light caught this one," he held my hand, "I knew."

"When I first met you, I realized you saw way more than I was comfortable with; it's true. Flash isn't me. You picked a ring that caught my eye when I was walking around. I'm impressed." I waited while he opened my door.

"I feel that I know everything about you and other times, nothing at all," Jake confessed, kissing me before closing the door, leaving me breathless.

Dinner was relaxed and excellent, and Angela had the waiter bring out a small wedding cake for us that she'd had a friend make at the last minute. It was precisely the type of wedding I would have chosen for myself and Damien, even if my mom had still been alive. It was simple, intimate, and easy. I loved that there were pieces of Damien here with us.

We toasted our sparkling non-alcoholic cider to Damien and Caleb, my mom, and Hector's brother before we split our ways and headed back to the hotel. Jake was over the top cheesy and carried me in, delighting the front desk people, and didn't set me down until we were in the elevator.

In the elevator, Jake pinned me against the wall and devoured me with a kiss that almost had me taking my dress off then. The chemistry between us was out of this world. When the elevator dinged on our floor, he lifted me, kept his lips sealed to mine, and carried me to our room, opening it and locking it behind us.

Then he broke away, closed the blackout shades, and turned on one of the lamps on its dimmest setting. "Take your hair down," he said huskily, loosening his tie.

"Oh no, I get to undress you." I batted his hands away before unpinning my hair.

He ran his fingers through it before tenderly kissing me again. "I'm all of a sudden nervous," Jake said shakily.

"Because it means something this time," I told him, understanding the feeling because I felt it too. I hadn't been nervous with Damien, though sex had meant something with him also. It had been beautiful and hot. It was unquestionably different now. And I knew that it was on Jake's mind, as it was mine. I did my best to separate the two. Jake deserved my attention on him.

Jake squatted down to grab the hem of my dress, gathered it up as he stood, lifted the gown over my head, and dropped it to the floor as he stared at me with naked lust on his face. Whatever shadows had lingered were gone. The lingerie was as white as my dress had been, lacy and sheer. The bra was strapless, and the panties were practically non-existent.

He dropped to his knees and pressed a kiss to my belly. "Sorry if you get jostled, but one day you'll understand." He gently slid my shoes off, his hands running up the backs of my calves as he pressed kisses to my knees and thighs. Exquisite torture, but I wasn't about to stop him. I'd get my turn.

He turned me around and groaned. I yelped when I felt him bite each of my ass cheeks, then he stood and unfastened my bra and moved me back around. I was holding it in place, and he let me but backed me up to the bed and waited until I crawled up on it, scooting back until my head was on the pillows.

"Beautiful isn't a good enough word for you, babe." He held himself over me easily with one arm and pulled my bra away with the other, a low growl leaving his lips as he settled on top of me, still fully clothed. "Not even in my wildest dreams could I have pictured this."

"You're a little too overdressed," I commented, wanting to feel his skin on mine.

"I'll stay that way for a little bit, or this will be over way too fast," Jake lowered his head and kissed me stupid again. He kissed, licked, and bit his way down my neck and between my breasts before turning his attention to the twin globes.

After the Wreckage

My hands clutched at his biceps as he lavished sweet torture between my breasts until I was mewling and begging him to go lower. I had no shame, I knew what I wanted exactly, and he took his sweet time getting there, but what a path it was.

He literally ripped the panties at the sides and threw them off the bottom of the bed. I would have used my finger and offered him a taste, but he'd moved his hands and wove his fingers through mine, holding them on my hips. I didn't know if it was a strategic move or just part of the foreplay.

I didn't care either. The moment Jake's tongue touched me, all thought fled my mind except him and what he was doing. He took pleasure to a whole new level and had me screaming out in no time flat. His attention then switched to kissing the folds as I came down before he dove back in again.

He took it slower and lighter, then would switch it up and increase the pressure of his tongue and suck, going faster and changing it up, so I didn't know what to expect. My body writhed and bucked as I exploded again, his name echoing against the hotel room's walls.

I gripped him with my legs and rolled us, my surprise move catching him off guard, but he went with it and smiled a sexy smile up at me. "I like hearing you call my name." Jake lifted me easily and slid up the bed, setting me back on him.

"It'd be strange if you wanted me to say someone else's." I bent forward and kissed him.

"Let's not try it," he suggested as I leaned back and unknotted his tie.

"No worries. I forgot my name for a second there," I smirked.

"I aim to please," he chuckled as I threw his tie on the floor with my torn underwear.

"I've heard a sniper has to have good aim." I bit back a smile at the expression on his face.

"Did I miss my mark?" Jake finally asked as I unbuttoned his shirt.

"Oh no, you hit it. I'll have you go back just to make sure it wasn't a fluke. You can never be too sure about these things." I pushed the shirt off his shoulders and waited until he rose a little so I could toss it with the rest of the clothes.

"That's one practice I wouldn't mind doing several times a day," his voice cracked as I dragged my nails down his chest. The sounds he made when I bit his nipples the way he had mine had me riding a high.

"It's like an artist sculpted you," I muttered, my fingers tracing each ridge and plane on his torso.

"I could say the same about you," Jake groaned when I traced my finger just under the waist of his pants. I didn't have the same patience he did to drag out the torture. We had all night to learn the nuances of each other; right now, I wanted him.

I unfastened his pants and pulled both them and the boxer briefs he had on down when he lifted his hips, having to stop to free his cock on the way. Then I had to stop and take his shoes off because I was too impatient.

When I finally had him naked before me, I took a small moment to appreciate his beauty. He was all hard muscles, smooth planes, and bronze skin. He wasn't hairy either. His legs were, and a tiny little trail led down from his abs. That's where I started.

Our playful banter fell to the wayside as my mouth had other plans, and Jake focused intently on what I was doing. I used every trick I had ever learned until all he could do was make unintelligible sounds and fisted the comforter in his hands as I used my clever tongue and hands to extract from him the same pleasure he got from me.

When he hissed out my name, I knew he was close and bobbed my head fast and sucked hard, swirling my tongue until Jake jerked under me and came hard, the low groan that tore from him as he pulsed in my mouth the sweetest sound.

Jake

Frankie was, indeed, going to kill me. I pulled her back up my body until she lay across my chest. "I have no idea how you did that, and I don't care. I will pull a play from your brother and punch anyone who looks at you."

She giggled, the sound making my heart happy. "They don't know I can do that."

"I'm far from rational right now, babe. We haven't even finished yet." I rolled us to our sides. "I wasn't expecting that. How do your ribs and face feel?" I caressed her face softly.

"I was; it was what I had planned exactly. Get that first round out of the way and spend the rest of the night trying to piss off the people in the rooms around us," she grinned wickedly. "I don't feel the injuries right now."

Heaven created Francesca for me. No question in my mind. "Let's be gentle. I don't want you hurting later. You have no idea how much I love you," was all I could think to say.

"Yes, I do, Jake," she rubbed her thumb across my bottom lip. "You love me enough to marry me, go along with my plans, pick out the perfect ring for me, get me the exact earrings I wanted, and just managed to seduce the hell out of me, which isn't easy to do."

"It's more than that, Frankie," I said quietly.

"I know that too. It's in the hundreds of things you do for me, each one a perfect little aimed dart that hits its mark and drives it home for me, just what the word love means. You embody that little poem about the sun and the moon," she said in a breath.

"The sun loved the moon so much that he died every night just to let her breathe," I quoted. "You nailed it. That's exactly how I feel for you."

"I don't want you to die for me, though. I want you to live for me," Francesca brought her hands up to my chest. "Not just for me, but with me. Next to me. I need you for me to breathe."

I rolled her under me, "We are stronger together, right?" I was hard again with those words and the look in her eyes. I worked my hips, rubbing myself along her folds, loving that her legs fell open even wider, and her knees gripped my hips.

"Yes," she moaned, "together." Her eyes blinked closed as I moved and slid in just a little, her plump lips parting and her soft sigh washing over my face. "More," she begged.

I held still until her eyes opened and latched on mine, then I gave her what she wanted and buried myself in her, the feeling unlike anything else I'd ever experienced. She fit me in every way. "Frankie, tell me you feel it," I rasped out. The friction as I moved slowly was enough to short circuit my brain.

"Jesus, yes," she groaned loudly. "Jake, please," her hips rolled, making me almost lose control.

"Do that again, Frankie," I grit out, desperately trying to hang on and not revert to a teenager having sex for the first time.

She rolled her hips again. Then again and again before shuddering under me, her body tightening around mine as she came. "That's never happened before," she gasped under me as I broke out in a sweat, trying not to come yet.

"More," I repeated Francesca's command to me. She reached her head up and kissed me, rolling her hips the same way she had done before. Twice, then twice more before I started to pump, my body finding the rhythm to match the roll and draw it out. That delicious friction and insane chemistry we had built until she tightened around me again.

This time I let go and came with her. My vision blurred with the intensity, and my arms shook so hard my body collapsed on hers. "I see a lot of that happening in our future," came the muffled words from under me.

I laughed weakly and rolled us to the side. "No arguments from me." I lost myself in the kiss she delivered; my brain was still buzzing from the most intense orgasm I'd had in my life. "What do you mean that's never happened?"

"I've never come from penetration alone like that, not that fast anyway," she told me, groaning as my body slipped from hers. "At least the wet spots are on the covers, not the sheets."

"The night's not over yet," I warned her, laughing. "Let's waste some water and clean up. I want to see my wife's beautiful face without the war paint on."

"War paint?" Francesca laughed.

"You are still beautiful with it, but you are radiant without it," I pulled her up.

"I love you even more now," she followed me, her legs shaking as much as mine were.

Chapter Nine

Francesca

"Is it wrong that I don't want to go back to the boat?" I asked Jake.

"Depends on the reason why I guess." He held the deli door open for me.

I thought about it. "I think it's because I don't want to sleep with you there."

"Then no, it's not wrong, babe. You had a life with Damien that was just starting. I wasn't comfortable sleeping in your bed for the same reason. What the two of you had was between the two of you. It's not the same as what's between us. We can get rid of the bed, but I think I'd still feel the same. The boat is Damien, through and through. I enjoy going there, and I think we should continue to do so. We just won't be having sex, and we'll be sleeping on the deck or out in the cabin," Jake looked down at me gently.

"It's why I want to move out of my house." The familiar guilt and grief came back in a flood of emotion, and I stepped into Jake's warm body.

"I know, Frankie. We'll grab your clothes and stay

at my house until we find a place. We can get all new furniture that we pick out together, a totally fresh start." He kissed the top of my head. "For the rest of our nights here, we can stay at the hotel or Hector's."

"Hotel," I voted. "But, I want to go back and see Hector." I studied the menu, my stomach protesting loudly at having starved it all morning.

"He's clearly better at getting you to eat than I am. That poor baby is going to be malnourished. We'll head back after lunch; we need to grab your vitamins too. We can close the boat up and hang with Hector the rest of the day," Jake suggested. "We can make him dinner."

That was a good idea. I placed my order, grabbed an ice tea then put it back, unsure about the caffeine amount I was supposed to have. I unhappily grabbed a water bottle instead, and Jake took a soda. We went and sat down, and I mentally went over anything we'd forgotten to do.

"License, social security card, oh, passport," I said aloud.

"Greg will handle that," Jake said. "We'll overnight the certificate to him on our way back with a copy of your new license and social security card. You don't have to fill everything out all over and restart the process. I'm almost certain there's just a form you fill out."

"Francesca Foxwood, I like how it sounds," I said, a goofy smile gracing my face. "Oh, by the way, don't think I didn't catch on to the fact that your initials are JTF."

"Your brother got a lot of mileage out of that," Jake smiled wryly at me. "Every time we formed a joint group, he had comments."

"Do you care if I continue to use Frances Gray for the assignments and project?" I thought to ask.

"Not at all. You didn't even have to take my name, but my ego got a little boost that you did," he admitted. "I wanted to talk to you about your project."

"What about it?" I asked, shredding a napkin.

"What do you think about broadening it from only talking to soldiers and talking to people who have PTSD from other traumatic events?" Jake stilled my hand, "It's not a criticism, babe. In my line of work, I encountered many people suffering from it because of a variety of things that happened to them. Even you, my beautiful wife."

He was right. On both accounts. "Not sure why either of those didn't occur to me. How would I find people willing to talk to me and let me take pictures? With soldiers, it was easy. I could go to the veteran's hospital and find several people."

"My support group has others. My club helps others as well. Two avenues we could explore," Jake suggested. "There are also local women's shelters and support groups that we could talk to."

"I think it's a good idea," I agreed quickly.

"You aren't going to argue with me saying you have it as well?" he leaned forward across the table to clasp my hands in his.

"Not now. I can see it, I guess. That thinking just made me consider other avenues for my house." I chewed on my lip as I thought. "Where does your club meet now?"

"The motorcycle club?" Jake asked me.

"Yeah. Where do you guys meet?" I asked again.

"Usually a bar. Why?" His fingers stroked over the insides of my wrists.

"I think we should make my house a meeting place for your club. You said you do work for the community, right? My house would give you a secure place to meet, and if you guys were helping someone who needed a place to hide, it could easily hold one of your club members and the person securely until they could get somewhere safe. You could also use it as a place for the PTSD meetings," I suggested.

"For that matter, we could use mine that way too," Jake followed my train of thought.

"Is your club a registered non-profit?" I started to build on my idea.

"No. We are a registered club, but not a non-profit."

"What if you were? You could head it, expand the people you help, and between the two houses, we could get classes and things set up, or counselors and things like that. You have the police connections as well," I added.

"You are brilliant," Jake cocked the side of his lips up in a smirk.

"I know. That's old news," I joked, moving as the waitress delivered the food. My stomach rumbled loudly again. "What are we going to make for dinner?"

"Let's get through lunch first," Jake laughed.

Michelle Lee

Jake

We'd been back home for two weeks. The distractions were lovely. Francesca had gotten everything personal moved out of her house, and it was sitting in my garage while the offer we'd made on a different place was gone over and waiting for inspections.

We'd picked out new furniture that would be delivered when we moved in and had started buying baby stuff. That had been hard for both of us; Damien would have loved doing that. It had cast a slight shadow over the day. We both had broken down over it.

It had also made me remember the box I'd carried upstairs when Damien moved his stuff here. Francesca was sitting outside watching sailboats, so I went to dig it out of the apartment's closet.

Once I found it, I opened it up and saw the banded-up letters. I lifted them out slowly. There wasn't a whole lot. Damien hadn't written letters the way Caleb did. Just when things had built up inside him to a breaking point.

I wasn't sure if these would help or hinder either of us, but Francesca's questions growing about Damien were the same ones I'd had for years. Maybe answers would lie in these letters, or perhaps they would do nothing but hurt Francesca and trigger me relentlessly.

I couldn't decide for her, and I didn't want to take the decision out of her hands. At the very least, they would help with her project, the best-case scenario, her questions get answered. I was heading back downstairs when my phone rang.

I hurried up and set the letters on the counter, pulling out my phone. "Yeah?"

"Foxwood, I need you to come into the station," the Chief said, his words clipped, but the tone was off.

"Why?" I asked defensively.

"Something has come up, and I'd rather talk to you about it in private before others come in and demand me to pull you in and question you. I also have a proposal to go over with you," Chief Stone's tone softened slightly.

"Is this about Damien?" My voice dropped, and my arm hairs raised as an odd sensation settled over my body.

"It is, son. I'm asking nicely, please come in and talk to me, off the record."

"I'll be there in twenty," I hung up. I grabbed my wallet and keys and flew out the back door. "Babe, something has come up, and the Chief wants to talk to me. Something about Damien. Please come with me," I said as her gaze landed on me.

Without question, she stood and followed me back into the house, folding the blanket and setting it on the back of a chair. "What's this?" she looked at the stack of letters before putting her shoes on.

I handed her the coat I had grabbed from the closet. "Letters. Do you want to take the bike or truck?" I gave Francesca the option. I hadn't had the pleasure of riding with her yet, and the weather was beautiful today.

Her eyes flashed with something I couldn't define, but she chose the bike. I was as protective as Damien had been when it came to her, but I also knew her independent streak was fierce, and I didn't want to push her buttons, so I let her strap her helmet on. I did check to make sure it was secure before I got on the bike.

"Are you nervous?" I looked back at her to check.

"A little." Her soft-spoken words had my stomach clenching hard.

"We can take the truck," I offered again, not wanting her to be scared.

"No, Jake, I need to do this while I can still fit on the back of a bike," Francesca's eyes flashed again, the fear easy to see this time.

I cursed under my breath and slid back off, and gathered her up in my arms. "We won't go anywhere near the route you were on, and I'm going to stick to two-lane roads, so it becomes obvious if someone tries to pull up next to us."

I took her hand and put it on the gun that my shirt concealed. Francesca wasn't flighty, so I wasn't concerned about her grabbing it because she was spooked. We'd already talked about her shooting, and she assured me she knew how and was quite adept at it and comfortable with them. The movement was so she knew it was there, and if she needed to grab it, she could.

"Do you care if I hold on to you the same way I held on to Damien?" she asked tentatively.

I wasn't sure what she meant, and my face must have shown it. "I'm wearing underwear," I said, remembering one of her conversations.

The fear disappeared from her face, and she laughed. "Not what I meant, but good to know. I mean putting my hands under your shirt, so they are against your flesh. Helps with the fear."

I grinned at Francesca's reaction. "Gotcha. You can have your hands on me anytime you want. Just keep them above the waist while we are riding."

"Kiss me," she requested. Not a hardship.

I got back on the bike, and Francesca slid her hands up under my shirt, and after a moment of wondering how the hell Damien had managed to ride with her hands on him like that, I got control and got us going.

She still flinched anytime a car got too close to us, and by the time we pulled up at the station, she was a little wrung out. I grabbed my phone and texted some of the club asking for an escort home, explaining a little behind the reason why.

I led her into the station and past a couple of the guys I knew, who gave us sidelong looks as we passed them. I maybe should have introduced Francesca, but I was selfish and reticent about my private life. They may have recognized her from the media as well.

I kept Francesca's hand in mine, and as I entered the office, the chief's assistant rose. "Jake!" Rebecca made as if she would embrace me and halted in her tracks as she saw Francesca, hand firmly clasped in mine.

"Chief is expecting me," I told Rebecca, keeping my voice distant.

A hurt expression crossed her face, and I felt a stab of guilt. Rebecca had always been interested in me, and I'd never overtly refused her advances, but I also never encouraged them. "Go on in," she said slowly, eyeing Francesca with interest.

I pulled Francesca in front of me and guided her into the office, closing the door behind me to the chief's utter and complete surprise. "Ms. Grayson," he stood.

"Uh, actually, it's Mrs. Foxwood now," I said uneasily.

"You married her?" Chief Stone's face bore a stunned expression.

"Francesca Foxwood," she held her hand out to the chief and shook it when he finally remembered his manners.

"Chief Stone. Forgive my rudeness. Please sit," he gestured to the chairs.

The Chief gave me a stern look as if I'd done something unforgivable, and I shifted uncomfortably in my chair. "We have our reasons," was all I said.

"None of which we owe you any explanations for," Francesca stood and moved her chair closer to mine.

"No, Mrs. Foxwood, you don't. It was just a surprise to me. Jake has never been impulsive like this, and I was trying to process the information," the Chief answered gently.

Pride blossomed in my chest for Francesca how she went to bat for me. "Chief, this is Caleb's sister. I assure you, it's a legitimate marriage with genuine love. Before someone killed Damien, he told me if anything were to happen to him because of those fights, he wanted me to promise to marry her and take care of her. I promised to take care of her, but I told him I couldn't promise to marry her because that was a choice that would have to be made by her. She proposed to me without knowing that part of it."

"Grief looks different to different people. Everyone navigates through it in their way," Francesca joined in. "My way happens to be to find a way forward. I already loved Jake. We can mourn Damien and build a life together simultaneously, which honors him and remains true to our hearts. It may sound callous or cold, but Damien knew, and he would approve. Please don't think less of Jake because of this."

"You misunderstand me, Mrs. Foxwood. I don't think less of Jake. I was simply surprised. There is going to be a trail of broken hearts behind him. Nonetheless, I wish you both a lifetime of happiness. He deserves that and so much more." The Chief came around and sat on the edge of the front of his desk.

"What's going, Chief?" I shook my head at the way Francesca won the hard man over.

He reached behind him, pulled a picture out of a folder on his desk, and handed it to me. "Do you know this man?"

I studied the picture, sorting through my memory, but nothing about him rang a bell. "Should I?"

"I don't know, son. It was a real question. I wasn't fishing. He was a veteran, served some of the years you did, but in the Army. Same general location. My intuition is telling me he is involved with the Damien Ocasta shooting. A fact confirmed with the suicide note recovered a few hours later in a separate location than the body. The coroner isn't sure if this is a legitimate suicide or a murder staged to look like one," the Chief glanced guiltily at Francesca's shocked face. "I'm sorry, ma'am. You can wait out in the reception area if you'd like."

"Francesca stays. She's aware of how her brother died. I told her. There aren't secrets between us," I handed the picture to the chief.

He stood up and rounded his desk to sit back down behind it, his fingers steepled. "I'd advise you not to say that if the NSA comes around again."

"I'm not stupid, sir." Francesca's fingers snaked around mine. "Why did you think the incident was involved before the note?"

He studied me quietly a minute before answering. "A tattoo on his body matches a date tattooed on yours."

My blood ran cold. "Caleb Grayson's date?"

"The same. Have you spoken with Darius Baker lately?" Chief Stone's eyes had taken on a harder gleam to them.

"Darius Baker?" Francesca asked quietly.

"Boomer," I responded. That was the only name she knew for Darius.

"The biker? The one that knelt and cried at the funeral? The black one?" Francesca further clarified because there had been more than one biker and tried to piece it together.

"Yeah. Boomer's name is Darius. No," I told the chief. "I haven't. Are you trying to insinuate that Darius killed this guy and staged it to look like a suicide?" That didn't fit for me.

"No, but others are. Word has spread that he's

looking for the shooter. There has also been a hushed rumor that this is something you are capable of; *that* is why I called you. I'm aware you have the skills, but ethically and morally, I do not believe this is something you can do." His voice was very low and insistent.

Francesca bolted to her feet, her face red and stormy. "Jake would *never* do something like that. He's been with me every single day since the day after Damien's funeral. If my word isn't good enough, we haven't been apart long enough for him to plan to murder someone."

I pulled her back down, fighting back a smile. "Chief's not accusing me, babe. He's sharing information he shouldn't be."

The Chief touched his nose and handed me the file. I flipped through it, took notes of essential things, glanced at the photos, and finally came to a copy of the letter. I read through it quickly and shut the file handing it back to the Chief.

"It's not Darius. Yes, he's looking for the murderer, and no, I'm not going to tell him not to. Darius wouldn't stage a suicide. He'd either beat the shit out of the guy and let him die bleeding out or put a bullet through his head. This death feels exactly like a suicide to me. I've seen more than one letter like this." My hand shook slightly, and Francesca pulled it into her lap and held it between her hands.

"If this letter is correct, then this poor soul wasn't the shooter but was in the vehicle with the shooter. What do you remember of the people with you on that date?" The Chief tipped back in his chair and held my gaze steady.

"I have the names of the people who died. Damien managed to get that before his murder. Darius has the same information; they were working together. This kid's name doesn't match any of the last names of those who died. I couldn't say whether or not it matched any of the ones that lived. We only focused on the losses. The president of the Prince's was sure that the person behind the rumors about Damien was a vet that had a grudge against Damien for not doing more to save more people that day." I huffed out a breath, trying to ease the tightness in my lungs.

"Easy, son." Chief Stone handed me a water bottle and waited for me to drink some down. "Jake, think very carefully about this. Is there a possibility that this shooter will also blame you or Darius?"

Full-blown panic slammed into my chest hard because if I was a target, Francesca was in danger. Hundreds of triggers instantly swamped my brain, and I couldn't shut them down. My body froze in paralysis, and my mind buzzed with the sounds of screams, gunshots, and explosions. Smoke filled my nose, and the stench of death and blood lingered under it. My eyes saw the faux pregnant lady as Francesca, and I heard a keening sound that I couldn't identify. It was me.

"Jake." Francesca's big brown doe eyes filled my line of sight, imposing her face on all the bodies in my memory. "You're safe. I'm safe." I felt her arms wrap around me. "It's in the past. We are safe. Look at me, Jake. Feel my belly; feel the baby in there. We are safe. Breathe with me." Her voice overrode the memory, and I matched my breathing to hers. It took a few minutes, but my heart rate slowed.

"Jesus, son. I'm sorry." I heard the Chief in the background, but I could only focus on Francesca.

"Stay with me, honey. I'm here. We are safe," Francesca repeated. My eyes focused on hers, and she brought me back, rooting me in the present until the sounds of that day faded from my mind.

Francesca darted, and a garbage can was in front of my face. I threw up. I have no idea how she knew that was coming, but I'm glad she did. The shakes set in then, and regardless of what decorum demanded, she sat on my lap and put her arms around me until I calmed.

"Talk it out, honey," Francesca suggested in my ear. "You're safe. I'm safe. It's just us three in here."

I took a slow breath in, holding Francesca in place. If the Chief wanted my help, she needed to stay exactly where she was. "I don't know. The rumors didn't mention either Darius or me. Only Damien, as he was the leader of our team. He was bleeding out, and he still managed to fight back the ambush, save six lives, and keep the remaining team alive."

The Chief was shaken by what he had just witnessed. "Had I known that would have happened, Jake, I wouldn't have asked."

"You can't know his triggers. I'm sure there are some even he doesn't realize he has," Francesca soothed us both.

"Chief, add my house to a patrol," I said, my voice shaking. "I will cold-blooded murder anyone that tries to hurt Francesca. Of that, I have no doubt."

"Relax, son. I haven't heard anything that makes me believe either of you is a target. That's why I am asking. If you feel there is a reason that either you or Darius is in danger, I want to know."

"Darius put the word out that Francesca gets protected at all costs. Everything I know about him tells me he's done that. I would know if he heard something about her being a target. As for myself, no. I have no reason to think I am a target, but whoever is behind this is unstable. As you saw with me just now, triggers happen unexpectedly. I was on the scene; my face got seen. Add my house to patrol. Hopefully, we'll be moving soon, and our names will get buried to make us harder to pin down. I'll beef up our security. Biking season is about over, so I'll be in my truck or Francesca's car." I went down a mental list starting in my head.

"Do you think the shooter suffered PTSD?" the Chief asked quietly.

I hesitated. My gut said this guy did; I nodded. Francesca did too.

"You think this incident ties to the ambush my brother got killed in?" I wasn't sure if she was talking to Chief Stone or me.

"My gut says that. I don't know what happened over there on that day, but my gut usually steers me right in these things," Chief Stone answered honestly. "I didn't even know that it was an ambush or that Damien saved people and was injured himself."

Tired of the secrecy, I spilled the memories of that day to the Chief. I watched his face as horror filled it, and understanding dawned in a way only someone who has experienced violence at that level before. He'd seen some nasty business during his time on the force.

"I can't say that me knowing changes anything, and I'm only guessing that is just a minuscule of the ugly shit you saw and were a part of, but I appreciate the trust. I agree that I don't think Darius shared any of that information with anyone, nor do I believe he had anything to do with this suicide. However, I believe that you, Darius, or both may become targets. If you could get word to him, I'd appreciate it. No more death needs to happen over this tragedy." The Chief ran his hands through his hair, making it stick up wildly.

"You'll add my house to a watch list then?" I asked.

"For sure. When you know your new address, I'll have it added as well if you want. Now, for the other reason that I called you in. I don't want the force to lose you. What if I offered you a desk job?" the Chief offered what I knew had been coming.

Francesca stiffened on my lap, reinforcing the answer I gave. "No, thanks. Not a desk job type of guy."

"No, I know. What about teaching the shooting classes?" the Chief revised.

"No offense, but that's how the other sniper guy they made a movie about died," Francesca snapped.

"Little bit of different circumstances, babe, this wouldn't be alone out in the wilderness. She has a point, though, Chief. I'm not willing to be the reason she doesn't sleep, eat, or has a stress-induced heart attack because she's worried about me. Truthfully, I'm on board with her idea of working with vets and PTSD sufferers in a non-profit capacity. Not having anything to do with shooting, period," I added, knowing the Chief would bring up the parallel with the sniper Francesca had just mentioned.

He deflated. "I don't blame you. It's admirable and honorable. You are going to be damn near impossible to replace."

"I happen to think so, too," Francesca pointed out candidly. My love for her only grew, and her tone solidified my decision.

Chapter Ten

Francesca

The escort's home had been sweet. Even more so that they each had two riders on the bikes, so Jake and I didn't stand out.

It hadn't distracted me from the episode in the office and how swiftly and viciously it had taken Jake down. The only other time he had been that far gone that I had seen was when he had picked me up from working at the hospital once and had broken down in tears. That had been about Caleb's death as well. I wondered if that was the only event that pushed him that far.

"I've asked Boomer to come by," Jake walked back into the kitchen and paused to give me a questioning look. "What's wrong?"

"Are you okay?" I reached for his hand.

"In which way?" He stroked his thumb over my wedding ring.

"I don't think I've ever seen you be hit that hard by an attack before," I said quietly.

"The last time you were unconscious in the road and the hospital," his voice dropped.

"You mean when Damien got killed?" I pushed for answers.

"That's when I'm talking about exactly." He stepped into my space and pressed his body up against mine. "I wanted to die, Frankie. You are the only thing that kept me here. Every single kill I made went through my head; every time Caleb or Damien saved my life replayed in slow motion. Every ugly thing we walked away from by force and ignored. All the death, bullets, screams, bombs, it was all there. Nothing got spared, and I was begging to die, to join my brothers."

"But you didn't. You made it through." I tried to hide how my throat had thickened, but Jake heard it.

"I didn't make it through it. The doctors sedated me. Before the reel could start all over again, your eyes were open and watching me." He pressed his lips against my forehead. "My goal was to remain in the present for you. It wasn't easy."

I didn't imagine it was. Jake was actively seeking help for PTSD, whereas Damien hadn't. Some of Damien's nightmares had been just as potent as what I saw hit Jake today, and there had been times I wasn't sure I could get Damien back out. When he finally returned, the ghosts haunting him shadowed his face. The episode today had put the questions I'd been forming about Damien back in the forefront of my mind.

"What are these letters?" I asked, fearing that I already knew the answer and wondering if I was brave enough to open them.

"Something we will open and read together." Jake kissed me again. "Damien wrote them and mailed them home to himself when he snuck out of the base. Neither Caleb nor I knew who he was writing to, but it was always after something big had gone down. I think this was Damien's way of trying to release the memories. I don't know what they say, he never opened them, and I only remembered them this morning."

They were just what I suspected they were. "Has any of the fallout gotten easier for you?" I reached around his waist and hooked my thumbs in his belt loops.

"Yes. The one thing that was the hardest for both of us was your brother's death. Honestly, airing it as I did with you, and now the Chief is a weight off me. Damien refused to talk about it. I held back because I was following his lead, as well as it was classified. I don't get why it matters now, the not talking about it part, but I think I always go to that event because I didn't get to let go of any of it for all those years." Jake gave me the brutal truth. "I know you have questions about Damien, and I do, too, in the spirit of honesty. We might find answers in those letters, or we'll just find more hurt, and I'll be in trigger hell."

I was the 'ripping the band-aid off' type. "Shall we start the letters tonight?"

Jake chuckled and buried his face in my neck. "You are hands down the strongest person I've ever met. We can if you want to. What do you want to do for dinner?"

"What time is Boomer going to be here?" I glanced at my watch.

"Probably in the next half hour or so. Why?" Jake leaned back, but my arms were still around him.

"I'll make up some burgers, and you can grill them. It will give you two a chance to talk, and maybe I can grill him with questions about the antics you three got up to and help put us in a better frame of mind before we tackle whatever heavy shit is going to come out of those envelopes," I suggested. "I can make up a pasta salad too, and we need to use that asparagus before it goes bad."

"I can help." He cupped my face and brought his lips a hair's breadth from mine. I closed the distance, sealing our lips together, needing the closeness, needing him.

"Later. More of that comes later." I moaned and pulled away before I took it too far. Jake protested but allowed me around the counter in the kitchen to get started. I had the patties made, asparagus prepped, dressing made, and noodles cooking in no time. Jake chopped up some carrots to add in, then opened olives and washed tomatoes.

I started making chocolate chip cookies because I figured I would need comfort food later. Jake cleaned up as I went along and then sat up on the counter, watching me work. We got the last tray in the oven by the time Boomer arrived.

Jake led him into the kitchen, where I was mixing up the pasta salad while the cookies baked. "Hi, Darius," I tried his real name out, seeing how it felt. I liked it a lot better than Boomer.

He gave me a startled look but smiled in response. "Heya, Frankie. Smells fantastic in here. You seriously going to feed me?"

"I am. It comes at the cost of telling me funny stories about the guys, though," I told him, sliding the salad into the fridge to chill and pulling the last batch of cookies out of the oven.

"There aren't too many funny stories of our time over there, but I can probably think up some of them. Most happened after they'd read one of the letters from you." Darius grinned at me and snatched a cookie up.

"First, we talk about what I learned today." Jake grabbed a cookie before I could smack either of their hands. "One, I'm no longer a cop. Don't do anything stupid and get arrested. I can't help you. Two, we might be in danger. All three of us."

"The immediate danger is if you two steal any more cookies before dinner," I interrupted and slid the plate of burgers over in front of them, then the prepped asparagus. "Go grill and talk."

I didn't need to be present for this part of it. It would only put me on edge and cause Jake to watch me for my reactions. I wanted him to focus on what he'd learned today. I wasn't there, I wasn't a part of what they'd been through, and my brain wiring didn't include the ways of military life. Chances are, I would miss something that Darius wouldn't.

Instead, I got the buns and condiments ready, fully understanding I was doing busy work to keep myself occupied, so I didn't tear open each letter. I was almost out of things to do when Darius walked back in, looking strained.

"Jake says he's about ready for the cheese and wants to know if we are eating in here or outside?"

Darius repeated his message.

"In here. I'm a little cold." I handed him the cheese and a clean plate for the burgers and got the table set. In the middle of the prep work, I started to miss Damien again and our dinners with Jake. There just hadn't been enough time for us. Guilt crept up, accompanied by the familiar pang of loss.

The sting of tears came on, and I busied myself cleaning up the remaining pans from the cookies, biting my lip as I furiously scrubbed. The pan was spotless, and still, I kept at it.

"Babe." Jake's arms slid around me from behind.

I turned and buried my face in his chest. "I miss him."

"We all do." I heard Darius say from the other side of the counter. "Even me."

"Get yourself something to drink and sit down," Jake told Darius, holding me.

"Sorry," I mumbled. "It just hit me."

"Don't apologize; it hits me about a thousand times a day like a punch straight to the heart. Grief doesn't ever go away. You know that. It changes shape inside us to resemble something different, but it's still grief. The dust hasn't even settled from your mom's passing yet, and this got shoved at you too. Give yourself time, Frankie. I know you want to keep moving forward, and you are, but it doesn't have to be at top speed." He tipped my face up to his, and I saw the pain I felt echo in his eyes.

I let him lead me back to the table while he grabbed the pasta salad and water for me. Darius studied me quietly, something in his eyes unnerving me in his unwavering gaze.

"Why do you keep staring at me like that?" I bluntly asked.

"I can see your brother in you. Caleb was my favorite person in the whole unit. He was real in a way that many of us were afraid to be. Caleb wore his heart on his sleeve, and his face was unreadable only when we were engaged in something. Your face is as expressive as his," Darius replied evenly.

"Be careful what you say. That's my wife," Jake warned him.

"No shit?" Darius gaped at him, then turned back to me. "Good for you. It's what Damien would have wanted to happen, your brother too. Jake's been in love with you for years."

My heart softened toward the hardened biker. "Thank you for saying that without judgment. It seems others only want to assume bad things instead of trying to understand why."

"I don't need reasons. I get it. Anyone that knew either of them back in those days would understand. Aside from already knowing how Jake felt, I can see you feel the same. I got eyes. Don't take a genius to figure it out. Doesn't detract from what you felt for Damien either," Darius shrugged. His honesty was refreshing.

"Tell me more about them," I begged with a small smile at Jake.

"I did think of one thing that gets me to laugh every single time I think about it. While in England, we went to a pub after one of our many strategy meetings.

The three amigos were drinking soda and eating fish and chips while I and a few others drank beer. This guy walks up to your brother, and I say that loosely because apparently, I'm the only one who knew it was a guy. They started flirting, and your brother was getting that bathroom sex look on his face. Jake and Damien looked a little jealous until I leaned over to tell Damien that it was a dude. Then Damien started buying drinks for this guy and smiling like an idiot at Caleb every time this guy put his hand on Caleb's leg."

I looked over at Jake, who was grimacing. "It's true. I didn't know either."

Darius laughed. "I'm not sure what happened in the conversation, but suddenly this guy laughs, grabs Caleb's hand, shoves it into his crotch, and declares super loud, 'Oh honey, you aren't drunk enough for me!' Damien about fell over backward off his stool; he laughed so hard. Caleb's face, though, man, it was priceless. He didn't talk to another female the entire night. Have to say, the two playboys of the group were quite shy the rest of the night. Once Jake realized it, they both went and sat in a booth with the rest of us on the outside like we would keep them safe."

I giggled because it was funny. "Damien set him up; that's hilarious."

"Now, it's funny. It was less funny then," Jake said with a sour expression. "I'm not a homophobe, but I also don't want to find out at the last minute that what I thought was a woman really wasn't."

"Dude had an Adam's apple; I don't know how either of you missed that. Plus, his hands were the same size as yours," Darius chuckled at the memory.

"Poor Caleb," I ate my burger, smiling.

"Don't feel bad for him; he was quite a practical joker and got the rest of us back plenty after that. Caleb truly was a standup guy, Frankie. Nights off in base, he'd go out with the other two monkeys, and they'd all play with the kids gathered outside the base looking for food. Or they'd go into town and talk with the elderly or women, making sure they were okay. They'd feed the stray animals and generally make the rest of us look like giant assholes with all their good deeds." Darius scooped a large scoop of pasta salad on his plate, not meeting our eyes.

"It wasn't just us, Boomer. You joined us sometimes, too," Jake argued quietly.

"Sometimes," he agreed. "When those guys wore the shirts and hats you sent, people outside our unit didn't know how to take them. A few guys looked interested in joining that man harem, and others that practically ran in the other direction. No one had the balls outside of our group to harass them, mainly because they were the three biggest badasses on base and didn't want their asses handed to them. With our group, though, the three husbands with their bromance were constantly ribbed."

"No lie. I can't tell you how many times I had condoms left under my pillow or in my pack color-coded for use on either Damien or Caleb," Jake shook his head slowly. "After I kissed Caleb, some of the guys weren't sure if we were serious or not."

"He did write that you weren't as good of a

kisser as you said you were," I remembered the letter fondly with a smile. "I disagree."

"I hope so. Wouldn't want to have to go practice," Jake fired back at me.

Jealousy flared to life within me. "You can practice on Darius," I shot back.

"Hey! Don't involve me in this." Darius gave me a level look that said he was serious. "You know Jake wouldn't ever step out on you, right?" I did know that. I nodded. "I mean, he got punched in the dick because of you."

"I heard about that too. I think Caleb enjoyed that one a little too much," I grinned. Damien mentioned the incidence too.

"Yeah, he did. I swear to God that I would have kept my mouth shut if I had known she was behind me. That hurt," Jake winced at the memory.

"That right there should tell you everything you need to know about how that man feels. Damien and your brother both knew Jake was genuinely in love with you. Hell, Frankie, I think we all were a little bit. Caleb had a damn good punch, so we kept our mouths shut most of the time. Not Jake. That pansy carried around one of the pictures you sent, one of the misty woods. Jake carried it everywhere we went," Darius continued to eat as if he were unaware he'd touched my heart.

"I think it's sweet," I said softly, glancing at Jake, whose eyes glued themselves to me.

"Back to business," Darius broke through our heated gaze. "Frankie, word spread throughout all clubs in the area that hell will rain down on their heads if a move happens against you or the baby you are carrying. I know you don't particularly want to hear about the club's activities, but our president and I knew Damien and respected him. Prince's are top dog around here, and we'd definitely know. I think you are safe."

"Add Jake to that, please. I'm not safe without Jake, no matter what you say. If I lose him, I lose my reason to breathe," I heard Jake take a deep breath. "No, Jake. Don't interrupt. I mean it. Can you add him to that watch list, please? As well as yourself? You are my last connection to my brother, other than Jake. If I find out you get hurt over this, I might have to kick your ass myself. Pregnant ladies are scary."

Darius's eyes went through various emotions, finally landing on humor. "Yeah, they are scary. I'll have Jake added now that he's not a cop. He's still covered, Frankie. The force would stop at nothing to find this guy if Jake got hurt. He's still one of them even if he quit."

"I think the shooter has left town," Jake said quietly after a pause. He'd pushed his plate away, and I gathered it up with mine, waiting until Darius finished eating before I cleared the table.

"I'm starting to think so too. Prez has been reaching out to other clubs across the states, putting the word out. Guy might be on active duty too. Whether I knew him or not, our brothers who served there are dropping. The suicide wasn't even on our list of names, and it makes me sick to lose another like this. Suicide, mental issues, or those like me that went the crime route," Darius listed off. He pushed his plate away, and I grabbed it and started clearing the table.

"Frankie, we can help," Darius stood. For the tough image he portrayed, the man had manners and was polite.

"Tonight, you are a guest. I got this." I cleared the table, stopping to kiss Jake because I sensed his tension. "Next time, I'll put you to work."

"Associating with me won't win you any friends," Darius warned. His tone held a guarded note that softened me more.

"I don't need friends. I have Jake, and now you, who help teach me about the person my brother became. Soon I'll have a baby. I don't need more than that." I walked into the kitchen to start cleaning up. I knew they needed a moment without estrogen fueling their emotions.

I arranged a plate of cookies, dished some vanilla ice cream, grabbed some toppings for a sundae, and brought it all back to the dining room. Darius and Jake both shot to their feet to help relieve my full arms.

"Jake, you are a lucky bastard," Darius said as he sat back down.

"I know it, too. Frankie's a dream come true." Jake kissed my cheek and sat me down next to him, our bodies touching.

"If my opinion matters, I think I'm the lucky one here." I scooped some ice cream onto a cookie to make an ice cream sandwich. "It's not every day a man is willing to reinvent his life for someone."

"He would if that someone was you," Jake said in my ear, snatched my sandwich, and made me another one.

"Jake's got a point. But I wouldn't have taken your cookie sandwich. That's just mean. You can come sit by me, and I'll protect your ice cream." Darius grinned evilly at Jake.

"No deal." I knew the flirtation was harmless. "Jealous Jake is scary," I laughed.

"Babe, you think I'm scary?" Jake asked half-seriously.

"Frankie's right. You scared me way more than Damien ever did. Caleb, though, he topped both of you. Shit, Frankie, if one person mentioned you outside of asking how your schooling was going, they got punched. Hard. Then on missions, Caleb was this totally different person. He was the Ghost they called him. Meeting up with him wasn't a good thing if you weren't on our team," Darius said off-handedly.

I wasn't sure what to do with that. Jake had stiffened next to me. "It's okay, Jake. I wanted to know who he'd become. That was part of him."

"Caleb was exactly who his letters said he was," Jake said, his voice slightly edgier than usual.

"He was," I gently agreed, "but he was also more. You don't need to hide that part of him from me. I saw it when he was back home on leave. Honesty, remember?"

Jake melted back into my side. "I'm honest. I just don't want you to think of him as a killer."

"We all killed, Jake. It's why we were there," Darius's tone held an edge this time. "It's not who any of us were. We saved a lot more than we killed."

"I know, Boomer." Jake's quiet tone hurt my

heart because I knew he was fighting back the memories.

"What are you going to name the baby?" Darius changed the subject, seeing the same thing I did.

"Damien wanted to name him Caleb. Now, I think I want to name him Damien Caleb. I haven't talked about it yet with Jake." I looked at him out of the corner of my eye and saw the soft smile playing on his lips.

"Going to keep his name Ocasta?" Darius sported his own soft look now.

"Damien Ocasta will be the father on the birth certificate, but Jake will be adopting him at birth. So, he will be Damien Caleb Foxwood," I smiled at its sound.

Darius started laughing until tears rolled down his face. I didn't understand what was so funny, and I looked at Jake, softly chuckling himself. He kissed the side of my head but didn't say anything.

Once Darius got control of himself, he gave me a sheepish look. "Sorry, Frankie. He's getting his husbands. I always knew someday those two men would end up with Foxy's name."

Then I got it. It *was* funny. "Does that mean we need to think of a different name?"

"Hell no," Darius answered. "The name is perfect. Damien and Caleb are laughing their asses off right now. That made my damn night. Keep the name."

"I agree, babe. The name is perfect," Jake kissed my head again, unable to stop the grin.

Chapter Eleven

Jake

I washed up the dessert dishes while Francesca said goodbye to Boomer, eliciting promises from him that he'd have dinner with us again. Boomer had already agreed to keep me in the loop on what they found out, and I'd share anything the Chief shared with me.

"Can we do this outside?" Francesca's voice sounded small from behind me. I turned to see her holding the letters.

"Won't you be cold?" I leaned against the counter, waiting for the explanation I knew was under the way she sounded.

"We can bring a blanket. I just know this will bring Damien back, and if he's in here with us, it will make me want to run again or not stay here. At least outside, I already have memories of him there. Convoluted thinking, I know, but my brain isn't entirely rational," she finally said.

I'd thought it would be something like that. Francesca never went anywhere near the apartment that held his items. It was just storage for his things.

Admittedly, it wasn't easy for me to go up there, even knowing he didn't ever truly move in there.

"Want me to start a fire?" I offered, staying where I was. Her signals were mixed between 'stay away' and 'hold me.'

"No. You, me, and the blanket will be enough. You run hot," Francesca moved into me then, setting the letters back on the counter and resting against my chest, her arms hanging loosely at her sides. She was with me but at a distance.

"Talk to me, Frankie. Let me in." I kept my arms resting on the counter, despite the overwhelming need to have them around her.

"I'm scared." She kept her face pointing away from me. "I'm scared they will trigger you, that what's in there will hurt us both and possibly change our opinions of Damien. What if my suspicions are true?"

"Baby, look at me, please. I feel like there's a barrier between us that I can't breach. You are here with me, but you aren't," I tried at first. My thoughts on the letters were mirroring hers; she finally looked up at me, her eyes filled with fear. "We don't have to do this, Frankie."

"I feel like I need to know." Her hands came up and made their way under my shirt, anchoring her to me in a way I felt deep inside my soul. "I have so many questions about glimpses of something I'd think I'd see in him, but Damien always pushed it away before I could question him. It won't change how I feel about him, but it might give me more closure."

"Will it change the way you feel about me?" I

asked selfishly.

"No. I don't think anything could change that, Jake. Even if all these letters are about you and the women you slept with, it won't change anything because you are here with me, not them. I want that gap between what I see and what I think I understand closed more. Not just with Damien, with you and Caleb too."

"And if what we learn hurts us?" I moved my hand to cup the back of her head.

"Then we love each other even harder, and we figure out how to help each other through it. I was Damien's forever; we just didn't know his forever would be as short as it was. You are my forever. I owe it to both of you to understand this piece of you both a little bit better. If what I find in these letters is what I think it is, I want to make sure it doesn't exist in you because I refuse to let my forever with you be short."

There it was. I knew Francesca would get there. "It won't be. I made you a promise I intend to keep. I'm not Damien, babe. Those layers you are about to peel back existed in all of us, but I wasn't as comfortable leaving them put as Damien was. I pulled them out and examined them every chance I got and changed enough to get past them."

"Okay." Francesca's face didn't convince me that she believed me, but she nodded.

"Frankie, we'll do this because you want to. But we are going to do this my way. That means I want you to touch me at all times, and I want you to ask questions if they come up. Don't assume. Me holding you as I plan to will help keep me where I need to be. Stronger together, right?" I rubbed the back of her neck and waited for her response.

"Did you think I wasn't going to be sitting next to you?" Francesca finally asked.

"I had hoped you would be, but you were holding yourself away from me when you came in here. Here, but not here. I want you with me in all the ways," I stared deep into Francesca's eyes.

"I'm with you," she agreed. "Always."

I had a deep-rooted feeling that the letters would hurt her far worse than they did me. For years now, I'd been seeing the same warning signs that she had seen in Damien. I expected them to become revealed in a manner of fashion in those letters.

"One more thing, when we come back inside the house, it's just us. We leave the memories, the hurt, the emotions, whatever those letters say or bring up, we leave it out there. When we come back in, it's just us, nothing hanging between us. We don't come back in until we agree it's time. When I go to sleep tonight, I want it to be with you and know you are here with me. I don't expect there not to be fallout, either in our dreams or in anything else, but we need to try," I practically begged on this point.

"I'll even agree to the letters staying here after we move," she said readily.

Somewhat relieved I wouldn't have to battle Damien's memory in my bed, I kissed her forehead and told her to stay put while I ran upstairs to grab us sweatshirts. She had gathered up the letters and the big blanket and met me at the back door.

I took the blanket from her and the letters, setting them on the table before pulling the sweatshirt over her head and then grabbing a chaise lounge and pulling it close to the back door for the light. I got my sweatshirt on, sat in the chair, pulled her down between my legs, and settled the blanket over us.

This setting would have been a comfortable scene if we hadn't been about to dive into Damien's personal thoughts. She leaned forward to tuck the blanket around our legs and then rested back against the front of me.

"Give me a minute," Francesca said quietly. "This feels so good, just sitting here like this with you. I want to soak it up."

My damn heart constricted in my chest at her easy words. "There are times it scares me how much I love you. Like earlier today, when the thought of you threatened triggered me. Then there are times like this when nothing in the world has ever felt more right, us sitting out here under the stars wrapped up together." I kissed the side of her neck. "Whatever we learn, Frankie, he was still the same Damien we knew and loved."

"I know. I'm just starting to think that my love wouldn't have been enough to root him here. I think he lost an important part of himself over there, just like Caleb had. And it hurts to think I wouldn't be enough, and he deserved that."

"Do you think the same about me?" The words hurt. Way more than I thought they would.

"I don't know yet, Jake," she gave me an honest answer. "My heart says no; it's just taking my brain longer to catch up."

As much as I wanted to argue and tell her that her love was enough to keep me firmly rooted, she needed to figure it out independently. Francesca may be right about Damien and Caleb; it wasn't the first time I'd thought that either. It just hurt to believe that. I knew how much that war had taken from us all exactly. No loss hurt less than the others.

"Even if it's true, Jake. I'm still in love with you. Just as I was in love with Damien, as I'm still in love with him, that's not going to change," she assured me and turned slightly in my arms to snuggle closer into me. "I know whose arms are around me. I know who takes care of me day in and day out. Your love is the best feeling I have ever felt. Don't doubt that."

For the millionth time since he died, I thanked Damien for putting the thought of marrying Francesca into my head. I cursed him for dying and then thought about how much I loved and missed him being a part of my everyday life. I didn't believe the pain of losing him would ever leave me.

"I miss him, Frankie. It's a big, living, breathing hole inside me that I haven't figured out what to do with yet. Sometimes I wake up and wonder how I'm not going to fall into it, and your breathing next to me pulls me from the edge. It's still there, that edge, every day. We got through Caleb's because we were still enlisted and had things to keep us distracted. Fighting to heal our physical injuries, talking strategy, things like that. Damien is ingrained in my survival skills, and we had each other. How did you survive it?" I said into her neck, my eyes burning with endless tears when I dwelled on Damien.

"I haven't gotten through my mom's yet," she answered me, bringing her arms up behind her head to encircle my neck. "Caleb's took me a while. It was months before I got to the hike with that wrecked airplane. It took me the whole hike up, staring down the cliff and wanting to throw myself over and wondering what my insides would look like even to recognize that I was drowning in it. The hole Caleb left is still there. Damien, and you filled a part of it. Even Darius. You're a step ahead of where I was."

"Think this little one will fill it?" I asked her. She took my hands and settled them on her belly, the life growing there a reminder that a part of Damien was still very much alive.

"I'm sure he will fill part of it. You're always going to miss him, Jake. So will I. You need to find a way to be okay with that. Healing sucks. It's painful and awful, messy, and we have a long way to go. There has yet to be a day I didn't want to break down into a sobbing mess, just screaming that I wanted my mom or Damien and berating myself that I didn't marry him sooner. We have each other, and it's a start. The loss will shape us into different people, and you started well by insisting on honesty, even though most of it hurts. Letting you in is hard, but it feels right now that you are in there." She kept her hands over mine on the barely-there swell of life she carried.

"They'd all be so proud of you." I pressed my head against hers and felt her breathing pause. "They are," I told her again. "I am."

She pushed her face into my neck this time, and we sat there for a few minutes, just breathing each other in and fighting through the pain that was closing in on us. "I know I don't say it enough, Jake, but I love you."

"I know you do, babe." I brushed my lips across hers. All those years wishing I could, and now I had the rest of my life to kiss her.

She sighed heavily, lifted the letter stack, and pulled the rubber band off. "If I know Damien, these are already in order," she voiced softly. I chuckled because it was true. "Keep your hands there, right over the life inside me," she instructed me.

I pulled a move from her playbook and moved them under the clothes, so my hands were against her flesh, warm skin on warm skin, the comfort of the touch magnificent to me. Chaos reigned supreme in my head, but her skin on mine was a laser that pierced right through it.

Chapter Twelve

Dear Future Wife,

We haven't met yet, but I have hope that someday we will. And when we do, you will probably have many questions about me. If I continue to write them, maybe these letters will tell you what you need to know about the asshole I am sure that I am. Or perhaps it's my position here. This place doesn't give a whole lot of options about that.

If these words are seen by someone other than me, I hope that not all hope is lost. The two most important people in my life are here with me, and I'm watching them unravel a little bit every day. As their leader, I blame myself for not keeping them safer.

I'm smart enough to realize that there's no such thing as 'safe' here. Some days I don't even know which part of hell we are in at any given time. My brother Ghost writes to his sister almost every other day, and it's keeping him somewhat sane. Her letters to him keep us all sane. Writing this right now, I can say I hope you are similar to how she is; she seems to get us.

My other brother Foxy is my big worry today. If I keep all this bottled up all the time, I will become a statistic. We were out on a mission earlier, sneaking up on a camp spotted by what upper brass is calling 'insurgents.' Lately, I've been questioning whether that's true or they want us to kill everyone.

As my future wife, it's vital that you know I'm a killer. I'm excellent at it in multiple ways. It sickens me. I hate what I've become. That said, please don't leave me. I need love, a lot of it. My biggest dream is to have a family someday, and I hope I don't screw up as badly as mine screwed me up. My dad was the biggest prick alive.

Shit. I'm off track. Today. We were sneaking up on this camp, Ghost moving just like you'd think the air would, without a sound and undetectable. I wasn't far behind him, and Foxy positioned back in one of the rocky areas keeping an eye on us. Our explosives guy behind me, the communications guy by Foxy, and the medic brought up the rear. I usually take point on these things, but Ghost is a master at getting in and getting out.

I didn't want us to go in guns blazing. I wanted proof they were indeed terrorists and not some nomadic people. We'd seen too much bad shit by this point, and the constant killing made us feel like mercenaries. I guess that's what we are; some higher-up cabinet members personal Navy mercenaries.

I have instincts that have kept me alive through this shithole of a place, and they had been screaming at me since we left Foxy. Ghost was up ahead of me and had come to a halt, which didn't mean anything good. The risk to my own life was worth sticking my head up to make sure he was okay, and I did.

If I am marrying you or have already married you, you already know how much I love these two men. You need to understand that their lives are more valuable than mine, and I would die for them. I would die in place of them. They would do the same for me.

You might have figured out by now that I'm not all that great at sharing. I'm doing my best, and it might not be good enough. It's a fear I live with every day. Maybe that's why you are reading this.

Anyway, when I rose up, I saw the glint of something and called out for the team to stay down. Ghost ignored me, and he kept moving forward, albeit cautiously. We used a series of clicks to relay messages when we needed to be silent.

I looked again and saw a kid. It was the only sign of life in this so-called camp we visited, a kid. Had to be a kid under ten too. Just sitting there, not even looking in our direction. Ghost was a bleeding heart and wanted to save everyone. He saw his sister in every person, and each death hit him like a ton of bricks. I knew why he was moving.

I also knew this wasn't a normal kid sitting there. He was too silent. The air felt wrong. It wouldn't be the first kid we'd have to kill, probably not the last either. It was disgusting. Each time we had to do it, it took a piece of our soul.

Foxy saw what we couldn't. He took the shot before Ghost could get there, effectively saving his life even if he doesn't see it that way. The kid's head exploded, his body moving, and then the camp exploded. Gunfire rang out from beyond, and Ghost came rolling back towards me as Foxy took out the rest of the base one by one. Maybe his highest kill count in a day yet.

What kind of people sat a kid on a bomb? Why does life mean nothing to these people? Even if their paradise is real, they certainly aren't going there after killing a kid. If that boy had fallen asleep and moved, he would have blown himself up. Now instead of them killing the kid, they blame us. We're the bad guys. Maybe we are.

If I wake you up at night screaming, this is why. These are the things I'm remembering. My brother rolling towards me, shot after my other brother had to kill a kid to keep us alive. I used to think we were doing good out here, ending the reign of terror striking across the globe. I'm less sure now.

As he shakes in his sleep, I find myself in a dark place, Foxy between Ghost and me here in our camp. I want to go off and just kill everyone because it makes me so mad. On the other hand, I want to grab these two men and run and never look back.

What would Ghost's sister think of us if she knew these horrors we had to do in the name of war? Would she still be as proud of us as she says she is? There's a worry in her letters to Ghost. Worry about his mental state. She's right to worry. He's been on edge too much lately. The same edge Foxy is flirting with right now. The same one I've been on for over a year. Probably even longer.

Days like today, I don't care if I die. If I keep living, I'm just going to kill more, and what difference is that sincerely making? My heart breaks for Ghost and Foxy, and is strangely silent about the shit going on in myself. That *can't be good.*

You need to know. If you are going to tie yourself to me, you deserve to know the reasons behind my broken spots. Maybe I'm incapable of loving anyone other than these two men. I hope you know I love you. I might be shit at showing it; I can't see the future. There isn't a future here. Just death. Violent and awful death.

Now that I realize what I've written here, I probably won't share this with you, future wife. I can only say that if I asked you to marry me, it means I can love. I never even told the last one I loved her. Please have patience with me. I think this war will get fought in my head for many years to come. Maybe even the rest of my life.

Maybe you should ask Foxy if I'm worth it. He sees far more of me than I want him to. Ghost too. I don't think Ghost would rat me out, though. He understands this dark place, and he's a part of it with me. We sit in the dark together. Foxy fights it. He clutches the picture that Ghost's sister sent and insists that there are still beautiful things in the world, even after he had to kill a kid and tore his soul out to do it.

I owe you so much more than these strung-together words. I have no idea where to start. I'll again beg you for patience. We wear scars outside and inside; I worry about them. I'm aware I need help, but fear keeps me from asking for it, a fear of showing who I truly am inside. The only relief I get is hand-to-hand combat, which isn't healthy either.

I know after today, I'm requesting time before they send us out again. I'll have to see how Foxy is in the morning. Routine training would give us time to get past it, at least.

Thank you for loving me. I think it gives me something to look forward to, the thought of a family.

Love,

Damien

Francesca

My voice caught several times reading the brutally honest letter. Jake had stiffened under me but didn't let me go. The staggered breathing let me know he was struggling. I folded the letter carefully, put it back in the envelope, and stuck it on the bottom of the pile.

There were twelve letters. If they were all as painful as that, we wouldn't have an easy time with this. It did give me an insight into where Damien's head had been over there. Also, a significant look at Caleb and Jake. My heart bled for them and what they went through.

"That wasn't pleasant." Jake's low growl had me turning more into him. His voice was thick, with emotion brimming under it. "He was farther in it than I thought he was. Damien clearly became excellent at hiding it from us. I knew he struggled, but I also don't imagine he thought he would ever share those letters."

"It's telling, but I don't think he was suicidal. At least not at this point. Needing a break and a change of scenery, for sure. Disillusioned about being over there, too." It was sad seeing the words that way. I saw Damien in the text of the letter, those pieces that I had gotten glimpses of at times. He'd been in a very dark place and was willing to take the risks of death, but he wasn't actively looking for it.

"That doesn't make you look at me differently?" Jake's voice was drawn and rough. He was on the verge of a breakdown.

"Not even a little in the way you are thinking. I feel awful that our government put you in the position you were in, but I can't judge you, Jake. I wasn't there. I didn't live it, and I didn't see what you did. It's not the first time I heard about kids getting used like that. I love you more for remaining human despite it." I turned to kiss his chin.

"I stayed human because of you, Frankie." Jake's voice was very strained now, and I set the bundle of letters on the ground and turned into him, letting him wrap me up as he trembled. "He loved; Damien was capable of love. It fucking hurts to think he didn't think he was. It makes so much sense now, his reaction to you."

"Damien was loved, he is loved, and he did love." I didn't have anything else to say to that. I knew Damien had loved, he was open about it, but he was also different from the person who had written that letter. Better in some ways and perhaps worse in others.

"I killed seventeen people that day," Jake said when he slowed down on the shaking, more in control. "Seventeen adults and one child. I rationalized so many thoughts in the span of five seconds as your brother moved closer. I pulled the trigger, believing that I was saving my team and that no one that meant anything good would put a child on a bomb. It still destroyed a piece of me doing it."

"Because you have a good heart, Jake," I murmured, stroking his chest. "No more letters tonight," I decided. I don't think if I opened anymore that Jake would be able to keep his promise of not bringing it in the house with us. I didn't know that I could.

I struggled with the picture the letter had painted, and I hadn't been there living it. Instead, I kept stroking Jake's chest until I felt those rigid muscles ease slightly. "You made Damien's life better, Frankie. Even if it was only for a little while, you showed him the beauty that still exists. There is nothing I can say to thank you enough for that. You gave him his every dream before he died. Maybe Caleb had a hand in that, as you said."

"And for you?" I asked quietly.

"I always knew it existed. Beauty came to life for me with each letter your brother read us. It didn't matter if what you told him was sad, your heart broken, how many people you dated, or the scenic places you went. I didn't care if you only talked about homework, Caleb's nightmares, or assuring him it was fine that he talked to you. It was your voice that came through those words and reminded us that life was precious and what we were in that hell hole fighting for; at least for me, it did. As for the thanking you, I plan to spend every moment I have with you trying to show you how fucking incredible you are," Jake turned his upper body into mine.

"You already do that," I told him with a smile. "My very own superhero."

158

His expression darkened only briefly, but it was enough for me to see. "I'm not a superhero."

"You are to me. You will be to our babies. Yes, plural. This one and the ones after. What happened overseas was tragic and awful, and yes, it shaped you. What you aren't seeing is this beautiful warrior that I see. You survived it, and you made your life good, still protected, and took care of people that probably didn't deserve half of the energy you put into making sure they survived whatever crime they were trying to commit. Since you met me, you've been taking care of me," I pointed out, my hand still over his heart. "You took care of Damien, too. He was a superhero just like you are."

"I don't agree, but I'll accept it." His green eyes stared into mine, unblinking for the longest time.

"You don't have to agree. A difference of opinions doesn't change anything that I feel. We will lay here until you think about nothing other than the dirty things I'm going to do to you when we get to bed." I thumped my fingers over Jake's heart with the promise.

Chapter Thirteen

Francesca

We'd spent the last two weeks moving into our new house and packing up things from Jake's. He'd enlisted Darius to pack up the boxes in Damien's room. After reading that first letter, neither of us could go in there just yet.

The letters, I'd packed those away and left them at Jake's house, as promised. I wasn't willing to let them go because they were a link to Damien, a very personal part of him he hadn't let Jake or I be a part of; they hovered there out of sight but never out of mind for either of us.

My birthday was in a week, my doctor's appointment in two weeks, and our trip to Ireland. I'd accepted two assignments while I would be over there, and I was excited about them. Jake was looking into survivor groups of trauma that were there to see if I could talk to anyone for my project.

I was busy but unsettled. I think it had a lot to do with those letters, too. I'd been abrupt with Jake and hadn't meant to be, and he'd left me alone to sort it out.

He kept popping his head up every once in a while to check on me, but he kept his distance.

It was one of the biggest differences between Damien and him that I'd seen. Damien wouldn't have left me alone, and eventually, I think I would have blown up at him for it. Jake let me have space while satisfying his need to ensure I was safe and okay. Mildly annoying but understandable given everything we'd been through up to this point.

The honesty part of our relationship was brilliant—what a concept. I may not have wanted to share everything, and Jake didn't make me do it all the time. He asked me for answers only when he felt like he needed clarification on something or that it would become an issue. I knew he'd ask about today because this was the first time I'd lashed out.

In return, Jake would ask me if I wanted him to explain something about himself, like a nightmare, an expression, or a reason he did something the way he did. I never turned him down because it helped me understand the place he was in better than I did before. We didn't walk on eggshells around each other. We flat out broke the eggs, threw the shells on the ground, and then stomped on them together and cleaned the mess up.

I didn't know what I was going to tell him this time. I owed Jake an explanation, and blaming it on pregnancy hormones might be valid, but it wasn't right. I was almost positive it was because of the letters. A piece of me wanted to read another one and a smaller, quieter part wanted me to ignore them because they hurt us.

Our hearts knew Damien was gone, but those letters gave us a very sharp picture of the dark shadows he'd kept hidden, and it was like he was there when we read them, alive again. That was something we both craved.

I sat down on the swing in the backyard and looked out over the water. The day was overcast and on the cooler side of things; the fall colors were in full swing, and we were lucky enough to have one of those trees with the bright red leaves in the back. When the sun hit it right, it looked like it was on fire or full of brilliant red gemstones with the sun glinting through them.

"Could sure use your wisdom, Mom," I said softly to the water. "I mean, really, you created me with all this intelligence, yet I have no idea what to do about my husband or the almost one that's up there with you. I'm every bit the lost little girl I was when I started college courses at sixteen in a room full of twenty-year-olds. Or better, when Caleb left."

I liked to think that the slight breeze that made the leaves rattle overhead was my mom's way of letting me know she was still with me. The Sound was mostly calm today, the sky gray and moody, and I suddenly desperately needed the ocean. I hadn't gone to put some of Damien's ashes with my mom's. Maybe I should.

"Why do you think you need to do something with me?" Jake's hand touched my back lightly, pushing me a little on the swing.

"I was unnecessarily mean. I need to apologize," I answered without looking at Jake. It was rare when I heard him move, so the sudden appearance of Jake didn't startle me.

"You weren't mean, babe. You do look sad. I can't resist staying away when you look like that." He continued to push me gently, the back and forth motion soothing. "Tell me what you need."

"My mom," I put my feet down to halt the swing and stood up. "Can we go to the coast?"

"Today?" Jake ran his hands down the back of my arms.

"I think that's what I need," I nodded. "With the letters and some of Damien's ashes." He flinched at that. "Jake, I can go on my own. You can stay here and get settled."

The security he'd added had all been finished earlier in the week; there wasn't anything that required him to stay home. I didn't want him to think I needed him to go everywhere or do everything I wanted.

Jake was studying my face, looking for an answer to a question I didn't know. "Do you want me to stay here?"

No. I honestly didn't. I wanted Jake with me. "I want you to do whatever you want," I said after a pause.

"That's not an answer, Frankie," he chastised me softly. "Am I treading on something you want to be alone for if I go with you?"

"No. I don't want you to feel obligated to tag along with whatever crazy whim strikes me." I closed the distance between us and slid my hands into the back pockets of his jeans. "Strangely enough, I haven't wanted to be rid of you yet."

"I know you don't need me," Jake pressed a kiss on my head, "but I like being with you."

"You're wrong. I *do* need you, Jake. I'm just not good at expressing it. When I ordinarily want solitude, I find myself looking for you. I don't know what happened to me earlier, but I think it has to do with the letters and what's inside them. I think needing my mom is pulling me to the ocean," I tried to explain.

"You didn't run and go on your own; instead, you asked me if *we* could go. It's progress, and I'll take it," Jake conceded with a smile down at me. "Not excited about reading another letter, but I understand the need to see what's in it."

"Does that mean that you will come with me?" I asked, hopefully.

"Nothing would make me happier," he replied. "Hotel it?"

"Yeah. I'll call and get a room," I hugged Jake. "Thanks. You're pretty awesome; you know that?"

"Yep. Sure do." He grinned down at me. Confident but humble. It got a laugh out of me because Jake was pretty humble most of the time.

Jake

I got to the coast right as the sun was starting to set. It had been overcast at home, but here the clouds were rolling through, and the patches of the sky lit with brilliant pinks, oranges, and purple. Frankie had grabbed her camera and tore out of the truck like it was on fire.

She scaled a sand dune like it was nothing, snapped pictures, and came running down it like a pro and headed for the water. All I could do was smile. If being here was what Francesca needed to free her mind a little, I'd make the drive every day or just move us here to make it happen.

I'd accidentally stumbled on Francesca talking to Damien how she spoke to her mom earlier today, and it gutted me every time. She'd tucked a letter inside her coat before getting to the beach, so I knew I would have to face that soon. At least here, it might be easier to let go of the emotional buildup that would happen from it. I hoped anyway.

I watched Francesca for a little bit, loving that she wasn't afraid to get down on the ground and get dirty to get the shot she wanted. I'd seen her do it in other places we'd been, even watched her wade out into an ice-cold lake to get the picture. Whatever she had to do, she did it, and it always paid off. Her photographs captured emotions and made you feel when you looked at them. Whether it was crowds of people, portraits, or scenery, she had an eye for the essence, waiting for notice.

There was a picture of Damien she'd gotten while he was working out on a bag, and in his expression, I could see all the demons he was fighting inside. Every one of them. That single picture proved to me that he was holding back on many things, and when I'd tried to get him to talk about it, I fell to pieces in front of Francesca.

Shaking it off, I kept heading slowly in her direction, where she'd finally settled on a washed-up log; her face turned to the sunset, one of her knees drawn up to her chest with her arms wrapped around it. She looked young and innocent, and I saw the girl in the letters to Caleb.

My heart tripped over itself. It was Caleb's Frankie. The girl who had completely captured my heart simply through her words and a picture of some woods. I wasn't a photographer like she was, but I wanted to remember this moment, and I fumbled with my phone until I got the camera turned on and took a picture of her.

Francesca turned to look at me then, and my heart not only tripped over itself again, but it also lodged in my throat. That love in her face was for me. I don't know what I did to deserve it, but I'd do it repeatedly to keep her looking at me that way. I almost ran to her when she patted the empty log next to her.

She grabbed my hand when I was close, pulled me down, and burrowed into my side. It took little to no effort for this woman to bring me to my knees in any manner of ways. She understood me like no one else ever had.

"When Caleb and I were kids, my parents brought us out here for a week every summer until my dad died. Caleb would chase me up and down the beach with those kelp whips or crabs, and we'd have to dodge jellyfish as we ran. We collected sand dollars, bright-colored rocks, and sea glass and occasionally tried to fly kites. My mom would sit in a chair reading a book, and my dad would try to make big grand sandcastles, but we were little assholes and always went crashing through them. We would create booby traps for the other to fall in, and then when we finally wore ourselves out, we'd sit still, leaning against each other and watch the waves or the sunset," she told me.

"Then we'll carry the tradition on with our kids," I said softly in her ear, breathing in the fresh scent of her skin.

"I like the sound of that. I'm going to hold you to it, too," she replied, those big brown eyes melting everything in me.

"I'll keep my word. For damn sure, I will do everything in my power to keep you happy and with me. You are a force, Frankie. Independent, strong, intelligent, funny, and so good. You're going places, and I will do my damn best to make sure I don't get left behind," I gave her the blunt truth of my deepest fear.

"If I'm going places, you will be right by my side. I might be all those things, but I'm also your wife. I'll go after what I want, but *you* need to remember that you are one of those things I want. I don't see that changing, Jake." She brushed a sweet kiss against my jaw.

"Absolutely bewitching," I murmured. I wished that Damien could see her like this. "Read that letter, babe, before we lose the last of the light."

My lovely future wife,

Thank you for loving me. As I sit here and write this, I'm pretending you are real right now and that someone is waiting for me at home, worried about me and praying for my safety. I got shot today, and all I could think about was how no one but Ghost and Foxy would miss me.

Ghost was pissed that I took the bullet for him. He's been bitching at me since. I tried to bribe Foxy to shut him up, but he ignored me. We've had so many close calls out here. I saw it as an even trade. I jumped to push him out of the way and took the bullet, and he, in turn, killed the fuckers that came at me with knives.

I'm not going to survive this place if I don't do something about this shit inside me. So, I'm putting up walls inside and making a fortress and going to shove it all in there and lock it down. Not the healthiest thing I can do, but I'm assuming you know they are there by now. Survival is why.

The constant kill or be killed. While we were doing a little recon in the city yesterday, we watched a woman get stoned to death. All because another man that wasn't her husband touched her arm to get her attention. The woman died brutally, publicly, and is now getting shamed in death for something innocent. What the fuck. We couldn't do anything. We couldn't intervene, we couldn't save her, we couldn't kill the bastards that thought this was right. Why the fuck are we here if we can't help in these types of situations?

Ghost and Foxy cried after, Ghost puked, and I became this walled-up, closed-down asshole that couldn't figure out how to process the senseless death. We aren't part of the solution here; we are part of the problem. They hate us. In cases like this, I can't blame them.

God doesn't exist in places like this. After watching that, I'm not sure God exists at all. This place has put my life growing up with my prick of a father in a new perspective and makes me appreciate life a little more. I may not have had much love from him, but I was safe. These women don't even have love, at least not that I've seen.

I've heard some other soldiers say things like they should just nuke this place off the map, and there are times I think they are right. Then I see these little kids, girls, and boys who don't know that life isn't supposed to be this way, and they are smiling and laughing, and I can't think that wiping them off the map will make it any better. I want to hope that if their environment changes, maybe they'll see that life doesn't have to be as cruel as here. This place kills hope, though.

I'm jaded and bitter before I've even hit my thirties. I have no idea how to go back to regular life after this. Hell, I don't even know what ordinary life is. All I've ever known is military housing, military schools, training, discipline, and having people try and break me. I'm going to see my grandpa next leave; he'll park me on the boat and try to shove love down my throat.

I want to say you'll get to meet him, but he's not doing good, and once he goes, the only tethers to this life I have are Foxy, Ghost, and the hope of you. Please have patience with me if all I can see is the underbelly of life. It's all I can see here. It's all I know.

Ghost reads his letters to us, and I see the other side for those little moments. Foxy clings to it with stars in his eyes. Ghost, I think he's sitting where I am. He's in the underbelly with me, Foxy straddles it, but Foxy is stronger than us. He's the good we no longer are.

I see the look in Ghost's eyes, and it echoes what I feel inside of me. Desolate, violent, empty. He's a better *soldier than all of us combined, but he's more sensitive because of his sister. I can't blame him. If I had a sister, I'd feel the same way. I'm doing all I can to ensure he gets home to his family. That's his saving grace.*

My dear wife, I can only hope you don't see me as empty as I feel. I hope you don't find these walls unscalable. I also hope you never need to reconcile the person writing these words with the one you marry. The walls are there to keep us all safe from this shit I'm trying to hide. These walls are for you.

I'm learning to hate the desert and trying not to let hate fill the rest of me. Would I have still chosen to be here if I had known the cost would be so high? Time will tell.

Love,
Damien

Jake

As Francesca's voice carried off the last words of the letter, I dropped to the sand and pulled her between my legs, enfolding her into me. How the hell could Damien think I was stronger than him or Caleb? That made no sense to me at all. It killed me that he didn't see he had the same stuff inside him that I did.

It confirmed my suspicion that Caleb had been hiding some pretty deep feelings inside him. It still didn't point to either of them being suicidal, and I guess even if it did, it didn't matter now with both of them gone. I didn't believe one little bit that Damien's mental state caused him to take risks with our lives. If anything, he was more cautious than either Caleb or I had been.

Because he was trying to make sure we made it home even if he didn't? I wasn't sure about the answer to that. Damien did risk his life an awful lot. I wasn't sure that hearing the letters made getting over his death easier. They told me more about the man I knew as a brother when I thought I had known almost everything.

The shadows inside of us had been profound, but I explored mine. Damien let his grow until he met Francesca, then he tried to bury them again, only to have them come back out when he was vulnerable. I believe that is because of who she was, a link to Caleb for him. He loved her before he knew that, but I think that connection is what the resurgence of nightmares was from; a part of me believes his soul recognized Caleb in her from the start.

"Damien never loved me as you did, did he?" Francesca's melancholic voice broke through my thoughts.

"You mean back then?" I tried to wrap my head around the question.

"Yes. I know Damien loved me after we met. He was very upfront and honest about that. He talked a lot about how the letters from me helped, but even in his letters, like with Caleb's, they both talk about how you loved me then, not him. Not that it matters, I'm just trying to get a feel for it all," she pressed her lips to my throat.

"Damien looked forward to them as much as Caleb and I did. They brought him hope, the same as us. But perhaps you are right. The way he felt about you then was affection, whereas what I felt was genuine love. I'm not sure I would have noticed if you hadn't brought it up," I truthfully answered as I thought about the distinction. "What did he say to you about them?"

"That they kept you all going, that I was a light in the dark; the same thing Caleb's letters said. It doesn't change anything. It does help me see that while, yes, Damien loved me, in the end, I was always supposed to be with you. I saw Caleb in Damien. I was drawn to Damien because he's like the dark horse, mysterious, and something for me to unwrap. In those dark moments where I'm dwelling on things, I felt closer to Caleb when I was with Damien when I think about it. It was instant familiarity, comfort, and natural from the start with you. I sound like I'm comparing the two of you, but I'm not. I'm working through the guilt and looking for the differences that tell me the truth of the situation," Francesca explained carefully."

"Damien's love was genuine," I insisted. It had been palpable. Not that mine hadn't, but I'd also been in love with her longer than Damien. I'd gotten used to the feel of it. That kind of love had been new for him.

"It was, and I treasured it. I always will," Francesca agreed. "I'm hungry. There's a great pizza place not far from here. You game?"

I wanted to argue with her about Damien, but I couldn't make myself do it. She saw it from a different viewpoint than I did, and she hadn't given me a reason to argue. She knew he had loved her, and it was real. Why did I feel like I needed to defend him then? Her explanation made sense because Caleb and Damien had carried heavy shadows in their hearts. Francesca missed Caleb, and if she had seen or sensed her brother in Damien, she migrated to him from the start.

"Hey," Francesca pulled my attention back. "I know Damien loved me. I also know now that it has always been different from how you loved me. That's all that meant. From where I'm sitting, you loved me enough to let me go. Damien wouldn't have unless I pushed. Those are very different types of love, both as equally real and strong."

The words halted my train of thought at the stark truth of them. Francesca was utterly right. Damien wouldn't have let her go the way I did. Damien wouldn't have pressured her; that wasn't his style. If she had told him she wasn't interested, he would have been upset if I moved in, and he backed down. Not that I would have, knowing his interest, but that had been my read on it.

Francesca's simple yet powerful words had caused a cyclone of thoughts to run through my head. I didn't know what to do about any of them. "I'm not ignoring you. I only need to think about that," I finally said. "Stand up, babe. Let's feed you."

Chapter Fourteen

Francesca

Jake was distant. He didn't take care of me any less than usual, but his mind wasn't entirely with me. I knew he was working things through in his head, but I wasn't sure which part. Jake had the heart of a warrior, while Damien had the soul of one, but his heart wasn't in it.

"Can we go sit on the rocks for a minute?" Jake asked as we left the pizza place. "Are you too cold?"

"If we grab the blanket from the truck, I'll be fine." I didn't mind sitting outside.

"Never mind. I want to lay down." He was agitated. I'd figured that much out. "Is that okay?"

"Of course," I agreed, letting him take the reins. The second letter brought me to several conclusions that I had been on the cusp of figuring out about Damien, how he loved me, and his relationship with Caleb and Jake. I think Jake was starting to put it together, and it bothered him.

When we got back to the room, he flopped on the bed, fisted his hands in his hair, making it stand out at odd angles, then held his arms out. "Frankie, please come lay with me."

I went to him. I didn't know how to ease the war inside his head other than just doing what he asked. It was a role reversal. Jake rested his head on me this time, let me hold him, and drew comfort from me. I loved that he did it too.

"Will you tell me what you've figured out about this?" he finally asked me. "You are far calmer than I am after that letter, and I've yet to figure out why it's hit me the way it has. Not to mention, I'm struggling with the statement about how Damien loved you."

I couldn't call it brotherly love because I wanted Damien in a non-brotherly way. I saw the same dark parts of Damien that I saw in Caleb. I couldn't help Caleb get through them because he died, but I could help Damien, and I think that was my initial draw to him over Jake. I tried to figure out how I could explain it, but I wasn't sure I could so Jake would understand the real meaning behind it.

"Can I show you?" I thought out loud. "It might be easier. I just need to grab my laptop."

He moved so I could get up, and when I sat back down, propped against the headboard, he curled into my side like I had done so many times to him. "Is this going to hurt?" Jake asked as the computer booted up.

"All healing hurts." I kissed the top of his head. It was the only thing I could think to say. I wasn't sure if it would hurt him or not. My initial reaction to reading the letter had been anguish because of how Damien had felt wounded, but it hadn't hurt me. It had made me unbearably sad.

"It feels like I'm missing something obvious," Jake mumbled.

"Because you are closer to the situation than I am. You were there for everything that happened, and you saw how it affected everyone. You lived it. I'm only learning things now, and I only saw it from Caleb's perspective and the few details he shared," I told him gently.

"Damien being in love with you makes you pretty close to that situation," Jake countered.

"Is that the part you are struggling with?" I asked, surprised by his words.

"Part of it," he admitted.

I flipped through my saved project until I landed on a picture of one of the older vets I talked to from the hospital. "David was a soldier in Vietnam," I started. "He's the first vet I seriously talked to about anything in depth. David also seemed to need it the most. He told me that some soldiers were in the service because they wanted to be. They wanted to help, make a difference, and stand up for all humans' rights. He said there was another side to that as well. Some joined because they had to, and while they did what someone ordered them to do, they got out once their tour was up. Further down on the spectrum, he talked about the soldiers there for the wrong reason. That they craved the violence, and killing was allowed this way. I don't imagine that's changed much?"

Jake stared at the weathered face on the screen. He was lying in the hospital bed, various machines hooked up to him told of his vital signs, but nothing of the damage inside showed on his face while he talked to me. A vacant look shadowed his eyes that doctors had said was a side effect of David's pain medication for cancer. I knew better because he was present, just locked in memories.

"Still true," Jake acknowledged slowly.

I flipped to another picture, this one a younger vet from the same time frame of Jake's service. He held himself up along the balance bars while he tried to walk on the prosthetic leg for the first time. Only his face showed raw anger. Pain bled from his eyes as he tried to walk again while he'd shouted and cursed the Middle East's existence that had cost him his leg, pride, and hopes.

"Sam here hated everything about the Middle East. He blamed everything going wrong in his life on the people there. Sam joined because he wanted to, but his reasons were muddy. He wanted out of his life, and he thought that was his ticket. His father was pretty harsh on him when he came back, saying losing a leg was the sign of a weak soldier. It manifested inside him and started to control his mind. This man was one of the vets that asked me out. He was sure I would say no because he was missing a leg. After I said yes, he started talking to me, wondering why I would say yes to what he considered an invalid. He's now married to this therapist who wants to bash him in the head with that crutch," I tapped the screen.

I flipped through to the next photo of a middle-aged man who was a veteran of the Gulf War. His face was hard, cold, and mean. Even when he smiled, something about him made you want to back up and move away.

"Jeff was one of those that liked the violence. Out of all the people I'd talked to, he was the most unpleasant because of how negative he was. Hatred dripped from his words when he spoke and left you feeling wary and uncertain if you were in danger or not. Jeff was effective at his job; what Jeff saw didn't bother him, and he enjoyed it. The reason he's in here is that his friend got killed, and he had nightmares about that. He got through them by drinking."

"I get it, but I'm not making the connections," Jake stared at Jeff's picture. "He looks like a bastard."

"He truly was. Jeff scared me. But let me go back to the first picture." I flipped back through the photos, and when Jake motioned, I switched until we were back at Jeff's. I then changed to a picture of Damien. "I want you to note what you see in their eyes."

I took this picture while Damien was working out. Sweat beaded on his face, his fists in motion; his muscled, inked body, a work of art that I knew intimately. It was his face that was arresting, though. There was something in Damien's face of each of the people I had just shown Jake. The same thing I saw in Caleb when he was home on leave.

The tormented pain, the haunted and hollowed eyes, the hatred and raw anger that had bled from him with each strike on the bag; each loss he suffered written there, every desperate thought about death and the war he was still fighting in his head. It was a picture that was horrifyingly beautiful and utterly painful. It was perhaps one of my best and worst.

Jake's breath caught as he started to see what I was trying to show him. Damien's body radiated a fury easily seen in the recoil of the strike, the grimace on his face speaking of the pain. Still, his eyes told an entirely different story that you wouldn't understand unless you had read those two letters.

In those moments of Damien working out, the walls he'd erected inside came down, and I don't even think he knew it. The first time I'd seen it, it was like someone had stabbed a hot poker in my heart. It was excruciating to watch the play of emotions, each second bringing a different pain to his face as he tried to beat it away. I'd fallen in love with him more then.

I switched to a picture of Hector I'd gotten while he leaned on the fence while he talked about losing his leg and losing his brother. It was poignant and touching because his face spoke volumes of the pain he'd gone through, but acceptance of what he couldn't change shone through his expression. Hector's eyes were sad but kind. His face was lost in thought but held the shine of hope for better things. It was heartbreaking and breathtaking. The shadows of his hat highlighted the different aspects of pain and love. It was almost the polar opposite of what the picture of Damien had shown.

I kept quiet and moved to the picture of Jake I'd gotten when he unpacked the image of himself, Damien, and Caleb that Damien had in his box. Jake's expression pulled at every single heartstring I had. The loss was plain to see, the love showed in the way he held his body, his eyes distant, but he was in the moment. Jake wasn't where Damien was, or Hector either, but he was closer to Hector's state of mind than Damien's.

"Do you see the difference?" I spoke softly. "You might not be at the peace Hector is close to, but you are not the tormented soul Damien was either. You are actively working through those emotions, moving closer to the peace side of it. Damien's picture shows it taking him apart. Your picture shows remembrance and love."

I scanned through some of the other photos until I saw one of Damien looking at me. Again, only after reading the letters did I truly understand what that look in his eyes was. His expression was one every girl wishes her man would bestow on her. Pure love and rapturous adoration, a brilliant smile that spoke of devotion with a hint of the sexy and sultry smolder that he exuded. Possession, some called it.

I found one of Jake looking at me and displayed that one. There was the same look of love and adoration, but his eyes spoke of a deep understanding of who I was and an enduring deep emotion that I now knew was passion. There was a fine line between the two.

I manipulated the screen until the photos were side by side and glanced down at Jake's face. His eyes rapidly flickered between the two images. His breathing quickened, then slowed down, and his body stilled. Jake grimaced at the look on Damien's face, not seeing what I hoped he'd see yet.

"Tell me what you see, Jake," I requested softly.

"Love," was his first answer. "There's darkness to Damien, though. That's not right; he'd never hurt you."

"Not intentionally," I agreed. "Keep going."

"I always just thought it was an intense love," Jake murmured. "I don't know what word to put to this."

"You aren't wrong; it was an intense love. The word I would use is possessive. I only figured that out today," I moved my hand and stroked his face. "What do you see in your picture?"

"Devotion," he answered immediately. "Not a genuinely fair question since I know how I feel about you."

"But have you *seen* it? There is a clear difference between these two pictures, and before today I would have said that your love was equally as strong as Damien's. That still may be true, but it's a different type of love." I tapped Damien's picture, "It was real; there's no denying that. It came from a different place than yours did. My love for him came from a different place than my love for you."

"Just so you know, the phrase a picture speaks a thousand words has never been truer than right now," he mumbled and rolled to his back. "No questions about it. You have a gift. I can see what you are talking about, but I do not understand what you are translating."

"What was the one thing Damien wanted more than anything?" I asked Jake.

"A family." A light dawned in his eyes. "You gave him that. I get that much."

"What was the worst thing that happened to him?" I asked more quietly.

"Caleb's dying," Jake's answer was immediate.

He sat up, grabbed the computer, flipped back to

the picture of Damien working out, and studied it. Then Jake switched to the one where Damien was looking at me and put them side by side. I let him sit and work it out rather than give my opinion. He knew Damien in a way I didn't, and there was a chance I was wrong.

Jake

Damien's words echoed in my head from things he'd said over the years, and pieces started to fall into place. I stared at the pictures that held much more than I had ever seen before. I hated what I was thinking, not because it wasn't right, but because it hurt.

Damien wasn't suicidal, but he hadn't cared if he lived or not after Caleb died, maybe even before that. He'd lost more of himself to that war than he had ever admitted. Damien's father raised him to be a soldier, but Damien never wanted that. He'd given up on happiness.

Yet, I saw pieces of each of the previous men echoed in Damien's face. Except for Hector. Damien hadn't made peace with any of it. He fought against it, bottled it up, and let it eat at him. Then Francesca walked in right when Damien decided to turn things around and presented a damsel in distress that he could help. She'd had that same fire to her that night we met that Caleb had when he tried to do something to make Francesca proud.

Then Damien found out she was Caleb's sister, and he suddenly had a piece of his brother back. He *had* fallen instantly in love with her, and it had been genuine love; you could see it all over his face. I knew it wasn't the idea of love he'd fallen in love with, but with her. There had been a real connection there—a powerful and deep one.

Francesca had said the word possessive. I could see that, too, now that she said it. Then it hit me. "Damien wasn't just dealing with trauma from the war; he was dealing with trauma from his relationship with his dad. He clung to you because you gave him what he'd lacked his entire life. Unconditional love," I spewed out. "That's why he was possessive."

"I think so," Francesca agreed quietly. "Damien's love was as real as yours, just as mine was for him. It came from a different place inside him, the same as my love for him. I felt drawn to him because I saw Caleb in him. I didn't realize it until tonight."

"Damien wanted to save you and protect you because he was saving a part of Caleb," I said, wanting to take back the words that made too much sense. She nodded. "That was always his biggest failure in his eyes. I called it survivor's guilt. You gravitated toward Damien for the same reason."

"I'm positive that was part of it. Everyone has a breaking point, and that might have been Damien's. He would have gotten over it eventually, but it would have been hard, and he'd have to want it. He was holding pretty tightly to that loss." Francesca scooted down until she lay next to me.

"You think I'm not in the same place?" I didn't think I was, but I needed to hear it from her. I desired the validation she offered.

"No, Jake. You miss Caleb, you mourn him, but you aren't stuck there. Maybe you were before you told me about it, but I don't think so. I became stuck in it for a while; not knowing what happened was the worst. Think about it. If Damien thought Caleb was in the same dark mental place, he would feel protective and closer to him. The loss and perceived failure would be that much worse."

Francesca had nailed that one. Damien was fiercely protective of both Caleb and me. The rest of the team as well, but the three of us had always been our own unit. "I don't want to read any more of those letters," I decided. "I have the answers I was looking for."

"I agree, except I want to read the last one." She put her arm across my chest. "I don't want to get rid of them, but we can pack them back up and store them at your house."

"In some other dimension, Damien's okay and living with you happily, right?" I turned to face her. "With Caleb and I?"

"I'd like to believe so."

"Then that's what I'm going to believe, and see some silver lining in that he was deliriously happy about the baby and had everything he wanted before he died." My heart clenched painfully again. I needed to laugh to break through the sorrow. "Somewhere, he's also laughing and calling me Uncle Daddy."

"If he is, he heard it from Caleb first," Francesca giggled. "That's totally something Caleb would say."

I laughed at the truth of it. "Tell me this, do you

think knowing what you know now that your relationship would have lasted?" I switched back to serious. I couldn't help it with the vortex of information swirling in my mind.

"Hard to say. I've thought about it. The problem I keep coming back to is my feelings for you were only getting stronger. I would have put everything I had in me into the relationship to make it work with Damien. But my heart tells me that it would have fizzled out at some point. I can't say whether it would be from my independence and wanting to pull away from the hovering, or the passion just disappearing or admitting that I wanted you, I can't say. I know that I wouldn't have just turned away from him; I would have poured my heart into making it work. I loved Damien enough to do that," Francesca moved to sit up and look down at me.

It was an answer I could accept. I still don't believe Damien would have let her go easily. "Okay, another question. Why do you want to read the last letter?"

"I don't need the details of all the awful shit Damien saw you guys through. I read the beginning of his letters, and the end will tell me where he was mentally before coming home, I assume. The stuff in between, when you are ready to talk about it if you need to, we can deal with that as it comes up. I don't need Damien's words about how you were. I can see it in your eyes. Reading all the letters will take us through a journey of how he came to be where he was, and it's important; I'm not disregarding that. I don't need to air it, though. Not right now. I loved Damien when I met him, and I understood he couldn't talk about what he'd been through for whatever reasons he had. The last letter will be a type of closure, I suppose."

I could see that. I wasn't sure when Damien had written the last letter, which meant I had no way to prepare for whatever was in it. I didn't think I could prepare even if I did know, but I knew that I would deal with it because Francesca needed it. I felt awful for wanting it to be over, but I didn't know how much more I could take before I drowned in the pain of his loss.

"Tomorrow, when we send his ashes off, we'll read it then."

Francesca moved and straddled my hips. She raised off me, straightened her legs to slide them under my arms, and leaned back against my legs. I brought my knees up behind her back, making her slide forward a bit.

"You don't think I'm possessive?" I had no idea where the insecurities were suddenly stemming from all of a sudden.

"Protective, yes. Possessive, no. What would you do if I were to tell you I wanted a divorce and walked away from you?" Francesca's soft question was a knife to the heart. "Hypothetically, Jake. I don't want a divorce," she said after feeling my heart rate increase under her fingers resting on my neck.

"I'd follow you to get answers, talk to you, explain my stance, try to reach a compromise, and if you still wanted to be away from me, not married to me, I'd give you what you want. Your happiness matters more to me than my own," I told Francesca honestly.

"What would Damien have done?" Her tone was

gentle, even if the question, or more accurately, the answer, wasn't.

I paused to think it out. My immediate answer was that Damien would track her anywhere whether she wanted him to or not. I would have followed at first, too, until I had answers, but in the end, I'd give her what she wanted. Damien would have followed her still. He wasn't the type to let go.

I sighed, giving in to the problematic response. "Damien would have followed you. I see what you are saying. Damien wouldn't have been dangerous to you, but he wouldn't have left you alone. Your happiness mattered to him too, and if you truly wanted him completely out of your life, he would have stayed a distance, but he would still follow to make sure you are safe."

"You wouldn't follow to make sure I'm safe?" The question was a sincere one.

"I would have gone about it differently. That would have been part of the talk I had with you before agreeing to stay away. I didn't push Damien to back off you, and I could have. I didn't because I saw how happy he was, and you were genuinely happy too. Yes, seeing you two together was hard for me, but I was happy as long as you were happy. Love is hard, and sometimes it requires you to do things you don't want to do. Letting you go was one of those things. I'd rather see you happy with someone else and get to remain a part of your life than lose you completely. You don't think Damien would have trapped you, do you?" I hoped not.

"No. Damien told me he would back off if that

were my decision but that he would always be a part of my life. But look at the difference between the two of you. You aren't possessive in the same way he was. There are a lot of similarities, but there are a lot of differences too. I loved him; I still do. Damien was a good man with a good heart," she pulled my hands into hers. "I don't know that this level of communication that you and I share would have ever been possible between Damien and me."

I sat up, dropping my knees, and she slid down between my legs, hers hooking around me for stability. "You are right about that; Damien was tight-lipped about the damage in him. I like what we are rebuilding together, Frankie."

"You only like it?" she joked. "I *love* it."

Her face changed slightly, and her breath caught, her eyes widening to big saucers. I didn't know whether to be alarmed, and her entire body went utterly still, her hands clutched around her stomach.

"Frankie, are you okay?" I whispered, fighting off panic.

She grabbed my hands and pressed them tight to her belly, holding mine against her skin. She kept me there for about three minutes, both of us still, with me not knowing what was happening until I felt a tiny little flutter-like movement and saw her face light with wonder.

"Is that the baby?" I croaked, wondering if I was pushing too hard on her belly.

"Yeah, I think he's moving. It feels strange and wonderful," Francesca grinned.

I pushed her back on the bed and knelt to put my head on the little swell. "Hey, little man, I'm your daddy number two. The one who made you is up in heaven watching over us. So, grow big and strong for him, and your mommy and I will tell you all about him. You are going to be so loved; it will be ridiculous. Hopefully, your uncle that's up in heaven with him will have bestowed his sense of humor on you and is driving him nuts." I turned and kissed the bump.

"Jake," Francesca's ragged voice called to me. "You're sexy as hell, and I'm pretty damn sure that I need you in me now."

No arguments from me. I kissed my way back up, stripping her shirt off on the way. "Any requests?"

"You," she panted, her pupils dilated with need.

Chapter Fifteen

Francesca

Sex with Jake might be the best thing in the world. I didn't think we slept more than a couple of hours last night, and I was okay with that. My body had a nice little electric buzz going through it, my heart was all tingly, and he smelled divine.

"Babe, if you don't stop looking at me like that, it will be very awkward walking out of here," Jake's low grumble penetrated the sex haze of my brain.

"I almost don't care, but I think if one of the females here looks at you, I might punch them," I gazed at the gorgeous man sitting across from me.

"I only see one female in the room, and I'm looking at her." Jake's soft response made me want to leap across the table and pounce on him. He stood and slid around outside the table until he sat next to me.

"You make me forget that I'm hungry," I mumbled, leaning into the kiss he offered me.

"Honey, that man would make anyone forget they are hungry," a scratchy voice said. "What can I get you?"

After the Wreckage

I smiled into Jake's lips, trying not to laugh at his grimace. "Pancakes, please, for me. Herbal tea, the non-caffeinated kind, I don't care about the flavor." The waitresses age was probably in her sixties and had the look of someone who smoked and drank a little too much in her younger years. Her smile was pristine, though, and her eyes twinkled with a fantastic sense of humor.

"Can you grab my camera out of the truck?" I asked Jake. She had that quality that made me want to ask her questions and take her picture. Jake placed his order, and she left with a grin over her shoulder at us.

He didn't question it, and I watched him walk out, ignoring everyone that looked at him, and when he headed back in, his eyes were only on me. It thrilled me stupid when he did that. He slid back in next to me and set the camera on the table.

"Got a feeling about her?" he smiled, a slow smile that skyrocketed my libido.

"Who?" I asked distractedly, wondering what would happen if I touched him under the table.

"Babe," Jake chuckled, "if you act on the look on your face, we will get kicked out of the restaurant. I have no problems repeating our night, but we need to fuel up before we do."

"Phew! You two will set this booth on fire," the waitress exclaimed, setting the drinks down. Her name tag read Margaret. "You got a keeper there, honey. The way he looks at you is every woman's dream."

Now Jake smiled. "Thank you, Margaret. Can my wife take pictures of you? She's working on a project

192

about PTSD in photos, and something about you sparked her interest."

"If it's okay," I blushed. "I would take your contact info and send you every picture I took and let you know the ones I wanted to use, and if you approved, I would add you."

Her smile didn't change, but the humor faded slightly from her eyes. "What makes you think I would know anything about PTSD?"

"A hunch." Jake squeezed my thigh under the table. I got it; he was using his charm to woo her. "My name is Jake, and this is Francesca. I was captain of a S.W.A.T. team in Pierce county. I've learned to recognize some things in people even if they don't know they are showing it."

"Go ahead and take pictures. We'll talk after you two lovebirds finish your breakfast," Margaret said cautiously, but the humor was back in her eyes. "I have a break coming up, and the breakfast rush will be over then." She walked off then to take care of other customers.

I grabbed my camera and snapped a few of her taking orders, her smile locked in place. I was careful not to get any of the other customer's faces in the frames, and then I looked back through them quickly to make sure.

"You are certainly good at charming women into getting your way," I said smoothly, putting the camera back on the table.

"My way? If I had my way, I'd be asking to use the office I am sure is in the back to get a quickie in with my wife, who has me so turned on that I can hardly string two thoughts together," Jake replied, his low timber igniting my libido again.

"Your wife is so lucky," I quipped, kissing his chin.

He put his thumb on my chin with his fingers under it, not gripping it, just tenderly resting them there. "I happen to think I'm the lucky one out of us."

"I think you both are pretty lucky," the waitress returned, setting our food down. "Hold on to that closeness. Life has a way of beating it out of you."

That was something we both already knew, but I didn't mind the reminder not to take it for granted. I stretched my neck up and kissed Jake. "I love you."

Heat flooded those green eyes, and an achingly beautiful expression came over his face at my words. "Through any distance, any dimension, any test, any span of time, my love for you will continue to grow," he whispered against my lips.

In the last twenty-four hours, I had stopped feeling guilty for loving Jake the way I did. The loss of Damien still hurt, and we both mourned him deeply, but I was no longer feeling guilty for loving and marrying this man.

We ate in comfortable silence as I remembered the first time I'd met them both. Jake had been taking care of me since then. Damien had been too, but not in the same way. I saw it clearer now, the subtle differences and nuances and what they meant.

We pushed our plates away, and Margaret came back, bringing more tea and coffee, and letting us know she'd be about ten minutes before she could join us and took our plates away. I formed a list of questions to ask her in my head.

"It's fascinating to watch you think," Jake interrupted my thoughts. "I can almost see how fast the thoughts are processing through your mind, your eyes get this introspective look, and you take everything in."

"You were staring at me?" I quirked my lips up in a half-smile.

"I usually do," he smiled back. "Why wouldn't I? Nothing else comes close to matching your beauty, and I get to go home and sleep with you."

"I can say the same thing about you," I laughed.

"Then Margaret must be right; we are both lucky," he kissed my nose.

"Of course, I'm right. I'm always right," Margaret slid into the booth across from us, a coffee in her hand. "Now, what exactly do you want to know about me?"

"What trauma looks like to you," I said, simplifying it.

"That's a broad statement." She tapped her fingernails on the tabletop and studied me. "Tell me what you are doing first."

"I'm a nurse and a photojournalist. I lost my brother to the war on terror and my dad too. After my brother died, I decided to start a book showing what the faces of PTSD look like in hopes I can get more people to recognize that so many are suffering and the world needs more kindness. It started being just about vets because so many war veterans get neglected. Jake helped me by suggesting I add more than just veterans to it because PTSD wasn't just for them," I tried to explain.

"Francesca is oversimplifying it," Jake clarified, reaching for my hand. "From what I have seen so far of what she put together, she shows how people have gotten through grief, trauma, some of the triggers, and what it presents as from someone seeing it. Instead of sweeping the disorder under the rug, she's shining a light on it. Through pictures and brief descriptions of people's stories. The pictures speak for themselves."

"Can I see some of the pictures?" Margaret asked me.

I grabbed my camera, scrolled through the ones I hadn't cleared off the memory card yet, and showed her how to navigate them. She paused and looked at me, her face sporting a frown as she set the camera down and slid it over to me.

"Is that you?" she asked.

I glanced at the picture and then over to Jake. I didn't know he'd gotten a picture. One that could rival mine with the emotion that it showed. It was me lying on the boat's floor the day Jake had shown up after I had taken off.

"Yes, it's me," I said quietly.

"I married early," Margaret told me, her voice and tone soft. "I was barely twenty, and he swept me off my feet. Two years in, the beatings started. First, he'd only hit me in the stomach because no one could see. Then he moved on, not caring anymore. I started drinking to ease the pain. I wanted to leave him, but I couldn't. I didn't have enough money to support myself or get far enough away that he couldn't find me. I didn't have any family to turn to, and my friends were afraid of him."

Jake had stiffened next to me, and it dawned on me how much he'd probably heard and seen stories like this while he was on the police force. He didn't comment, and his hand's grip on mine didn't change; he remained as gentle as ever.

"Abuse was one of those things that people didn't talk about forty years ago. Not like they do now. We lived in a rural part of Virginia then, and at that time, the doctor in the area wasn't one to rock the boat or report the abuse to the authorities. I grew distant, drank more, and took up smoking to kill my appetite when it hurt too much to eat." She paused to take a drink of her coffee and looked out the window.

I snatched the camera up and got a few pictures of the look on her face. It was the look of someone who remembered every detail of the abuse and overcame it in her way. She radiated strength and vulnerability at the same time that touched me deeply.

"I lived with it for about ten years when one day, the postman dropped off a package at the front door and saw me lying on the floor. After damn near beating me to death, Andrew had left me there and then had taken off for the local bar. The postman was new to the route, probably to the area too. I didn't get out much anymore at that point. I felt like a laughing stock. I'd heard the comments about me being too stupid to leave or being someone who liked that type of man. Anyway, he saw me and came inside the house, knelt next to me, and asked me if I wanted to live or die," she stopped to take another drink of her coffee.

That was a point in life I was familiar with; it was a breaking point. I didn't want to interrupt her, so I stayed quiet and let her go at her own pace.

"I couldn't answer him because I didn't know. He carried me out to the delivery truck, set me in the back, and went back in for a bag of clothes. He brought me to his house and nursed me until I was well enough to walk, talk, and think. That little bit of kindness from a complete stranger helped me see I wanted to live again. He got me out of the state and to one of his family member's houses in Oklahoma, where they found me a job doing the exact thing I'm doing now. I saved enough to file for divorce and moved clear over here to put distance between us. In that process, I turned to drugs to escape what would happen to me if I smelled his cologne or saw a truck like the one he drove. It numbed me well enough until that postman showed up here to check on me."

Jake's thumb had started stroking my hand softly. I wasn't sure if it was a comfort thing for him or me. I was just selfish enough to want him to keep doing it.

"He was so angry with me that it put me back in that mental place I had been in with Andrew, and I shut down. It never fails to amaze me when I run into someone with a soul like his. There's still kindness in the world, and there's still love. He again helped me clean up, and I got sober, deciding I wanted to live again. He went back to Virginia, but he called me every week. He talked to me, checked on me, and became one of my best friends. It was that connection to him that got me through it all. That's not to say I don't have a moment of fear when I smell that cologne, but it won't take me to the ground anymore." She tapped her nails on the table again, then smiled. "I stuck with doing this as I was good at it, and this type of work helped me confront the fears. I encounter all sorts of people daily."

Margaret's story replayed in my mind. I pulled a piece of paper out of my purse, asked her for her contact information, and promised to let her see what I put together. She went back to her shift after that. Jake paid the bill, and we headed back to the truck.

Jake

Margaret's story was one of many along that vein. I hated hearing about it, and I saw too much of it while on the force. I was willing to bet that we could walk down the street, and any female we passed was the victim of some sort of assault. Francesca was oddly quiet about it, lost in thought.

"Frankie, were you ever assaulted?" I remembered Caleb talking about it once.

"Didn't we have that conversation?" she replied, distracted.

"Maybe you talked about it with Damien," I answered her quietly, unsure of how to take her response.

"Oh, right," she sounded apologetic. "Not like Margaret, no. The first guy I dated tried to paw at me and got pushy, but a neighbor kept it from going too far. I just had scrapes and bruises from him dragging me outside. Then, when Caleb returned on leave, he beat the crap out of him. It could have been worse, but I was lucky. No rape or sexual assault, either."

"Are you okay?" I asked after a pregnant silence.

"Yeah," she answered, staring out the window, her mind somewhere else. "Just thinking. I guess I didn't put it together that people going through things like that would have PTSD, but I should have been aware. Margaret's triggers of the truck and cologne make sense. I'm just thinking now that there are probably so many people trying to find their way through their trauma, and you'd never know unless you saw them get triggered."

"Do you automatically assume that all vets have PTSD?" I wondered.

"No, but I can usually spot signs of those that do. I now understand why you can spot signs of other things so easily, having seen so much of it while on the police force. It blows my mind that I missed that connection," she said again.

"Stop beating yourself up over it; you know it now. I think what you are doing is fantastic because you give a voice to those who can't do it themselves. You are giving hope to those going through it that they can get through too. Frankie, it's amazing." I reached for her hand and kissed her palm.

"Can you set me up with some people to talk to, not veterans?" She looked over at me.

"I'll get my guys on it," I promised her. "We still have the time scheduled for the next week's support group meeting."

"Thank you," she squeezed my hand. I pulled

down the road that we had gone down yesterday and parked the truck. As soon as I got my seatbelt off, Frankie climbed across the console and sat sideways in my lap, leaning against the door. "Needed some cuddle time," she told me.

"I'm not ever going to argue with you about that." I nestled her into me, treasuring the closeness and vulnerability she offered up to me. I thought she fell asleep, which I wouldn't have minded either.

"Wherever we are, anywhere, it doesn't matter; I'll always be home. You are my home, Jake. Did you know that?"

It was moments like these that completely unraveled every fiber of my being and remade me into something else. Something more substantial with Francesca's love woven into me that made me feel indestructible, safe, and cherished. Nothing could compete with the way she made me feel.

"Ditto, babe. We could have wanderlust for the rest of our lives and never stay in the same place twice, and I'd still be home," I kissed her head.

Francesca's hand slid down my chest and under the waist of my jeans. "Have you ever had sex in your truck?"

"No," I growled as she stroked me. For sure, this woman was going to kill me.

"You're about to." She maneuvered until she straddled me, undoing my jeans. I lifted my hips to help her get them down and then pulled her leggings down. It took some work and horn honking, but it was worth it when she lowered herself down on me.

After the Wreckage

She rode me fast and hard, not caring that anyone could see us. Her body demanded pleasure from mine that I was only too happy to share, and when we came, it was so intense that my ears rang for about five minutes after.

"Thank you for asking me to marry you." I pulled her toward me and drowned her in a kiss. I grabbed the wipes out of the console, and she cleaned us both up, bagged up the dirty wipes, and threw them in the back seat.

"I might be unconventional, but I do know what I want, and I'll go after it," she replied when I let her go. "Let's go get some closure."

Chapter Sixteen

Francesca

Once again, I found myself standing out in the surf, saying goodbye to someone I love. The only difference was this time, I wasn't alone. Damien's death was beyond tragic and senseless. He'd been loved and had given love. His life had just been getting started.

"Damien, I love you. I loved what we had and what we started. I loved that you protected me and made me feel safe. I loved that you were a gentleman; you were ridiculously happy about the baby and romantic. I loved the way you loved my brother and Jake. I loved that you took care of people, and I even loved the darkness in you. You were an amazing man, and our little boy will grow up knowing who you were. He will learn to treat people the way you did, with softness and kindness. I even love that you tried to force Jake to marry me. In reality, it was I who threw myself at him. Thank you for everything, Damien. Thank you for your countless sacrifices, selfless love, and the strength that poured off you. My fervent wish is that you are now with Caleb and my parents and have found a family with them. Nothing would make me happier," I said to the sky. "By the way, I'll take care of Jake."

"Demon, brother, we had some good years and some super shitty ones." Jake clutched my hand tightly in his, and his body swayed slightly with the ebb and flow of the waves. "Through it all, we had each other. Always. I always knew you had my back. This baby is going to know you. I'll do right by him and by Frankie. I know you've got my six still, Caleb too. It's our turn now to do things to make you guys proud. That's my goal. I love you, brother. Give Caleb a big old wet kiss from me; I know he misses them."

Short and sweet, but the heavy emotion in Jake's voice told me all that hid behind those words. He didn't need to say more. Damien knew how we both felt; he knew all the complicated emotions inside me. That was certain in my mind.

Jake stepped into my back, his body pressing into mine as he undid the container's lid we'd brought. He poured some of the ashes into his hand, then handed it to me, and I dumped the rest into mine. Together, we let Damien's remains trail into the vast Pacific, joining my mother and returning to the earth.

It was heartbreaking and poignant to say goodbye to two people you loved in six months. Damien had been a significant presence during my time with him. He still was, in a way. He opened me to love. Real love. To be fair, it wasn't just Damien. Jake had too, but I wouldn't have seen Jake in that way if it hadn't been for Damien. I wouldn't have recognized the things I do now.

A tiny bit of guilt crept in because I felt like I was

comparing them again, and I wasn't really. I had wanted both of the men from almost the start. Damien had wormed his way in fast and taken over, while my feelings for Jake had only continued to grow. Regardless, Damien had been life-changing for me. In good ways.

"Lost in thought, babe? Anything good?" Jake asked as we walked back to shore.

"Thinking about how big of a presence Damien was," I told him.

"That he was. Overseas, the only one with a bigger presence than Damien was your brother. I may have known Damien a couple of years longer than Caleb had known him, but those two were on a different level. I understand it now after those two letters pointed out they were in the same place mentally, but you are absolutely right. Everywhere Damien went, he was a large presence," Jake agreed readily.

"I hope he's at peace." I turned and looked back out over the ocean spread out before us.

"I'm sure he is, or he's close to it. The only thing that might keep him back is he's waiting to make sure our little guy is born and is healthy." Jake rubbed my belly, a soft smile on his handsome face.

I quickly sat on the log we had been on last night before I jumped him again. "How the hell I ever managed to land the two sexiest men alive, I'll never know," I mumbled.

"Well, with Damien, you only had to walk into the bar. With me, you wrote a letter to your brother," Jake sat down next to me, putting his arm over my shoulders and pulling me to him. "If I remember right, you called me pretty. I've moved from pretty to sexy?"

"Okay, Damien Junior will not learn how I met his father or his uncle daddy," I quipped.

"I have to admit the tequila filter was pretty hilarious." Jake kissed my cheek, then tucked my head into his chest. "Do you ever wonder what would have happened if you rode back with me?"

"I *know* what would have happened. You would have gotten laid if I could have gotten through your gentlemanly ways," I answered automatically.

"No doubt you would have worn me down in about two seconds. Damien was always more of a gentleman than I was." He buried his face in my hair.

"Liar. You are just as much of a gentleman as he was. I know the truth about you," I sighed.

"You do know the truth of me, babe. Even before you knew me, you did. I swear that sometimes as I was listening to Caleb read the letters, you talked to me," Jake's tone turned nostalgic.

"Sometimes, I was. Caleb had known. He'd thank me for it when he came home and talked about all the awful things he'd seen. I talked to both you and Damien. Foxy, and Demon. When Caleb wrote about you guys and the struggles, I'd speak to you. I'd carefully word sentences based on what I knew of you two and hope that my message of hope came through."

Jake was quiet for a few moments, then he released me and moved sideways a little so he could look at me. "How much of an asshole does it make me if I say I think we were always supposed to end up together?"

"I don't think it makes you an asshole at all." I

didn't hesitate in my answer because I believed it as well. "I believe the same thing. I think the fates, or the universe, or God, whoever, could have gone about making it happen in a better way than killing Damien, but I believe in my heart that I would always end up with you. These past few weeks have shown me that. I even think that Caleb knew it too."

"I think on some level Damien knew it too." Jake's smile was both radiant and sad. "Come on, let's get this letter over with." He dropped down to the sand again, leaning on the log like last night, and pulled me between his legs.

The future love of my life,

I'm coming home. General Allen said the word is they are going to pull troops in the next year, but I'm wounded and taking the training gig they offered us back in California. I can't do this anymore. More nights than not, I believe that this place, this war, has broken me permanently.

You may never know who I used to be capable of being. I don't even know anymore. I have no idea how I will adjust to life outside the military. It's all I've ever known. Boomer told me about a motorcycle club he's in, and I might look them up. He's in Washington, close to where Foxy lives, so it works out well. Still haven't decided what to do with that house of mine yet.

We are going to start searching for Ghost's sister pretty hard too. I need to fulfill my promise to Ghost. Plus, Foxy is head over heels in love with her. Maybe he'll get a happy ending. Ghost is a constant in both of our minds, and he's a weight in my chest that won't leave. A hole in my heart that will never heal. It's more painful than any injury I've suffered in this fucking war.

I'm sorry the man you are marrying is a broken mess. I'm sorry that I might not ever be who you need me to be. I promise to try. I'm going to spend some time on the boat before I go home. I wonder what you would think of it? To me, it's pure magic. I'd drop it in the ocean and sail wherever the tide took me if it were seaworthy.

Regardless, I'm coming home. I'm not sure it will ever feel like home, but I'm leaving this place and never looking back. I don't want ever to pick up a gun or knife again. I'm terrified. Would you think I'm weak if I said I was scared?

I don't know the last time I had a peaceful night's sleep or if I ever will. I only know I want to go to bed and not worry that someone will try and kill me in my sleep. I don't think that's unreasonable to ask for after all I've given.

Home. Are you my home, future wife? Will all this shit settle down once I have you? Am I doomed to torture you with my nightmares, or will they cease in your loving arms? However long it takes me to find you. I'm going to do it. I need to try. I need to prove I'm not my father and that I value relationships.

Foxy said he would apply for the police force once he's out. He wants me to do that with him, but picking up a gun and pointing it at someone makes me sick to my stomach. I can't do it. I can barely do it now to keep us alive, and I still have a team depending on me.

Foxy will go far. He'll probably even find Ghost's sister. I hope he does. I hope someday I can be the man he is. She deserves to know how fantastic Ghost was. Foxy deserves to find love too. This last tour over here has proven to me how strong he is. He still carries a picture Ghost's sister sent. He takes it everywhere he goes.

I wonder if she meets us, will she hate me? Will she hate me because I couldn't save her brother? I hate myself for it. I wouldn't blame her. It's laughable to think we'll find her. For all we know, she's married. We don't even know what she looks like; Ghost was so protective of her.

The thought of you, future wife, is what's keeping me going. I'll apologize in advance for clinging to you because I'm sure I'll latch on like nothing else when I find love. I've never had the love of a good woman. Jenny wasn't good, and she doesn't count. She didn't love me, anyway.

Be ready for me, future wife. I hope we have oversized closets to store all my baggage because I come with a lot of it. You'll have to love Foxy, too, because he is a permanent part of my life. I won't negotiate on that. Right now, he's the only human on this planet that I love. Hopefully, we'll meet soon, and I can add you to that list and contemplate burning these letters, so you never know how fucked up I truly am.

I'm coming home, and I'll be looking for you. I hope you are looking for me too.

Love,
Damien

After the Wreckage

Jake

We sat there in silence for about an hour. Holding on to each other and staring at the waves, the rhythmic crashing sound soothing our raw hearts. That letter was far less painful than the others, but I still heard their desperation. It was hard not to.

Francesca had turned sideways and cuddled into me as she had in the truck. I wondered if Damien had thought about these letters after meeting Francesca and had contemplated showing them to her. Especially after seeing the way she'd preserved the ones from Caleb. He *had* to have thought of them.

They were brutal. I was glad this was the last one we were going to open. What's truly sad is that so many soldiers come home feeling that way and ultimately take their own lives because of it. I was lucky that hadn't happened with Damien, given what I now know about his mental state.

Damien wasn't as weak as he thought he was, or he would have given in to the darkness that festered inside him. Damien fought against that darkness despite what he thought about himself; weak wasn't a word I would have ever used to describe him. It bothered me that he felt that way about himself.

I sighed as the first raindrops fell, but Francesca didn't move. I let myself smile a little at that. I'd sit here and get wet as long as she wanted me to. The rain was more comfortable to tolerate than the desert heat I'd been subjected to over the years; as I thought that, the skies opened and drenched us in minutes.

Francesca started laughing and turned her face up to it, the rain washing away the traces of tears I'd seen on her face. I had to admit it felt cleansing in a way. She wasn't one to bend her will unless she wanted to, and she wasn't going to let rain chase her off. I followed her cues and remained sitting there with her.

Soon enough, the squall passed, and we were left sitting there, soaked to the bones but ultimately lighter than we had been. Francesca pushed herself to her feet and held a hand out to me, pulling me up with her. We headed back to the truck, where I pulled out the towels I had in there, thankfully, and wrapped us both up before we climbed in and blasted the heaters to warm us up.

My phone rang as we pulled out onto the road, and I answered automatically without looking to see who it was. I cringed as Lisa's voice screeched out, "You got married?"

I glanced over to see Francesca's eyebrows raised and a curious look on her face. I truthfully had no idea how to handle this. I had never made promises to Lisa and had been completely clear on my intentions.

"I did," I replied slowly. "What can I do for you, Lisa?"

"Explain how you were coming over here to sleep with me a little over a month ago, and now you are married!" she screamed.

"How did you even know?" I asked stupidly.

"I went to the station to check on you." Lisa's caustic voice made my ears want to bleed. "One of your team told me you resigned and got married."

For the life of me, I couldn't read Francesca's face. I had no idea what she thought of this or how I could get out of it without being a dick. I had never wanted to hurt Lisa, but I also never wanted a relationship with her.

"Nice to meet you, Lisa. I'm Jake's wife, Francesca. Did Jake make any promises to you?" she asked sweetly.

A spluttering sound came across the speakers. "No, he didn't. He was quite clear about it only being sex. Did he tell you about me?"

"There's no reason he would have if it were only sex. I'm well aware Jake wasn't a virgin, and neither was I. However, he's been in love with me since probably oh-three. I don't fault you for being angry at him, but he didn't, *doesn't*, owe you any explanations."

"You're her? The one he's been chasing all these years?" Lisa's quiet question floated through the air.

"She is," I answered. "I never misled you, and I never meant to hurt you."

"I wish you all the happiness in the world," Lisa's tone changed to fake sincerity. "Goodbye, Jake." She hung up.

"Frankie, I'm sorry," I started to apologize, and she halted me.

"Why? I was engaged to Damien. It wasn't like I could take the edge off for you. You don't owe me any explanations, either. I've come to know you well enough to know that you would have told her the truth if you had made promises to her. That was pure angry, jealous female right there. If I had you on a line and lost you, I'd feel pissed too." Francesca reached for my hand.

"I wasn't in the market for a relationship because I was in love with someone else. I never lied to her. I told her from the start it would only be sex. I didn't give her any other details, but it was terms she agreed to. I never invited Lisa to my house; she didn't even know where I lived. I only went there when I needed the release," I told her, even though she said she didn't need the explanation.

Francesca lifted my hand to kiss it the same way I kissed hers. "I'm not stressed about it. You're mine now. I'd only get angry if she tried to come between us."

"I wouldn't allow that to happen. Are you going to get any of those phone calls?" I shot her a look.

"No. There wasn't anyone after Kevin. Well, sex-wise, there was. When my mom died, I took an orderly to a supply closet and fucked him. Grief sex. Nothing more. No one after except Damien," she said without shame.

"Grief sex? I didn't know that was a thing," I smiled at her.

"Sex was my go-to outlet. Sex with you is addicting," Francesca warned me. "Be prepared, I guess."

"Babe," I groaned, "I'm yours whenever you want."

Chapter Seventeen

Jake

"Club meeting, Mike. We'll meet at my house. Francesca will propose her idea, and she said she'd cook dinner too. Can you gather everyone?" I asked the co-founder of our club.

"Yeah, give me a time and text me the address. I don't think I've ever been there," Mike answered, sounding tired.

"You okay?"

"Rough night. Some kids decided to set off a ton of fireworks," Mike's weary voice came over the line.

"Oh shit. Trigger a flashback?" I breathed out. Thankfully the fireworks didn't trigger me quite as badly as they did some, and I think it was because I still went shooting at the range, so the sound was typical. However, there were times when the sound of fireworks had me diving to the ground.

"Yeah, you could say that. The way they were going off, it was like I was right back in the middle of a fight. I started screaming at my family to get down, and I tackled my daughter to the floor. The dog thought it was some sort of game and was trying to play, which was good because it quickly brought me back out of it, but I was on a serious edge. Scared the shit out of my wife," Mike filled me in.

"Bring her with if you can get a sitter. Actually, you can bring the kids, and I'll let Francesca know," I revised the offer, thinking quickly.

"I'd rather find a sitter. I'll bring Susie. What time?" he asked again.

"Hang on. I don't know." I jogged back into the house, "Babe, what time do you want them to come for dinner?"

"Um, how about five?" Francesca thought out loud. "If they arrive around five, I'll have it ready to eat at about five-thirty?"

"She said to have people arrive around five," I told Mike.

"Do you want me to have them all bring their spouses? That will be about twenty people," Mike said, hesitating. "That's a lot of work for a pregnant woman."

"Sure. I'd rather have spouses aware of what's going on than not. I'll help Francesca, so she's not doing it all herself. I won't have booze, though, for any of those who drink. If they want that, they'll have to bring their own. Make sure they know they'll need to be prepared to vote," I added. "I'll text the address as soon as I hang up."

Before I got back on the phone, I texted Mike the address knowing he'd make sure the ones that needed to show up would. I needed to make two other calls, but I'd wait until I was back outside.

"I told him it was okay to bring spouses, which means at least twenty people. I'll help you with dinner," I moved over to slide my arm around her. "What were you thinking?"

"Pasta. Twenty people? Hmmm, let's add a prime rib to that then. Give me twenty minutes, and then we can head to the store and over the house. I just want to finish this part on Margaret and e-mail it to her for approval," Francesca said distractedly.

In the past week that we'd been home, her belly had gotten a little bigger and now showed when she wore more fitted clothes. It was adorable. She also held her hands over the small bump now that movement was happening.

"Twenty minutes. Got it," I kissed Francesca and headed back outside.

I pulled out my phone and called Greg. "Hey, Greg, it's Jake. Francesca will pitch her 501(c)3 idea to the club today over dinner. Did you want to be a part of it?"

"Not yet. If the club goes for it, then at the next meeting you all have to talk about logistics, and how it will get run, I'll take part in that. The lawyer has all the paperwork drawn up, and we'll need to add specifics on a board of directors and officers for the group. How's she doing?" Greg asked.

"Good. Francesca has been working on her project a lot. Bump is showing now, and the follow-up appointment is next week. Her birthday is in three days. You going to come to the surprise party?" I checked back over my shoulder to ensure Francesca couldn't hear me.

"Yeah, we'll be there. Your new house, right?" I

could hear the smile in Greg's voice.

"Yep. In two days. Ireland is all booked and ready to go, right?" We were leaving the day after her appointment for our impromptu honeymoon.

"All set. I'll bring her new passport, the itinerary and everything else needed. I've got to say, Jake, I am thrilled that you've proven me wrong."

"About trusting me?" I wasn't sure what I had proven him wrong about; that was the only thing I could think of off the top of my head.

"I had serious qualms about you and Damien. While I didn't get a chance to get to know Damien, you have proved exceptional in all the ways that Frankie is. Her mom, Carolina, would have loved you," Greg doled out the rare high praise.

"Thanks, Greg. See you in a couple of days," I replied, humbled.

Next, I called Hector. "Hey man, how are you doing?" I asked when he picked up.

"Good. Party still on?" Hector had a smile in his voice too.

"Yep." I'd sent the e-tickets, but sometimes Hector wasn't quite as technologically advanced as he liked to think he was. "I'm just checking in to ensure you got the plane tickets I booked for you guys."

"I got them. Angela printed them for me. She's about as excited as can be. Are you sure you don't want us to stay in a hotel?" Hector asked again.

"Hector, we have three houses to choose from; personally, I think you would like mine. It will give you privacy and an awe-inspiring view of the water. Frankie's house is also private but more surrounded by woods. If you stay here with us, you might hear sounds you don't want to hear, but there is also a fantastic view of the water. Any of them is fine with me. You'll use Damien's truck; I'll have one of my club members bring it to the airport and park it in the short-term lot. He'll wait there with the keys. All you have to do is tell me where you want to stay, and I'll make sure you know how to get in."

"Your house is close to the one you are in now?" Hector asked.

"Both mine and hers are about the same distance, just from different directions. Both houses have separate bedrooms and bathrooms for you, and both have security systems," I told Hector. "Thirty minutes max driving time."

"Then I think yours with the water view would be a nice change of pace," Hector decided.

"Great. It's programmed on the GPS of Damien's truck already, so you'll be able to get there. I'll text you with the security info. Make sure Angela remembers it's a surprise. Frankie's got a little bump now, Hector. It's precious," I couldn't help adding.

"You will be an amazing dad, Jake," Hector laughed warmly. "Damien would be proud of you. I gotta get back to the farm now. See you soon."

I hoped Damien would be proud. I glanced back at the house and decided to make one more call. "Hey, Boomer," I said when he answered.

"No leads yet, man," was his clipped reply.

"Not why I'm calling. Frankie's birthday is three days away, and I'm having a surprise party for her the day before. Interested?" She liked Boomer for some reason, so him being there would make her happy. To be fair, he was a different guy around her, and he wasn't so bad.

"Seriously?" came the quiet question.

"Yeah, seriously," I returned. "Why would I joke about that?"

Silence, then, "I'm in. Thanks for including me. Text me the details."

I headed back in to finish the chores I'd started, namely the laundry, since Francesca's favorite thing to wear now was leggings, and they were all dirty. There was also an old Navy sweatshirt of Damien's that she loved to wear. I had just dumped the clean clothes on the bed when she came up behind me.

Her hands slid around my waist, over my abs, and straight down the front of my exercise pants. She stroked and cupped my balls while that precious little bump pushed into my back. I swear, the first touch of her fingers on me had me hard as a rock.

"Gotta say, I love it when you don't wear underwear," she purred and yanked my pants down.

I'd been with many women in my life, but none of them had the skills to make me forget my name until Frankie. Not only that, but she also could make my legs so weak I could topple over. Luckily, she seemed to know when that would happen and pushed me back on the bed so I didn't crush her.

The moment her mouth closed around me, I had no control over my body. She owned me and worked me until I begged her to stop. I didn't know if it was the pregnancy hormones or what, but she had worked herself up as much as she had me, and she couldn't get her pants off fast enough.

It was enough time for me to regain control of my body, shove the clean clothes off the bed and have her flipped and under me, her eyes heavy-lidded and her face flushed. "So beautiful," I murmured.

"Now, Jake," she pleaded.

I wanted to draw it out, but I couldn't. Francesca had me in a frenzy already. I knew the places to touch on her body to bring out maximum pleasure, and I set out to do that, knowing this would be quick. She was bucking up into me in no time flat. Just like that, it was over.

Once our breathing returned to normal, we trudged to the bathroom and showered off. "Babe, is this all pregnancy-related, or are you normally that active?" I asked her.

"I'm not sure. Until Damien and you, no one ever really got me that worked up before. Damien said he wanted to wait until I had feelings for him because it would make a difference; maybe that's it? I don't know. I only know I see you, and I want you. It hits hard and fast." She stepped out from under the opposite showerhead and moved towards me. "I'll tell you this and stroke your ego; nothing compares to you."

I wondered briefly If death by sex was a thing. "If you hadn't already drained me, we'd be going again," I groaned as she pressed into me.

"Later. We need to get to the store so I can get things going. What should I wear? Something nice?" Francesca stepped out of the shower.

I wrapped a towel around her. "Depends on if

you want them to pay attention to your words or your curves."

"Are you saying I should wear your clothes then?" She laughed warmly. "Mine are all tight right now."

I almost growled because when she wore one of my t-shirts, it had to be the sexiest damn thing ever. "Definitely not my clothes or I'll be too distracted to join the conversation. What about that stretchy green dress?"

"Oh, yeah, that's not uncomfortable." She dried her hair while I dried her off, then myself. I came back in and put the necklace I'd gotten her on our wedding day around her neck. She wore the ring Damien had given her on her right hand, and I loved that she kept it.

I went to put on some nice jeans and a shirt, and she was coming out of the bathroom, fresh-faced, smelling like heaven, and stunning in her naked glory with that green stone hanging right above her breasts. She was a vision.

"Jake, keep that up, and we will be right back at it again, drained or not," she warned with a gleam in her eye.

She walked into the closet and, a few minutes later, came out with the green dress on, a pair of green Converse, and a little white sweater to keep her arms warm. Her small bump was pushing against the dress's fabric just enough so that you knew it was there.

I fell to my knees, kissed her belly, and then stood up to do the same to her lips. "I love you so much. Do you know how excited I am to hear the heartbeat?"

"It was pretty amazing," she smiled. "I'm excited for you to hear it too. And see junior." She stretched up to kiss me again. "You look hot. If one of those grocery store ho's hits on you, I can't be held responsible for my reactions."

Francesca

I've never cooked for this many people before; it was a tad daunting. The easy way Jake and I worked together in the kitchen was fantastic and offset the nerves. We needed at least two hours for the prime rib to cook, and I got it seasoned up, and Jake got it prepped in the pan. We had at least an hour before it needed to go in.

I was making the sauce, and Jake had moved on to cutting the broccoli, cucumber, and carrots. This domesticity was bliss to me, pure domestic bliss. Damien had tried in the kitchen, but he was useless short of things he could put in the crockpot. He tried, though, and I had loved that too.

The house was a mix of smells that had my stomach growling like crazy. I finished the sauce, started making a spice cake and got that cooking in the oven while Jake cleaned up his mess and then sliced apples for me. He made me a peanut butter and jelly sandwich while I cooked the apples on the stove and fed it to me. Peanut butter was my new all-time favorite thing.

We pulled the cakes out when they finished, and Jake set them to cool on some racks while I made caramel. When the cakes were cooled and assembled, it was time to put the prime rib in the oven. I started making a salad, put it back in the fridge, and made the dressing. Jake got the broccoli in a pan and sliced and buttered the bread.

We finished with the prep work, so we got plates and silverware out and set them up buffet style on the bar end of the counter. When we completed that, we went to sit quietly outside. Jake started a fire in the firepit, and we cuddled, moving only to stir the sauce every so often.

Aside from sex, I think these quiet times like this were my favorite with Jake. We meshed so perfectly and didn't need words. Yet, when we did talk, the conversations were intelligent, and we could talk about anything. Jake was everything I had ever wanted in a partner when I had dared to allow myself to think of being married.

"Think they'll like me?" I asked Jake.

"Who?" he paused, rubbing my belly.

"The women. I've never really had female friends. I find so many of them are catty," I explained. "I do not see a ton of reasons to cut people down because of insecurities. I was on the receiving end of that too much."

"The women aren't the ones that will be voting on your proposal, and I've only met a few of them. The ones I have met were genuine and nice. Fuck them if they don't like you. If I hear cattiness, I'll make damn sure their men know I have no problem asking their spouse to leave. Not all the guys have spouses either. Some just date and those probably won't bring the girlfriends,"

Jake declared.

It wasn't much longer after that that we heard the low rumble of bikes approaching, and my nerves went through the roof. Large groups of people weren't my thing, and I tended to be very uncomfortable in those situations.

"Relax, babe. You've met Mike and Dave. This group of guys is very similar in attitude to how Damien and I are—were; God, I'm not used to that yet, as well as your brother. They want to help, are all vets, and are good guys." Jake kissed my head as we sat up.

We made our way inside, and I uncorked the wine we'd bought; someone might want some even though we didn't drink. I drew the line at beer or liquor, wine at least I could cook with if it wasn't drunk.

Jake went to answer the door, and the house filled with noise. It was startling because, for the most part, Jake and I were quiet. The volume would take a bit of getting used to if we were to entertain. I'd only met Mike twice, but I'd taken to him the first time. He was large, loud, and a teddy bear.

Mike came bustling into the kitchen to give me a boisterous hug and look me over. "How you feelin' sunshine?"

"Good," I grinned, "how are you?"

"Hungry! It smells fantastic in here!" Mike peered around me to see what was on the stove. "You went and got wine?" his eyes landed on the open bottles.

"I figured some might want it," I shrugged. "If not, I can always cook with it."

"Resourceful. Whatever you are doing for Jake,

keep doing it. I haven't seen him look this alive and healthy in years. Happy healthy." Mike hugged me again and moved out of the kitchen. "Here's my wife, Susie. Susie, this is Jake's wife, Francesca."

Just like that, the shy me from high school and college came screaming back to the surface. Susie was like a supermodel type of beautiful. "Hi," I said quietly. "Nice to meet you."

Mike gave me a confused look, then glanced at his wife. "Susie won't bite."

"Ignore this buffoon. You have no reason to be shy around me, Francesca. I'm nothing like the expression on your face says you think I am. Is there something I can help you with?" Susie offered, the genuine sincerity of her voice breaking through my frozen state of mind.

"No, I've got it under control. Sorry about that, I'm a bit shy in large groups of people," I apologized.

"Don't worry. The wives are cool. I'm not sure about the girlfriends. I don't know too many of them, but you've got me as a buffer. I'm a take no shit kind of woman." She eyed me in a friendly way, "Something tells me you are the same way."

"She is." Jake came in and moved around them to take up a position next to me. "Not only is she badass like that, but she's also got a heart of gold."

Susie looked between Jake and me and smiled an angelic smile. "This I like. You two are a unit, and damn, what a gorgeous couple you are. Do what you need to do, Francesca. I'll guide the loud group outside. I see a fire going."

"Told you," Jake said in my ear. "You might have just found yourself a new friend. Susie is good people."

"She also looks like a lingerie model," I muttered. "I haven't frozen like that in front of someone in a long time."

Jake moved to stand in front of me. "Babe, I would rather look at *you* in lingerie than Susie. You are what my fantasies consist of."

I blew out an exasperated breath. "You are one sweet talker, Jake. Go, entertain them while I finish up."

"Nope. I'm in here with you, helping you; that's where I'll be. Mike and Susie can entertain them. That wasn't sweet talk, babe; that was the truth." He kissed me quickly and then got the broccoli going while I started the pasta.

In what seemed like no time, we had dinner ready, spread out on the counter, and Jake was leading me outside, my hand held tightly in his. He let out a shrill whistle that had the group falling silent fast. I was impressed.

"First, before I set you loose on the feast my wife made, I'd like to introduce you to her. This beautiful woman is Francesca. Francesca, this is most of the Knights of Dawn, the motorcycle club that Mike and I formed," Jake Introduced me. "Now, like good soldiers, as you make your way inside, say hi to Francesca and tell her your name."

I almost laughed at his mocking tone, but I held it in. They did as Jake instructed exactly. They filed up in a line and introduced themselves and their spouse, if they had one, before going inside to get food. Mike, Susie,

Jake, and I were the last ones inside.

"Damn, Francesca, you did a lot!" Susie exclaimed. "You're like a wonder woman, aren't you?"

"You can call me Frankie," I told her, blushing. "Jake helped me."

"The Frankie thing is just for you two," Jake added. "Only friends call her that."

I loved how protective he was of me and my emotions. Susie grinned at me and winked. "Never thought I'd see the day this happened. Jake, you are whipped."

We all heard the sound of another bike. Jake glanced at Mike, who shrugged, "Probably, Matt."

"I got this," Susie put her plate down, "you've earned your food. Get yourself a plate." She moved around us and went to get the door.

I started dishing up some salad when I heard Susie curse. Both Jake and Mike instantly dropped their plates and made their way to Susie. Jake was in SEAL mode. His moves were stealthy and his body coiled with instant tension.

I rounded the corner to see Susie headed directly for me. "Let them handle it," she tried to steer me away.

"Hell no. Whatever is out there affects me if it affects Jake," I argued.

"What do you know of his past?" Susie whispered in my ear.

"Enough. Why?" I turned to look at her concerned face.

"Matt showed up with a new girlfriend, who happens to be someone Jake used to, um, see," Susie tried to word it carefully.

I suddenly laughed. "Not concerned even a little. Don't take this as me being cocky, but Jake loves me in a way he has never loved anyone else. That's a guarantee I'd bet a lot of money on."

"I knew you were tough," Susie smiled. "I never liked her. Jake only brought her to a few parties, but I always wanted to hold her head in the punch bowl until she stopped screaming."

"Okay, definitely call me Frankie," I hugged her, then moved to the front of the house where Jake looked about ready to pop a vein. I flicked my gaze over the woman, a fake smile plastered on my face.

The guy, who must be Matt, looked at me and smiled. "Hi, I'm Matt. Sorry, I'm late. Mike said I could bring a date, and since I had one scheduled already, I figured I'd just bring her."

"Hi Matt, I'm Francesca," I held out my hand, my other arm winding around Jake's back. "Dinner is ready, so go grab a plate." Matt's eyes were warm, but he gave Jake a concerned glance.

"Lisa, if you start shit, you can find your way to the door and sit on the porch until our business here is concluded," Jake's cold voice chilled me. So, this was the face behind the phone call.

She was curvy, which told me Jake liked this body style, but other than that, she looked used up. Bleached hair, fake tanned skin, lots of makeup, and dull brown eyes. Slightly taller than me, but other than curves, no similarities.

Lisa followed Matt without replying, and Jake

looked down at me. "Matt is new to the group, and he wasn't around the few times I brought her to some parties, so he didn't know there was history there. Her, on the other hand, I have to say, I think she planned this. I'm sorry, Frankie."

"Don't be, Jake. I can handle her. If she gets out of hand, I'll let Susie drown her in a punch bowl," I snickered.

Chapter Eighteen

Francesca

Dinner was a success. Mike and Dave did the dishes while Jake and I cleaned up the leftovers and made bags for some of the guys to take home. The only one that seemed to find fault with anything was Lisa, which I had expected, and it didn't bother me in the slightest.

"Ready?" Jake asked me with a soft smile.

"No, I'm suddenly nervous," I admitted. I felt like I would puke up the dinner.

"You shouldn't be. After that meal, half of the guys *and* their spouses are in love with you. You could ask them all to dance naked through the fire, and I think they would," Mike said, butting in. "You got this, Frankie."

"Pitch first before you offer them dessert," Dave said. "Otherwise, they will hear nothing because they are focused on the food."

"That's no lie," Jake laughed. "The cake she made for dessert would have them all groveling at her feet."

"Damn, woman, you make a cake?" Mike

stopped drying the pan and looked over at me.

I opened the microwave where I had stored it and pulled it out, the eyes of both men popping out. It was three layers of spice cake, with the apples Jake had sliced up, and I cooked between each of the layers. The caramel I made would get drizzled over the top.

"Yeah, talk first," Mike agreed. "I'm gonna run away with that while she's talking."

"No, he won't," Susie walked in. "I'll kick his ass if he even tries it."

I laughed along with Jake at the way Mike scowled at his wife. I slid it back into the microwave as Lisa walked in, asking for a restroom. Susie offered to show her with a nod at Jake, some sort of silent communication between them.

"Be right back, babe," Jake took off out the back door, and I saw him in conversation with Matt.

"Just telling him the lay of the land," Mike said from next to me. "She's tried to make Jake jealous by openly flirting or hitting on other club members. Lisa doesn't seem to get that he doesn't care. Jake never invested himself in her."

I put the pans away and wiped the counter down while Mike and Dave dried off their hands and flanked me as Susie returned with a surly Lisa in tow. Susie winked at me again, and led her back into the yard.

"She won't leave Lisa alone in the house. Susie doesn't trust her as far as she can throw her. That's the type of woman who will snoop as much as possible," Mike explained.

"There's nothing here of Jake anymore; it's all at

our house," I said quietly. "I'm thrilled we decided to do it here and not there."

Mike laughed wholeheartedly. "Come on. Let's get your pony show over with so I can eat that cake."

Dave socked him in the arm. "You have to share."

The baby chose that moment to make a bunch of movements that had me halting in my tracks, my hands flying to my belly. Jake cleared the yard in less than two seconds. "You okay?" he whispered, his hands settling over mine. His face lit up at the movements, and he crushed his lips to mine.

One of the guys whooped at the display, and I felt my face heat up. Matt walked up to us and interrupted the kiss.

"Hey, I called a car to come and get Lisa. If I had known, she never would have been brought here. Can you hold off on whatever business we are about to discuss until she's gone?" He looked down at his phone, "The car is five minutes out."

"I don't care if you date her, Matt," Jake nodded. "Just be sure of her motives."

"Look at her face, man. Lisa's not here because of me," Matt said without looking back. "I'm going to take her upfront and wait."

I agreed with Matt's decision, as well. I didn't want Lisa to know more about our lives than necessary, not if she was willing to go this far to strike back at Jake. "We'll wait," I told him. Matt gave me a grateful smile and left to escort Lisa out to the front.

"Looks like we both made some bad choices on who we horizontally danced with," I said with a quiet smirk.

"Did you only do it horizontally?" Jake grinned down at me.

I laughed a big belly laugh, drawing attention to us. "Oh no, stud. I'll be happy to teach you other ways to dance."

Mike and Susie snorted in quiet laughter as Jake scooped me right up into his arms. "Challenge accepted, babe."

Matt returned a few minutes later, apologizing profusely for the interruption and the unfortunate choice of company. Susie patted his arm and said a few quiet words to him, putting him back at ease.

I glanced at Jake, who had sat us down on a chaise lounge with me in front of him. "Guys," Jake said, drawing their attention. "I want you all to promise me confidentiality on what you will hear. Not because of law, but because of brotherhood and respecting privacy."

A round of agreement went through the group, and I took a deep breath in, my belly fluttering like crazy. I pulled Jake's arm around to settle it over my stomach. For whatever reason, Jake's touch soothed the little guy inside me.

"I'm going to tell you about myself before I propose my idea," I started. "The number of people that know my story I can count on one hand. But, for you to understand why you should consider my proposal, you need to understand where I'm coming from; I'm speaking to you now as Francesca Grayson, not Jake's wife."

Only one face seemed to register that name, which told me that someone else in Jake's club either knew Caleb or knew about him. My pause was long enough to make Jake start rubbing small circles on my belly, one of the things he did when he felt my emotions go haywire.

"My father died in the 9/11 attack. That itself is public knowledge. What wasn't public knowledge was that he was in the Pentagon, not the south tower, as the records say. I had just turned fifteen when my brother decided to join the military because of that event. Caleb Grayson was my brother. He was also my best friend. He applied for SEALs and made it through their program with all eyes on him. He got recruited to be a part of an elite team that few knew about," my voice broke a little.

"I'll fill in a bit here," Jake spoke from behind me. "Caleb was recruited to my team. Some of you know that 'elite' doesn't cover what we were, but you also know we can't speak much about it. Caleb was probably the best SEAL to have ever come from the program. Damien and I found ourselves another brother in him. The three of us were our own unit."

When Jake's voice cracked, I took back over. "Needless to say, when my brother died on a mission, it hit hard. Through his years enlisted, Caleb had become the one person alive I was closest to. I was a misfit. I graduated high school and had my AA at fifteen. Before I was sixteen, I enrolled in programs at college to get my bachelor's in nursing. I was twenty-two when Caleb died. At that point, my life took a radical turn."

Jake stepped in again. "What she didn't tell you is things I have mentioned to a few of you about my time in the service. Caleb and his sister wrote letters to each other frequently. Through these letters, we learned about Francesca, and she, in turn, learned about us. Those letters kept more than one of us going through pretty dark times. When we lost contact with her after Caleb was gone, we suffered. We'd made promises to Caleb to find her and watch over her. We never could find her."

"I had been working at the VA hospital with vets," I said when Jake paused. "I quit. It hurt too much. I instead took on temporary jobs in nursing, filling in when needed at various places. I started taking on photojournalist assignments and dragging my mother with me to places. One was a hike where I went to look at the wreckage of an old crashed plane."

"Holy shit, you're F. Gray," one of the guys burst out loudly.

"Guilty. That's the assignment that gave me an idea. Caleb's mental state had been declining the longer he was overseas. He'd have bad flashbacks, nightmares, and moments where he was utterly paralyzed and inconsolable when he'd come home. It couldn't be just him that this was happening to, and I knew from his letters it wasn't. I started to seek out vets and ask questions about it. From there, I decided to use photos to show faces of PTSD."

I took a breath, and Jake spoke again. "They aren't just photos. She's telling a story, showing faces if the person wants, and it becomes evident that people need to pay more attention to those around them. It showed me Damien in a way I wasn't expecting. I'm getting ahead of myself, sorry."

I stroked Jake's fingers. "Flash forward to this year, June. My mom had just died after a series of debilitating strokes. I was at the ocean spreading her ashes as she had wanted and having our yearly tequila shot to celebrate Caleb's birthday. A bad day for sure, made worse by events I couldn't have foreseen. I walked into the bar out of my mind with anger and grief, and I met Damien."

"The door to the bar slammed open," Jake reminisced with a smile. "I've never seen Damien react to a woman as he reacted to Francesca. My reactions had been the same, but at that moment, they only had eyes for each other."

"It's true. Damien told me that it was love at first sight for him. I was a bit slower on the ball with that, but I fell nonetheless. He asked me to marry him shortly after, and I said yes. The day we found out for certain I was pregnant was the day he died." My voice broke utterly then, and I had to swallow several times.

"You already knew I saw the whole thing," Jake said softly. Every eye was riveted on us as we bared our souls. "Things had been stirring with the Prince's, and someone was purposely trying to set Damien up because they blamed him for deaths that happened overseas; unjustly blamed him. Boomer and I were with Damien for the events we had gotten it narrowed down to."

"Jake was all I had left in the world. As much as I had loved Damien, I loved Jake just as much." I was terrified I was going to get judged for this. "I had repeatedly been told how much Jake had loved me in the letters I had received from Caleb. What I hadn't understood was that he was serious. Jake had been in love with me since back then. It was something I had started to see as I got to know them more. After Damien's murder, I latched on to Jake like you wouldn't believe. I couldn't even breathe if I was away from him. That scared me."

"Damien had tried to get me to promise to marry Francesca if something had happened to him," Jake added. "Damien always knew how I'd felt about her, and he knew I would take care of her. I wouldn't make the promise because I can't force someone to marry me. Even if I wanted to, and believe me, I did, and the guilt was tearing me up over it."

"I took the decision away from Jake," I started when I had control of my voice again. "I took off the day after the funeral, I needed air, and I felt like I was losing my mind. Grief and I were old pals, and after Caleb died, I floundered for months, trying to figure out how to get through it. I found what worked for me. Underneath it all, life never stopped, it kept going, and that's what I needed to do."

"I knew she was going to leave, Caleb used to get the same look on his face when he was overwhelmed, and Damien and I would schedule leaves to get him back on track. I hadn't expected to come back and find the house totally unlocked and no sign of her anywhere," Jake spoke of that day's memory. "Thankfully, Francesca texted me when the security on her house showed me frantically running through it."

"In that time between me leaving and Jake arriving, I'd made several decisions and plans and started to put a few of them in motion," I informed them, my eyes landing on Susie, who was wiping tears from her face. "I'd contacted an adoption lawyer because no matter what, this baby would have Jake as a dad, whether he wanted me or not. I'd decided to find a new place to live because my house had too many memories, and I'd decided to use my house as a base for a charity I was dreaming up."

"None of this I had been privy to before showing up and finding her lying so still on the floor that I thought she had died for a moment. There was a storm outside, and she'd had all the windows open. Once I realized she was breathing, I took a picture with her camera to prove that she was suffering just as much as I was. I picked her up, and we talked," Jake wound his fingers with mine.

"I asked him to marry me," I couldn't help the smile spreading across my face. "Despite the grief of losing Damien, I still loved Jake. I knew it would be hard, but we would navigate our way through it together, and I believed in my heart it was what Damien would have wanted."

"Wait," Mike interrupted, "you asked Jake to marry you?"

"Sure did," I smiled. "Best decision I have ever made. The next day, we got married, started looking for a new house, and started talking about my ideas for mine. Jake decided to add his to the idea, and we moved, and now here we are." Some of the guys looked at us like more than one donut was missing from the dozen, but no one said it.

"Every woman I dated was chasing the memory

of Francesca. No one held up to her; she had always been what I wanted. Once we realized who she was, I was resigned to a life with no love. At least no real love because Damien had claimed her. Their love was genuine, and I have pictures that show it. My love for Francesca is just as genuine. We might not have waited a respectable amount of time to do what we did, but rest assured, I wouldn't have married her if she hadn't been clear-headed when she asked me."

Susie sat up and looked over the group challengingly. "If one of you thinks they are wrong, take it up with me. Have you ever seen Jake look as happy as he does right now? Even after hearing that brutally heartbreaking story?"

I smiled at the woman. "Now for the proposal. I talked with Jake about making your club a federally recognized 501(c)3. You all do volunteer work to help out the community already. If we make you a charity, donations will get used to help you achieve your goals. Both houses can become safe houses or transitional places for vets needing to ease back into society or to hide a woman trying to escape a life of abuse. Either could get used as a meeting place, and we can get the word out to police stations, shelters, support groups that you guys are here, and what services you can offer."

"Offer, how?" one of the guys asked. "If it's charity work, we aren't paid."

"Correct, but people wanting to donate can donate, and those funds can go to pay someone in need of a job, even if it's just yard work. The donations can fund a salary for the charity's officers and maintenance on vehicles that get used in the line of work. To buy food for people temporarily housed. My original idea was for the charity to help vets since that is closest to my heart. Jake opened my mind to helping and including others, not just in this, but also in my project."

"Aren't investors hard to find?" someone else asked.

"Normally, yeah," I hesitated before answering. "I already have one. If you guys don't want to do this, I'll just start a charity. I only figured I'd ask you guys first because you already do this stuff. I've already talked with a lawyer and gotten the paperwork started for it."

"If it's a charity or not-for-profit, how will you offer to pay someone? I'm not following," Matt said.

"Investors' funding goes towards the not-for-profit, which gets funneled back into the charity. The board and officers won't have a paid salary. Not at first, I don't think, but we can offer paying jobs for assignments. For example, hypothetically, Mike is the president because Jake will be busy having lots of sex." There was a lot of laughter at that, and I continued. "Mike won't get paid for being president. But if he gets notified through a support group that a vet needs help transitioning into civilian life, there is something we could do to help. We could then offer a temporary job, say, clean the house and maintain the yard for three months, and provide room for him for those three months until he could find a job and a place to live. Or, if a woman was fleeing an abusive marriage, we could hide her and pay her to do something, based on her situation, until she was safe to come out of hiding. Along those lines, we could post a position internally for a bodyguard for a set time, and one of you could take the job and get paid to be a bodyguard. Follow?"

There was a round of agreement, and Jake posed a vote to see if they were interested in becoming a not-for-profit club. "Majority carries it," Jake clarified. It was unanimous, every guy there was excited, and for those with spouses, I was sure every one of those guys would get very lucky tonight.

I got up. "Now, I'll offer you dessert."

"Wait, you were holding dessert hostage until we agreed?" came a voice I couldn't name.

"Not until you agreed, moron. Just until you listened," Dave told the guy. "It was my idea."

"Good call on that," Susie stood to help me.

Chatter broke out behind us as we walked in, and I left Jake there to field questions because it had been hard to open up and share my story. As soon as we were clear of the door, Susie grabbed me up in a hug.

"Take no shit from anyone on your choice to marry. You and Jake are perfect for each other, and I'm not saying that to disparage Damien. He was a good guy, too," Susie pulled away to see tears in my eyes.

"He *was* a good guy, no worries about taking no shit. I loved Damien, Susie, I truly did. I also loved Jake more without even realizing it. I damn near snapped the head off of Jake's Chief for questioning our decision." Tears spilled down my cheeks, and soon hers joined mine.

Before I knew it, there was a kitchen full of wives sandwiching us in hugs. It was overwhelming, and I was happy to have Jake rescue me amidst all the protesting of a man butting into girl time.

"I'm allowed to help my wife." Jake ushered them all back out of the kitchen until it was just us. "You okay?"

"Yeah, I think so." He set me down on my feet and kissed me, framing my face with his hands. "We better stop, or the sex demon inside me will make a scene."

"Certainly, one of the guys will walk in, wondering where dessert is," Jake chuckled. We worked together to prepare the cake and then brought it outside and spent the rest of the night talking and eating. I wasn't alone anymore.

Chapter Nineteen

Jake

Today was Francesca's surprise party, and I was beyond nervous. Hector and Angela had arrived yesterday and settled in at my house. Now I needed to find a way to get Francesca out of the house so they could come and get set up.

They'd cooked up a storm this morning in preparation; that had been Angela's condition on agreeing not to tell Francesca. She got to cook. Since Francesca was crazy about Mexican food, I wasn't going to argue.

The last-minute invitation to Mike and Susie was a stroke of genius after I saw how Francesca had taken to her. Susie also knew a friend who would make a cake, and they would bring that. I had to get her out of the house first.

"Frankie!" I called out, not sure where she was in the house.

"You bellowed?" She popped her head out of the office.

"I need air. The weather is perfect, a little cold,

but I need some air. Want to go for a quick ride?" I tried. I didn't need to hide the nervousness in my tone; she would just take it as a sign I was struggling with something. Francesca didn't need to know my struggle was finding a way to get her out of the house.

"Okay. Do I need to change?" She stepped out of the office. She only had on leggings and a t-shirt.

"Yes, you need jeans and at least a coat," I marched towards her.

"Ugh, my jeans are all tight," she complained.

"Just don't button them," I suggested, leading her down the hallway.

"Only if you do the same." She grinned at me wickedly.

The thoughts that popped in my head weren't going to get us out of the house. "Ride, not crash, babe."

"Killjoy. Fine. Can I wear these shoes?" She had her Converse on.

"Not without socks." I turned, picked her up, and tossed her on the bed. I had her shoes and pants off in no time at all. "Hi, baby boy. We're gonna go for a ride. Want to get you used to a bike early." I kissed her belly.

I stepped away before Francesca could distract me from my mission and grabbed a pair of jeans and a thick pair of socks. "You grabbed the stretchy ones, good call," she wriggled them on, and my brain fried at the vision she presented.

"Socks," I reminded her and turned to grab one of my police sweatshirts that she looked better in than I ever did. "Sweatshirt *and* a coat."

"Yes, sir," she mock-saluted me. "Can we go to

my house? I want to check it over and make sure I didn't leave anything too personal there."

That was perfect! "You got it. I'll take the long route to get there. I'm going to grab our coats." I practically ran out of my room, texting Hector that I was leaving the house within five minutes. After getting his acknowledgment, I shoved the phone in my pocket and grabbed both heavy coats from the closet.

I turned in time to see her walking toward me, and I couldn't stop the smile from spreading across my face if I wanted to. "You are perfect." The sweatshirt hid every one of her curves, but I knew what was under it.

"You are perfect for my ego," Francesca let me help her get the coat on her. She had a mischievous look on her face. I grabbed her wallet and stuffed it inside of my coat pocket.

"Hands above the waist," I told her, seeing the heat in her eyes. "Later, they can go wherever you want them to." I locked up and got us going. The ride felt good as it always did; it also helped get my nerves under control. I'd never planned a party before.

By the time we arrived and parked in the driveway, she was frantic to get inside. "Need to pee!" Francesca shouted, running past me to enter the garage code and practically dove under it to get inside. She didn't even stop to silence the alarm. I shut it off and tried to keep from laughing.

"I'm going to go check on the back, make sure all is okay," I called out and headed towards the shed. We'd taken the gear out of there when we moved, but I still wanted to check it. I did a slow prowl around the back and, seeing nothing wrong, went back inside and locked the back door.

"Frankie?" I called out, not hearing any noise.

"Out front," she answered.

I walked back out the front and stopped dead in my tracks. Francesca had obviously forgotten the cameras we'd placed all over here, and I made a mental note to erase the footage after giving her what she wanted. She sat there on my bike, completely naked.

"Before you ask, no, I've never had sex on my bike or had a naked female on it. And yes, I can see that's about the change," I answered, stripping my pants off. "Maybe I'll keep this tape," I said quietly.

"What tape?" she frowned and then remembered the cameras. She tipped her head back and laughed. "Can't believe I forgot about that. I don't care right now. I want you, and I want it on your bike."

"There is no way I'm about to let this fantasy go unfulfilled," I told her. I'd never been naked on my bike before; it was different.

"Wait, this is a fantasy of yours?" Francesca asked, her eyes dropping to my lap.

"Babe, I think this is wet dream material for any guy that owns a bike." My voice came out like a growl. "Not only that, but this is also going into my top five of best times. All positions held by you."

I scooted her forward until she hooked her legs around me. I pushed between her breasts until she lay back over the seat, her body open for me and on display. She writhed as I rubbed myself along her.

"Jake," she begged, panting.

"If someone comes down your driveway, they are getting shot." This time I meant it to come out as a growl as I pulled her down on me. She locked her legs behind my back and started that roll of her hips that drove us crazy. I wasn't going to stop her; it felt too damn good.

I put my thumb over her sensitive nub and applied a small amount of pressure, so the friction made her cry out when she rolled her hips again. The positioning wasn't easy because I didn't want her to roll off the bike or lose balance and topple us.

I timed my strokes to her hip rolls. So that spot inside her rubbed just as much as my thumb was doing. Five minutes later, under the slow torture, she came apart, crying out and bucking her hips wildly. That was all it took for me to join her. The sight of her coming was enough for me under any circumstances. On top of my bike, it was even more potent.

"I don't think I ever have to worry about mediocre sex anymore," she panted.

I leaned forward to smash my face between her breasts and chuckled. "Certainly not if you keep doing things like that. I don't think I've ever taken off a pair of pants that fast before."

She ran her hands through my hair. "After I proposed, I had a thought that our sex life would never be boring, and I'm happy to announce I was right."

"Were you planning this before we left?" I asked, remembering the mischievous look on her face.

"Maybe. I didn't need to come here, but now that I'm here, I came," Francesca grinned and sat up, pushing me up. "By the way, we are certainly doing that again. You made a mess, though, and now I need to clean up, or the bike's vibrations will make all this mess come out and make a bigger mess all over your pretty leather seats."

I howled in laughter. "Oh babe," I clutched at my sides. "If I had known then that you were like this, I would have taken the first discharge they offered me and hitchhiked across the ocean to get back to you."

"I wasn't like this then. Not to this extent, but the potential certainly existed. Probably would have come out with a blast at the sight of you," Francesca admitted as I swung my leg over the bike and helped her up.

"Where are your clothes?" I asked.

"You walked right past them," she laughed. "They're inside on the floor."

"Give me a break. There could have been twenty elephants around us, and I wouldn't have known once I saw you on my bike like that. Not one rational thought existed." I patted Francesca's ass as I picked up my discarded clothes.

I locked the door behind us, followed her inside, and watched as she swung her hips, walking down her hallway. I'd done something right in my life to deserve this woman. Now I just needed to figure out what, so I could do more of it to show my gratitude.

Francesca

Jake had ridden us all along backroads, windy roads, hilly roads, and long stretches of nothing. It was wild. His riding wasn't anything like Damien's, who had gone fast, but not like this. It was exhilarating and scary both, and I loved it.

My adrenaline was running high when we got back home, and I couldn't stop bouncing in place, waiting for Jake to get off the bike. "That was amazing!" I squealed as he finally got off, throwing myself at him.

He chuckled lightly and unstrapped the helmet I hadn't even remembered I still had on. "I didn't scare you?"

"A couple of times you did, but then I knew I was okay because I was with you, and you wouldn't do anything to hurt me," I babbled excitedly. "It was thrilling. I want to do it again!"

"We'll do it again the next time the weather is nice. Once things ice up, the bike stays in; it's not worth the risk," Jake unzipped my coat and took my hand. "I'm glad you liked it."

He led us into the house and hung our coats up; my blood was still zinging in my veins. "Even the baby is excited," I gushed, the fluttering in my belly going crazy.

"He is? Maybe we'll make a biker out of him yet," Jake pushed his hand up under my shirt to press on my belly. "I love feeling this."

He pulled me towards the kitchen where smells emanated, confusing me since we'd been gone for over two hours. Jake flipped the light on, and several voices screamed out, "Surprise!"

I jumped about a foot in the air and stared open-mouthed at the gathered people. "Holy shit! Sex on the bike *and* a surprise party?" I blurted out.

"Madre de Dios! Hija!" Angela chortled happily. "Happy birthday! Sex on the bike?"

I blushed madly, realizing what I'd said out loud. Jake was biting his lip to hold back, and I heard the sound of muffled laughter from behind Hector. I moved and saw Mike and Susie grinning with Darius next to them, smiling widely. He waggled his eyebrows at me.

"Oh my God," I groaned. "That was without tequila. JTF, you are in trouble," I mumbled and pushed my face into his chest.

I heard Darius boom out a laugh. "Just like her brother! I can't believe she just called you JTF."

Hector came around the counter wearing a broad smile. "Amiga, you look beautiful. Happy birthday. Let me see that bump Jake keeps talking about."

Happy not to be talking about bike sex, I pulled off Jake's sweatshirt and pulled my t-shirt tight across my belly to show him off. It was still small, but it was there. "Feel, he's moving," I grabbed Hector's hand. "That's your godson."

Even Darius got up to feel, and then I noticed Greg. He smiled and waved. I was torn between happiness and embarrassment because I knew he'd heard my words. I made my way over to give him and his wife a hug.

"You've got yourself a good man, Frankie." High praise indeed from Greg.

Suddenly the adrenaline wore off, and I felt my knees sag. Someone caught me from behind before I dropped. "Whoa, Frankie. I gotcha," Darius said as he lifted me and carried me to the couch. "Sit for a minute."

Jake appeared instantly. "Babe, what's wrong?"

"She's fine," Susie pushed them both out of the way. "Excitement wear off?"

I nodded, then my stomach growled, and I shivered. I almost laughed, watching how fast Darius moved and threw the sweatshirt to Jake, who then had it over my head in a flash. "Nice teamwork," I told them.

"She's just hungry. With all the excitement she mentioned, I'm assuming her energy wore out." Susie grinned at me, "At least tell me it was parked."

I laughed at her expression. "Yep. I'm brave, but not that brave. What smells so good?"

Jake stood, looking sheepish. "Hector and Angela flew in yesterday and stayed at my house. They spent the morning making a Mexican feast and brought it over here after we left. Angela insisted she cook."

"Wow," I breathed out. "You guys all came here for me? You planned all this?" I looked back at Jake.

"Yes, to both," Jake bent to brush his lips over mine. "Do you want to come and sit at the table, or do you want me to make you a plate and sit right here?"

I held my hand out to him for him to pull me up. "I want to see the food. You might shortchange me. All this sex you keep demanding is wearing me out, and I need sustenance." I didn't even blush that time, but Mike and Darius roared in laughter.

Jake spluttered but pulled me up. "I think you

might be confused about who is demanding what, but I'm not stupid enough to complain."

"If he complains, Frankie, I'll come and take his place," Darius smiled at me and winked. I knew he wasn't serious.

Jake shot him a look that made me laugh. "I'll keep that in mind," I said, earning me a look from Jake. "What? We can set him up with Lisa."

Jake almost tripped. Darius lost his smile. "No. That bitch is crazy."

Now Susie laughed. "See? I knew it all along."

I tugged on Jake's arm. "This is unbelievable. I'm so happy that I could pee my pants right now, but I'm more hungry than anything else. Thank you!"

"Don't sneeze, hija. You *will* pee your pants," Angela advised, and Susie and Greg's wife laughed and agreed.

We ate dinner, talked, and laughed so much my sides hurt. I felt torn between laughing and crying; I was so happy. I wished Damien could have been here with us. It was the life I had always dreamed about having, and Jake made it happen. Darius, Mike, and Jake cleaned up after dinner while the rest settled in the living room.

Greg talked about the Knights of Dawn and the meeting he would set up for when we returned from Ireland. Susie and Mike both asked intelligent questions, and Darius listened with an attentive ear but didn't say anything.

When they all came back into the living room, Jake pulled me up from the recliner and then sat down in my place, pulling me on top of him. "Just making sure

Boomer doesn't have any openings."

Darius snickered and sat on the couch next to Angela, who gave him an appreciative look that he didn't know what to do with that made me giggle. Mike and Susie sat together in the other recliner, and Greg and his wife took up the other end of the couch. Hector sat on the fireplace.

"How's your project going, amiga?" Hector asked me.

"Pretty well, honestly. Jake's lined some good things up for me, and it's coming along nicely. I've gotten some of it laid out now. Want to see?" I asked. A resounding yes came from the room.

"Before we do that," Jake interrupted, "Greg has something for us."

I looked over at Greg expectantly. "Your passports, updated. Your itinerary and a gift from Annie and me," Greg handed me the envelope.

I pulled it open and looked over the itinerary. "Did you plan this, Greg?"

"Not entirely. Jake gave me the stops that your brother was in love with, and I planned around those and added some that I knew you would enjoy," he gave me a soft smile. "Hopefully, I'm not wrong."

I glanced it over excitedly. "It looks phenomenal to me." I opened the other envelope and gasped, looking back up. "You guys are sending us to Scotland?"

Jake made a surprised sound and looked down at the picture in my hand. "A castle?"

"Annie's family has a distillery there in an old castle. They rent out the upstairs rooms for special

255

parties, so we called them and had them reserve them for you. It's in a beautiful location, not far from Loch Ness in Inverness. Then you'll move down to Edinburgh. The highlands are amazing; it's one of my favorite places. Edinburgh is beautiful, too," Greg told us.

"Have you been there?" I looked at Jake, who looked stunned.

"No. We only went to Ireland, and your brother fell in love with it, so we didn't make it farther than that," Jake looked over at Greg. "This is amazing. Thank you."

"Well, since we are doing this now," Angela stood up and went and grabbed a bag I hadn't noticed. She handed it to me. "I started this shortly after I met you."

I pulled out a beautiful quilt. "You made this?" I gasped. A patchwork of designs made up an extensive design in the center, hand stitching throughout. It was incredible.

"I did. I wanted you to have a wedding quilt. I almost stopped when Damien died, but I kept going when Hector told me you were marrying Jake. Unfortunately, it wasn't in time for the wedding, but it is in time for your birthday," Angela gave me a beatific smile. "I put some mojo on it to give you lots of babies."

Jake laughed at that and pushed me up a bit so I could get up and hug her. "I love it, Angela. Thank you. I already told Jake he had to give me lots of babies."

"You say that now. Get through that one first, " Susie giggled.

"That's what I told her," Jake grinned back at Susie. "Not that I'm not going to give her exactly what she asks for; we will fill the world with life."

"Famous last words, brother," Mike quipped. "Get used to no sleep."

"I'm already used to that," Jake's tone was a bit more somber then, and I went back to his lap and tucked the blanket around us. "Should I call that the baby maker blanket?" he asked Angela.

"Well, you can, but it won't work until the other one is out of her," Angela laughed.

Susie got up and brought me a card. I opened it, read it, and then saw the gift card. "Pregnant massage," I said out loud.

"Save it until closer to your due date. Trust me, you'll need it," Susie said wisely.

"Thank you!" I slid the gift certificate back into the card so I didn't lose it. "You guys didn't need to do anything like this. Dinner was perfect."

"Sometimes, amiga, you touch people without even knowing you've done it," Hector said gently and gave me a gift.

"Ditto to that," Darius joined in and set another gift on my lap.

Jake moved his hands to my belly and started rubbing small circles on it, sensing my emotions were about to boil over. I opened the gift from Hector to see a picture of Damien, sprawled out on the boat's deck, relaxed, gorgeous, and almost peaceful looking. The shadows still showed in his eyes, but this was a very true-to-life picture of Damien in his favorite place, and it had tears forming in my eyes before Jake even looked.

I pushed off Jake's lap again and hugged Hector

tight. "It's perfect, thank you," I whispered.

The picture had hit Jake hard too, and his glossy eyes met mine as he stood to thump Hector on the back and set the photo on the shelf in the room. Darius swallowed and looked down at his lap, saying nothing. There wasn't anything to say, and while it was emotional, it was also a beautiful gift.

"Maybe you should wait to open that one," Darius said softly.

"Nonsense," I chided him just as softly. I pulled the paper off to reveal an album. I braced myself for another picture of Damien, but instead, I saw my brother smiling back at me. My throat closed up, and Jake sat forward, holding me tight.

Various pictures of Caleb from overseas lined the pages, with brief descriptions under them. Jake wiped the tears from my face before they fell on the pages, and together we looked at each picture. Some made me smile, and others were ripping at my heartstrings. Darius brought him back to me. He gave me a piece of himself, along with Damien and Jake.

I tapped Jake's hands, and he let me go, and I curled onto Darius's lap and hugged him while I cried. "There is nothing you could have given me better than that. Thank you, Darius. I love it."

"We all loved him, Frankie. Through him, we all loved you. Hector said it; you have no idea how many of us you touched. I don't even think you know how much of him you have in you. Sadly, playboy, he was completely in love with you as much then as he is now. My favorite memory is still him getting punched in the dick for saying he loved you," Darius tried to ease the emotions in me.

Jake chuckled. "I think it was Caleb's favorite memory too."

"Can I see?" Greg asked. Jake handed the book over, and Susie and Mike joined them in looking through the pictures.

I kissed Darius on the cheek. "Thank you so very much. That couldn't have been easy to put together. Not with both of them gone and you being there for both."

"It was easier knowing you were with Jake. I'll admit that freely. That man will be by your side for everything, Frankie. That's why I did it. I knew you wouldn't suffer as much seeing those pictures if Jake was with you, and it was a way to bring a little of Caleb home to you," Darius let me go and pushed me back to Jake. "Go back to your man before he tries to punch me for feeling you up."

I laughed through the tears. "You already felt me up earlier, and Jake didn't punch you."

"He wanted to," Darius said with a smile. "Now show us your project. I don't know what it is."

I grabbed my laptop and settled back down on Jake's lap while he set the TV up to mirror the screen, and I took them through the pages I had laid out. The most emotional pictures were of Damien. I hadn't added Caleb's yet. Hector and Margaret showed so much hope that it shone through the memories.

Mike cleared his throat roughly. "Damn, Frankie. You should have just shown this the other night, and every single person there would have agreed without the story. I know a couple of people I can ask to talk to you if you want."

"Me too," Darius offered, a distant look on his face.

"Jeez, I want you to take pictures of Mike and me now. You are good," Susie breathed.

"Anytime," I offered. "Goes for any of the club. It doesn't have to be for this project."

"You don't have Jake in there," Angela pointed out. "Why?"

"I just haven't gotten there yet. Same with Caleb." I flipped through the photos until I found the ones of Jake I wanted to use. "He'll be in there."

"Babe," Jake whispered urgently, "Boomer is almost triggered."

I shut the program down immediately and stood up. "Darius, help me scoop ice cream." He stood up woodenly and followed me, Jake right behind us. I plopped a container of ice cream down in front of him, and Jake grabbed a cake I hadn't even seen. "Where'd the cake come from?"

"Susie brought it; she has a friend who makes cakes," Mike called out.

I handed Darius a scooper and set bowls in front of him. "Scoop ice cream into each bowl. Stay with me, Darius. Whatever is fighting you is in the past. You are safe here, in our house. If there's something you need, tell me."

"You're doing it, Frankie," Darius said in a low and dangerous tone. "Keep me busy."

I pulled the cake away from Jake. "After you

scoop the ice cream, slice up the cake. We aren't going to sing because if I learn that Jake can sing, on top of the way he looks and moves, I'm going to chain him to the bed."

"That's sexual harassment, babe," Jake protested with a smile.

"Maybe so, but you like it," I fired back at him. "I mean, come on; you can't be perfect."

"Oh, he's not. That boy can't sing to save his life," Darius said, the tone a little too even for joking, but he was trying.

Chapter Twenty

Jake

"Frankie, are you packed?" I called out to her from the bathroom.

"No," a forlorn voice called back. "Nothing fits."

I stifled a laugh. "Pack your leggings. You can wear all my t-shirts if you want to. I happen to think you look sexy, so don't tell me you don't."

"You're biased. You have to think that," Francesca walked in, pouting.

"No, I don't. When you were sick and didn't know you were pregnant, I thought you looked dead." I went with brutal honesty.

"Point taken," she laughed. "All I have is leggings. We might need to stop at the store on the way back from the doctor's appointment."

"We'll do whatever gets you packed and on the plane tomorrow," I promised. "A honeymoon without you would suck."

"A honeymoon without me would get you a very pissed-off wife." She hopped up on the counter while I finished shaving. "I liked the stubble."

"It'll be back. I need a trim too. I'll get one while you shop," I decided.

"What?" Francesca cried. "You can't cut your hair!"

"Trim, babe. Not cut. I don't want short hair again, but I don't want it as long as Damien's. You'll still be able to pull it when I'm not behaving." I leaned over to kiss her. "Mmm, you smell good."

"That," she murmured, "will make us late for the appointment. Finish your primping."

"I just heard Caleb come out of your mouth!" I called after her retreating form.

I came out to see her sitting cross-legged on the bed, wearing one of my sweatshirts, leggings, and green shoes. She looked impossibly young and stunning. This woman made my insides melt; I turned my back to her. "Hop on. I feel the need to give you a piggyback ride."

"If you wanted my legs wrapped around you, just say so. I'll be late for that appointment," Francesca grinned widely.

"If you don't know by now that I always want that, then I can't help you. Now zip it, and hop on," I retorted.

We made it to the appointment with minutes to spare, and I eyed the stirrups on the table with mild discomfort. Francesca laughed at the look on my face. "Be happy you aren't a woman and subjected to those evil things for the rest of your life."

"I'm well aware you are the stronger sex," I admitted freely.

"Nice to see you again, Captain Foxwood," my

head snapped around as Dr. Waters walked in.

I stood to shake her hand. "Likewise, Dr. Waters."

"Francesca, how are you feeling?" Dr. Waters settled onto the stool at the end of the exam table.

"Horny, tired, and sometimes restless," she listed off.

"All to be expected. Anything that concerns you?" Dr. Waters crossed her legs and looked between us.

"Francesca got very weak the other day out of the blue. Weak enough, she dropped," I told her. "Is that normal?"

"Depends on the circumstances. Fill me in," Dr. Waters pulled out the tray to the computer and made some notes.

"Well, I hadn't eaten in a while. Went on an exciting motorcycle ride, had some outstanding sex, came home to a surprise party, then dropped," Francesca summed it up. "Not quite in that order, but the dropping."

"Certainly, the lack of food can cause that to happen, especially coming down from an adrenaline high. You need to remember to eat regularly. Is that the only time that's happened?" Dr. Waters made a few more notes.

"Yes," Francesca told her. "We've also been feeling little flutters, which I didn't think would happen yet. Jake's touch seems to calm him down."

"Each pregnancy is different. It's not unheard of to feel movement at this point. No pain during sex, cramping, unusual swelling, or spotting?" Dr. Waters listed off.

"No, nothing," Francesca told her.

"I'm going to do a physical exam, and then we'll do an ultrasound. Scoot forward and into the stirrups." Dr. Waters stood and helped put Francesca's feet in the contraptions. I stayed up near Francesca's head while the doctor rooted around down there.

"He's sitting in a different position than normal, but it's nothing to be concerned about; if he shifts, you'll probably start to show more. Right now, he's kind of growing towards your back. You might have back pain or feel like you have to pee a lot if he rests on your bladder," she stated. "Your uterus isn't tilted; he's just shifted around."

"It doesn't mean anything bad?" I asked, trying to keep the fear out of my voice.

"Not at all." She stood and took Francesca's feet out of the stirrups and moved her back on the table. "Your blood work is normal. Your hormone levels for estrogen are on the low side of normal. I'm not concerned and will continue to watch it. I do want you not to fly after you return from your trip."

"Do we need to do Lamaze classes?" I thought to ask.

"I'd recommend it. Do you know how you would like to have the baby?" she asked Francesca.

"Natural would be my preference, though I will do whatever you suggest. Jake has to be in the room with me. I talked with an adoption lawyer, and Jake will be adopting him, but we'll put Damien as the father on the birth certificate. Jake and I are married now, too," Francesca filled her in.

Dr. Waters looked at me levelly. "I'm glad you took my advice."

"What advice?" Francesca looked between us.

"To heal together," Dr. Waters told her gently.

"I remembered our talk from when your husband died. Damien and I are together in a different dimension. This one, I'm supposed to be with Jake," Francesca's shy voice came out.

"I think so, too," Dr. Waters patted her hand. "How about we take a look at your little guy? Are you ready to see your son, Jake?"

A thrill went through me at Dr. Waters's words, and I imagined how Damien felt when he was in this spot. "Sorry, I just got thrilled and sad simultaneously," I choked out. "I'm ready."

Francesca grabbed my hand and held it to her cheek as Dr. Waters spread some gel over her little belly, and then the tiny little rapid heartbeat filled the room. "Look, right there," Dr. Waters pointed to the screen. "That's your son."

I burst into tears. "I'll give you as many as you want, you amazing woman."

Dr. Waters printed off some pictures for us. "This was no less emotional than your last appointment, but I'm sincerely happy to see the love between you two. Six weeks, be back here unless something concerning happens. Have a good trip."

"Thank you, Dr. Waters," I reached out to grasp her hand again.

"Be happy, Captain Foxwood," Dr. Waters said gently. "See you two soon."

I helped Francesca sit up and waited while she put her pants back on and then swooped her up to plant kisses all over her face. "I know I didn't make him, but I love him like I did."

"That's what makes a true father, Jake." She clung to my neck and held me.

Francesca

"I need to walk a little bit," I stood and stretched as much as I could in the space between seats. At least we were in first class. "Want to join the mile-high club?"

"I do," the elderly gentleman across the aisle answered me. I bit my lip at Jake's scowl.

"I think my husband might object to that very kind offer," I winked at him.

"I don't blame him. If I see you head to the restroom, I'll trip anyone who heads that way," he offered slyly.

Jake finally laughed. "The last thing she needs is encouragement."

"Live a little, kid. I miss my wife every day," he gave me a conspiratorial wink. "He won't turn you down."

"I know he won't," I held back my laugh. "Will they get mad at me if I pace?" I asked Jake.

"Not likely." He turned to face me, "Turn around."

I turned, and he rubbed my lower back for me. We still had about four hours of flight time left, and sitting in the same position was getting to me. My hips were stiff, my back was sore, and my shoulders were tense. I was ready to lay flat on the floor in the middle of the aisle.

"Hips," I told him quietly. His hands moved to rub over my joints, and I let out a small groan. My belly also went crazy with movement. "Wow. Jake, feel."

Jake slid his hand around my belly, and I heard his quiet exclamation sound. "He's active."

"Stir crazy, probably like his mom. I'm not used to sitting still this long," I said softly. "I also suddenly want an apple, and I know that's a bad idea because the resulting gas might blow the plane up."

Jake let loose with a surprised laugh. "I love you, Frankie."

I bent forward to kiss him and then slid past him and paced a little bit until the people in front of us glared at me as if I were invading their space. "Jeez, no compassion," I mumbled, moving back to sit down.

Jake turned sideways in his seat as best as he could. "Move the armrest and lean up against me. Try to rest, maybe."

I did as he suggested, and he slid a hand around me to rub my belly, the soothing motions soon putting me into a sort of sleep state. I was woken up a couple of times by some bad turbulence, but Jake had the magic touch and was able to lull me back to sleep until we started to land.

"Flying while pregnant is not fun," I told him,

anxious to get off the plane.

"I don't imagine flying with a baby or toddler would be either," he pointed out.

I almost ran off the plane when they let us disembark, but the thought of being tackled by security wasn't exciting, so I managed to maintain control. I was just happy to be up and moving around. "Do you know how to drive here?" I turned to ask Jake.

"It's just the opposite side of the road. I think I can manage that. We don't have to, though; Greg arranged a driver for us." Jake led us to the baggage claim, and we waited for our luggage. Jake waited, that is. I jogged in place, stretched, and paced.

"Foxwood?" I heard and turned around to see a man about our age, or Jake's age, standing there. He wasn't as tall as Jake, and his eyes were a glacier blue color. Muscular but lean and with a messy head of dark red hair.

"Yes?" I answered, glancing back at Jake.

"I'm Finn. I'll be your driver while you are here," his smile was slight, and he held out his hand. I took it out of habit, and a chill went through me at the contact. Handsome and cold. Something about this man felt dangerous to me.

"Francesca," I answered, pulling my hand back. "My husband, Jake, is the one wrestling with our suitcase."

Like magic, Jake materialized behind me as if he felt my unease. "Jake," he held out his hand, his posture unusually stiff. His SEAL persona slid into place quickly.

"Dublin is usually safe, though there are a lot of

petty thieves. Keep your purse safe or hidden," Finn advised coolly.

"My wife is perfectly safe in my presence," Jake clarified. "Thank you for the words of caution, though; I appreciate it." Something flickered across Finn's face that Jake caught. "She'll be in my presence all the time."

"I don't know what's happening here, but this is our honeymoon. It's supposed to be fun. If you are going to be creepy and keep us from having fun, I think I'd rather take my chances driving. I'm pregnant and irritable at the moment from ten hours on a plane, which is not a good combination. I'm not some helpless female, and I'll rectify that if someone gets too close to me for my comfort. If someone touches me, you can be damn sure that Jake will be intercepting that. Think you can chill the fuck out and get us to wherever we are supposed to be going?" I snapped.

"Aye," Finn finally smiled. "You'll be fine." Finn led us out to a Mercedes and loaded our suitcase and bags. I tuned out while Jake talked with Finn and just took in the scenery as we drove to the hotel.

"Babe, are you listening?" Jake's voice broke into my thoughts.

"Nope, sorry. What?" I turned to look at him. After ten hours of flying, the man looked perfect. Damn him.

"I'll need an explanation for that look you just gave me," he started. "Finn was telling me about a few places that aren't on the itinerary that he thinks would be great for your assignments."

"Is there a question in there?" I realized I was

grumpy, but my back was sore, and I wanted a bath and to lay down.

"Are you interested, or do you want to stick solely to the itinerary?" Jake chuckled.

"I'm down for whatever. After a day to recoup. Nothing until tomorrow, or I'm going to be downright bitchy," I said with no apology in my voice. I stared at the city around us, but Jake was paying attention to me now. "I'm okay," I told him.

He quietly scoffed but took my hand in his and rubbed my palm while resuming talking with Finn. Dublin was a sight. A mix of modern and old, and I loved it already. I really couldn't wait to get out and explore, but I needed rest and a little bit of Jake.

Chapter Twenty-One

Jake

Once Francesca had gotten over the flight, she was a whirlwind. We'd been to so many places in the three weeks we'd been here in Ireland, and it was dizzying. Giant's Causeway, Cliffs of Moher, Blarney Castle, Ring of Kerry, National Trust Carrick-a-Rede, the Dingle Peninsula, Newgrange, I was losing track of all the places we went. She had a blast on a tour of the underground tunnels and reveled in the ghost stories and legends.

Finn took us to local spots for some views that left you breathless, and it was in these places Francesca fulfilled her assignments, along with including some of the popular attractions. Much like Caleb, she felt drawn to the cliffs of Moher.

"I swear I can see faeries dwelling here or hear a banshee's wail," she said, looking over the pictures.

"I don't think I want to hear a banshee's wail. If I remember right, that's not a good sign," I kissed the top of Francesca's head.

One of the contacts I'd reached out to had finally

gotten back to me and had a person willing to talk to Francesca about their story of being sold into sex slavery. I worried because she had woken up from nightmares about Damien's death twice. Woken up with such violent screams ripping through her, it had almost sent me over the edge.

I didn't know why they were happening now, she'd had a few immediately after Damien's death, but there hadn't been any since we'd gotten married. Her screams had been loud enough to rouse Finn from two rooms over, and he'd practically kicked the door in, thinking we'd gotten attacked.

Greg hadn't just hired us a driver; he'd hired us protection disguised as a driver. Finn had been part of the Irish army, but that's all I'd gotten from him. He was more close-lipped about it than Damien or I had been about our time in the service. Finn stayed in the same places we did and kept us in sight without intruding.

Ireland was far safer than many places back home and worlds different from what I had seen in the Middle East, but I appreciated Greg's gesture. Especially now that I had seen the baby and heard his little heartbeat, I'd do anything to keep Francesca and our little one safe. I no longer thought of him as Damien's baby; he was ours. All three of ours.

I felt terrible thinking that way at first, but it faded as the memory of Damien's last words echoed in my head. He'd been telling me that this baby was all of ours. Unquestionably, I planned on giving Francesca one of my blood; the thought of many kids with her was thrilling.

"What do we have left to see?" I asked, laying back on the bed.

"Carrauntoohill, The Burren, Croagh Patrick, and I think there was some other cliff thing that Finn mentioned we should see. Are you bored?" she closed the computer and rolled into me. Her belly was getting a little more pronounced now, and I loved it.

"With you? Impossible to be bored around you, Frankie. Seeing things through your eyes is wild and exciting. Your enthusiasm is palpable, and I've never felt more alive. I could do with fewer suspension bridges, though." I stroked my hand down her side.

"I agree," she shuddered. "I can't believe I made it over without peeing my pants."

"You stopped to take pictures!" I exclaimed. "I about had a heart attack from the bridge and because I was worried about you falling. Did you not notice how much I was sweating? And there you were, showing your usual no fear will stop me face."

"I had to get a picture," she declared. "Because that was a once in a lifetime thing. Not doing that again, but I'm glad we did." She giggled. "I doubt Damien would have let me cross that bridge."

"You are right on that," I tapped her nose. "Damien probably wouldn't have let you get close to the cliffs either. Not with this little one in there." I moved to rub her belly and felt movement. It awed me to no end feeling that.

"Tell me about this person we are meeting tomorrow," Francesca urged me.

"I don't know a lot other than she was sold into

sex slavery and is no longer a part of it. I don't know how or anything else, but she was willing to talk with you. I have no idea how to pronounce her name, either. She spells it S-a-o-i-r-s-e. Sersee, maybe?" I tried.

"Probably not correct. I'll find out tomorrow. Right now, I think I want to make you my sex slave," she rose and straddled me.

"Babe, you owned my ass the minute I met you," I said lightly.

"It's a pretty nice ass, too," she stretched to try and pin my arms above my head, but she wasn't tall enough. "Damn it. This scenario isn't working. I was trying to be sexy and dominant."

"Want me to hold them up here?" I asked, trying to be helpful and not laugh.

She looked down at my face. "You better not be laughing."

"I wouldn't think of it," I managed to say without a chuckle, but it wasn't easy.

"Liar. Don't move," she ordered me. Francesca took over complete control of my body. I'd say I lost more of my soul to her, but she owned that too, along with my heart and body. Francesca was a storm, not one that destroyed and wreaked havoc. She was a storm that people chased just to watch its beauty.

After she wore us both out, I was thankful for the peaceful night's sleep, with no dreams. I had a feeling today's interview was going to be a hard one. We ate breakfast quietly, and then Finn drove us to a quiet neighborhood in a remote village.

I could smell the sea air on the breeze, and the

houses were all small and quaint, well kept. It gave me the impression of a place older couples would live, but that could be my thoughts as places like this at home mainly were elderly.

Finn stayed back in the car while Francesca and I went up to knock on the door. Maybe only a few years older than me, a man answered the door to my complete surprise. It just proved that I shouldn't base things on how they look.

Francesca beamed at him and introduced herself, his rigid expression thawing under her relaxed tone and manner. I introduced myself, standing behind Francesca, content to let her run the show. We followed him inside, me having already forgotten his name, and I took in the home.

Clean, modest, and simple, yet warm and inviting. The man offered us tea, and Francesca accepted. He left us in the sitting room, as he called it. "What was his name?" I whispered to her.

"Colin." She elbowed me lightly.

A stunning creature chose that minute to walk into the room, silencing us. Beautiful for sure, but broken inside. I'd seen the look in the woman's eyes many times across the years, and it never failed to invoke the beast inside me that demanded I protect.

She was tall, willowy, with eyes the color of steel. Her hair was mid-length, stick-straight, and a light brownish color. She exuded a fragility that spoke to me on a base level, and yet there was strength to her that told me she wouldn't break easily again.

"Francesca," my wife introduced herself. "This is

my husband, Jake. I'm sorry, but neither of us knows how to pronounce your name."

"It's pronounced ser-she," she told us with a distant smile. "I understand you want to take pictures; do you mind if we do that out by the sea?"

"Whatever makes you comfortable is what we will do," Francesca assured her.

Saoirse was satisfied with that answer. "I was born in an impoverished area. My father worked the land, and my mother was too sick to do much of anything. She ended up selling me," Saoirse started immediately. "My father didn't know until they came to take me. He didn't argue either. I was one less mouth he had to feed. I don't know how she found out how to sell me, and in the end, it doesn't matter. I was ten."

"Ten?" Francesca asked, shocked.

"Ten," Saoirse confirmed with a nod. "There's quite a market for young girls, especially young virgins. I could no longer claim that title within weeks of being sold. They sterilized me at thirteen after I got my period. Sex was never something I learned to like. I didn't get shown pleasure; I was there to provide it. I didn't get a say in with who or how. What I did learn was how to make it quick so that it would be over sooner. My captives caught on and punished me severely for that."

I felt sick. Francesca paled, and her hand went immediately to her belly. I wasn't going to be very helpful in this interview, and I had no idea how to combat this. Whenever we'd seen something like this happening while we served, our reactions were to kill the bastards doing it, but we couldn't.

"The joys of motherhood are not something I will ever experience." Saoirse's eyes caught Francesca's movements, and a sad longing flickered over her face. "I don't even know that I would be capable of it even if my captors hadn't butchered my body inside. I'm telling you these things so you can help others understand this needs to stop. I'll let you show my face and my scars. No child deserves to have their life taken from them in this way."

"I understand," Francesca swallowed audibly.

Colin came back in and handed us both teacups and sat silently near Saoirse, within touching distance but with enough space not to crowd her. There was an interesting dynamic between them that I was still trying to figure out. Colin loved her; she was where I was drawing a blank, though.

"When I became an adult, the men changed. They were more violent, and I was fed drugs in various ways to make me complacent. I had never once experienced an orgasm or the touch of love. Whether men or women who used me, there was never anything pleasurable. When I turned twenty-four, the police raided the place they held us. I escaped, barely. Naked and beaten, I slept in a barn I had found. Colin found me." The tiniest bit of emotion crept into her voice at the mention of him.

I understood. Saoirse loved Colin but was still learning what love meant and how to navigate emotions that were foreign to her. It broke my heart and made me want to love Francesca even harder than I already did.

"Colin hid me, helped me physically heal, and

protected me. I didn't understand his reasoning for this, and sometimes I still don't. I assumed he wanted sex from me because that's all anyone wanted me for, no matter how many times he told me otherwise. He sold his farm and moved us across the country to this house. He's never raised his voice with me, never shown me anything other than kindness, and it took me ten years to understand that he loved me. That entire time, he didn't touch me once unless I asked him for help," Saoirse said quietly, the coldness in her eyes fading a bit.

"How did you learn to understand or get through what had happened?" Francesca asked quietly.

"I understood it very slowly. Kindness and love weren't words I understood the meaning of in my life. Colin took the time to show me, and I realized that love didn't mean I had to give him my body. For a while, I thought that Colin found me repulsive because of what my life had been." Saoirse reached for his hand. That, in itself, was a substantial telling gesture.

That statement was one I could understand and had seen many times while on the police force. It was one of the more complex things I'd had to deal with when victims of sexual abuse were at play. The treatment the victims became accustomed to and their emotional states were some of the biggest tragedies I'd encountered.

"Colin asked me to marry him last year, and I did. For the first time, he touched me, and I knew what pleasure was. I don't know how I got through it to answer your question. But I know that Colin led me, never pulling or pushing, just being with me. I may not have gotten through it, just moved past it," Saoirse replied, correcting herself.

"What do you mean?" I asked, then cringed because it wasn't my interview. "Sorry."

Francesca grabbed my hand and wound her fingers through it tightly. "If Jake hadn't asked, I was going to."

"I was kept in the basement of an old building when not forced to work. There were about twenty or so of us girls down there. It was dark, damp, moldy, cold, and stank like sewage and sex. We shared two mattresses between us; there was no peace or quiet. Someone was always crying, complaining, talking, or moaning in pain or sickness. There was no privacy. We had three buckets to use to relieve ourselves, and we had to be the ones to empty them. There were always at least two men on guard who took their liberties when they saw fit," Saoirse painted a horrid picture. "There was more than once they hadn't even realized someone had died."

I was barely in control of myself at this point. Francesca's hand in mine was the only thing keeping me rooted. "Do you know what PTSD is?" I hated how the words came out of my mouth and how they sounded harsh when I didn't mean them to be. My voice was rougher than usual as emotions choked me.

"I do. If you ask if I have it, I believe that answer is yes. That is why I say maybe I haven't gotten through it, as Francesca says. Instead, I only moved past it because of where we are. Colin moved us to the coast; fresh air blows here constantly. There is no noise, no commotion. The house is simple and clean but warm. The weather may be damp, but it isn't inside here. We have a lot of windows so I can see the light. If I go into a city, I panic at the sounds. I don't feel safe, and I feel hunted and preyed upon there. If I smell mold, I feel trapped, and my instinct is to run. You call these triggers, yes?" Saoirse looked at Francesca, who gravely nodded.

"You see, Colin gave me everything, so I would not have them. I don't go to the city. We go to the coast four minutes from here when I feel caged. Wide-open spaces and the surf's sounds are the only loud thing, and it calms me. I often wanted to throw myself over the cliff, but I didn't because I felt like I would disappoint Colin, who had completely altered his life for me. Sex is still difficult, but he has shown me pleasure is possible. However, for example, if Jake were to come too close to me or touch me without me inviting it, I think the results would be bad for me. Even knowing he didn't mean me harm," Saoirse explained. "This is why I say I may not have gotten through it."

I desperately needed some of that fresh air she talked about then. "I think I need to step outside for a moment," I said roughly. I knew she had been using me as an example because I was a stranger in her home, but the thought of anyone feeling unsafe because of my mere presence made me deeply uncomfortable.

Francesca glanced up at me worriedly. I was well aware of the company we were in, so I didn't kiss her. Instead, I caressed her face gently, letting her know I just needed to breathe without saying the words. She kissed my palm, and feeling like a coward, I fled the house and dropped on the porch, my head down between my knees until my heart stopped pounding in my chest.

Francesca

Saoirse allowed Jake time to calm down, and then we all headed outside to walk to the coast that was near. It gave me time to think about all I had heard of her tale. Why I had never once thought about the trauma the girls experienced is beyond me. I knew that Caleb, Damien, and Jake had seen girls sold, and I knew the trauma it had caused them.

I owed Jake a massive debt of gratitude for opening the door to broaden this project of mine. Saoirse's story was heartbreaking and brutal, and I thanked God that I had never experienced anything like what she had gone through.

Saoirse had taken time to change into a flowy skirt before we left because she said that scars might hint at something ugly, but that doesn't mean you have to see them that way. I noticed that she stood as far away from us as possible, which I understood.

The cliffs she lived by were not as dramatic as the cliffs of Moher, but with the blustery day, they made a fantastic place for a photoshoot. I quickly explained some hand motions to her so she understood if I wanted her to move or not.

Saoirse, in turn, gave me a very guarded look, which I immediately wanted a picture of, and I asked her to keep that look and snapped a couple of pictures.

"Francesca, please understand this, no one since Colin found me, including doctors, has seen my body. I am doing this so others can understand," Saoirse told me in an even tone. I didn't understand what she meant until she pulled off her top.

Jake cursed softly and buried his face in my neck, and I felt the tremors running through him. He kept his gaze off her but allowed me to move to get the pictures I needed to. Jake's volatile reaction had sparked fear in Saoirse, and that was what I needed to see precisely to get going.

Scars marred her small breasts and torso, and her back looked like someone had flayed her open with a whip; it was so scarred. Saoirse looked out at the water with fear tightening her face, and I got a few superb profile shots. I had her turn her face and twist her body a little, so only the curve of her breast showed and displayed her back more. I had her change position a few times, and I felt I got what I needed.

Saoirse's face showed fear, and I had her get dressed. "You said you don't go out, right?" I asked when she walked back up to me.

"Correct. I can't handle it. I feel like I trap Colin sometimes, but he never protests, and when we need things, he goes himself," Saoirse told me frankly.

"I'd like to offer to take a few photos of you together. This place is a fantastic backdrop for it," I offered. "They would be just for you two. I wouldn't use them."

"I think I'd like that," she smiled shyly. The first genuine smile I'd seen on her.

I moved them to the best lighting, switched between color and black and white, and got some stunning photos of the handsome couple, the best was one where they were looking at each other, and her guard was down. It was the most expression I had seen on her face, and the love on his was pure gold.

"Why didn't you ask about the scars?" We headed back, and she turned to me and asked.

"I don't need to. Why make you relive something that left its mark on you forever?" I answered simply. Jake's hand trembled in mine again, and I knew it was time for us to go. His eyes were glossy with unshed tears, and he hadn't spoken.

I wanted to hug Saoirse and tell her how brave she was, but the words were unnecessary, and the touch wasn't welcome. I gave her my heartfelt thanks, took the contact information from Colin, and promised to send the pictures and what I came up with for her part of the story.

Once we were back in the car, Jake broke down, and Finn looked pale. Too late, I realized he had probably followed us as a precaution and seen Saoirse and didn't have the context to understand what we both had learned. To his credit, he didn't ask, just took us back to the hotel, where it was my turn to comfort Jake.

When he fell asleep, I pulled the camera out and downloaded the pictures to my computer, immediately starting to edit them. I did the ones of Saoirse's body while Jake was sleeping. The stark brutality of what she had lived through showed clearly. It was a direct contrast to the beauty around her.

I finished those photos quickly and started on the images of the couple together. I'd gotten more than one good shot and edited them all to send to them, but I chose the best three and quickly got them uploaded somewhere local I found online to get them printed for me. I was sure we could find frames for them and get them sent off to Colin and Saoirse. I had just finished composing an e-mail to Colin attaching several of the photos and a link where he could download the rest when Jake woke up.

"Wow, that's a good one," Jake pointed at the screen.

"I sent it to a local place to print; we can pick them up in an hour. I was hoping we could find somewhere that sold frames so we can frame them, then send them via post," I shared my idea.

"I think Saoirse would love that," Jake agreed. "Did you already do the others?" his cautious question had me looking at his face.

"I did them while you slept."

"Can I see them?" he asked tentatively.

I slid the computer over to him, and he scrolled through the pictures. I observed his face for signs that it was too much for him, but the images were apparently more comfortable to look at than it was to see in person. I got that also.

"You should for sure use this one," Jake's soft words pulled my attention back to the screen. It was one of the ones where her body twisted to the side. The light fell on Saoirse in specific ways that illuminated her face and some scars, while shadows and profile hinted at the rest. Her expression was almost abject fear in that picture, yet you could also see the sheer willpower shining through holding her together.

"Then I will," I answered him, trusting his judgment.

"Cigarettes and belts make those scars." He closed up the computer. His quiet words jolted me. "Let's get Finn, take him to dinner, and have him help us find a place with frames and get the pictures." That's just what we did.

Chapter Twenty-Two

Francesca

I loved Scotland every bit as much as I loved Ireland. The Highlands might be my favorite place ever, next to the cliffs of Moher. Loch Lochmond was beautiful, as were the countless castles and Edinburgh. Loch Ness was super cool, and we took a stunning boat ride.

I swear my belly had doubled in size in the past month we'd been over here, and I was not looking forward to the next day's plane ride. We had sent a couple of cases of whiskey back from Annie's family that we planned to give out as gifts, and I made Jake buy a kilt.

He wasn't in it long, and Jake looked so good in it that I almost ripped it off him. I learned rather quickly that those aren't easy to get off, much to Jake's amusement.

Thanks to Finn, we had some great photos of Jake and me, both in Ireland and Scotland. Jake had offered Finn a place to stay if he ever wanted to come our way, and they exchanged information. Now I watched Jake pace as he had taken a call from Darius.

289

The rigid way he walked told me it wasn't good, and part of me didn't want to know.

Aside from some vivid nightmares, things had been normal for us. It was nice. We had fun, learned more about each other, had a ton of sex and ate good food. It was everything a honeymoon should be. The Saoirse part was a bit unsettling, but we got through it.

"Darius said the president of the Prince's has a lead on the shooter he is following," Jake told me after he hung up. "He's pissed that the president isn't letting him go down to California to see what he can find out."

"California?" I asked.

"They think he's still enlisted. Fort Irwin is what Darius said. The first lead they've had. The president thinks if Darius goes, he'll do something foolish and get arrested. I don't think Darius would act unprovoked, and he's top-notch at gathering information, but I don't want him to wind up in a situation that lands him in prison either," Jake sat down heavily.

"What is the president guy going to do?" I moved to sit next to him.

"Gather information from the sources that gave him the rumor. He has his contacts and ways. He hasn't escaped prison this long for being stupid. Darius also let the General we served under know, and he will do some digging. If this is an enlisted guy, he can pull strings we wouldn't be able to." Jake flopped back on the bed and let out a sigh.

"How can I help?" I stroked my fingers up and down his chest.

"Let's just stay here," Jake sighed again. "It's

been nice just being us. There are no reminders of how we came to be a couple and the shit we've dealt with along the way. I also want to put this to rest, though." Jake moved and pulled off his shirt, pressing my hand over his heart and holding it there. "Darius also said he wants to be a part of your project."

"I can do that," I agreed. I had figured Darius would be after how he was at my birthday party. I also had a few ideas for doing his photos without showing his face. I'd make the same offer to him that I did to Saoirse of taking some portraits of him that he could have. Darius was shadows, hard angles, and a cold exterior unless he let you in, and then you saw the softness he contained inside. I was lucky enough to know that part of him.

Jake put his hand on my belly, and the baby moved and kicked like crazy. "He's active," Jake smiled softly. "Hey, little man, you will grow up knowing to respect a woman's magic, her power, and all that she stands for. Just like both of your daddies and your uncle. That means stop beating up your mommy's insides."

"Stand up. Let's go for a walk since I will be stuck for at least ten hours tomorrow." I giggled and then immediately had to pee. "The baby found my bladder, that's for sure." I bolted for the bathroom. I came back out in time to catch the sad look on Jake's face.

The moment Jake leaned forward to kiss my belly, the baby started kicking again. "I think he likes me," Jake looked up at me with a wondrous expression.

"He loves you," I insisted and pulled him up. "Just like his mom, who is telling you that now so when she's stuck on the plane tomorrow and driving you crazy, you at least remember at some point, I loved you."

"I know you love me, and I'm used to you driving me crazy." Jake laughed and followed me out the door.

I paused, unsure if I should be offended, but he looked so yummy that I threw myself at him instead. Finn heard us out in the hallway and decided to walk with us. We ended up walking quite a ways, and then when my back started to hurt, we caught a taxi back to the hotel.

I was going to miss these two countries and the mystery and magic the land held. I was also excited to be going home and in a familiar place. I had several interviews lined up with vets, people from the PTSD group, and contacts at the police station between Mike and Jake. Several police officers, firefighters, and EMTs as well. With any luck, the next few months would give me time to complete the project and submit it for publishing.

Jake

I managed to talk to the flight attendant and get our seats changed to the front. That way, if Frankie stood up, she wouldn't be bothering anyone, and I wouldn't have to punch them for being rude to my pregnant wife.

She worked on the project for several hours, putting the stories together and laying them out. She had yet to add Caleb or me. Saoirse and Damien were the most heartbreaking stories with the most emotionally hard-hitting pictures, but Caleb would be right up there too.

Halfway through the flight, the restlessness kicked in, and Francesca's back was cramping up. One of the flight attendants brought her a hot towel, which helped ease the pain. I got her resting across the seats against me again and rubbed her back.

The same flight attendant came, covered us up with blankets, and brought me a pillow because it was nighttime. Most of the others in the cabin were sleeping. Instead of sleeping as I'd hoped, Francesca decided to begin stroking me through my jeans.

The vixen had a napkin in hand and the blanket's cover; she had no fear of being caught. I stopped trying to fight it. It made Francesca happy, and that was my goal. It almost became too much when she freed me, pulled the blanket over her head, and wrapped her lips around me. When she did this, I always made noise. Trying to keep a lid on it was my biggest challenge and kind of erotic.

Especially since she was doing her damn best to try and break me, I'd get her back for that, just not on the plane because I knew she wouldn't be able to keep a lid on it. As I plotted out my dirty revenge, she slid her hand down and stroked a spot that left me hissing through my teeth as I exploded in her mouth.

She kept sucking until I was ready to cry when the flight attendant came back by us again. "Everything okay?" she asked quietly, assuming Francesca was asleep.

"Can I get water?" I croaked out. "Dry throat."

"Sure thing," she rushed off. I pulled Francesca's

head off me and tucked myself back into my jeans.

"You are evil, babe." Her sly grin had my heart thumping hard.

"Now, you want to take me to the bathroom and have your way with me?" she whispered the question.

"If you hadn't just drained me dry, I would have considered it. Now you have to suffer," I whispered back.

"That's what you think," her words teased me. She put a finger up to my lips, and I sucked it in, tasting her. "I took care of me while I took care of you."

"Fuck," I groaned quietly. "You're going to kill me."

She pulled her finger out of my mouth and curled up against me. The flight attendant brought back the water and two more pillows.

"Have her put her head on your lap." I almost choked on the water. "Stick a pillow under her back, and it might be a little more comfortable for her."

I helped Francesca rearrange, gave her a drink of water, and thankfully she fell asleep. I rubbed her belly a bit when little Damien started moving around, and he settled back down. My whole life was now resting here in my arms.

"Ghost, Demon, I hope you two asses enjoyed that display of torture," I whispered out the window to the black sky. "I don't want it to bother either of you when I say some deity made her for me. She was. I miss you two like crazy, and I wish you were both here to enjoy it with me. This experience has been the worst ride ever, but it had the best outcome because I've never wanted anything as much as Frankie. Keep watch over us, brothers. I'm going to give you a lot of kids to be guardian angels for."

"Give me a sign," I pleaded. I wished just once to get an answer in return, something to let me know that neither of my brothers was angry or that they were at peace and together.

Francesca shifted and let out a little moan, grabbing my attention. I put my hand on her belly and felt the fluttering, and I started rubbing again until he calmed back down. I had a feeling these last three months were going to be hard on her.

That was my last thought as I drifted off to sleep, waking up when we landed. The sudden movement of Francesca no longer being on me woke me up. The flight attendant had her sit back up.

"Frankie, you okay, babe?" I asked sleepily.

"Tired," she replied. She slumped over against me, safely buckled in her seat.

"We'll be home soon," I kissed her forehead softly. "Wanna take a bath when we get there?"

"Hmmm," she moaned. "Together?"

"That was my idea. I owe you some payback," I said in a low voice.

"I'm game." She gave me a wicked smile and sat up, her eyes showing how tired she was. "Damn. I think I'm addicted to you."

"I will not look for a reason to stop feeding that addiction. The feeling is mutual, babe." I rested my hand on her belly when she shifted again. "Mike is going to pick us up. I'll text him when we pull up to the gate."

"Think it would get awkward if I jumped you in

his vehicle?" her weary voice was still filled with the humor I loved so much.

"I think that would push the boundaries of our friendship with him, yes," I chuckled.

"Betcha Susie would be okay with it," she mumbled good-naturedly.

I sent the text when we landed as we were approaching the gate and got confirmation back that he was on his way. We disembarked and made our way through customs to baggage claim, surprisingly quickly this time.

We were standing outside when I heard a horn. I looked up to see Mike pulling up and then jumping out of the truck to sweep Francesca up in a hug. "Frankie! You grew!"

"Telling me I'm large is not the way to win my affection." She smacked his arm lightly.

He helped her up into the back where she could lay flat, and I climbed in the front, twisting to check on her. "I'm fine," she told me. "Counting minutes to that bath."

"Me too, sweetheart," I growled playfully and turned around.

Francesca

Veterans Day was tomorrow, and Jake's birthday was in another couple of days. Hector and Angela were going to come back out, but it wasn't a surprise. I was officially six months pregnant, huge, always horny, and now hungry all the time, but half the smells of food made me want to puke.

I asked Mike and Susie to come over and then extended the request to Darius. Darius suggested that I invite the Chief and a few guys from the force, so while Jake was working out, I went through his phone and called the Chief, asking him to bring whoever he thought should be there.

We had a doctor's appointment in a few hours, and I just wanted it over with; the exhausted feeling never stopped. Baby Damien was one active little guy. He got excited no matter how much I talked to him, rubbed my belly, or tried to soothe him. Then when Jake did it, it was like he fell into a trance and just calmed right down. I'd be annoyed if it wasn't so sweet.

We were also starting Lamaze classes now. Amazingly, Jake had asked Darius to join us as a backup. I couldn't imagine a situation where we'd need a backup, but the way Darius's face lit up made me not question Jake's call on it. Jake had obviously seen something that I hadn't.

I finished making my shopping list for Jake's birthday dinner; he'd picked lasagna. I hadn't made that in ages, and hopefully, it wouldn't suck. We'd decided to do a club Thanksgiving for those who didn't have families to celebrate with, and I wanted to pick things up for that. I also needed to get some black sheets for the photo sessions with Darius.

"Frankie, you look absolutely gorgeous," Jake came up to me, grinning like a fool.

"Thank you." I blushed because he wasn't just

saying that to make me feel better. He genuinely meant it.

"Meeting for the club with the lawyer and Greg is set up for next week," he pulled me to him and kissed me until I forgot my name.

"I don't care what Caleb said. You are a good kisser," I breathed out, dazed.

"Glad that I could prove him wrong." Jake laughed and kissed me again.

I shook my head to try and get my thoughts back. "I drafted a letter of introduction for the club to send out that we can add the decided-on services we'll offer and fill in the blanks on who the board and officers will be. I also put together a list of places for you to look over and see if there are any I forgot."

"You are so on top of this, and it's kind of nuts. Making my job a little easier," Jake brushed the hair out of my face.

"It's only fair since you spend most of your time taking care of me." I'd thought about asking for some nursing shifts but quickly realized I doubted I'd be able to be on my feet twelve hours a day. I needed something to do with my time.

"Okay, doctor appointment, Lamaze, then what?" Jake wrapped a sweatshirt around me.

"Grocery store, and somewhere we can find black sheets." I handed him the list, so I didn't lose it. "I think we should have a club Christmas too, just like Thanksgiving. We can do it secret Santa style or pick-a-number and choose a gift thing. I like secret Santa better. More personal, and that way, everyone gets a gift."

"Whatever you want to do is fine with me," Jake agreed. "Almost all the guys in that club that aren't married are awestruck by you."

"More likely, they are afraid you'll kick their ass if they don't play nice with me," I replied.

"They are probably more afraid of Susie doing that than me. She's frightening when she's angry," Jake shuddered. "Let's go."

Darius was already at the hospital when we got there, so I invited him to the appointment. He looked uncomfortable but trudged along behind us. There wasn't anything embarrassing that was going to happen. Dr. Waters would do another ultrasound, go over my blood work, and answer the litany of questions Jake wanted to ask.

She did a 3D ultrasound, and we saw the baby in real-life form for the first time. Both Jake and I cried, and Darius looked like he wanted to, but he held his tough-guy image together. Dr. Waters told us to set appointments every four weeks for the next two months, then every two weeks. She was a little concerned that the baby would be too big for a natural birth, but she would monitor it.

Lamaze was interesting. What amused me to no end was how both Darius and Jake were riveted and memorized everything said. It was what I got for having two SEALs be a part of this. Operation: get the baby born. I giggled, and they gave me glares because I interrupted their learning.

Plus, I kept getting looks from all the other women because these two dedicated men were hell-bent on getting me through the delivery with no problems. Not to mention, Jake looked like an Adonis. Then there was Darius, who was the bad-boy type of good-looking, his mocha skin ink dipped a lot more than Jake's but less than Damien's had been.

Darius sat behind me, propping me up while Jake was in front of me, being my focus point. I focused on him, not the way they wanted me to. A flurry of movement from my belly had both men melting into piles of gooey SEALs.

Chapter Twenty-Three

Jake

We visited three cemeteries for veterans and put flags on the graves that didn't have them, and Francesca took several pictures. We ended our rounds at the wall where Francesca's family was and now Damien. Here we left flowers and flags, spoke a few words, shed some massive tears, and left.

Darius was coming over to do his photos in a bit. I helped her drape the shed in black sheets, mute the light, and then sat there while checking the results. We altered a few things as needed, then went inside, where she profusely thanked me for my service to our country.

The days had passed fast. The president of the Prince's had not come up with any useful information, nor had General Allen. Now the club, some force members I hadn't known were coming, and Darius gathered to celebrate my birthday.

Susie had brought a giant cake, and Francesca and I had made several pans of lasagna that were all gone. There wasn't one bit of food leftover. The Thanksgiving count and Christmas count had just gone up after they ate her cooking again.

Now Francesca was over talking to one of the club guys, standing in the corner. I knew she was safe, but the way he had her boxed in was unnerving me. I guessed it was for Darius, too, because he hovered not far away. I almost laughed at the way he had taken up Caleb's place. That was why I'd asked him to be a part of the birth stuff. He loved her as Caleb had. She had a new brother and didn't even know it.

Her delighted peal of laughter rang across the room like a siren call for me. I made my way over to her, giving Darius a nod of thanks. I knew he understood and elbowed Steve out of the way. "Is there a reason you are crowding my wife?" I growled at him.

"He was asking me for a favor," Francesca scolded me. "One that I am looking forward to."

"Care to fill me in?" I shot a look at Steve.

"Do you know what a doudoir shoot is?" Francesca laughed again.

"No," I said slowly, not sure I was going to like this.

"It's a sexy photoshoot of guys, a play on the word boudoir. He wants to have one done for his wife and give it to her for Christmas." Francesca was enjoying this. There was a twinkle in her eye.

"You want to strip for my wife and have her take sexy photos of you?" I turned to face Steve, not sure how to feel about this.

"Not all the way naked unless she thinks that's how it should be," Steve winked at her.

"This is legitimately a thing?" I looked back

at Francesca.

"It is. I've never done one, but I'm up for the challenge," Francesca laughed. "You got a deal," she held out her hand, and he shook it. He saw the look on my face and left before I hit him. "Relax, he won't be naked. He isn't anywhere near as sexy as you are."

"Not exactly comforting," I grumbled. I wasn't seriously jealous.

Thanksgiving was over, and Christmas was rapidly approaching before I knew it. We had the club set up, the board of directors in place, and officers voted in. Greg suggested rotating positions so officers would serve two years, and then we'd vote on new ones.

The board consisted of Greg, Francesca, me, Mike, and Susie. Greg, Mike, and I spent many hours with the lawyer getting the by-laws and policies set up, with input from Susie and Francesca along the way. They had sent the letters to several organizations, and then they set out to plan a fundraiser party as a kickoff for New Year's Eve.

Francesca started a winter clothing and blanket drive that would have the club out delivering to shelters and specific areas where we knew several homeless vets hung out. She was unstoppable. The guys loved it because it was apparent that they were now a part of something bigger that made a difference in the lives of others.

Even Darius got involved, despite his affiliation with the Prince's. After Francesca had shown him the pictures she'd taken of him, he was behind her one hundred percent. They were good. They showed him shadowed in darkness as she had envisioned; a warrior whose emotional scars were exposed in the pictures by the muted lighting, positioning of his body, and posture.

Francesca also got one of him and me while we stood talking out by the water. I can't say we looked friendly, but we had been talking about Damien. She loved the picture, and I thought we looked like two hardasses. She was going to frame it and give it to Darius for Christmas, along with one I hadn't even known she'd gotten of him on his bike. She was sneaky.

Francesca

I finished printing out my little gift certificates for each of the people in the club and set them in a stack on the desk. I sent Darius out to do my shopping for me since Jake watched me like a hawk to ensure I wasn't overdoing things.

We'd promised to do simple gifts for each other since there wasn't anything either of us needed. I wanted to get Jake a new pair of riding gloves, a leather jacket, and boots. I also wanted to get a coat for Darius, which meant I had to send one of the club members after him to see what he looked at and report back. It wasn't going to be easy since Darius was continually looking and aware of everything around him.

I had my dinner list ready for Christmas, and Jake and I needed to do that. My secret Santa person was Matt, and I was at a complete loss on that one. I hardly knew him, so I had Jake do my dirty work. It turned out

Matt was a reader; Jake had picked out an e-reader for him.

Today, blankets and winter clothes were on the schedule to deliver to shelters, safe houses, and the homeless. Our New Year's Eve party garnered a lot of attention, and we had quite a few RSVPs. It made me genuinely glad that Susie and I chose a hall instead of a house to have it.

I'd been married three months now, and each day the grief we carried inside us seemed to ease up more. We still had moments where something would catch us off-guard, and the ache became visible, but we got each other through it, each breakdown bringing us closer.

I loved being married to Jake. I loved being pregnant, and I loved what our lives had become. I had genuine friends now and a sizable non-blood family. Darius was like a long-lost brother, and I had fun with him. Life was good.

I had one interview left before I was considering calling my project complete, and I was just waiting for Jake before we headed out to get it done. A guy in his PTSD group decided he wanted to be a part of it.

Jake said he was one of the guys who had let it go untreated for so long that his brain altered significantly, and he had a hard time functioning in everyday situations. Jake wasn't sure about the interview, but I pushed him into it. He kept telling me the guy wasn't stable enough for this. My argument was if it was his idea, maybe he was, and Jake just didn't know it.

I finished sealing the envelopes, addressed them,

and dumped them in the box we would bring to Jake's old house, where we would have Christmas with the club. Jake had invited Darius to come over and have breakfast with us on Christmas morning if he wanted to. Hector and Angela would be with their families.

I grabbed my grocery list and headed out to grab my camera and a notebook that Jake said I should use to take notes since my memory was all over the place lately. He wasn't wrong, and he was pretty amused by it most of the time. I found it less entertaining.

"Babe?" Jake called.

"Coming," I yelled back, looking over my shoulder to make sure I hadn't forgotten anything, like my phone that I had left sitting on the desk. I went back and grabbed it and met Jake in the hallway.

"Wind has kicked up. You need a coat." He kissed me and steered me to the closet.

"Can't I just use your body heat to warm up?" I protested.

"Not while I'm driving, and not while you interview Clancy. When we get back here, you can use my body in whatever way you want to," he backed me up into the wall. "As many times as you want, too."

"You might regret saying that," I grinned, stuffing my ice-cold hands down the front of his jeans. The cold didn't bother him, but it was still fun for me.

"I never regret offering my body up to you." He lifted me and pinned me to the wall with his hips. "Nor do I care if we are late. Damn, Frankie, you smell good."

"I'm going to smell like sex if we keep this up," I moaned as he kissed my neck.

"Nope, I have more self-restraint than that." Jake let me slide down.

"Not fair," I whined, but I let him wrap my coat around me and lead me to the truck. "I have zero control when it comes to you."

"I like it that way." Jake chuckled as he helped me up.

Soon he was leading me down the hallway of a church not far from our house to a small room. There was a man probably ten years older than Jake sitting on a chair, the leader of the PTSD group next to him, and two chairs across from them.

Jake leaned against the corner of the door, and I gave him a confused look. "It's for his comfort," he said softly.

"I was sexually abused by a man most of my childhood. I need space when there are many people in the room," the guy I assumed was Clancy said. He was thin and pale, with jet black hair and dark eyes. His voice was somewhat higher-pitched.

"I understand," I replied gently. "Has it been explained what I am doing with this project?"

"Yes. I'll only share what I can. The church is one of the places I feel safe," Clancy said, his eyes shifting wildly around the room.

It made me think of someone strung-out on drugs. I kept my eyes on Clancy instead of looking back at Jake, which is what I wanted to do. I could feel Jake behind me, and without a doubt, I knew he would never leave me alone with this man. Only these few minutes in here, and I understood why Jake wasn't comfortable with it.

"My father was sadistic," Clancy started without me asking him anything. "He liked touching things. Kids, women, boys, men, it didn't matter. Sometimes he did it to cause pain, and other times he did it to bring pleasure to himself. It started when I was four, I think. I can't remember, but I was young. It was before I started kindergarten."

"It will be helpful for you if you talk about the things he did," the group leader said. I couldn't remember this man's name for the life of me.

"He would pull on my penis." Clancy nodded at his statement.

"Clancy, do you mind if I take pictures while you talk, or would you rather wait until you finish, and we can get some in the church?" I asked him.

PTSD had rewired Clancy's brain, it seemed. There were moments when he looked all there and acted his age, and then out of nowhere, it was like I was talking to a child. Unstable appeared to be an appropriate word, and I wasn't sure if he was dangerous or not.

"You can take pictures," the adult Clancy was back. "Where was I?"

"You were telling Francesca what your father would do to you," the leader steered him back on track.

"Oh yeah. My dad would get mad if I cried, and then he would pinch my testicles. Because if I was going to cry, there should be a good reason for it." Clancy's face shuttered closed, and I grabbed a few pictures. My camera captured his flip between utter despair, fear, and absolute rage. "I'm not gay."

Startled, I almost dropped my camera. "I didn't say anything," I replied evenly.

"I saw it on your face. You think I liked it. I probably did something to deserve it. Did I deserve having to suck my dad's penis?" Clancy suddenly screamed. It was the side of PTSD I had only seen in the veteran's hospital, and always with orderlies or doctors around to sedate or restrain the patient.

"Clancy," the leader moved calmly, stepping into Clancy's field of vision. "Francesca didn't say anything at all. She only took your picture. No one is accusing you of anything, and no one thinks you deserved the abuse. Focus on me, Clancy. Where are you?"

"Church," the child Clancy was back.

"Are you safe here?" the leader continued.

"I don't know," his childlike voice answered with a simper.

"Yes, you do. You are with your support group. You are safe. Name the states that start with A," the leader instructed Clancy.

"Alaska, Arkansas, Alabama, Arizona," Clancy recited, and his eyes cleared. "I'm sorry, Francesca."

Tension radiated off Jake, but he didn't move. I think this was more heartbreaking than Saoirse's story. She was able to come through the trauma. Clancy was stuck and stuck deep. I swallowed down my heart and kept my tone even.

"I understand, Clancy. We can stop if you'd like," I offered, unsure what to do.

"I want to help you," Clancy insisted. "I think this project is important."

I didn't know what to do. I didn't want to ask questions and upset Clancy. I wasn't even sure what the trigger had been. I was in unknown territory with Clancy, and I understood why the group leader thought it was a good idea. Showing what PTSD could do if left untreated *was* important. Not all cases would be like this, but showing the best and worst-case scenarios was good. It just left me feeling unsettled.

Clancy closed his eyes and went on. "The abuse continued until I was a teenager, but it had evolved. He raped me, would force oral sex on me, made me masturbate in front of him then shamed me for it. He was sick in the head. When he got mad, he hurt me, usually in the genitalia area, in some way. By the time I graduated high school, I had severe depression, social anxiety, and panic attacks. People couldn't touch me without me losing my mind. I would cut myself."

"You are doing great, Clancy," the leader coaxed him to keep talking.

"I wanted him dead," Clancy suddenly snapped. "I would pray to a God I don't believe exists that he would die." Spit was flying from his mouth, and I was able to get a few pictures of the madness. "I was afraid to be in the house and be out of the house. I tried running away and telling the police, but they didn't believe me. My dad told them I had a history of mental health problems."

I was more than a little scared of Clancy. My heart broke for him, but he wasn't okay. I wanted to tell him he was brave for sharing his story, but I was terrified to open my mouth.

"I started to hurt myself to remind myself I was still alive," Clancy's voice went soft, and his eyes unfocused. "The blood dripping was beautiful. It was like art, the way it would roll and splatter on the ground. The pain was nice because it was a pain I controlled."

I heard Jake's teeth grinding and realized he hadn't known this. Clancy never had a childhood. He didn't have a chance to understand that life wasn't always bad. No one had ever helped him. His brain had shut down sometime during his childhood and stayed there to try and protect itself.

"What happened after that?" the leader asked Clancy.

"My dad died. I was twenty-seven. He had me handcuffed to a pipe in the bathroom. I screamed for days until someone kicked the door down. They put me in a mental hospital. No one believed me; no one believed a grown man was held hostage by his father and sodomized. They had to put me to sleep to do exams because they couldn't touch me. They found the damage then. They listened then," Clancy shot to his feet, "but it was too late!"

Clancy lunged for me, his eyes showing him unhinged, pupils blown out dilated, and Jake was in front of me with lightning-fast reflexes. "Clancy, stop." Jake's voice was stern and commanding.

I leaned around Jake and snapped a few pictures feeling slightly unhinged myself for doing it. Jake's tone had frozen Clancy in fear. The leader was trying to get through to him, speaking softly in his ear. I heard him ask to recite states again, then music, and circled back to where we were, why we were here, and what had happened.

"I think the talking is over," Jake softened his tone.

"No," Clancy pleaded, "I'm sorry. I'm okay now."

"Clancy, you helped me tremendously. It was courageous of you to tell me your story," I said gently from behind Jake. The sad reality was that Clancy wasn't ever going to be okay. Jake wasn't budging, and I didn't want him to. I also loved that he never threatened Clancy or moved aggressively toward him. He only stepped in front of me.

"I helped?" he asked in the little kid's voice.

"You did. So much. You should be proud of yourself." I peeked around Jake again.

"Shall we get a few pictures out in the church?" the leader suggested. "It's your favorite place to relax."

"That would be nice," adult Clancy was back. "That was harder than I thought it would be. Would it be possible to get a picture of me sitting in a pew? I think I'd like to put that on my dresser."

"Of course," I agreed quickly, standing and staying behind Jake. "I'll follow you out there. You do whatever feels natural to you."

"Thank you, Francesca. I think today has helped me," Clancy said calmly and walked out of the room.

"We'll talk when he leaves," the leader assured me. "I'll fill in a few of the blanks since he signed the waiver that he was willing to talk about the experience and have it included in the book."

There were no blanks, in my opinion. Clancy's

father had ruined his life. It was pretty self-explanatory, but I simply nodded and followed them out to the central part of the church. I snapped pictures automatically.

Jake

It had taken exceptional control not to flatten Clancy when he moved towards Francesca. The only thing that stopped me was understanding that he wasn't doing this. His PTSD had become a mental illness. I'd only known parts of his story, and while I still only knew pieces, it was pretty horrific.

When Clancy's caregiver came to pick him up, he was as calm and rational as he was in the meetings. Francesca felt rattled, and I felt the need to shoot something.

"Jake," Tom said, breaking my stare. "Don't let this trigger you."

"It's not. That was just disturbing and fucking wrong. Clancy only seems unstable at the meetings sometimes, nothing like that," I gestured to the door. "I wouldn't have agreed to this had I known that was possible."

"I can't say I knew either." Tom sighed, "Francesca, I'm sorry. I didn't think you would be in danger. Clancy is one of those cases where PTSD became so deeply ingrained in him that it did indeed rewire his brain into mental illness. He's had intensive therapy over the years, enough to believe he is fine to live independently. He does, but a caregiver also comes in once a day to check on him. Clancy doesn't drive, he doesn't grocery shop, his public outings are to meetings, appointments with therapists, and sometimes he goes to church."

I couldn't stand not having my arm around Francesca right then, and I kept her close. "I understand," she told Tom. "I guess if I am going to show the faces of PTSD, it was important that I see this."

"It is. Again, I apologize that it got away from me." Tom shook her hand. "It's very nice to meet you, by the way."

"Nice to meet you too," she said, her voice polite but distant. "The state thing, that's pretty ingenious."

"It helps to refocus the mind away from the track it was on. It forces thought. It works with my other clients better than it does with Clancy. I have to get his eyes to look at me first, and then I can usually get him with that one. Other times, I have to ask him to name songs off his favorite album."

"Do you mind if I use that?" she asked.

"Not at all. Clancy is quite lucid and aware of his surroundings; he's intelligent and can carry on conversations about various topics. His triggers are what he can't control, and he can't identify them either, most of the time. Touch is one, and personal space, for obvious reasons. Tone inflections as well, as you saw with Jake. There's been a couple of meetings where I've had to have Jake use what Clancy calls his soldier tone. I rarely use it because it's a fear inducer, but with Clancy, inducing fear usually brings him to a screeching halt."

"I hate doing it," I muttered. "Clancy's been

scared enough in his lifetime." Francesca burrowed into my side in silent support.

"I know. See you at the next meeting?" Tom asked gently.

"Yep. I'll be there." I needed to get out of there. "If Francesca has any questions, I'll relay them. Thanks for the help, Tom."

"You're welcome," Tom smiled at us both, and we went our separate ways.

I rushed Francesca out of the church, lifted her into the truck, and rested my lips on her belly. "Hey, DC, no one will get away with doing awful things like that to you. I give you my word on that."

"DC?" Francesca's hands wove into my hair, massaging my scalp.

"Damien Caleb," I looked up into her eyes. "The way he kicks it could be Demon Child or Demon's Child."

"I love it," she laughed. "DC it is, then." She tugged my head up and kissed me. "Now, I seem to remember the promise of sexual favors."

"After grocery shopping," I told her with a wicked look. "I never promised when we would get home, just that you could do what we wanted when we got there."

"That's evil," she cried, laughing. "By the way, your soldier voice has a very different effect on me, and if you are lucky, I'll show you."

"I already know I'm lucky." I pushed her into the truck, chuckling.

Chapter Twenty-Four

Francesca

We got through Christmas and New Year's with smashing success. We had several people decide to donate funds to the club, we got publicity for them, and people sought us out to help. I was deliriously happy about it too.

Many of the club members had been calling in their photo coupons, luckily not for doudoir shoots. It had been fun, and Steve was a good character, but it also felt awkward. However, one of the shots had turned out great, and his wife was over the moon happy and had been showing it around, which was hilarious because Steve was embarrassed.

My due date was four weeks away, and DC was giant. Now Valentine's Day was staring me in the face, and the remaining club members who hadn't used up their coupons were all trying to get photo's taken as gifts. Jake was amused and annoyed both.

I still craved sex like I was approaching a deadline of not being able to have it, and I guess, in a way, I was. Dr. Waters had warned that I would need six weeks to recover from birth and probably wouldn't want sex anyway.

I doubted that, but it was getting harder to have sex now that there was a gigantic belly in the way. It didn't stop me. It just made me more creative. I was betting that Jake was ready for a break. He denied it.

I was stuck on what to do for him for Valentine's Day. Utterly baffled and clueless. It was sad. I sat back in my desk chair and thought about kicking my feet up on the desk, but I was sure I would topple over backward and be stuck on the floor until Jake got home.

"Frankie!" I heard Darius bellow from the living room.

"In the office," I called out. I hadn't even heard Darius pull up.

"Girl, what are you doing?" he strode in.

"Trying to think of a gift for Jake for Valentine's Day," I muttered. "Any ideas?"

"You are speaking to the eternally single. That answer is a resounding no." Darius dropped a stack of mail on the desk. "I grabbed that on the way in."

"Where's Jake? I thought you were with him." I thumbed through the mail, pulling out the junk and tossing it.

"Jake's at the house. He needs you to come back and help him pick out something or other. I don't know. I wasn't paying attention." Darius plopped on the end of my desk.

"Oh my," I whispered, a tremble running through me. My hand stilled at an envelope from one of the publishing companies I had sent my project to for publication. It was the first response I had gotten.

"What is it?" Darius went razor-sharp at my tone, looked down at the envelope, and frowned.

"It's from one of the publishing companies I submitted the book to," I whispered, afraid to move my hand.

Impatient, Darius snatched it up and tore it open, unfolding it without looking at it, and placed it in front of my face. "What does it say?" he demanded.

Suddenly, I knew what to give Jake for Valentine's Day. I yanked the paper out of Darius's hand and glared at him. "Do not say a word about this to anyone!"

"Fine," he huffed, "at least clue me in!"

"They want the book," I breathed out.

Darius whooped, hopped up, and did a little dance around the office. "Why the hell wouldn't you want anyone to know?"

"This will be Jake's gift," I said quietly, looking for a place to hide the letter.

"Jake's not a snooper. Just put it in the drawer under something else," Darius understood what I was doing. "He is a worrier, though, and if we don't get going, he will think something is wrong."

"Jeez, you guys are bossy. Do they teach you that in the SEALs or something?" I grumbled, holding my hand out for Darius to pull me up. "I feel like a whale."

"It's a natural skill we are born with," Darius grinned. "You aren't a whale, but you carry a giant baby created by a giant man. He might be born four feet tall."

"I will find a way to curse you if he is. You'll be a prime babysitter." I waddled down the hallway, Darius close behind.

We were walking out the front door when a courier service pulled up, and Darius growled something and whipped out his phone to send a text, presumably to Jake. "Now what?"

"Francesca Foxwood?" a young kid bound up the porch steps, faltering slightly at Darius's formidable scowl.

"Ignore him. That's me." I held out my hand to sign for whatever it was, and the guy took off. I looked at the envelope and drew in a sharp breath. "It's from another publishing company."

Once again, Darius ripped it open and dangled it in front of my face. "They want it too, right?" he asked snarkily.

"Yep. Gotta hide this one too. Damn it. I will have to get the mail every day now to make sure Jake doesn't see them," I frowned.

"Stay put. I'm going to go put this one with the other one," Darius ran back into the house and was back out seconds later. "Come on. We'll figure out the mail thing later. I'll stake out the damn mailbox if I have to."

"Jake might notice that." Darius boosted me up into his truck as I laughed.

"Girl, you haven't gained enough weight," Darius said as he climbed in the driver's side. "For as big as that belly is, the rest of you is the same damn size."

"Shut your mouth. I've gained plenty, and Dr. Waters said everything is fine," I huffed at him.

"I know, I know," he mumbled.

We drove in silence the rest of the way as I tried

to figure out how to get the mail without Jake knowing I was up to something. There seriously wasn't a way. The man noticed everything. He'll even be aware I'm hiding something from him now.

"Stop worrying about it, Frankie. Just tell Jake there's a gift coming in the mail, and he's not allowed to check it. He'll listen." Darius parked. "Stay put until I'm around and can help that monster child out of my truck."

"Calling him a monster child isn't helping," I told him after opening my door. With his hands under my armpits, he pulled me out and set me on the ground as if there weren't twelve watermelons stuffed in my belly.

Darius walked me to the door carefully, standing slightly behind me as if I would fall over. I pushed open the door and was about to snap at him when a loud, "Surprise!" made me about launch into labor.

Speechless, I stared in shock and *did* almost fall over backward, but Darius's bulk caught me. "What the hell?" I asked, stupefied.

"The club wanted to throw you a surprise baby shower," Darius whispered. "You better start walking forward before your man leaps over everyone in that room to see why you aren't moving."

I glared at Darius and let him push me forward. "Wow! You guys! I can't believe this!" My emotions caught up to what was happening.

Susie started cracking up laughing, which only confused me. "You have two different shoes on!" she exclaimed. "I remember those days!"

"Why didn't you tell me?" Now I turned fully to glare at Darius.

"Unless they were different colors, I wouldn't have noticed. They are both white," Darius defended himself.

Jake wove through the room. "I didn't know they were doing this until today. It was a surprise for me too. How are you feeling? What's wrong?"

"I'm embarrassed because Darius let me leave the house with two different shoes on," I told Jake. "Now I have to pee again. By the way, you aren't allowed to get the mail until after Valentine's Day," I decided to use Darius's idea. "I have a gift coming, and I don't want you to know."

"Is that why you have your secretive face on?" Jake gave me a calculating look.

"Bathroom, now." I laughed and almost peed myself.

Jake scooped me up, carried me down the hallway, deposited me in the bathroom, and closed the door. I knew he was standing right outside it, waiting for me. A sharp pain hit my back as I washed my hands, and I cried out.

"What's wrong?" The door opened immediately, and Jake's worried face checked me over.

"Back pain," I said, panting through it until it eased up. "I think I sat too long earlier."

Jake wasn't having any of it. "Susie!" Jake yelled down the hallway, his tone demanding. She came walking at a clip, Darius on her heels.

"What is wrong with you now?" she asked Jake, eyeballing me. "Frankie looks fine."

"She had a pain in her back," Jake insisted.

"Oh, for the love of Pete. She's pregnant, of course, she had a pain in her back, you ape. You are giving me one in my ass. Come on, Frankie, let's sit. Darius, Jake, if you hover, I will have Mike lock you outside," Susie threatened.

"That won't happen," Darius responded. "He can't take one of us, much less both."

Susie glared at him, one of those scary glares that were so effective against the men. Darius backed down immediately, and Jake laughed.

"I get to sit by Frankie; it's my baby too."

"You get to rub her back and behave yourself. That's what you get to do," Susie told Jake smugly.

I laughed as Susie led me to the couch, sitting me in the middle, Jake sitting close on the other side of me. Darius lurked not far away but far enough to not tempt Susie to yell at him. Jake immediately started rubbing my back, and every man in the place fell silent.

"Francesca's fine," Susie burst out laughing. "If she were in labor, her water would have broken, and those back pains would be a lot closer together. Relax. They could be Braxton Hicks too."

"Want something to eat?" Jake asked in my ear. "Drink?"

"I would kill for a Coke," I told him. "I'll settle for water."

"I made a delicious punch," Susie told me. "Darius, bring her some punch and water." I quietly giggled how he snapped to attention to do as she asked precisely.

"That's a neat trick. How did you make that

happen?" I asked her.

"Fear. He's afraid of me," Susie chuckled. "Get mean, and you'll get the same reaction."

"She's right. Let Darius see that feisty side of you that scares doctors, and he'll shake in his boots," Jake smirked as Darius brought drinks.

"Get your own," he told Jake.

"If he gets up to get a drink, you have to take over back massage duty," I told Darius. He looked doubtful for a moment, then glanced at Susie and went to get Jake a drink. "Darius would have rubbed my back, but I don't think he wanted to sit that close to Susie."

The baby shower was fun, noisy, and full of happiness. Susie had a cake made in the shape of a baby, wearing boxing gloves in honor of Damien. It was perfect. We had so many gifts that Jake and Darius took a few trips to get them loaded in the truck.

"Any more pains?" Susie asked when they walked outside again.

"One, but it wasn't as bad as that first one," I told her. "DC might be trying to come early, but I'll be paying more attention now."

"Nesting yet?" Susie checked to make sure they weren't back inside.

"Sort of," I shrugged.

"You know what to watch for; take it easy and stay off your feet as much as possible. It's still too early for DC to come and meet us. You need at least two more weeks," Susie gave me a worried glance. "That means slow down."

"I know what it means," I shot back as Jake came

in, a worried look on his face. "Shit. I know that look doesn't mean anything good."

Susie glanced up as Darius boomed out, "Foxy! Get your ass out here!"

"Help me up," I said immediately. Susie didn't argue with me and pulled me to my feet as Jake bolted outside. I followed as quickly as possible to find Jake in cop or SEAL mode, trying to pull rank on Darius.

"Spill it, now," I demanded as they walked up to me.

"General Allen has a solid lead on the shooter," Jake told me quietly. "He ordered Darius to stay here and stay out of it."

I didn't need Jake to say more to understand why the general would want that. "He's right, Darius. I need you here," I thought frantically of a valid reason to keep him close. I didn't want him to end up committing murder, which was what his eyes were showing. "That was a labor pain I had earlier, which means that this kid could pop out any moment."

It was only a slight lie. It *had* been a labor pain, but it was most likely Braxton Hicks, as Susie had said. It worked. Darius instantly transformed into concern. "Isn't it too early?"

"It is. If it happens early, I need you here to help keep Jake sane," I hoped Jake understood what I was doing.

"Fuck. Frankie, I know what you are doing, but it's quite effective. You aren't shitting me? That was a contraction you felt?" Darius held my gaze evenly.

"It was. Will you stay at the house with us?" I felt

Jake's hand on my back, so I know he felt the contraction rip through me. I almost pitched face-first into the ground.

"Jesus Christ, get Frankie in the truck," Jake snapped. "Hospital."

Darius flew into action, and they got me laid across the backseat. "Don't you go having your water break in here," Darius said weakly.

"It's leather," I panted. "It'll clean up easily."

Jake called Dr. Waters's emergency number and left a message that we were headed to the hospital because I had labor pains. I was reasonably sure it was a reaction to the stress and overdoing it, but that last pain had been intense.

Thankfully Dr. Waters called back, letting us know she was already at the hospital and would meet us in the ER. Darius pulled right up front and was out the door getting a wheelchair before Jake even got out of the front seat.

They got me inside, and Dr. Waters gave me a slight frown but took me back right away. Darius stayed out in the lobby until we were behind the doors, then I hoped he went to move his truck so he didn't get towed. That would make him very unhappy. I told Jake to text him.

Jake

I was barely keeping my shit together. That contraction had scared the hell out of me. I knew if the baby was delivered now, that meant a hospital stay for both of them, and I didn't think I'd be able to tolerate that. This place didn't hold good memories for me exactly.

Dr. Waters did an exam and had a frown on her face more than once, which didn't help the anxiety boiling up inside me. "Jake, go get your friend," Dr. Waters told me gently. I didn't question her; I just did as she asked.

"Boomer," I said from the doors, jerking my head for him to follow me. "Doctor told me to come and get you."

"Why?" he tripped over his feet. "Is Frankie okay?"

"I'm sure she is. I don't know anything. I think she told me to come and get you to give me a chance to try and get my shit together because I'm freaking out," I admitted.

"Then I'm sure Frankie's fine, or she wouldn't have let you leave the room. That doc knows what's up between you two." A calm look spread over Darius's face at my words.

A small breath escaped my mouth at his declaration. It was true. If something were wrong, Dr. Waters wouldn't have sent me away. She saw me at my absolute worst. She knew what Francesca meant to me, what I meant to her, better than any other doctor.

I knocked at the door, and after being told we could come in, I opened it slowly. Francesca was sitting quietly, her pants back on. Darius and I flanked her as soon as we crossed into the room. Dr. Waters let out a small laugh.

"Sit down, gentlemen," she instructed us. "For two of the Navy's finest, you sure let this one woman run all over you. You are both well aware that the baby coming now is too soon. It's not quite as traumatic as you both are thinking, but it would result in a stay in the hospital. To avoid that, she needs bed rest, off her feet and laying down on her side, lots of water, and no stress. She needs two more weeks minimum before we can safely deliver this little guy and send you home."

"I told you. Fine, I'll be staying with you now," Darius glared down at Francesca.

"Strict bed rest, or can she move to say the living room so she doesn't try to escape out the window?" I asked Dr. Waters.

"No more than five to ten minutes on her feet in say six hours," Dr. Waters gave me a time frame to reference. "That's not to say Francesca can't get up to go to the bathroom, but just to remain in close proximity to one to minimize the time she's up."

"Were those the fake contraction things?" Darius asked.

"No. That's why this is serious. That was a real contraction. The baby has dropped a little, and he needs to stay put for a while longer. The more she's up and moving around, the more he will drop. Francesca isn't dilated yet, which is good, but the more she moves, the better the chance of it happening. It's either bed rest at home or here."

"Sex?" I asked, knowing Francesca was still gung-ho about that. I nodded at the threat of hospitalization.

"Honestly, that's up to Francesca. Vigorous sex, I

would say no," Dr. Waters advised.

This whole time Francesca hadn't said a word until then. "What do you consider vigorous sex?"

"I don't want to hear this," Darius groaned.

Francesca elbowed him. "Dr. Waters?" she pushed.

"Stick with going slow and not standing," Dr. Waters shook her head and laughed. "Oral is good too."

"This is like my little sister you are talking about; I don't need to hear that," Darius cursed.

"You realize she's pregnant, right? How do you think she got that way?" Dr. Waters raised her eyebrows at Darius.

"The stork," he retorted, scowling. "Fine. Frankie, if I see you on your feet, I will lock you in your room and not let Jake in. You know damn well I can do it too. I'll carry you where you need to go."

"I had doubts about this little birthing team of yours, but it's quite amusing, and I'm sure I can trust that they'll keep you down for a while between these two." Dr. Waters stood and patted Francesca on the leg.

"What do I need to watch for?" I asked before Dr. Waters left.

"Cramping, spotting, her belly getting really tight and low, pains in her back. Francesca knows the signs; she just needs to stop being stubborn and listen to her body. There's a reason she's so tired. It's because Francesca's doing too much," Dr. Waters said bluntly. More quietly, she said, "She'll be fine, Jake. The baby isn't in any danger, and if she behaves, neither is she."

"Thank you." I nodded, grateful for the extra

words that eased my thudding heart.

"If there are more contractions, call me, and I'll give her a drug that slows labor. The more she rests, the better everything will be. She can move around in little bursts of time, but she needs to be sitting or lying on her left side," Dr. Waters reiterated. "The baby's lungs need at least two more weeks to develop enough for early birth. Four is ideal."

"Hey, Doc," Darius called out. "Shouldn't she eat more?" I smothered a laugh as Francesca elbowed him again.

"Her weight is on the lower side of normal, but still within reason," Dr. Waters answered Darius.

"Told you," she muttered. "Like Jake hasn't checked daily?"

"Take her home, Jake," Dr. Waters told me, then left.

"Come on, Frankie, in the wheelchair," Darius picked her up and set her in the chair.

"You seriously aren't going to try and carry me everywhere, are you? I'm not about to be your daily workout. I can walk places," she argued. "You heard her."

"I heard every word out of that doc's mouth," Darius said. "Staying off your feet means no walking. Five minutes in six hours. Don't think I won't time your ass."

I sighed. The following two weeks were going to be hell. At least Darius wasn't taking off to Texas now. That's the lead. The guy had gotten discharged a week before he shot Damien, if this is the same guy. Fort Irwin was his station, so the lead Darius and the president of the Prince's had was right in that regard.

Darius wheeled Francesca to his truck, arguing with her the whole way while I followed behind them. "Come on, sweetheart, give Boomer a break. You scared the shit out of him," I told her, getting her settled in the backseat again while Darius brought the wheelchair back.

"Did they honestly find the shooter?" she asked me.

"General Allen thinks so. We'll find out more later," I promised her. "Let him coddle you a bit. It's keeping him here and out of jail."

"Fine. If Darius tells me to eat more again, I will punch him," she warned. "Better yet, I'll have Susie come over and boss him around."

I grinned. "It would work."

"Quit plotting, you two. I'm on to you, Frankie." Darius climbed in the driver's seat and started the truck.

Francesca

"Darius! I swear to God you will be the reason I go into labor! I will call Susie to come over here right now and tear into your ass if you don't stop telling me what to do," I threatened him. "Give me the damn letter."

"Sit your ass down," he repeated.

"Argh!" I screeched, dropping to the couch. "Happy? Give it to me."

"Keep making noises like that, and Jake's gonna come see what the fuss is about, and your surprise is gonna get ruined," he chortled but handed over the letter from another of the publishing houses.

"Shred it, please, or let me up so I can do it." This one was a rejection, which I had kind of figured.

"If you think I won't yell at you, think again. Stay down," Darius growled, tore the letter from my hand, and stomped down the hallway.

"You're worse than Caleb," I yelled after him.

"Damn right, I am," he snarled when he walked back in. "I learned from him and then perfected it."

"You better be out of the house tomorrow night, or you're going to hear sex," I told him with a smile. "Lots and lots of sex. I'll be extra loud too."

"Evil. Pure evil. That's what you are," Darius stomped into the kitchen and came back with a water bottle. "Drink it, or I'll dump it on you."

"DC, this mean old man is your uncle. When he's babysitting you, have lots of blowouts," I said to my belly.

"Pure evil," Darius repeated. "I'll be gone. Don't you worry about that."

Between the two men, I wasn't left alone at all. Jake was far less surly than Darius, but I could bend Darius. I couldn't bend Jake. Not even a tiny little bit. Four days is all it had been, and it felt like a lifetime.

"Did you see the finished book?" I asked Darius suddenly.

"No. I'll wait until it's published," he answered warily. "It's not that I don't want to, I'm just too stressed right now, and it almost triggered me last time. After the baby is born and I know you both are okay, we can look at it."

I immediately softened and moved over. "Put on a movie, make some popcorn, and sit down. I'll stay put at least five minutes until I have to pee again."

"My pick?" he brightened a little.

"Sure," I answered. I didn't care what Darius picked. I liked pretty much everything. "Wait. Nothing sappy. If you make me cry, I'm going to torture you."

"Nothing sappy," he promised and went to throw a bag of popcorn in the microwave. Three minutes later, he came back out, popped in a Marvel movie, DeadPool, and sat on my left, so I leaned against him the way I was supposed to lay. They were undeniably methodical in their approach to taking care of me.

This Darius was the one that reminded me so much of Caleb. That squishy teddy bear side of him that came out in these moments. He was going to be a great uncle. He threw an arm over me and rubbed the side of my belly as he demolished the popcorn.

"I've got you, baby. Let's go to bed." I must have fallen asleep because Jake's arms were around me the next thing I knew.

"You guys can't carry me everywhere," I murmured sleepily.

"If I could carry Damien's big ass around, I can certainly carry yours," I heard Darius mutter.

"You ate all the popcorn," I accused Darius, my brain clearing a little. "Wait, did you just say I had a big ass?"

"You fell asleep!" Darius stood and stretched, ignoring the last question because he wasn't stupid. "Are you hungry now? I'll make you some macaroni and cheese."

"Put me down, Jake," I told him, interested in Darius's offer. "We have the stuff to make macaroni and cheese?"

"Not from scratch. I'll make you a box of it," Darius clarified. "I picked some up on my last Costco run."

"Did you eat?" I asked Jake. He shook his head no. "Deal. Let's make three boxes of it. Feed us all. I have no idea why that sounds so good, but it does. That okay with you?"

"I'm good with it," Jake agreed, keeping his arms around me.

"Then I'll do it," Darius took off for the kitchen.

Chapter Twenty-Five

Jake

The past couple of days had been like clockwork. I set a vase of roses on her nightstand while she slept. Put a small wrapped gift box next to it that I had Hector pick up from Sam and stood a card up against the vase. She'd wake up soon. I knew that because it was usually every two hours that she got up to go to the bathroom.

I went down to make a quick pancake breakfast for her. Before working out, Darius had cut up a bunch of fruit she loved for a fruit salad. I'd leave a plate of pancakes for him in the oven; he was going out on a date tonight at Francesca's prodding, leaving us alone.

I'd managed to withhold sex for the past four days, and I knew that streak was over. I didn't like holding back from Francesca, and sex made her feel more connected. Aside from that, I would make enchiladas for her for dinner. My sole goal was to pamper her today and make sure she felt how loved she was.

I wanted Francesca to know that every day, not just Valentine's Day. It was the first one I'd be spending with someone I loved. Before Francesca, it was a holiday I avoided like it was the plague. Damien and I would hibernate in the house with our phones off. Now, my life was drastically different, and I never wanted to look back.

"You might just be the sweetest man I have ever known in my entire life," Francesca said as she walked into the kitchen. "I'm probably the worst wife in history. I didn't even get you a card."

I turned and sat her at the bar and kissed her. "To be fair, you are creating a life inside you who is just as bullheaded and impatient as his father. He has to wait until March to join us; you hear that, DC? Not yet, buddy." I poured Francesca a glass of orange juice and water, setting both in front of her and then adding the bowl of fruit Darius had cut up.

"You cut up fruit?" she asked, surprised.

"No. Darius did. He knows those are your favorites," I told her, turning back to the griddle. "Happy Valentine's Day, babe. I love you."

"I love you, too," she said quietly. "I'm going to cry."

"What? Why?" I spun.

"Because you are impossibly perfect, and I'm not even close. That card," Francesca paused, "wow."

I quickly flipped the pancakes onto a plate, slid them into the oven, and crossed back over to her. "How on earth can you not think you are even close? You have gotten us through a wall of grief that felt like it was drowning us by pushing us to do things for others. You transformed it. You honor Damien and Caleb with

336

everything you do. You love me with this intense strength that pulls me back from the edge and bathes me in your radiance and grace. You shine a light on our cracks and make them look good. Frankie, I wouldn't be who I am without you."

"See? Impossibly perfect." Tears filled her eyes, she held her arms open, and I walked around the bar to step into them.

"Never perfect," I corrected her. "But, the good in me is because of you."

"You two are disgusting," Darius walked in.

"Moment ruined," Francesca laughed lightly, wiping her eyes. "Thanks for the fruit."

I went back to making pancakes and then sat down with them at the bar to eat breakfast. Francesca bantered back and forth with Darius in their usual way. It was comfortable, homey, and warm. I'd be glad to have the house alone with her tonight.

Darius got up and cleaned up the breakfast dishes and then disappeared down the hallway while Francesca and I went to sit in the living room. She hadn't opened the box I had left for her yet, but she carried it.

"No contractions, right?" I asked as she nestled under my arm.

"Nope. None. He's behaving for the most part. Kicking the hell out of my bladder. This kid is a fighter already," she said wryly.

"Frankie, what's this?" Darius walked into the room, dropped down next to her, handing Francesca a large envelope and holding a gift in his hand.

"Looks   like   a   present   to   me,"   she

shrugged innocently.

Darius looked at the box and then tore the paper off. When he opened the box, he got a perplexed look, and I felt Francesca trying not to laugh. I knew what this was because I went and did it for her.

"What the hell is this?" Darius pulled out a diaper bag.

"It's your babysitter kit," she giggled. "Open it."

Darius had a hilarious, wary expression, but he unzipped the black leather bag that looked like a saddlebag. He pulled out a onesie that read, 'Boss Baby Nephew.' Then he pulled out a t-shirt that read, 'World's Best Uncle.' Darius snickered. "DC's only gonna think he's the boss."

Then his face changed, and he looked every bit the teddy bear that Francesca accused him of being. He pulled out a camouflage baby carrier, pacifiers, wipes, bibs, and everything he would need to babysit.

"You seriously trust me to watch your baby?" Darius finally asked us. "I know nothing about babies."

"Why would we not trust you?" Francesca asked him. "You don't know anything about women either, and you take care of me," she joked and shoved him.

"Trust is there, Boomer. You're his uncle. Don't try and recruit him, though." I understood where he was going with this.

"No. Wouldn't do that," Darius chuckled. "You're wrong, Frankie. I know what women like. They like me. Don't argue. You know it's true. Now give your whipped man his gift."

She shoved him again and looked at me

sheepishly. "I really couldn't think of anything to get you, total blank. I told you, bad wife. This was all I could think to show you that you complete me because this wouldn't have happened the way it did without you."

Francesca handed me the envelope, and I pulled out eight pieces of paper. I skimmed through the top one, and my heart sped up. I flipped through the rest and looked at her. "They all want it?"

"Those do. You get to pick who takes it on. Without your help, your advice, it wouldn't be what it morphed into; this wasn't just me," Francesca took my hand and held it.

"Holy shit, this is incredible." I flipped through all the acceptance letters. "This is why I couldn't get the mail?"

"Yeah, man. I joked that I would have to stake out the mailbox, and then I was worried Frankie would take me up on it. Only two rejected it, the idiots." Darius snarled but then looked at his bag in wonder. "You know, this bag better not jinx me."

"Never know; it might get you laid." Francesca burst out laughing.

"Are you trying to kill my sex life?" Darius set the bag down and gave her a narrow-eyed look.

"What sex life? You've been here taking care of me," Francesca fired back.

"Shut up and open your gift. I want to see what whipped men buy," Darius growled.

"Calling me whipped doesn't bother me," I told him with a smirk.

Francesca pulled the bow off the box and

unwrapped it slowly. When she finally pulled the box open, she saw a white gold circle with a single gemstone hanging off it. Francesca looked at me with a question in her eyes. She pulled it out and held it in her hand.

"Is this the March stone?" she finally asked.

"It is," I answered her gently. "The chain is under that. Sam said to bring it back when we have another, and he'll add another stone for that one. He can add whatever stones you want. It's a circle of love. There's no beginning or end; it's just continuous for you to fill with what you want to fill it with."

"I love it," she breathed out.

"Sam left the chain off because he said you could use a smaller chain and make it a bracelet if you want, or use it on a necklace. Do what you have to do to keep DC in there until March, or we will have a lot of stones to change around," I said gently.

"I'm a diamond, by the way," Darius told her. "Suits me, right?" He elbowed her softly.

"Of course, you are," she said with a full laugh. She turned back to me and pulled me down for a kiss. "Perfect."

Francesca

One more day. I needed to make it through today, and tomorrow would be March, and I could start moving around again. The only thing that has gotten me through is Jake stopped holding back on the sex. Otherwise, I would have been so bored that I would have driven both men completely insane.

Jake had selected a publishing house, and they were working on getting the book published in time for Memorial Day. I had approved the edits, made the dedication page, and added a page to the back with numbers to call for help for veterans, suicide, domestic violence, sexual assault, and a personal plea for those suffering PTSD to please reach out for help. Overall, I think it would be beautiful, but that was my opinion.

Jake was meeting with the publisher today to go over a promotion schedule that started on Memorial Day. I didn't want to be in the spotlight and struggled to agree to it. Jake had negotiated with the publisher that every person featured in the book got a copy for free, and I was excited about it. I wanted to see the results myself.

That was why Jake was the one in meetings about it instead of me. I will have a newborn then, but I'd worked so hard to stay out of the spotlight to keep the crazy people away from me that it seemed counter-productive to shine a light on myself.

Even Darius agreed the promotions were a good idea because the proceeds would funnel into our charity, Knights of Dawn, and another that helped veterans. There was also a particular section of the book solely for Damien's squad. Not all of them had PTSD, but all the remaining of their sixteen agreed to talk with me. They'd even e-mailed me pictures, and I promised to use only first names and give no specifics on their missions.

I knew most of the important ones between Darius and Jake, but I still wouldn't speak the details I wasn't supposed to know. Except for Caleb's death.

After the Wreckage

Every one of them had agreed it needed to get verbalized. That had been the last part I'd done on the book and the hardest.

The raw sting of Damien's death had faded, but we were now fully engrossed in the 'rebuilding our lives' part of the grieving process, and it was in the quiet moments where both Jake and I were silent at the same time would we talk about him.

Not in terms of the loss of Damien, but stories about him that filled us with love and smiles. The ache of his death was still there, but we both believed that Damien would be happy with the way things were turning out. Including the fact that Darius was a permanent fixture in our lives. I think Damien would have loved that, despite their differences.

Signs of spring were starting to pop up, and Darius and Jake had been fine-tuning their bikes when they had free moments. I was a little excited to ride with Jake again on one of those fast and windy roads like he had done last time. It also meant that Darius or Susie would have to babysit.

"Earth to Frankie!" Darius broke into my thoughts.

"What?" I said, irritated.

"Are you hungry?" he asked, apparently again.

"Is the pope catholic?" I fired back, making him grin. "No junk food, though, gave me heartburn last night."

"I'm sorry. Did it keep you awake?" Darius lost his grin.

"I'm always awake," I grimaced as a back pain

swept across my back. "I think I only sleep when I'm on the couch with you while you stuff your face with my snacks."

"I make a mean tuna sandwich; we'll have that and sit on the couch. See if you can get a nap in, maybe." He raised his eyebrow at me.

"Can you text Jake and tell him I think I just had a tiny contraction?" I said, my breath a little short. "Also, note the time; it only lasted about two seconds."

Darius's SEAL mode was different from Jake's, but it was still intense. Darius put off a lethal vibe, but Jake changed the very air around him. "Sit, or I'll put you on the couch," Darius barked gently. "You still gotta get through today to be considered a safe early birth."

"I know," I huffed but planted myself on the couch. Darius bent over, lifted my legs, and stuffed a pillow between my knees and one under my belly as I lay on my side. "I still want food."

Darius snorted and knelt in front of my belly. "Hey DC, if your real uncle were here, he'd tell you to cool your jets. There's no rush. Stay put for another day."

"Darius, you are his real uncle too," I tried to smack him, but he dodged me.

"Fine, DC, as your other uncle, calm down. I don't want to clean up no broken water mess. Don't play me like that, kid." He stood up, smirked at me, and went to make lunch for us. I had no idea where my phone was, or I would have texted Jake so he didn't freak out.

I flipped the TV on and rubbed circles on my belly. The baby's movements had slowed, which worried me, but Dr. Waters said it was normal because he was getting ready to come out and join the world around him.

"Jake is headed back. He told me to sit on you if I had to," Darius returned five minutes later with some sandwiches and a bag of chips. "No pickles on these," he set the pickle ones on his side. "Doing okay?"

Darius propped some pillows up against his side and had me lean into him as I sat. He ate with one hand and had his other resting against my belly. I ate one sandwich but felt unsettled, and I wanted to make sure the baby's room was ready. I started to get up, and Darius kept me in place.

"Nope. I *will* sit on you, Frankie," Darius threatened.

"I want to make sure the room is ready," I protested, knowing full well he would indeed sit on me.

"The room is as ready as it's ever going to be. You feeling the nesting thing now? He's coming soon, isn't he?" Darius tried to pull my attention back to him.

I guess I was nesting, as much as they would let me anyway, which wasn't a lot. "Yeah, I think he's coming soon. Impatient kid."

"Just like his father," Darius quipped good-naturedly. "He knows what he wants, and he will do it."

"Promise me you'll keep Jake sane if things get stressful," I begged Darius suddenly, my brain thinking ten steps ahead of where I was.

"Things won't get stressful, but I got him. Jake will keep a level head," Darius said gently.

"Thank you for being a part of this, Darius," I mumbled before falling asleep against my new brother.

I woke up later as a severe pain ripped through

me that had a scream tearing through my throat. "Breathe, baby. Breathe through it, look at me, look at me, Frankie. Breathe, baby. Breathe like we are breathing," Jake's calm voice drew my attention. "That's it, just like that." He held my hand and told Darius to write the time down and then the duration.

"Four hours between the two," I heard Darius say. "But that first one wasn't anything like that one. Jesus, I felt that shit."

"Something doesn't feel right, Jake," I whimpered. "Help me up."

Darius and Jake both moved and helped me sit up, but he shot off the couch, cursing when Darius moved the pillow from between my legs. Blood covered the cushion. "Call the doctor now!" he shouted. "I'm getting her bag."

Jake left an urgent message for Dr. Waters, and when Darius came back into the room at a full run, they got me standing and heading towards the garage when my water broke. The only lucky part about it was I was standing on an area rug when it happened.

"Fuck! There's blood," Darius shouted.

"Francesca's car," Jake instructed him. "She's not going to be able to get into either truck."

Darius took off to open the doors, and Jake scooped me up. "Clothes," I told him. "I can't go like this."

"I know, baby. Let me get you in the car first, and I'll come back and get a clean pair of sweats for you, okay?" Jake kissed my head. "Bottom drawer of my dresser, go grab a pair of my sweats, the top drawer of hers, get a pair of socks, and grab her flip flops," Jake barked out orders, and Darius flew into action.

Jake got me lying across my back seats, stripped my leggings and socks off, cleaned me up as much as possible, and then pulled a pair of his sweats over me when Darius returned. It was better than I had been, but I could still feel blood.

Darius drove, and Jake sat in the passenger seat and turned towards me, watching me the entire time. Another intense pain gripped me, and Jake helped me breathe through it. Dr. Waters called when we were halfway there, telling us to go to the ER, and she was on her way.

"Park, so you don't have to come and move the car. I'll carry her in," Jake ordered Darius, who didn't argue. "You are with me from here on out."

"Call the lawyer," I panted. "Get him here. Now." Jake cursed but did as I asked, leaving a message that we were at the hospital for the birth, and his presence was requested. "No matter what, you sign those papers, Jake."

"I will, Frankie. I promise," Jake told me. He carried me in, and thankfully Dr. Waters had called them and told them I would be there. They got me on a gurney and wheeled me back into a private room, bringing the paperwork to Jake for him to fill out as they got me hooked up to monitors.

They got Darius suited up and sterile after they tried to get him out of the room, and I yelled at them, then followed with Jake after the admission papers were taken care of and filled out. Darius stayed up by my head and rubbed my back for me; his presence was unnaturally quiet.

Dr. Waters came in with a flurry of activity as she called out to the nurses and immediately started to examine me. "He's definitely on the way, and you have dilated to a three, which isn't enough. I'm going to give this an hour and check back. It could go slow, or it could go fast. Are you still wanting to go with natural?" she asked me.

"I will do whatever you think is best," I told her again. "That was a lot of blood, Dr. Waters, and I don't feel right."

"Sometimes it happens, but we are watching closely. I've got monitors on you and the baby, and we'll play this by ear. For now, let them coach you through the contractions, as you learned in Lamaze class. Women's bodies are miraculous things, Francesca. I'm here with you through it all. I won't be far away," Dr. Waters promised me. "I promise you I will get you and your baby through this."

Jake

Francesca looked too pale. We were nearing midnight now, and she'd hardly dilated anymore, but the contractions only got stronger. Darius and I were barely hanging in there, but we stuck to the Lamaze plan and got Francesca through each one.

"Hell week has nothing on this," Darius muttered. "I swear to God this will break me when those drill instructors couldn't."

Francesca laughed weakly, her hair pulled back and face beaded with sweat. I was losing my shit inside but trying to remain outwardly calm for her. Truthfully, she was doing fantastic; Darius and I were struggling.

Dr. Waters came back in, rechecked her, and stood up. Her face was closed-off, which made my heart pound. "Francesca, you aren't dilating. I'm going to ask you to consider a c-section. We can wait another hour if you want, but I'd advise against any longer than that."

"Why another hour?" I asked, trying to rein in the panic.

"If her body starts to dilate, we can go with the natural course, but if she still isn't dilating and these contractions only get stronger, it's putting a lot of stress on her body and could harm the baby. Talk it over. I have a team prepping an operating room anyway. I'll allow you both in there if we go that route, but you have to remain out of the way and near her head," Dr. Waters said softly.

She left us there to talk about it. "Frankie, what are your thoughts?" I smoothed her hair back from her face. She'd been at this seven hours already, and it was only half an hour from midnight right now.

"We just need to make it to midnight, so he's born in March," she closed her eyes, her face lined with exhaustion. "Beyond that, I don't care."

The contractions were six minutes apart, and she should have dilated a lot more than three. There was also still blood, and she was so pale. So very pale. Her body shook with tremors, and I was terrified out of my mind.

"I love you." I bent over to rest my head against

hers. Darius watched me closely for the past couple of hours, which told me I was showing some of the stress I was feeling.

Chapter Twenty-Six

Francesca

I had another two contractions that made me feel like I had gotten run over by a cement truck. Jake's phone had rung, and I could see he wanted to throw it at the wall. He was worried about the baby and me, but he answered it with a gruff, "Yeah?"

His body went still, and his eyes shot to Darius, then to me. He said a few more words, made a grunting sound and hung up. He faced both of us. "They have the shooter in custody and are transporting him back here to get charged with attempted murder for Frankie and murder for Damien. Since she was pregnant at the time, they will count the attempted murder charge twice. General Allen said they would ask for life."

My ears buzzed, and my head swam. They'd found him. Damien could finally rest. I tried to smile, but my body seized as the most violent contraction yet slammed into me, and I screamed, the monitors attached to us going crazy.

I didn't even hear the door thrown open, and Dr. Waters rushed in. A flurry of movement and commands barked, and all I heard was the doctor saying the baby was in distress and my body pushed too far.

"Frankie, baby, look at me," Jake's face filled my vision. "We are going in for an emergency c-section. Stay with me, baby. You're going to be fine. DC is going to be fine."

"Sign the adoption papers," I begged him.

Jake

"Jesus. She blacked out!" I shouted.

"Jake, calm down, man," Darius was at my side in a flash. "Let's follow them. Doc said we could be there. We promised Frankie we would be. Come on."

Words were being pushed around and spoken hushed and urgently that I didn't understand. Except for the hemorrhage, I understood that. There was way too much blood. I followed blindly, forcing the tears back. There was going to be no saving me if I lost Francesca.

"Jake. Captain Foxwood," Dr. Waters snapped her fingers in front of my face. "Hold it together. I'll have them take you out of here if you can't. I know how much Francesca wants you here, and I know what it means for both of you. I need you to stand here and don't move. Either of you. I will *not* let your wife or baby die."

"Why so much blood?" Darius asked Dr. Waters quietly.

"I think her uterus has torn. This baby is large, and she's not dilating. We need to get him out of her, and I need to get her stitched back up and get the bleeding under control. It is going to be scary for you, and I understand that. Let me do my job," she spoke to both of us as we precisely stood where she told us.

This situation was almost too much. The authorities caught Damien's murderer as his son was trying to be born. "Demon, you better be watching over us right now, brother," I whispered, and Darius jolted. "If there ever was a time we needed a guardian angel, this is it."

Darius put his hand on my shoulder, and we stood there, watching as an oxygen mask got put in place; sheets were draped, blocking our view of that glorious belly that held life. Had it not been for Darius, I would have dropped straight to the floor, sobbed hysterically, or threatened to end every life here if they didn't save Francesca.

"Heart rate is in the danger zone," I heard, and my body coiled in tension, tears spilling down my face. "Clamp that, *now*. Suction, get blood down here." Commands were issued in clipped tones by Dr. Waters.

"Frankie needs us to be strong, Jake," Darius said in my ear.

"No pulse," I heard, and my knees buckled. Darius yanked me back to my feet, his face a controlled mask as his gaze fixated on mine. He put my hands on Francesca's head and held them there.

Amidst the frenzied movements and issued orders, Dr. Waters remained calm and focused even though the words that penetrated my fear added to the panic flooding me. Then the most beautiful sound rang out above the noise. The scream of my baby. Damien's baby. Ours.

Darius caught me again, and a nurse came up to us with a gooey and swaddled up tiny baby. "Here's your son," she handed him to me.

Dr. Waters didn't look up but spoke to Darius and me. "Captain, you stay there. Keep your hands on Francesca. Darius, go with the nurse and get the baby cleaned up. We'll be out to join you soon."

I gazed down at the red-faced baby who no longer screamed but stared right into my soul. "Hey, DC, happy birthday. You're going to go with your uncle Boomer now, and your mommy and I will see you soon." I kissed his head and handed him to Darius, who looked ready to cry.

"I've got him, Foxy. Take care of Frankie," Darius followed the nurse and left me staring down at my wife, who hadn't met her son yet.

"Work your magic, Ghost, keep her on this side. Demon, keep your baby safe," I whispered. "Frankie, you stay with me, baby."

Francesca

I woke up sore and exhausted. It took me a minute to realize that I no longer had the baby inside me. Jake was next to me on the hospital bed, and when I turned to look at him, I saw him sleeping with the baby cradled gently in his arms.

"You're awake," Darius said from the other side of me. I rolled my head to see him sitting on a chair, watching me. "He signed the papers, Frankie. I made sure of it."

"Thank you," I whispered. Darius handed me a cup with a straw, and I sucked down the much-needed water.

"You scared the shit out of me. None of that was in that damn birthing plan," Darius said softly. "How do you feel?"

"Like I've been sliced open," I answered truthfully. "How long has Jake been asleep?"

"Fifteen minutes," Darius smiled a half-smile. "He looks like Damien. The nurse kept telling me how big of a baby he was, but shit, that little thing is tiny. This little fragile human with a big set of vocal cords has me in knots. He looked a lot bigger in your belly."

"How big?" I asked him, glancing back at the infant happily asleep on his daddy.

"Ten pounds six ounces and twenty-four inches long. DC certainly made a dramatic entrance to this world in true Damien style," Darius stood up and moved closer to me. "He's beautiful, Frankie."

"Did they name him? Put Damien as the father on the birth certificate?" I asked, my eyes filling with tears.

"They did. We both made sure it was all exactly how you wanted it. I'd move DC to your arms so you can hold him, but I'm pretty sure Jake would wake up and knock my ass out if I tried to take that baby from him," Darius grinned. "Jake didn't leave you once, Frankie."

"Have you gotten to hold him?" I looked back at Darius.

"Yeah. The doctor sent me from the room with

the baby when they had to fix you up. I got to be there when we got DC all cleaned up, the nurse showed me how to swaddle him, and she let me hold him. No doubt, I'm in over my head, but I love him," Darius dropped a kiss on my head. "I'm also beat, and now that I've seen you are okay, I'm going to head home to shower and nap."

Darius snuck out of the room, and I looked back at Jake, who had opened his eyes. He gazed at me with so much love that another wave of emotions swept through me. "You made this," Jake said quietly and put the baby in my arms. "Frankie, meet your son, Damien Caleb Ocasta Foxwood, or DC for short."

"Hiya, DC, I'm your mom." My heart soared at the feel of him in my arms.

The nurse came in a few minutes later and showed me how to breastfeed, gave me tips on what to do if he wouldn't latch on, and left us alone as little Damien ate his first meal. Jake cried with me that Damien wasn't here with us for this, but there were happy tears, even though there was sadness.

"He does look like Damien," Jake took the baby after feeding and patted his little back. "We're going to give you siblings, I promise. You made a mess trying to get out, so we have to let your mom heal up first, then I'm going to keep her pregnant because she makes pretty incredible babies," Jake cooed to the baby that fell asleep on him again.

"You have the magic touch," I whispered. "DC calms right down for you, just like he did in my belly."

"He waited until March," Jake shifted, putting

baby Damien back in my arms. "Twelve seventeen AM, they pulled him not breathing from your body. I don't know how long it was from then to when he screamed, and I almost dropped to the floor, but it was March. Two weeks early, but Dr. Waters said he is fully developed. She's having him kept under the light just in case, so we'll need to put him back in the baby bed soon."

"That's fine. I'm exhausted," I kissed Damien's head and handed him back to Jake.

"Want me to move and give you room?" Jake asked after putting the baby in the bed next to us.

"No. I want you to stay right here with me," I said, not moving my body but moving my head to lean against him.

"Go ahead and sleep, babe. I'll watch over you both," Jake kissed me, finally, and I drifted off to sleep.

Chapter Twenty-Seven

Jake

We had been home for a month and were getting into a routine with the three of us. Damien was a pretty good baby, except when he didn't get fed when he wanted to eat precisely; then, he exercised those little lungs. His volume rivaled his dad's when we'd been overseas.

Francesca pumped as often as she could, so we had a reserve of milk that we froze, and her body healed up for the most part. Today, she had an appointment with Dr. Waters to go over everything, and I knew she would be asking for the all-clear for sex.

I was nervous about it, but Francesca wasn't, not even a little. I was glad to know that her desire wasn't just pregnancy-related as she had been assuring me that it wasn't. I had no idea why I was worried about that, but I was.

DC liked to stare at my face when I read stories to him, and if I thought my heart had been whole when they handed him to me for the first time, it had only gotten fuller since then. I saw Damien in him, and it filled a hole in me that I didn't think could be filled.

I was head over heels in love with the way he calmed for me, something I was sure would change in the future, and how he seemed to pay attention when I spoke. When his little fingers held onto one of mine, I felt like a hero.

Darius, who had moved back to his room at the Prince's clubhouse, seemed to think it was hilarious, but it was no different when he held DC. He was just as natural with DC as I knew he would be. Also, as protective.

The sun was shining today, even though it wasn't quite warm yet, and Darius was going to watch DC for us while I took Francesca to her appointment. She wanted to go on the bike, which I was nervous about, but she kept assuring me it was okay; she healed.

I'd do it, but not the way she wanted me to. Not until I heard from Dr. Waters that it was okay. The memory of the possibility of losing both her and DC was still a little fresh in my mind. Francesca insists she was never in danger, but I'd heard the issued commands. I wasn't going to argue it, though.

I let Darius in before he knocked so he didn't wake DC up, who curled himself in the crook of my arm. We'd spoil him, but he'd be loved and disciplined. This Damien would grow up knowing he was loved, wanted, and used to touch. Even if Francesca hadn't voiced those words, it was something I was planning on doing.

"They're going to call to schedule depositions with all of us," Darius said as he walked in.

"Do it at my old house," I answered immediately. "It's not in use at the moment. Schedule ours for either before or after yours."

"That was my next question. Did you want us all to do it in the same place and day? Got it. When they call, I'll assume I can schedule yours as well. Got a calendar that has things already filled in?" Darius set his bag down.

"Frankie's office. She has one going on the desk," I told him. "Hey, hands-off. When we leave, you can have him; until then, he's mine."

"Chill, uncle daddy," Darius smirked at me.

"Being a dad to this baby is the best thing ever," I said quietly. "Pull away from the Prince's, don't make this kid have no uncles."

"Low blow, Foxy. I've pulled back quite a bit. They are my family, and I can't just walk away as Damien could," Darius shifted uncomfortably.

"We're your family too," Francesca popped in and scooted around me to hug him.

"Yeah, I know you are. I'll say that much. I've stopped doing the things that the law finds questionable. They are my brother's, though. They got me through some bad times," Darius hugged her. "Now, hand over my kid."

"Your kid?" I almost laughed but held back when I saw the raw need on his face. "I'll let it go this time," I handed over Damien.

"We won't be gone too long, or my boobs will leak," Francesca informed him bluntly, making him wince.

"If you schedule the depo's, write it on the calendar so I see it," I told Darius and led Frankie out to the garage.

"Depo's?" she asked as I put the helmet on her head and let her fasten it.

"Depositions for the trial. What this guy's lawyer will use to try and tear us apart and poke holes in our story," I answered. When she climbed on the bike, I slid on and got us going.

I didn't go as fast as she wanted me to, and I kept to the quickest route because I still had doubts that she should even be on the motorcycle. I trusted that she knew her body; it just made me nervous.

"I know you held back," she gave me a look as she got off the bike. "You better not when it comes to sex because if you do, I'll feel forced to tie you up and do whatever I want to you."

My body responded instantly, and I cursed under my breath. "I wouldn't hold back on you," I tried to argue.

"Liar," she kissed me and then looked at my crotch. "I know you would only because you are worried about me, but your body misses mine as much as mine misses yours. I want to rectify that."

"Frankie, you're killing me, babe," I groaned. I waited a few minutes until I was back in control of myself, and then we went in for the appointment. When Frankie got the all-clear, she whooped and gave me a pointed look.

"Told you so," she smirked at me. "Dr. Waters, can you refer me to a good pediatrician?"

"I'll do his first set of shots in a couple of weeks, but yes, I'll have a few names for you then," she winked at Francesca. "Have fun."

Francesca

I hung up the phone and stared at it for a moment, wondering what I had just agreed to do. I moved Damien to my other breast so he could continue to nurse and then set the phone down, thinking I'd lost my damn mind. I'd studiously avoided the public eye since my dad died.

I don't think Jake realized the marketing piece when he signed the contract. My belly fluttered nervously. Damien picking up on my unease stopped drinking. "It's okay, DC. Finish eating. I'll calm down."

We'd given our depositions last week, the lawyer Greg hired to protect our interests sitting in on each, as well as for Darius. The trial was looming, and now I'd have to appear on a local television show to promote the book and most likely answer questions I didn't want to answer. Not on TV anyway.

"Where's your daddy?" I looked down at the beautiful baby boy in my arms. He took after his biological dad all the way, except maybe his hair color. "You are going to be a heartbreaker; you know that?" I tickled his lip to get him to drink some more. "Your daddy was gorgeous too. But so is your other daddy. I lucked out there."

"You forgot to remind him how beautiful his mother is," Jake's sultry voice came from the doorway.

"Remember this, son; your daddy is also stealthy and sneaky. You'll never get away with anything if he's around," I kissed Damien's head. "Your uncle too. Sorry, kid. You're kinda screwed there." I moved him around to burp him while Jake sat next to me.

"I love seeing you two sitting there like that," Jake leaned over and kissed my cheek. "What had you worried?"

My brain had momentarily paused at the feel of his lips and jolted back to the moment. "Oh, I have to do publicity for the book. Did you know that? They have me going on the local talk show, a televised talk show. A live talk show," I emphasized.

"I knew," Jake said cautiously. "We talked about it."

"Damn. I wondered if you were going to say that. Lack of sex translates to a lack of brain function. Remember that for the future," I said with a straight face. "Is it smart to do that? Put myself in the public eye?"

"Is it the harassment that makes you nervous or the attention?" Jake astutely asked me.

"Both," I sighed.

"For one, we are publishing the book under Frances Gray, and you are now Francesca Foxwood. Two, you aren't alone in dealing with the harassment anymore. Three, yes, your face will be recognizable, but that's a good thing since it's tied to the Knights of Dawn. All the rest is just white noise that I will help filter out. It's scary, but it's not a bad thing, Frankie. The publicity will be good for the club and the book. All contact will get funneled through the club. Someone would have to go through layers of guys to get to you. Not to mention they'd have to get through Greg," Jake tried to reassure me.

I shifted Damien down to see his angelic sleeping face. "He's so perfect," I murmured. "Do you think big Damien is in love with him as much as we are?"

The swift change in topic caught Jake off-guard, but he rolled with it. "I'm positive he is, same with your parents and your brother. This little one has a whole lot of guardian angels." He looked up, "Is that it? You are worried about putting him in the spotlight because of all this?"

"Is it easy for you to just see right through me?" I asked him, a small smile playing on my lips.

"No," Jake chuckled. "Not in the slightest. It took me a long time to read between the lines of your letters to get to the level your brother was. Then after I met you, I got good at reading your expressions, remembering there was a lot left unsaid in those letters. The rest is just being in tune with you."

"What if all this stuff makes Damien a target?" I whispered one of the fears plaguing me.

"DC's born of pretty tough stuff. Look at what he survived already. He will grow up knowing how to stand up for himself, know he's loved, and be protected. Frankie, we take it as it comes." Jake moved and took the sleeping infant from me. "Let's put him to bed and take some much-needed alone time."

"Adult playtime?" I stood, my worries forgotten.

"Very adult," Jake nuzzled my neck. "By the way, Darius's birthday is tomorrow."

"I knew that, too, didn't I?" I groaned.

"I'm not sure. I got us covered. Now, on to important business that includes worshipping at the altar of my wife," Jake said, laying Damien down and turning on the monitors.

I ran down the hallway, shedding my clothes as I went. "I'm ready," I called back, hearing Jake laugh. I loved this man as I had never loved another, and I was finally okay with it.

Chapter Twenty-Eight

Jake

I felt sick to my stomach. Francesca was beside herself with anxiety, and DC was unhappy with our moods. I almost felt sorry for Susie. Almost. Darius said he would meet us at the courthouse, and he warned me that the Prince's president and a few other members would be there as well.

I might have moved past the wall of grief over Damien's death, but facing his murderer presented a host of other problems. All of which made me feel sick. Either Darius or I would probably have some sort of outburst, and I was worried one of us would go in for the kill. The wound was still fresh, no matter how much progress we'd made getting through it.

"Baby," Francesca drew my attention. She rarely called me pet names. "Look at me, please," she requested, and my eyes landed on hers. "We can get through this the same way we've gotten through everything else. We face it together, stare it in the face, and refuse to bend to what we know is wrong."

"I want to kill him, Frankie," I said the words aloud.

"I know. Darius does too. What would little Damien's life be like if you did? What would happen to me? What would you do if I jumped over the railings and tried to attack this guy?" Francesca's soft words had a grounding effect on me.

"Darius shouldn't be here," I looked out the truck's window.

"Darius's going to sit on the other side of me and hold my hand as he promised me he would," Francesca reeled me back in. "You are going to be doing the same on the other side. We will get through this for Damien and bring his death closure in the view of the law. We just keep doing what we've been doing for our hearts."

"I don't want you dragged through the mud," I muttered.

"Because of what? We haven't done anything wrong. They can try to discredit us all they want; we aren't the ones on trial. We might not even get called to the stand; they have many witnesses to exactly what happened. Where I'm weak, you are strong, and when you are weak, I am strong. Together, there is nothing this guy can do to beat us down. I'm terrified of seeing his face too, but Jake, all those bad thoughts you are thinking, are just a reaction to that fear."

"Fuck fear," I quoted Francesca from the first time Damien and I had met her.

She let out a little laugh, "Exactly."

"Stay put. Let me open the door for you," I decided to face it all. I walked around and opened the door, and helped my wife out like the true queen she was. "I wish I had the words to tell you how goddamn much I love you, but everything feels inadequate."

"I already know, baby. Hold my hand because I want to puke." She jammed her hand in mine. "Let's go find Darius."

Like magic, Knights of Dawn and Prince's members surrounded us as the media noticed our approach. "Keep your heads down," one of the Prince's told us. "We'll get you to the doors, but we aren't going in. Boomer and the Prez are already in there."

The small act of kindness and humanity was almost my undoing, but Francesca kept me rooted in the moment. I knew we both were going to have to relive Damien's death over and over today. I knew we would have to see pictures that I never wanted her to see. I even knew one of the witnesses had gotten a video of my complete breakdown when Damien died. Above all that, I knew she would remain a pillar of strength to keep both Darius and me upright.

The Prince's peeled off as we got to the doors, and the Knights of Dawn moved in around us, blocking the media that was flinging insulting questions and trying to shove cameras and microphones towards us. Once the doors opened, my old brothers in blue took over for the club and ushered us inside.

Darius practically tackled Francesca, his nerves strung beyond tight. "Darius, hold my hand, and don't let go," she told him quietly. "You stick by me, okay. I might need to lean on you." Smart woman. He instantly transformed into the SEAL I remembered him to be.

After the Wreckage

We entered the courtroom, found our lawyer, and sat on the bench behind him. The judge approved some media to be in the courtroom, and I heard the quick shutter sounds of pictures taken when we walked in. Darius and I squished Francesca between us for the peace and strength she brought to us than for her protection.

Francesca gasped when the murderer came in, her eyes riveted to him. She said nothing, didn't move, and quietly listened to the defense lawyer as he talked about how this guy was a victim and insane.

He didn't know what he was doing. I called bullshit. It was pretty organized and thought out to follow someone, pull up next to them in traffic, and shoot from a moving vehicle to another moving target with precise accuracy.

They called me to the stand first, grilled me about my expertise as a sniper, a S.W.A.T. captain, my role in Damien's life, our time served, and questioned the events of the day that Caleb died. Thanks to the government's gag order, I had very little to answer on that front. They made me walk step-by-step through the events leading up to Damien dying in my arms, and I wasn't unaffected.

I broke down into tears on the stand, and my eyes stayed locked on Francesca as she cried with me. She heard the sounds, she listened to my screams, but she never looked away from me, keeping me grounded in her eyes. They made us watch the video, and instead of watching, she held my gaze.

They called her next. Francesca kissed Darius's

cheek and stood as I walked back, kissing me as she proudly walked up to the stand. After she got sworn in, the defense attorney tried to take her apart, and not once did my fabulous wife break. She did ask permission to make a statement; the judge granted it, his curiosity getting the better of him. She had that effect on people.

"I've dealt with PTSD a lot. With patients, my mother, brother, myself, and members of the squad my brother belonged to. I can plainly see the effects of it on this man here. He didn't act out of insanity; it was cold-blooded, premeditated murder born of grief. However, he needs help. He needs help with getting through PTSD. Life in prison isn't going to give him that, and we often see it end in suicide. There isn't justice in that. Damien deserves justice. Instead of throwing all these life sentences at him, get him help. The justice comes in him feeling remorse for what he did. It comes when he atones for it, changes his thinking and ways, and sees how wrong it was to end a life that shouldn't have ended. Yes, he needs to serve his time for what he did, but he needs help. You are free to believe whatever you want about Damien's life. Damien wouldn't want this to go down this way. He knew firsthand what living with PTSD was like, and when he saw it in people, he tried to help. That's all."

After closing arguments, the judge called a recess, and people filed out of the courtroom, but we remained right where we were sitting. Francesca stood when the judge dismissed her and made her way back to us, sitting right between Darius and me and taking our hands. Darius and I both broke down once again after the gravity of Francesca's statement sunk into our bones.

Her statement was correct. Damien would have wanted this guy to get help. Darius and I both knew it. It was the same thing he did for others he saw stuck where we had been. Whatever happened today, this was the closure we needed. We faced his murderer; we spoke our truth and bore the weight of grief again publicly. We broke down even, but we didn't surrender to it.

We left before the sentencing. The Prince's president stayed, and our lawyer. They'd let us know what the outcome was. We were all anxious to return to the little life that carried Damien's blood and soul and let his little body soothe our pain.

Francesca

I bolted to the bathroom and threw up. Public speaking had never been my thing. Seeing all the lights and feeling the heat, the cameras freaked me out. The makeup person assured me it was a normal reaction, but she had to fix what she'd already applied.

Jake, Darius, and Damien were out in the audience. I wished Jake was back here with me. I hated this. I wasn't born to be in the spotlight. I may have a gift for photography, but not in front of the camera. I belonged behind it. I sucked down a gulp of water, hoping it stayed put.

"Why so much makeup?" I asked again.

"It looks different under the lights and the camera. Trust me, you don't look like a clown," she smiled kindly at me. "Keep your eyes on the hosts; don't look out at the cameras. Ignore the audience, and don't forget to breathe."

"Do people do that?" I asked, shocked.

"Forget to breathe? You bet. We get people passing out all the time," she patted my shoulder. "Would you sign the book for me?"

"What?" Caught off-guard, I gave her a blank look.

"Your book," she held the tome out to me. "Would you sign it?"

"You bought my book?" I sounded like an absolute idiot. I took it and the offered pen and scrawled my name on the inside cover.

"I did. It's for a worthy cause, and I know a few people who suffer bad flashbacks from trauma in their life." She tapped the book and smiled again. "You have a way with a camera that shows soul. That is important."

I shouldn't be surprised. I mean, I wanted people to buy the book. In publishing it, that was the point to give voices to those people. "Thank you," I answered sincerely, feeling more at ease than I had until someone came and gave me a two-minute warning, which had me wanting to throw up again.

"Breathe through it," she said, fanning my face. "You've got this."

Some assistant led me to a chair, seated across from the two hosts whose makeup was getting retouched, and then suddenly, they talked to the cameras. I froze.

"We are here with Frances Gray. Her book about

PTSD was released today." The guy whose name I couldn't remember was holding up the book. "Looking Through the Shadows, the Faces of PTSD. Welcome, Frances."

I almost corrected him on the name but caught myself just in time. "Thank you. It's a pleasure to be here." My voice came out small and timid.

"Tell us how this book came to be." The woman smiled at me. Why couldn't I remember their names?

"My father died in the 9/11 attacks, resulting in my brother joining the military. He became a decorated SEAL and ended up dying overseas. It was a huge blow to my mother and me, and we struggled with his death for quite a while. So many people, veterans, are looked at as if they have an illness because the trauma they saw, or experienced, changed them. I came up with the idea of documenting PTSD stories of other veterans to honor him, and the project morphed into an idea for a book. I wanted to show others that may be struggling with it that there is a way through it," I said, my voice getting bolder.

"You included yourself in here. Did you have PTSD as well?" the man asked.

"I did. Still do. Triggers are present in anyone with it and can activate out of the blue. That is why it was so important to me. You don't know what those triggers may be in some, and we shouldn't judge others by what we don't know. When you look at the first page of the book, you see a photo of a busy street in downtown Seattle. You don't know these people; the faces you aren't seeing are the same faces in the book. You can probably look out over your audience and not be able to spot someone with PTSD," I warmed to the topic.

"There are some pretty brutal stories here," the woman said, her face shuttering slightly. "How did you find some of these people?"

"Some of them found me," I answered. "Others, I just put the word out at places I worked that I was interested in hearing stories, or my husband helped me find them through his contacts."

"Interesting. You also lost your fiancée in the recent past, and he's in here too. As well as your current husband," the man went on. I didn't even think he was listening to me.

"They are." I wasn't saying anything the book didn't. "Both men were a part of the SEAL team that my brother was on."

"You were at the trial of his murderer, correct?" the man continued.

"I was, yes," I answered warily.

The woman interrupted whatever her co-host was going to say. "Your statement about him getting help was powerful. How did you get through the grief and triggers of PTSD?"

"I refuse to back down. It takes time, patience, and a lot of tears. The grief is the same. Only, with Damien's death, I had Jake. We had each other and a mutual love that has shown it can withstand the worst storms. He is a hero in every sense of the word. Jake is who I had been waiting to find my entire life, and it took the death of Damien to help me understand that. Grief looks different for everyone. There is no right way to get through it; you just survive. Some don't. When you look at a tragedy like that, you grab on to whatever you can and hope for the best. I got the best in my case, and he's sitting out there with our baby and my new brother." My words were soft, but the audience had gone quiet.

"What do you say to those who think you got married too fast or didn't love Damien if you could turn around and marry his best friend so quickly?" the man asked, clearly being one of the people he mentioned.

"I say it's none of their business. My journey isn't their journey. I decide what's right for me. If my journey crosses yours, I hope it's a happy crossing. But if not, I have no problems with keeping moving forward. We all loved Damien, and we all mourn him. Deeply. We still do. I can also tell you that Jake wouldn't have married me if he didn't love me, nor would I have married him. No one gets to decide what's right for us but us. And I honestly don't care what others think of me or my life," I stated plainly.

"Well said," the woman replied, clearing her throat. "The proceeds of your book are going to a few different charities, is that correct?" she redirected the conversation.

"Yes. One of the charities is the non-profit that Jake and I started with his club. There are a couple of veteran's charities as well. The overall goal is to help veterans get the help they need. Whether it's to reacclimate to life outside the military, overcome PTSD, get physical help for wounds they received, or anything. Jake opened my eyes to adding people that aren't veterans to the book, and our club helps those people as well. Police, firefighters, first responders, and victims of abuse, we leave no one out. I'm all too aware of what it feels like to be alone and face overwhelming loss. My message to others is, 'I hear you, I value your story, and I'll sit with you so you don't feel alone.'"

"That there might be the most important message to get out there." The woman turned towards the camera, her eyes holding unshed tears. "You aren't alone. There are people out there willing to listen. Pick up a copy of Frances's book today. Thank you, Frances, for the reminders we all needed to hear."

The lights dimmed, and they went to a commercial break, and when I stood, Jake was barreling up the stage to sweep me off my feet. "You are a goddess, and I love you," he crowed, the audience behind him cheering.

The woman wiped her eyes and thanked me. The man said nothing. We beat feet out of there as fast as I could after washing my face off. Darius followed behind, with Damien telling him how crazy his parents were.

Chapter Twenty-Nine

Francesca

"Get your asses down here now!" I yelled up the stairs to Darius and Jake. We were supposed to be headed to the coast to have our tequila shot in honor of Caleb. Well, now Caleb and Damien. We would stay the night, so we weren't really in any hurry other than I just wanted to go. The ocean air called to me.

I yanked my phone out of my pocket as it rang. "Hi Greg," I answered, checking to see who it was.

"Frankie, a woman is coming to see you. I gave her your address, and I've vetted her. Please give her a chance," Greg said immediately.

"Um, okay," I said, hesitating. "Today?"

"Yes. Hopefully soon. Call me later. Anytime," Greg added before hanging up.

"Weird," I slid my phone back into my pocket as Darius appeared with Damien. I took him while Darius juggled the diaper bag. He was three months old now and had grown so much. Too fast. I wasn't ready to not have him as a baby yet.

"Who was that?" Darius finally asked, setting the

bag down by the garage door.

"Greg. He said he sent some woman here to talk to me. Guess we aren't leaving just yet. He gave me no other information than that and that he vetted her," I bounced Damien around as he smiled and giggled at me. "Best sound ever," I kissed his chubby cheeks.

"I'll agree with that," Darius grinned. "Baby laughs are the best."

We walked into the kitchen, and I grabbed the bottle I had prepared. "What's taking Jake so long?"

"He was showering. He watched the baby while I showered, then it was his turn. Our workout was sweaty," Darius grabbed a banana and peeled it. "You aren't in a hurry now anyway. Relax, Frankie."

I didn't have time to respond because there was a knock at the door. I shot a nasty look over my shoulder at Darius and went to answer it, curious about the woman now. I pulled it open to see someone about my height but slight in frame and pale. Her eyes looked bruised and were sunken in a bit.

"Francesca Grayson?" she asked, and my heart slowed slightly.

"Yes," I said slowly, sensing Darius behind me.

"I know you," Darius said, standing slightly behind me. "From where?"

She ignored him, her body showing nervous tension. "I saw you on TV about the book. It took me a week to get through to someone, but I seriously need to talk to you."

"Do you want to come in?" I asked, trying to step back but bumping into Darius. Damien found it funny and kicked his legs.

Suddenly time stood still. My heart stopped and then pounded fast as blood rushed through my body, and my ears started to buzz. A boy had stepped out from behind the woman, and he was the spitting image of Caleb.

My head swam, my body swayed, and I whispered, "Caleb," before dropping.

"Jake!" I distantly heard Darius bellow as I felt him catch Damien and me before blackness took over my body and mind.

Jake

Darius's scream sent panic flooding through me, and I barreled down the stairs to see him holding my passed-out wife with our baby in her arms. My gaze rose to see a boy that slowed my pace to a halt and a vaguely familiar-looking woman.

"Jake!" Darius demanded. "Either take the baby or her." I snapped back to attention and grabbed DC while Darius hoisted Francesca in his arms. "I think you both better come in."

I gave Darius a shocked look, and he shook his head at me as he carried Francesca to the living room. "Do I know you?" I asked her.

"We've met," she responded elusively, following us in.

It was the boy who drew my attention. I swore he looked like Caleb exactly. My step faltered as it clicked. "Holy s...cow," I exclaimed, eyeballing the kid, then looking back at the woman. "You were seeing Caleb." My eyes landed on the boy again, and it suddenly made sense why Francesca had passed out.

"I was. Amelia," she held out a shaking hand. "I'm sorry about Damien."

I shook her hand, and that's when her appearance seemed to penetrate the fog my brain was creating. She was very pale, sort of emaciated looking, a hat on her head, dark circles under her eyes, and her body trembled, not just her hand.

"You're sick," I whispered. Amelia nodded slightly, and I directed her to sit down. "Can I get you anything?"

"No, thank you. I came to talk to Francesca, but it seems I caused a bit of a reaction," she said apologetically.

"Give me the baby, take over for your wife," Darius stood, looking shaken. I swapped with him and sat with my legs under Francesca's head.

I looked back at Amelia, trying to piece it together. "Air Force?" I asked her.

"Yes." She didn't say anything after that, and I understood she wanted Francesca to be awake before she spoke. Darius had his eyes glued to her as he bounced DC around.

DC was super strong, and he was already lifting his upper body from the floor and moving around a lot. He was a pretty happy baby and liked everyone, and I swear he would have his mother's brains. He decided he wanted to miss nothing.

Francesca started to stir on my lap, and I stroked her face to wake her up. "Wake up, sweetheart," I crooned softly to her.

"Jake, I think I'm pregnant," Francesca said as her eyes cracked open. My heart picked up its pace again.

"Why do you think that?" I helped her sit up, and her eyes widened as they landed on the boy, then swiveled back to me.

"Is that a hallucination?" her voice wavered.

"No, we have visitors, Frankie," I told her quietly. "Why do you think you are pregnant?" I asked again, not caring why this woman was here, not after that little bomb dropped.

"My breasts hurt. I've been sort of sick, but not like last time. Dizzy a little and no period," she listed off, her eyes trailing back to the boy. "I'm sorry. You startled me. I'm Francesca."

"My name is Amelia. I've been looking for you for a while now. I saw you on TV for the book you did and had to get pushy with several people before I ended up talking with someone named Greg. He gave me your address and sent me here right away," she explained.

"He called and told me he was sending someone," Francesca's voice was tentative. "We were just headed out. If he hadn't called, you would have missed us. This dazed man is my husband, Jake, and my new brother, Darius, but something tells me you know them already."

"In a way. We've met before. I'd like you to meet Franco," she tugged on the boy's arm, and he stepped forward shyly.

"Franco," I said, my body jolting. "It's nice to meet you, buddy."

"Hi Franco, I'm Frankie." Francesca dropped to her knees before him.

"You're my aunt," Franco stepped toward her as if they were two magnets.

"Oh my God," Francesca breathed out and enfolded the boy in her arms, tears streaming down her face. "No, no, don't cry. These are happy tears, Franco."

"My mom calls me Frankie," he said.

That was it for me. I was on the floor behind Francesca, pulling her into my lap, folding both boy and wife into my arms as Darius dropped to the ground beside us, DC flapping his arms against his cousin and giggling happily.

"How?" Francesca asked Amelia through her tears.

"I was about two months along when Caleb got sent out on that last mission. I hadn't told him yet because we had only just started seeing each other for two months. It had to have happened our first time together, even though we were safe. There wasn't anyone else. Caleb talked about you all the time. At first, that first couple of dates, I couldn't figure out if you were a love he left behind here or family, then he explained you were his sister. Francesca Grayson disappeared. I lost track of the remaining squad members after they were injured," Amelia started her story.

"Caleb never mentioned you. Why?" Francesca stroked Franco's arms. The boy looked enthralled with her.

"Relationships in the military, especially ones involving groups like his, don't last. He was literally afraid I'd fly away since I was a pilot. Instead, *he* didn't come back, didn't get to know he created life. I was discharged and had Franco. You were the most important person in Caleb's life, and I wanted his son named for you. I know he called you Frankie or Frank, but he also told me your name was Francesca, so it seemed right to me when he was born. I tried to find you for a couple of months, but I got sick. Breast cancer." Amelia started fidgeting, and Darius plopped DC in Francesca's arms and went to sit on the arm of the chair next to Amelia and put a calming hand on her.

It was the strangest thing I'd seen yet. With as many women that threw themselves at Darius, he'd not reacted like this with anyone except Francesca. "Franco, this is your cousin, Damien. I call him DC. We named him after his dad and your dad," I said, watching Francesca.

"You knew my dad?" Franco sat down in front of us, and Francesca lowered DC so Franco could hold him.

"He was my best friend, along with DC's dad, Damien. Darius, over there, was part of our group too; we all knew him. He was the best. He and your aunt used to write letters all the time, and they'd pick on each other and tell jokes," I told him.

"You look exactly like him," Francesca told the boy softly.

"He does," Amelia agreed. "Anyway, I went into remission and have been fine for the past five years. But cancer has come back now. I came back here to try and find you again and then I saw you on TV. I saw Caleb's picture and Damien's. I knew it was you. Here I am. I want Franco to grow up knowing his family," Amelia left the unsaid words hanging in the air.

"He will," Francesca promised. "Are you living here?"

"No, I have a lousy apartment in Nevada. Things got rough with treatment, and it was all I could afford. I had to come when I saw you," Amelia's voice shook. "I'll sign anything you want."

"Hey, you aren't going anywhere, so stop that," Darius said gruffly.

"Darius is right. Hang on, let me make a call." Francesca used me as leverage to get to her feet, and she walked out of the room.

Franco played with DC in front of me, and my eyes went back to Amelia, with Darius taking up a guard over her. There wasn't any way we would let this woman and child out of our sight. We now had Damien and Caleb back with us, whatever the universe was up to.

Francesca was gone about five minutes and came back in, fresh tears on her face. "Greg, the man you spoke to?" she waited for Amelia's nod. "He's going to help you. When we get back tomorrow, he's going to help you find a house close to us for you to move into; and he's going to get you enrolled in the cancer treatment place here. It's excellent, and we are going to take care of you. I don't want any arguments. Caleb's money that passed to me when he died was the money used for this. It's now Franco's money."

Amelia paled. "I can't accept that. It's too much."

"No," I told her gently, "it's not enough." I

nodded at Franco. "This is the biggest gift any of us could have ever expected. It's Frankie's way of making sure you are around to see who he will become."

"Yep," Darius agreed. "I'd also like to take this moment to ask you out on a date to the coast. You turned me down last time I asked, hoping this time will be different."

Francesca and I sat there stunned, looking at Darius as if we had no idea who he was. Franco had a slight smile on his face. "My mom is strong and brave," he told us.

"She sure is," Francesca said quickly. "Want to come to the ocean with us? We are going to celebrate your dad's birthday. It's today."

"Really? Do you have a picture of him?" Franco asked excitedly.

"I sure do. I have a bunch. For now, look over the bookcase. You'll see some of the photos." The boy hopped up and ran over to the case as Amelia stared at us helplessly. "You aren't alone anymore, Amelia."

Francesca

"We need to stop and get a pregnancy test," I told Jake as we pulled out.

"You genuinely think you are pregnant?" Jake asked me quietly.

"I'm almost positive. I thought my being sick at the studio was from nerves, but I think it was morning sickness. I've woken up nauseous a few times since but didn't think anything of it. Not sure why seeing Franco made me realize it, but I'd be willing to bet on it," I answered with a smile.

"Call Darius and tell him we are stopping at the drugstore and for him to keep going," Jake told me. He pulled into a drugstore and ran inside while I made the call. Jake was back within minutes and then drove across the street and made me go into the fast-food place to use one of the bathrooms.

Jake was so excited. I did as he asked and went back out to the truck, handing him the test that already showed a positive. "You're going to be a daddy again," I kissed him.

"Jesus, can men get morning sickness? Why is my stomach all in knots now?" Jake asked in awe.

"Because you made this one. Damien is still yours, but you made this one. We have a part of Caleb back, Damien's baby, and now we will have yours. Jake, our family is growing," I kissed him again as my phone rang.

I looked down to see Darius's name and handed it to Jake. "Bro, you will be an uncle again," Jake told him, the sweetest smile crossing his face. "Looks like only you and I are taking shots tonight unless Amelia thinks she can." He paused, "Yeah, man. I am."

"You are what?" I asked when Jake hung up the phone.

"The happiest man alive. Call Dr. Waters and make an appointment," Jake grinned and pulled out of the parking lot and headed to the coast.

Chapter Thirty

Eight months later

Jake

"Jake," Francesca called out.

"Yeah, babe?" I wrestled with DC to get his diaper on.

"Your baby is trying to be born," her voice had dropped in pain.

I shot to my feet, and a bare assed baby ran the opposite way. I grabbed my phone to call Darius. "Meet us at the hospital. You've got to take DC; the baby is coming."

"On it." Darius hung up, and I raced after DC.

"You seriously are a little demon, aren't you?" I snatched DC up. "Mommy's about to give you a little brother or sister, and you are running around with your butt hanging out. Let's get this diaper on and get mommy to the hospital. Uncle Darius is going to come and grab you. Feel free to run around without a diaper on for him. He'll love it."

"Unca," DC grinned.

"Yes, Uncle Darius. Come on." I quickly got DC's diaper, hoisted him up, and ran to grab Francesca's bag.

"I can walk," Francesca said as I moved to help her. "I cleaned up; my water broke."

"Okay, babe, let's go," I put my arm around her. "Holy cow. We are going to have another rascal to chase after now."

"Maybe this one won't be quite as active?" Francesca laughed.

"I'll chase around twelve of them all day if it means I get to spend every night with you." I loved this woman with every fiber of my being.

"Might turn out to be the case with your super sperm," Francesca laughed again as DC flung himself at her. "Hey, little man, will you torture Uncle Darius?"

"Unca!" DC cried out and then kissed his mom. He was so much like Damien, and it thrilled me to pieces.

I got us to the hospital in record time, and Darius met us in the parking lot, catching DC as he hurled himself at Darius. Franco followed close behind. "Where's your mom?" I asked him.

"Not feeling great today, but she's doing better," Franco told me. As much as DC was like Damien, Franco was just like Caleb. Which meant this kid trying to join us now might be just like me. That was a scary thought.

"Well, thanks for helping Darius out. DC is a handful," I patted Franco's shoulder.

"How can I get Darius to marry my mom?" Franco asked me. Both Francesca and I stopped to look at him with raised eyebrows.

"Talk to him about it," Francesca told him.

"Darius is pretty straightforward, and he won't get mad."

"Okay. Good luck, Auntie Frankie," Franco beamed at her and followed Darius in while we checked in, thankfully with less fanfare than last time.

Shortly after we settled in, Dr. Waters came into the room and checked Francesca over, "This looks good. You are dilating properly, and the baby is in position. You made it to full term, and it shouldn't be much longer. How are you feeling?"

"Excited," Francesca told her. "Ready to meet this little one."

"You know what to do, Jake," Dr. Waters smiled at us and left to check on another delivering patient.

"Are you truly excited?" I asked Francesca, rubbing her back and reminding her to breathe through the contractions. "You don't hate me for making you go through this again?"

"No," she panted. "I like being pregnant. This one was easier than last time, and I can't wait to meet our baby."

"Me too. I think my heart is about to beat right out of my chest," I admitted.

"Kiss me, Jake," Francesca ordered me. "Kiss me before I start cussing you out because these contractions hurt like a bitch."

"I love you," I whispered. I chuckled but sealed my lips to hers in a promise to always be what Francesca needed me to be. She stole my breath away and drank me in.

"I know. I love you too," Francesca smiled, then

winced as another contraction hit; this one a lot closer together.

Dr. Waters came back a few times and finally came in and gave us a bright look. "It's time," she pulled up the stool and told Frankie to push. I held her legs and watched as the head crowned, the miracle of life unfolding before my eyes. "Keep pushing, Francesca, give me a big one," Dr. Waters called out.

Sweat dripped down Francesca's red face, pain etched into her eyes, but she did it. She pushed through like she always did, and I heard the most beautiful wail as our baby came sliding out.

"Congratulations, you have a baby girl," Dr. Waters announced, and I almost fell over.

"A girl? I have a daughter?" I shook as Francesca laughed weakly.

"I knew it," she declared.

"Jake cut the cord," Dr. Waters instructed me. A nurse quickly cleaned my baby girl up, swaddled her, and gave her to me.

"Oh my God, Frankie, she's an angel." I moved next to her while Dr. Waters did whatever she was still doing down there. "She's tiny."

"Well, compared to Damien, most babies are tiny," Dr. Waters said with a small laugh. "Let's weigh her," she led me over to the scale. "Five pounds, seven ounces, and twenty-one inches." She let me pick the baby back up. "Go on back to her," Dr. Waters prodded me and went back to cleaning Francesca up.

"She's beautiful, baby. She looks like you," I stared down into the tiny face.

Francesca laughed. "She looks like a little alien, but a beautiful little alien."

We waited for a little bit before going to get Darius and Franco and then brought them back. "Oh, no. Are you kidding me? It's a girl? You are my niece?" I watched Darius melt as he spotted the pink hat. "Oh, baby girl, your life will be filled with men who will not let anyone near you. I'm just gonna apologize now. If your daddy decides to let you date for some unknown reason, they will have to get through me, Franco, and Damien. And if that little dude is like his daddy, that ain't ever gonna happen."

"Darius, we need a name for her," Francesca told him, holding my hand as the tough biker crumbled.

"You want me to pick out her name?" Darius looked flabbergasted.

"Her first name, at least, I have a middle name picked out already," Francesca glanced at me. We'd decided to let him name the baby a few months ago when he'd been cycling through possibilities.

Darius glanced down at the baby lying in his arms peacefully while Damien settled next to his mother and watched us, unsure of what was happening around him. Franco stood next to Darius and stroked his hand over her cheek.

"She's so small and fragile," the ten-year-old said in wonder. "Darius is right; I'm going to watch over you."

I bit my lip to stem the flood of tears that wanted to pour down my face. Caleb was with us in this room, no doubt about it. Damien was, too, his eyes watching from his son's face. My family was growing. "Hey DC, come here, buddy. Want to meet your sister?"

Damien crawled over to me and leaped into my arms as I pulled the chair over to Darius. I held his little hand in mine and put his fingers against her soft cheek. He stilled, and I saw him again, his father staring out of those eyes.

"This is your baby sister, buddy. You will help us take care of her, love her, watch over her, and not let Uncle Darius scare away all her friends," I told Damien.

"Isabell," Darius whispered. "She should be named Isabell. This girl is my Izzy."

"Isabell Jaclyn Foxwood," Francesca repeated. "I love it. What do you think, Franco?"

"I like it," he said. "Isabell, it's nice to meet you."

"Jaclyn?" I asked Francesca.

"Female version of Jake," she said quietly, her gaze soft on mine.

"Izzy, Damien," Darius said to my son. "Say, Izzy."

"Issy," DC repeated, too damn smart for his own good.

"Good job, little man. I'm Uncle; this is Franco," he pointed, and Damien's eyes followed. "This is Izzy, that's daddy, and that's mommy."

"This is our family, buddy. What do you think?" I looked down at the toddler, who gazed back at me with his father's eyes.

Damien's hand moved excitedly. "Issy." He went to touch her, and Darius caught his hand.

"Gently, little man. You only ever touch a female with a soft hand. Like this," he moved Damien's hand and touched baby Isabell softly.

Darius handed her back to me, and I returned to Francesca, sitting next to her on the bed, cradling my newborn daughter. "My life is perfect," I whispered to her.

"This girl will sucker you men at every turn imaginable," Francesca laughed. "You're loved so much, baby girl."

Chapter Thirty-One

Three years later

Francesca

"I swear on all that's holy. If you two don't sit still, I will lock you in a room and not let you be a part of this," I growled at the toddlers.

Amelia laughed, "Have Franco come and get them. Sit down before you fall over."

"I'm trying to help you get ready," I grumbled. I waddled over to the door. "Franco, come get these monsters."

"Still want more?" Amelia stepped into her gown and turned so I could zip it up.

"I don't have much choice, do I?" I zipped it up and stepped back while Franco grabbed the baby from the floor where he'd been trying to crawl under Amelia's dress. "Damien, Izzy, you go with Franco and help watch your baby brother."

"You look beautiful, Mama," Franco kissed his mother while William squirmed in his arms.

"Thanks, baby," Amelia beamed. Her hair was

chin-length now, and after all her treatments had finally ended, it grew curly and fine.

Darius had asked her to marry him after William was born and two years of being hassled about it by Franco. Jake liked to call him uncle daddy now too. Our family had grown more extensive, and now we were officially adding Amelia. I was ecstatic about it. At the end of eight months, I was pregnant with our fourth child.

Life had turned out even better than I had thought it would when I made the snap decision to ask Jake to marry me. That first year had been challenging. So terribly hard. There had been so many moments of guilt, sadness, flashbacks, and tears, interspersed with moments of pure joy and happiness. Jake had learned the trick somewhere along the way of tightening the lid on the peanut butter when I got mad, so I had to talk to him. It worked every time too.

Then along came Damien, bringing us the rest of the way through it. He was every bit of his father. Jake was beyond proud of him, and we talked about Damien all the time, making sure DC knew precisely the kind of man his father was. One day, he'd understand that Jake was his dad in all the ways that mattered, but he would also appreciate the man who created him and the brief shining love we had shared.

Damien and Izzy were two peas in a pod, with Damien being the instigator in most things. Still, Izzy apparently inherited both Jake's intelligence and mine, and she outthought Damien somehow, making them more diabolical than he would have on his own. Not a great thing to deal with in toddlers, but we laughed about it secretly.

We didn't know what this baby would be, but I suspected another girl. Damien was four, Izzy was three, and William was one. Franco was thirteen and so handsome. Doppelganger for his dad, but with Amelia's gentle disposition. Jake said he had Caleb's personality too. I saw it at certain moments.

Life was indeed beautiful, and the day the doctors had declared Amelia cured after two scary bursts of cancer coming back, Darius proposed. They didn't know if she'd be able to have another baby, but he often declared that he would keep practicing until it stuck.

Somehow with the cousin magic that Franco had in him, he corralled the kids and got them through the ceremony without a fuss, and we watched as Darius blissfully kissed his new wife. He had pulled entirely out of the Prince's and was fully engaged in the Knights of Dawn and going to classes to become a social worker.

As Jake led me around the dance floor during the reception, our kids trailing after us, dancing with each other, I wished I had my camera. This moment was everything I had never allowed myself to dream of; these kids ran us right into the ground, but I wouldn't change it for anything.

Susie appeared at my side and dropped a handful of napkins on the ground. "I'm on duty. I've got the kids. Go bring this one into the world."

Jake looked up, surprised. "What?"

"My water just broke," I grinned at him.

"Jesus, Frankie, were you going to tell me?" Jake

stepped on the napkins and cleaned up the mess.

"Yeah, when we finished dancing," I gasped as a contraction hit. "Okay, good luck, Susie."

I caught Darius's eyes and pointed to my belly. He gave me a face-splitting grin and a nod. "Text me, and we'll help with the kids."

Dr. Waters was going to do a tubal ligation while I was still here in the hospital. Both Jake and I had agreed on that. It'd be nice to have even a larger family, but I wanted time to enjoy Jake. Our bond and love had only grown, and the sex was beyond fantastic when we weren't interrupted. And we were off—no more kids after this one.

"Frankie, this one will go fast," Dr. Waters warned me. "We don't have much time for anything. You are fully dilated, and the baby is trying to crown."

"Okay, let's get this impatient one out then," I leaned forward, well versed in birthing now. We welcomed our second daughter into the world less than an hour later. Bright green eyes stared up at us as we settled in for the night, trying to get her to breastfeed.

"What do you want to name her?" I asked Jake.

"Scarlett," he answered. "She was so red when she screamed. It was all I could think."

"Scarlett it is," I looked down at our newest addition. "I think our wreckage has rebuilt into something quite beautiful."

"That it has, all because of you, my love," Jake kissed me tenderly. The kind of kiss that got us a ton of kids. "Filled the world with life."

"Us, Jake. It was both of us. Together as a team.

Just like we promised each other. Now we give them wings and teach them to fly," I snuggled into him as he moved Scarlett off of me. "Better find a babysitter for six weeks from now."

Jake chuckled. "Already done, baby, and the countdown has started. I love you."

I said a silent thank you to Damien for loving me the way he had. Without question, I was where I was because that beautiful man had shined so brightly in my life, even if it was for such a short time.

Resources for Veterans

DoD Safe Helpline
is the sole secure, confidential, and anonymous crisis support service specially designed for members of the Department of Defense community affected by sexual assault.
www.safehelpline.org
877-995-5247

SAMHSA: Substance Abuse and Mental Health Services Administration
www.samhsa.gov
1-800-662-4357

www.988lifeline.org
Call or text 988

www.veterancrisisline.net
dial 988 and press 1
or text 838255

www.crisistextline.org
text HOME to 741741